YANKEE INVADER

"Darling Cam, I know for a fact there was no one before me. And we both know no man will ever succeed me in your arms.

"What an arrogant Yankee bastard you are!"

Her whole body was trembling, not from anger so much as from his nearness. "You don't own me, Tate Carruth! No man does! And don't you think for one minute that what happened between us gives you the right to me. I am not some property that can be bought or sold or traded!"

He closed the distance between them with slow, determined steps. His nostrils flared with deep, heavy breaths. There was no mistaking the thoughts going on inside his head.

"Don't you come one step closer. I'm warning you, Tate. You take another step, and I'll make you regret it. I swear I will."

"Shut up, Cam!" His hands locked against her spine. Reclaiming her lips with savage intensity, he crushed her to him. . . .

JOLENE PREWIT-PARKER

LEISURE BOOKS NEW YORK CITY

This book is dedicated to
my son,
Jake Hamilton Parker,
born January 12, 1987.

A LEISURE BOOK

Published by

Dorchester Publishing Co., Inc.
6 East 39th Street
New York, NY 10016

Printed in the United States of America

RECKLESS
ABANDON

1

July 4, 1876—Caesar's Head, South Carolina

Sitting proud and erect atop her chestnut stallion, Cam Tranter anxiously awaited the call for steeplechase riders to line up. It was growing late, much too late for her liking. The race was supposed to have been run at two o'clock but had been postponed first one hour, then two, and they were still waiting for it to commence at five o'clock. Already the sun was dipping low in the west, and the hot summer sky was splashed with purple and orange.

Growing short on patience herself, Cam could tell by the muscles tensing underneath her that Traveller was ready to spring to action. The tiniest urging from her and all the other horses would be left behind in his dust. But until the cross-country event began, she had every confidence in the world that he would behave like the perfect gentleman he was.

Since four o'clock, the start of the race had been delayed three times because of uncontrollable mounts tearing out into the crowd and frightening the onlookers. The horse she had figured all along would give Traveller the most trouble—an ominous-looking black that snorted fire and pranced on his hind legs—had been disqualified when he crashed into the judges' platform after being terrorized by a yelping puppy. Poor Mr. Summers had been sent sprawling to the ground! But as far as Cam was concerned, it was nothing less than he deserved for having barred her from last year's race.

Thank heavens Traveller had plenty of sense and wasn't easily spooked. He might not be able to hear a rifle go off in front of his nose, but he was honest and willing, and he trusted her judgment without question. Few could boast of a steed that had such faith in its rider. The fact that Traveller was deaf mattered little. As Cam had so often told him, she had ears for the both of them!

Cam leaned down to pat Traveller's thick neck. She owed him a lot, and she wasn't about to forget it! He was her friend. A horse like hers was a once-in-a-lifetime find, and nothing would ever make her part with him.

"Won't be long now, sweet pea," she whispered into a big red ear that was standing at attention. "We'll show them a thing or two this year, just like we did last time. It'd serve them right if we won again, wouldn't it? They just barred us because they were scared we'd beat them." Her cheek nuzzled his mane. "You just do your best, fellow. That's all I ask."

Cam glanced around to make sure none of the other riders had heard her. Confident her secret was still safe, she searched yet another time for any telltale sign that might give her away. So far, so good! Her mask was still secure over her eyes and nose, and no dark strands had escaped from under her cap.

Growing more restless with each passing minute, Cam surveyed the swarm of people in the field. It looked like everyone from Greenville County, and a few others besides, had turned out for the race. The fact that it was the Fourth of July could hardly account for the hundreds of spectators. There was no reason for anyone in South Carolina to celebrate a centennial of independence, not as long as Union troops still occupied the state.

No, folks hadn't come to Caesar's Head from every corner of the state to talk politics, Cam decided as she sat even taller in the saddle and felt all those eyes on her. News of last year's hair-raising escapades by a masked rider had spread like wildfire. Each month, his exploits had inspired a tale more romantic and more exaggerated than the last. Some believed the masked rider to be a farm boy out to make a name for himself. Others had him a Union soldier who was trying to win the hand of his Southern belle. Whatever the story, all were in agreement. That they had never seen anything like it! How strange that not one of them had even considered the possibility that a woman could be astride the big red stallion! One day, she would take off her mask and enjoy watching their mouths drop open. For the time being, it was enough fun just to keep them all guessing, but when that day came, she'd give anything to see each and every one of their faces the instant she jerked off her mask! Maybe she'd do it even sooner than she planned. What a ruckus she'd raise!

Her gaze focused on a pretty little blonde the same age as she. It was all she could do to keep from waving at Abbey Sullivan. She had thought her best friend would surely recognize her, but the girl's heat-flushed face was as baffled as everybody else's.

Frowning, Cam scanned the rest of the crowd. It looked as if somebody was expecting trouble. Fellows sporting the Union blue mingled conspicuously with the crowd. Not far behind were the Red Shirts, who were firm in their determination not only to protect Southern heritage but to administer justice to anyone who committed crimes against their Dixie. Over the years, most of the Union boys had grown accustomed to their presence, and when the red shirts were exchanged for white robes at night, the Yanks just looked the other way.

Where on earth is the Senator? Cam asked herself as she stood up in the stirrups to get a better look. Her father had left home a good hour before she had, and he had been nowhere around all afternoon. It wouldn't be like him to miss the steeplechase, not the way he liked to drink and gamble and carry on with his cronies. No doubt he was hiding, trying to dodge Widow Ward's blackberry wine and amorous advances. Poor Senator! Just about every old maid and widow around—and a few who were still married—would give her eyeteeth to latch onto him, but Cam knew all too well that he had had his fill of women sixteen years ago when his young bride walked out on him, leaving him with a newborn baby to raise.

Her scowl deepened. She had never been able to think of the woman who bore her as her mother. The truth was, she couldn't remember thinking much of her at all. She didn't hate the woman, or miss her for that matter. She felt nothing, nothing at all. If she had thought no more of her daughter and husband than to run off with some turpentine merchant from England, then she and the Senator were much better off without her. Good riddance! Besides, they had Ludie Mae, and she more than enough made up for all the hurt that miserable woman had caused them.

Cam peered harder into a group of men that had assembled outside the refreshment tent. Even from where she waited, it wasn't hard to figure out who was the center of attention. The way Strothers Bennett was circulating among them, one arm extended in enthusiastic handshaking and the other slapping backs, one would have thought that he, not Wade Hampton, was running for governor.

The longer she watched him, the angrier she became. What a scoundrel! The way folks bowed and scraped to him was disgusting. Poor Abbey! Even she got all starry-eyed when he was anywhere near. Could no one see past that big grin of his, or was she the only one who knew him for the snake in the grass he really was? When he'd arrived from God-only-knew where, he was as poor as Job's turkey, but it hadn't taken him long to worm his way into what was left of Greenville's elite society. Rumor had it Strothers was quite a lady's man, but how he could appeal to any woman in her right mind was beyond Cam's comprehension. No doubt once the wives of prominent men had been courted and charmed by him, their husbands had lined up to be next. How else had he convinced them to finance one business scheme after another? Eventually, the businesses he had begun all wound up in Yankee hands, and though Strothers swore it was all a coincidence, she doubted him. He always made a pile of money on the deals, and no one could make her believe he hadn't sold out his Southern pride to do so. As far as Cam was concerned, Mr. Strothers Bennett had about as much charm as a rattlesnake fixing to strike, and the next time he tried to get all lovey-dovey with her, she was going to kick him in a place that would bring him to his knees a whole lot faster than the uncontrollable love he professed for her.

The moment the Senator came into view, her grimace faded, and Strothers Bennett was quickly forgotten. With thumbs hooked under his arms and an ivory-tipped pipe dangling from his mouth, the Senator looked as if he were carrying on a little politicking of his own. The excited way he was rocking from his heels to his toes alarmed her. It didn't do his heart good to get so excited, but she knew she could talk herself blue in the face, and he'd never hear her. With so many South Carolinians all in one place, he'd have no better chance to spread the word about his choice for President. Removal of Federal troops from Southern soil was mandatory, and since Hayes had sworn an oath to pull them out, he was the lesser of the two Yankee evils in the Senator's eyes.

Cam made no effort to hide her smile. How

she loved watching her father in action! Dixie had never had a more loyal son. No older than she at the time, he had been a major force in the fight for secession in '32 when tariffs on British goods made the North richer and the South poorer. He had argued for secession again and again in the '40s despite other states' reluctance to join South Carolina in withdrawing from the Union. It wasn't until Lincoln's election in 1860 that he finally succeeded. He had served faithfully in Jeff Davis' Confederate cabinet and had only escaped imprisonment after the War ended because the Union soldiers sent to get him couldn't find him. By the time they finally did, the powers in Washington figured he was too old to worry about. Greenville had been left standing during the War because of all the Unionist activity there, but that did not account for the Yanks steering clear of Caesar's Head. Folks around the South Carolina mountains took pride in saying no one in blue was man enough to lock horns with Senator Cameron Tranter! He was loved and respected by just about everyone in the state, maybe even the whole South, but Cam was certain no one adored him more than she.

Once more, she wished she had let him in on her secret. Many times since last year's running of the steeplechase, the temptation to confess all had been great, but each time she had decided against it out of fear that the news would bring on another of his chest pains.

All at once, he looked up and caught her stare. Their eyes held. Cam grinned in spite of herself.

His gaze still intent on her, the Senator scratched his nose, then gave his right ear a tug.

Her whole face broke into a smile. That gesture had been their own special signal for "I Love You" ever since she was a little girl. Obviously, the identity of the Masked Rider was no mystery to the Senator after all!

A few minutes later, Mr. Malone summoned all the riders with several blasts from his bugle, and Mr. Summer stepped up to the platform to make the long-overdue announcement.

"Ladies and gentlemen," he began at last in his loud, deep voice. "May I present you this year's participants in Caesar's Head's Second Annual Steeplechase." He turned to address the riders. "Gentlemen, please line up in the order in which you are called. Jeff Long. Pete Borough. Charlie Stanton. Ford Addison . . ."

Cam felt one last time to make certain her mask was in place and that no hairs were sticking out from under her cap.

"Jim Story. Carl Simon. Elliot Peak. Marcus Jones . . ."

She sat back and tried to calm the nervous jitters flitting about in her stomach. It would be a while yet before the Masked Rider was called. The previous year's winner would be the last to take his place among the field of contenders, and if her count was accurate, eighteen names still had to be read out.

"Nice-looking horse you got there, mister."

Cam didn't bother turning around to see who was atop the horse that jogged up alongside her. She'd recognize that long, slow drawl anywhere. Frank Chambers had been a plague on her ever since she was in braids.

"Yes, siree. Mighty fine looking animal

indeed." The rail-thin man beside her spat a stream of tobacco out between his horse's ears. "You're not looking to sell him, are you?"

Wishing desperately that he'd go away, Cam shook her head. It was all she could do to keep from sticking her tongue out at him. Even if she were planning to sell, he was the last person on earth she'd approach. He was always poking fun at Traveller. His heartless goading had made her cry at first, but that was before she had pointed Traveller at a jump and found out her big fellow could jump higher and run faster than any horse in the county.

Deaf old plow horse, indeed! She'd show him!

Frank edged his bay a little closer.

Even though she dared not look at him, she could sense he was eyeing Traveller very closely.

"Say, you know the Tranters from up at Willow Creek?"

Cam shook her head. She held her breath, hoping that Traveller's one painted stocking would keep her secret.

Frank looked down at Traveller's left hind leg. Laughing, he looked back up. "There's more than a leg's difference between those two. Yes, siree. This here is one magnificent animal. You let me know if you ever decide to sell him, hear?"

Her lip gave an angry twitch, but she held her tongue and nodded instead. Over my dead body! she shouted silently.

"James Slater. Marcus Calhoun. Frank Chambers . . ." Line up, please."

A hush fell over the crowd.

Cam took a deep breath. Her time had come.

Mr. Summers cleared his throat one last time.

"Ladies and gentlemen, may I present last year's winner, who I might add left in such a hurry he forgot to claim his winnings. Ladies and gentlemen, the Masked Rider!'"

Cheers and applause loud enough to be heard in neighboring counties erupted across the fairgrounds.

Biting her lip to keep from laughing at such an introduction, Cam stole a quick look at the Senator. If he didn't wipe that silly grin off his face, he'd give her away for sure!

Gathering her reins, she trotted into place beside Frank's reddish-brown mare and gave Traveller one last pat. He might not be able to hear the roar of the crowd, but he could surely sense the excitement building. Every tightly strung muscle was ready to spring into action.

Frank turned to appraise her horse once more, then shot a smile up at her. "May the best man win."

Or woman, she wanted to fire back.

Forcing her concentration to the task at hand, Cam leaned forward into a racing position. Heels low in the stirrups and hands high on her horse's neck, she mumbled a quick prayer. *Please Lord, keep us safe, and don't let me do anything foolish!*

The gun sounded.

Traveller shot out of the line with the rest of the field.

After the first turn, most of the horses had pulled ahead, but Cam took extra pains to keep Traveller's smooth, easy stride to a canter. There'd be plenty of time later to pour on the steam. For the time being, all she wanted him to do was feel out the lay of the land. Just like last year, once his confidence peaked, she'd give him his head. Until then, all she had to do was hang on and enjoy the ride. She wouldn't have to lay her whip to him once. She never did! Her big fellow as born to compete.

Seat out of the saddle, Cam stretched out over Traveller's neck and pointed him at the first obstacle. Power churned in his great limbs as he sailed over a five-foot hedge, clearing it with a good eighteen inches to spare. Unlike several of the other horses, he didn't shy at the ditch a few feet beyond, but flew over it, too, without giving it a second look.

"Good boy, good boy," she praised her mount, patting his neck.

Counting strides carefully, she urged him on through a mud pit that had been laid out to slow down the horses. Unlike the rest, Traveller charged right through it.

Cam was positive she knew the course as well, if not better, than those who had designed it, for she had spent every free hour during the past week walking it and picking out the distance from one jump to the next.

Like a winged steed in flight, Traveller glided over a stack of logs piled ten-high. He dropped down into the gulley on the other side, but the instant all four feet were planted firmly beneath him, he lunged back out without missing a stride.

How proud she was of him—her own magnificent Pegasus! Nothing could stop them now. Frank Chambers and those other louts would soon be eating their dust.

When Traveller flung himself, snorting, over a ditch at the quarter-mile steeple marker, it took all the strength she could summon to maintain control. More and more power was gathering under her with each loping stride. Head tossing wildly in anticipation of what lay beyond the next bend, he soared across the packed dirt wall in one enormous leap. Hardly touching the ground, he bolted on toward a row of barrels.

At every jump, Cam thought they would become airborne for sure. The course was Traveller's own domain. It was as though each obstacle had been constructed with his great ability in mind. Spectators and judges who had gathered at each jump were there solely to applaud him. Already halfway into the race, he had outdistanced all but three of his rivals without even breaking sweat. Everyone else was so far behind they were mere specks where she and Traveller had once been. Soon there would be no holding him back. He was built to jump higher and run faster than the rest.

By the time they approached the final jump, only one horse and rider separated them from the lead. But many a race had been won or lost at the end, and more than one rider had fallen prey to greed and ended up with a lame horse. Special caution had to be observed. Frank wasn't above trying something funny. He was out to show he was the best man, regardless the cost, so for the moment, Cam was content to hang back. Their time would come, and when it did, there'd be no stopping them.

The final obstacle was the one all riders dreaded, and with good reason, for it was a natural one and the most formidable. It was only a small creek, seven feet wide at most, but if a horse slipped on the wet stones bordering the water, the animal could break a leg or its rider's back.

Cam pulled up on the reins. Traveller slowed on command, just as she had known he would. Common sense demanded she wait until Frank was across where she could keep one eye on him before making her move.

As soon as Frank had cleared the stream, she picked her spot and, keeping a firm hold on the rein, charged across. She held her breath, scarcely daring to blink until they landed safely on the other side.

Without a moment's hesitation, Traveller raced up the bank and out in front and down the other side. Cam could hear Frank close on their heels, stinging his bay's backside with his whip, but the louder Frank cursed, the faster Traveller galloped.

Soon, all that lay between them and victory was a half-mile straight. Cam eased up on Traveller's mouth. She had held him back long enough. The time he had been waiting for had come.

A split second later, she thought for sure he was going to surge right out from under her. Foaming at the bit and tossing the froth back behind him, he released all the energy that he had kept harnessed inside him since the start of the race. He hit the stretch at a dead gallop. Even if she had wanted to, Cam wasn't sure she could stop him. The ground shook beneath him. There was no stopping him now!

Cam glanced back under her arm. The bay was lengths behind. They were home free! She let out a loud whoop, but then remembered what would happen if the judges found out she was a girl and cut it off abruptly.

Spectators waving and cheering them on welcomed them across the finish line. Cam paused only long enough to hear the Masked Rider proclaimed the winner, then sailed out of the arena and into the woods surrounding it. Maybe next year, or the year after, she'd stop long enough to claim her winnings; for the time being savoring the sweet taste of victory was enough.

Cheers and applause still ringing loud in her ears, she spurred Traveller far into the woods until the noise from the fairgrounds was only a whisper through the trees. She halted suddenly at a fork in the trail, then jerked off her mask and flung it into the shrubs in hopes of misguiding any pursuer. With a quick change of rein, she whipped back around and trotted in the direction from which she had just come. A few hundred yards away from the fork, hidden underneath a clump of dead bush and fallen limbs, she found what she was looking for—a narrow footpath that could easily go unnoticed if one didn't know exactly where to search. Her scheme had worked last year, and there was no reason to believe it wouldn't now.

A quick look behind her, and Cam dismounted. After running up the stirrup leathers and looping the reins over his head, she led Traveller through shoulder-high bulrushes and across a soft, miry patch of ground that yielded with each step. In the clearing beyond the quagmire was her place of refuge. All that remained of what half-a-century before had been a busy mining camp was a few rotten timbers to mark the entrance to the shaft. There she would wait, just as she had done the year before, until night fell. Then she would make her way back to Willow Creek in the dark. She wouldn't be missed at the party that evening. Her friends would think she was still sulking about not being permitted to enter the race this year or last. Only the Senator would know better.

The supplies she had dropped off the day before were right where she had left them, hidden in a clump of sawgrass. It took nearly a half hour of hard scrubbing before the turpentine lifted the white paint off Traveller's leg. Afterwards, to ward off cramps, she vigorously massaged the solid chestnut limbs with a linament-and-vinegar mix. The saddle was left on in case she needed to make a quick getaway.

"That should take care of you for a while, sweet pea," Cam mumbled with soft affection as she blanketed her horse to keep off the cool breeze. With a hug and a kiss on his nose, she left him munching contentedly on a straw bale she had brought there yesterday with everything else. There was no need to tie him. He never ventured far away.

Wishing she had thought to bring herself something to eat, she slid down in front of a pine tree. She had a long wait ahead of her. There she must remain until night had completely fallen. Only then could she risk making her way home. She hoped there would be enough stars out to light the path, but even if there weren't, she felt confident they would manage just fine. Luckily, few people ever ventured into the marsh past dusk. Losing one's way in the sinister maze of gnarled tree branches was not the only threat the marsh held. That neck of the woods was said to be haunted. More than one poor soul in a drunken stupor had stumbled onto the wrong path by mistake and had been greeted by the ghost of a miner who had lost his head and his wife to the gold mine's owner fifty years before. Legend had it the miner would never rest until both his possessions were returned to their rightful owner.

Cam shivered in spite of herself. She didn't believe in such nonsense. Not really. The mine had been closed down because there was no gold to be found. Granted, the unfaithful wife had committed suicide a few years later, and the mine's owner did drink himself to death, but a headless ghost could hardly be held responsible for their self-destruction.

No sooner had she leaned back against the tree than a twig snapped. She caught her breath, then released it in a relieved sigh. There was no ghost, only Traveller shifting his weight from one leg to the other.

Once again she settled back. The tension was slow in draining from her weary limbs. Every sound she heard was magnified ten times. Each shadow was the headless ghost coming after her.

A quick glance into the clouds curdling overhead brought an immediate grin. Everyone knew ghosts haunted only during the full moon, and tonight the low-hanging moon was curved like a sickle.

Another frown creased her mouth a moment later. Last month's full moon had proven fatal for poor Clayton Griffin. Most folks agreed that had it not been for the full moon, his horse would never have gone crazy and trampled him to death. Old man Griffin might not have given anybody the time of day, but he had a way with horses. The Senator said he had been decorated numerous times for his valiant performance as a cavalry officer. How ironic that he should die in such a horrible manner! Poor Jackson had gone nearly crazy after finding his long-time employer lying in the stall with his head bashed in.

In the distance, she could hear the fiddler warming up. Best to get her mind off such thoughts as deaths and ghosts, she told herself yet again. If she wasn't careful, her imagination would run away with her for sure.

The picking and singing she heard in the distance meant she would have a safe passage home. Everyone in and around Caesar's Head would be at the dance. If anyone had been out looking for the Masked Rider, they would have given up and returned to the festivities by now. As Frank Chambers had told her last year, a fellow would have to be crazy to leave good music, good whiskey, and good women to go off in search of some fool daredevil who wouldn't show his face.

"Won't be long now, sweetheart, before we're both tucked in our beds," Cam whispered as she adjusted Traveller's saddle. She ran her hand down the length of his muscular neck and kissed his shoulder. "You deserve a nice, long rest, and you'll get it."

A warm nose nuzzled her cheek. She giggled softly. Sometimes she wondered if he were really deaf or just play-acting. Most always, he acted as if he could hear her and knew not only what she was saying but what she was thinking. Maybe he could just sense the love she felt for him. Even if he had turned out to be nothing but the clumsy old plug Frank called him, she wouldn't trade him for the finest eventing horse in the state.

Cam swung herself up into the saddle, picked up the reins, and trotted Traveller into the night. Was it the next bend or the one after where they veered north? she wondered a few minutes later. If she could only spot that tree stump, she'd know for sure. Angry at herself for losing that keen sense of direction she usually prided herself on, Cam stopped to have a look around. All the trees looked the same, and if there was an old stump out there, she couldn't see it. There weren't enough stars out to light her way after all. How stupid not to have planned for such an emergency! The box of matches she had left on the water pump wasn't doing her much good now.

Convinced she was going around in circles after seeing the same knotted trunk twice, Cam dropped the rein. Traveller's quick and certain steps eased her anxiety. It was plain as day he knew the fastest way to get to his bucket of oats.

Shooting straight up in the saddle a moment later, she jerked on the reins. Traveller froze in response to her sudden tension. Had she imagined hearing hooves thumping, she wondered, straining to see into the darkness, or was there really another horse approaching?

Not waiting to find out, she yanked Traveller off the path and into a stand of trees. Struggling to make out each little sound, she waited, hardly daring to draw a breath for fear of it ringing through the woods. The thumping faded into the distance. If it was another horse, it was going away from her after all.

She leaned down to give Traveller a reassuring pat. "Everything's fine, honey pie. Nothing to worry about." Even as she mumbled her soothing words, she didn't doubt for a minute that they were intended to calm her as well.

She waited a few moments longer, but except for the hammering inside her chest, all was quiet. She caught sight of that elusive old stump at last and breathed a sigh of relief. They were hardly more than a stone's throw from the front porch of Willow Creek.

The slightest nudge was all it took to urge Traveller into a canter.

Won't be long now, she sang to herself over and over. Won't be long before I'll be sitting down to a plate of Ludie Mae's hot biscuits and red-eyed gravy.

They rounded the curve at a gallop. All at once, Traveller stopped dead in his tracks. A white horse bolted out of the night in front of them. Something black was sitting atop it.

Cam pulled on the reins. Her heart dropped to her stomach, and a scream stuck in her throat. Man or demon? She couldn't figure out what. A white horse! Clayton Griffin had a white horse!

A low-hanging limb caught her neck as Traveller lunged forward again. She tried to duck, but it was too late. She could feel herself toppling off backwards.

She had no recollection of hitting the ground, but when she tried to pull herself up, every muscle and bone ached. All of the wind had been knocked out of her. For an instant, she forgot exactly what had caused her fall, but then, when she sensed someone's presence behind her, she remembered. The figure in black! She spotted Traveller standing a few yards away, munching at some grass. If only she could reach him, they might still have a chance of escaping!

Cam scrambled to her feet. Blood rushed to her head, and the dark woods began spinning. She could feel herself sinking lower and lower.

Two arms reached out for her. She tried to fight them away but collapsed right into their hold instead. *Who are you? Who are you?* she wanted to cry out. But her demands gurgled in her throat.

"Easy, easy there, young fellow."

She felt her limbs uncoil as she was stretched back out onto the ground. Ghosts didn't talk, did they?

"Let's see if anything's broken."

No, of course they didn't. If he meant her harm, he'd certainly not be concerned over her injuries, she reasoned, still feeling groggy.

Cam squinted up at the black-caped figure hovering above her. Everything was a blur. She blinked several times to bring the figure into focus. The shadow was a man. There was no doubt about that. His touch, his voice, everything about him was firm and decisive. If only he'd lower his hood and show his face. Was he someone she knew? Probably not. There was nothing at all familiar about him.

Exploring hands began to roam over her.

A moan escaped from between clenched lips. Those hands—how strong they were! How powerfully they massaged the feeling back into her legs. Under their masterful guidance, life began seeping back into her. Her whole body came alive and awake. How wonderful the sensations his touch evoked! She should stop him, scream for help, but she could not. He might very well have come from beyond the grave, for his touch was definitely not of the earth she knew. It was sheer heaven.

Strong fingers slowly made their way up her waist, their power giving comfort to the aching limbs they were rubbing. But what was going on inside her? Whatever the tumult building inside her, it was wild and wonderful, and she wanted it never to cease. Her chest rose and fell with each labored breath. At any minute, the plump, rounded breasts she had tried so hard to hide were going to burst right through the bandage underneath her shirt.

Indigo eyes closed languidly; her head sank deeper and deeper into the cool earth. Surely he wasn't—yes, he was undoing buttons! Even if she could manage somehow to move, she wasn't sure she would, not as long as such delicious shivers were shooting up her back. All that was left to do was languish in his embrace. Surely heaven could be no sweeter!

"What the hell?" exclaimed a voice filled with surprise and anger.

Shame scarleted her cheeks. Her eyes flew open. She wasn't dreaming after all. There really was a man kneeling beside her. What on earth had gotten into her? How could she possibly have permitted him such free access to her body? Any decent girl would have wrung his neck or died trying. Only a hussy would let him do such unspeakable things and get away with it!

He jerked off her cap.

A cascade of thick black tresses tumbled out.

"Well, I'll be damned!" Shaking his head in disbelief, the stranger remained frozen in his half-kneeling pose. "You don't have to be afraid of me, m'am," he told her, his voice becoming much gentler. "I'm not going to hurt you. Can you hear me?"

Even if she could speak, she was too embarrassed to utter a word.

The man started to reach for her, then quickly pulled back his arm. "Where do you hurt?"

"Everywhere," she managed, her voice barely a whisper. She sat up slowly. "As soon as I catch my breath, I'll be fine."

Squinting up at him, she tried to make out his face, but leaning back made her neck hurt even more. The harder she tried to distinguish his dark features, the hazier they became.

"Who are you?" she finally asked.

He smoothed back the hair from her eyes. His touch proved far gentler than she had expected. "You don't know me."

Bracing her against him, he helped her to her feet.

"My name is Cam—Camille Tranter. What's yours?" She leaned against a tree for support. If only the woods would stop whirling around so she could get a better look at his face!

He acted as though he had not heard her question. "I'll get your horse, Miss Tranter."

"Oh, no, please don't bother. He doesn't like it when . . ."

Sure enough, just as he was about to take hold of the rein, Traveller kicked out and leapt forward, then took off in a gallop.

Cam gave a weak smile when the stranger returned. "What I tried to tell you is that he doesn't take kindly to anybody but me handling him." Taking a deep breath, she took a few steps away from the tree. "He knows how to get home. It's not far. I can walk."

Her legs gave way beneath her, but the man caught her before she fell again.

"I don't think you can walk anywhere," he told her, ever so gently. "Here, let me help you."

Authoritative fingers closed tight around her waist. The pressure flowing from their tips made her legs all the more unsteady.

"There, how's that?" he asked kindly.

Cam could do little more than nod as he turned her around to face him. Her arms reached out for his, and she held on tight. If she let go, he'd vanish for sure. Even though she could not see them, she knew his eyes were intent on hers. Something had locked them together. If only she could look deep into his gaze. Then she would know if he was experiencing the same all-encompassing sensations that she felt. Was she the cause of his unsettled breathing? she wondered. He was certainly to blame for hers.

As though she had willed it to be, his head lowered to hers. Still she could not distinguish his face, but it didn't matter. Not really. She knew he was no ghost, and feminine intuition assured her he was no Yankee renegade who used his job as an excuse to take liberties with whatever or whomever he desired. It wasn't necessary to see his face to know he was as aware as she of the special moment passing between them. A strange, consuming force had swallowed them both. Even had she had the strength to walk away from him, she would not. The closer he drew her, the nearer to him she wanted to be.

Deep down, she knew she was about to be kissed. Against her better judgment, too, she knew that she would utter not one word of protest. Her heart pounded louder and louder. Head tilted back, eyes closed in anticipation, she waited—waited for that one moment of ecstasy she was sure would come.

A moment later, her eyes opened. Disappointment swelled inside her. What had gone wrong? She could sense his piercing gaze on her, but what was his look conveying? If only he would make known his face. Then she could read the message surely spoken in his eyes.

After what seemed an eternity, he finally spoke. "I shall see that you get home safely." Disentangling his arms, he stepped back, then turned away. "It's the least I can do for the—for the inconvenience I've caused."

Her heart cried out for him to return. Surely he could perceive the turmoil mounting inside her. Was he immune to such feelings? Her face was not hidden from him. Could he not see the longing written all over it? How cruel he was!

"I can find my own way home, thank you."

Determined not to glance twice behind her, she walked away as fast as her shaky ankles would permit. How dare he dismiss her so abruptly! Who did he think she was anyway, some kind of tramp who waited in the woods and preyed on unsuspecting strangers?

Her heart sank lower and lower with each labored step. Of course, he did! What else was he to think? After all, her behavior was not what one might expect of a girl with her upbringing. Even if she could find the words to do so, would he believe her if she told him she'd never been kissed before? Had the fall jarred loose her good sense as well?

"Miss Tranter, I . . ."

A hand came from nowhere and grabbed hold of her elbow. "I don't know what to say. I can't begin to explain what got into me."

Go on, go on, she wanted to cry out, but her dignity forbade her showing her true feelings. "Yes?"

He let her go. "I'm sorry."

Her arm dropped back to her side. She affected an air of indifference. "There's no cause for apologies, sir. Now if you will excuse me, I must be getting home."

What was intended to be a dismissal just as unfeeling as his own dwindled into stammers. How could she possibly convey to him what she was at that very moment experiencing? She hardly understood the alien sensations herself. Maybe when she was older . . . her heart sank. Older? After tonight, she'd probably never see him again.

"Wait here."

Even though she knew better, she did as he requested. He returned a moment later leading his horse.

Before she knew what had happened, he had lifted her into the saddle and swung himself up behind her.

Cam dared not utter a single word as they galloped toward Willow Creek, for the slightest sound would surely have given her away. Leaning back into his embrace, with her head resting on his chest, she knew she could languish there forever. She was so close, she could feel the pounding of his heart. It was in unison with her own. So close, and yet so far, far away.

Hot breath filtering through her dark tresses singed her ears and sent shivers of fire coursing up and down her spine. Surely he was as aware as she of the tremendous swelling inside her chest. If only she could capture that moment and hold it in her mind always!

Much too soon, the lights from Willow Creek were beckoning to them. A few more minutes and he'd be lost to her forever.

"Please, won't you come in for a bite of supper?" she asked as he halted his horse in front of the house. She tried to turn around. Perhaps she might get a glimpse of his face so it would be imprinted on her mind forever. How she loved the strength enveloping her! "Please, say you'll stay. Just for a while."

"You're most kind, but I cannot." His arms held her firm in their determination that she look nowhere but straight ahead. "This must be good-bye, Miss Tranter. At least for now."

Her hand clamped down on his wrist. No! She would not let him go. Now that she had found him, she'd never release him. "Please, you must stay," she choked. "You must."

"I shall return." His cheek grazed hers. "I promise."

A soft moan escaped her lips. "When? You must tell me when."

"When the time is right, I shall return."

His answer did nothing to comfort her. How was such uncertainty supposed to be interpreted?

"Days? Months? Years?" she begged him. "Can you tell me that at least?" She sank back farther into his hard chest. Oh, how she longed to press her mouth to his, just this once! To kiss and be kissed by him would surely be a hundred, no a thousand times more wonderful than she had ever thought such an act would be.

Cam couldn't bring herself to let go of his arm, and she could tell it had taken every ounce of determination he could summon to remove her from his hold. Tears she could no longer control streamed down her cheeks. Whether he was real or a dream, he would soon be lost to her forever. She couldn't bear even thinking it, much less having it come true.

He leaned down to her. His hood remained in place.

Suddenly, it dawned on her how odd it was for someone to be dressed in a heavy cape and hood on such a sultry summer night. What did he have to hide? Try as hard as she might, she still could not distinguish what lay beyond the shadows covering him. Was he afraid of showing his face for fear she would find it repulsive? Even if he were scarred, she'd love him all the same. What was he trying to hide? What if he were some fugitive from the law? It didn't matter. She couldn't, she wouldn't, let him go!!

Holding her hand to prevent it from lowering his hood, the stranger kissed one cheek then the other. "I must go."

"But you cannot." She fought to hold on to his hand. "You cannot! I won't let you!"

His lips grazed the palm of her hand. "I shall return when you are older." Without warning, his lips found their way to hers and whispered a kiss across them. "You have my word as a gentleman."

With that, he whipped his horse around and charged back into the woods without another glance behind him.

"But I don't even know your name. . . ."

With the realization that she never would, at least not until he wanted it to be known to her, she sank down onto the porch. "Who are you? Where did you come from?" she wondered aloud.

Cam lifted a quivering finger to her mouth and ever so lightly traced the fullness of her lips. His presence could still be felt there, his lips imprinted on hers for eternity. Her lips were no longer hers alone. They belonged to him as well, and one day he would return to take possession of what was rightfully his. One day. How long would she have to wait for the storm brewing inside her to be quieted?

Cam smiled through tear-clouded eyes. She'd wait just as long as she had to. There was no reason to be sad. He'd come back to her. He had given her his word as a gentleman, and she believed him. No true Southern gentleman ever broke his word.

Her spirits soared. Besides, she *knew* he would come back to her. She had a feeling he would. Not just any ordinary feeling, but a very special feeling, and when she had one of those, she was hardly ever wrong. Feelings like those were heaven-sent gifts, and she had been born with a veil over her forehead that caused her to be blessed with a unique power to perceive an event before it actually happened. Of course, her second sight was her and the Senator's and Ludie Mae's secret. As superstitious as mountain folk were, they'd think her some kind of a witch if they knew.

Preacher Evans said faith could move mountains, and right now, Cam had all the faith in the world that her mysterious stranger would keep his promise.

2

Two Years Later—Summer Of 1878

Hugging her pillow close to her breast, Cam snuggled down farther into the bed and luxuriated in her sweetly wicked surroundings. The room was quiet, so quiet the wax could be heard dripping from the sole candle on the bedside table. Eerie shadows danced on the wallpaper's pink roses, but there was no reason to be afraid. She welcomed the coming of midnight and greeted it with arms opened wide. Only at that magic hour could true happiness be found.

All that covered her was a thin sheet, its fine-spun folds cooling her bare skin from the heat of the night. Thick, long masses of hair the blue-black of a raven's feathers lay over her like a mantle. Anxious eyes piercing the darkness with tourmaline intentness were fixed on the window, watching the moon play hide-and-seek with the clouds.

It won't be long now, she told herself confidently. Soon, very soon he would come to her, just as he had done every night for the past two years.

Closing her eyes, she relived all the wonderful nights the two of them had shared in that very room. Recalling each kiss, every caress, in vivid detail sent hot flashes flaring across her.

Then, all at once, as if her willing it had made it happen, her black-caped lover appeared beside the bed. Arms outstretched, she beckoned him nearer. Though she could still not distinguish his face, she could sense the look of love in his gaze. In answer to her silent pleas, he knelt down and kissed her.

Pulling him closer and closer, she yielded to lips as hot and as hungry as the night.

He pulled away, but only for a moment—just long enough to snuff out the candle.

The room became pitch black, just the way he insisted it must always be. Cam could sense his every move. She knew them now by heart. Off came the cape and the hood that kept his face a mystery, then his trousers and shirt.

Gently, tenderly, he drew back the sheet. Penetrating eyes feasted on the sight that welcomed him. "Camille, Camille, my Camille," he whispered over and over. Scooping her into his arms, he held her tight, so tight she thought her breath would be cut off. Ripe, eager breasts were crushed by the stone hardness of his chest. "Camille, my darling Camille."

Fiery passion smothered her lips with a kiss that was long and deep and searching all the way to her soul and beyond. Hands as powerful as they were masterful explored soft plump curves, discovering places she had never before dared to think even existed. Pebble-hard peaks rose to their highest, and the swollen mounds supporting them begged to be molded into whatever shape he desired. Every muscle, every nerve ablaze, she ached for more, so much more. In his arms she was driven by a desire that begged his total, absolute possession. He was her king, she his courtesan who found happiness only in pleasing and serving him.

Lips breathing fire teased a path of kisses across her belly's roundness and into the silk between soft, warm thighs before slowly making their way back up to her mouth.

Flattened by his weight, Cam locked him to her in a vise-like grip and threw her legs around him, clamping them onto his hips.

Stroking the fire burning rampant inside her, her lover laid claim to what had been his ever since the night near the old mine.

His limbs became her limbs. Every breath and heartbeat were shared. Hot blood raced through one, then coursed onto the other where it pulsated with the same rejuvenating vigor before reversing its route. He was her life, her love, her sole reason for existence. His burning urgency set free all the secret longings held captive within her. Vibrations tremoring inside the secret spots he explored sent her into awesome shudders. Cries of delight which could no longer be contained burst forth and were smothered by one kiss after another lest their midnight meetings be discovered. And afterward, as she slowly drifted out of this world and into one of divine ecstasy, her mystery lover began it all again.

"Why, Cam Tranter! Are you going to stay in that bed all day?"

Cam came awake with a start. Where was he? What had happened to him? One moment he was lying there with her and making such sweet love, and the next he was gone. Once again he had vanished and left her behind.

Frowning, she shielded her eyes from the jabs of sunlight and searched the room. He truly was gone. He always was when she awakened. All she had left of the man she loved was the man in her dreams. Soon her fantasies, too, would fade away into the night. She could hardly even remember the sound of his voice.

After another moment, her eyes came into focus on the red-checkered pattern of the apron-bibbed figure hovering over her. "Please, Ludie Mae. Do close those drapes. That sun is blinding me."

Cheeks as bright as the checks on her apron puffed with early-morning enthusiasm. "Come on, little darling, you got to get up some time, so it might as well be now."

"If it's all the same to you, I'd just as soon it be later." Cam rolled over and buried her head under the pillow. The coming of another day was a battle that had to be fought every morning. If only she could prolong the night so he could spend a little while longer in her arms!

"Rise and shine, pudding!"

Cam remained in hiding. She dearly loved the housekeeper, Ludie Mae, who was the closest thing to a mother she had ever known, but the sound of her sweet chirping voice never failed to depress her early in the morning. It seemed always to mark the end to her lover's visit.

"Why, if I didn't know better, I'd think you were pining away over some man, the way you waste away your days in that bed," Ludie Mae scolded her.

Cam threw back the covers. "You of all people should know better than that. There's not a man around these parts worth giving a second thought to, much less losing sleep over."

Troubled eyes settled on the pendant Cam always wore around her neck. "It's not the ones around here I'm worried over," Ludie Mae said.

Cam sighed. She knew what had prompted Ludie Mae's observation. When she began talking about her black-caped mystery man two years before, both Ludie Mae and the Senator had been convinced that her fall had caused more damage to her head than a sore spot. They had listened patiently while she recounted how a black-caped stranger whisked her through the woods on his giant white steed, but from the looks on their faces, she knew they were just humoring her by saying they believed her. They probably really believed he was a figment of her imagination, one she would outgrow as she got older. The trouble was, she was a grown woman now, and her sweet obsession remained. Perhaps they'd believe her when he returned to her, as he promised he would.

Cam slipped the gold disc out of sight the moment Ludie Mae turned her back. Between her breasts was where it belonged. That was where it had been ever since the morning after their encounter, when she had returned to the spot they had met in desperate hopes of finding some clue to his identity. Lying in the clearing near the mine was a button the size of a coin. Something was engraved on it—a lion, an eagle—some sort of animal. The picture had faded with age, but it didn't matter. He had placed it there for her to find as his way of telling her he truly did intend to keep the promise he made to her. One day she, as well as the button, would be returned to their rightful owner. Until then, as long as she had it with her, a little part of him would remain close to her heart, right where he belonged for all time.

Her face erupted into smiles. How could she have forgotten? Caesar's Head's Fourth Annual Steeplechase would be run today, and tonight—tonight would surely be the night when she would once again revel in the embrace of her wonderful black-caped stranger. He had promised to return when she was older. Well, she was a woman now, a woman who could give and receive love. It was time for him to make good on his promise!

Two years! Had it really been that long? So much had happened. More than once she had thought she would lose the Senator when horrible chest pains had him doubled over and gasping for breath. But each time he had fought his way out of it. Thank the good Lord that he was a fighter, but he had been under great pressures. The tobacco harvest of '76 had been the best ever—so good in fact that the Senator had left half of it curing in the barn two years longer than usual to command an even higher price. But last year's crop had been a total disaster, thanks to root rot. Getting by was about all they had been able to manage since then. Their savings had been depleted, and there was hardly enough money left to pay wages to the skeleton crew they had to keep on to tend the fields. But they'd make do. They always did!

And Abbey! Two years ago they had been inseparable—the tag-along twins, Ludie Mae used to call them. What a shame their life-long friendship had ended abruptly on Abbey's wedding day!

"Have you been listening to me at all, young lady?"

Cam looked up, grinning sheepishly. "I'm sorry, Ludie Mae. I must have been day-dreaming."

"As usual." Ludie Mae cast a disapproving scowl in her direction before going on about her business. "Frank Chambers was asking after you yesterday. He wanted to know if you'd be going to the race." Ludie Mae sounded casual enough as she closed the bottom drawer of the mahogany bow-front chest. "He's a nice fellow. His pa's doing real well with those general stores of his. Reckon they'll one day belong to Frank."

"I wonder how long it'll take him to run them into the ground." Legs curled under her, Cam sat on the edge of the bed hugging the foot post. He'd come to her tonight. She just knew it. After all, he was her intended.

Smiling, she caressed the curved wood. She had never put much stock in "dumb suppers," but that was before she attended one at Sue Wilkerson's last month. After a repast of salty cornbread, the man she was to one day wed was revealed to her in a dream, just as the old wives' tales said—and that man had been garbed in a black cape and hood.

"What about Jim Ryan?"

It took a moment for Ludie Mae's question to register. "You'd have me tied up with *him*?" Cam protested. "I thought you were my friend. Why, Jim Ryan sniffs after everything in a dress!" Indigo eyes twinkled devilishly. " 'Course, I reckon he'd do—if a girl doesn't mind being treated like a cow that needs milking."

Ludie Mae expelled an exasperated sigh. "Hush up, girl. How you go on! Why, the Senator would turn you over his knee in a minute if he heard you talking like that."

"He's never done it before, so I expect it's too late to start now." Cam hopped off the bed with a sudden burst of energy and stretched her arms high into the air. "Could be that's why I'm such a hellion."

Cam couldn't resist the urge to give Ludie Mae a hearty squeeze as she passed her. No doubt she was at that very minute blaming herself for failing to make Cam into a proper lady. Since she first came to Willow Creek to tend to the Senator's wee babe while he was off serving his state, Ludie Mae had considered it her sole mission in life to see that the infant didn't suffer because her mother had abandoned her. And, Cam suspected as well, that in the back of Ludie Mae's mind was the firm conviction that she'd do all that was needed to make certain she didn't turn out like her mother and break the Senator's heart. Ludie Mae had no worry on that account. Cam would die before causing her father one moment of grief.

"Cami, you all right?"

She gave the kind hand reaching out to her a quick pat. "Of course I am. I was just thinking about how awful I've been to you, that's all."

"Well, if you were my daughter, young lady . . ." began Ludie Mae as she folded Cam close to her bosom. "Awful as you are, I wouldn't change one thing about you."

Cam kissed the furrow across her housekeeper's forehead, then hid her face in her shoulder as she had done as a little girl when creatures in the night got after her. For all practical purposes, Ludie Mae *was* her mother. She had raised her, had tea parties with her under the weeping willow, and had been there whenever she needed her. A natural mother could not have done more.

"I love you, Ludie Mae. You know that?" Long black lashes batted up at her old friend. "And the next time you tell me how incorrigible I am, I shall quote those very words of yours."

"Yes, I'm sure you will."

Cam returned to her bed and sat back down. She pretended not to notice, but she knew her old friend was standing with her lips pursed and her hands on her hips, looking at her and debating whether or not to leave well enough alone.

"You may as well say it and get it over with before you burst," Cam finally told her. It was not hard to figure out what kind of speech Ludie Mae was about to deliver. She had heard it so often that she knew it by heart.

"You're eighteen, Cami, nearly nineteen," Ludie Mae began, predictably. "If you don't want to end up an old maid like me, you'd better find yourself some nice young man and settle down. Raise a family, maybe."

"You've said it yourself time and again, there's not a man in this county who could put up with me," Cam said. She could see immediately that her attempt to be humorous had no effect at all on Ludie Mae.

"Just don't you waste your life away."

Cam sensed Ludie Mae was about to attach "like me" to the end of her advice. Poor dear. What a sad life she must have led. There had been a man once, a man she loved very much, but when he married another, she had been heartbroken and swore never to love again. Too bad the Senator had soured on women years ago. A woman like Ludie Mae was a rare find indeed.

"Somebody'll come along," Cam ssured her, hoping to cheer her up. "Then all your teaching will finally pay off."

Ludie Mae fluffed the pillows. "Pity you let that nice Strothers Bennett get away. He'd have made a fine catch."

Cam gritted her teeth. If she wasn't afraid of giving Ludie Mae a heart attack, she'd tell her just what a fine catch Strothers Bennett really was, what a refined gentleman. He had cornered her in the barn and tried to entice his fiancee's best friend into a few rolls in the hay the day before his wedding, and when his rattlesnake charm failed, he had resorted to force. How shocked he had been when Cam rammed her knee right between his legs as hard as she could. Believing that Abbey ought to know the kind of swine she was marrying, Cam had then told her exactly what had happened, hoping she would call off the marriage. But by the time Cam got to her, Abbey had already heard Strother's version of the story and accused her friend of lying. How hurt Cam had been that Abbey believed that "fine gentleman's" lies. According to him, Cam had lured him into the barn and thrown herself at him, pleading that he marry her instead.

"Strothers Bennett is far from nice." Just saying his name aloud left an awful taste in her mouth, just like when he slobbered all over her that day. "Aside from the fact that I loathe and despise the man, he happens to be married to my oldest, dearest friend."

"Don't see Abbey much around here anymore," remarked Luddie Mae, looking over her shoulder.

Cam pretended it didn't matter, but that made it hurt all the more. "I guess that's what happens when you have a husband to answer to."

As much as Cam loved Ludie Mae, there were times when she'd just as soon not discuss certain details with her, and what happened with Abbey and Strothers was one of them. All along, she had pegged him for just what he was —an opportunist who would do anything and use anyone to get what he wanted. Not long ago he had come around Willow Creek trying to court her, but she hadn't wanted to be bothered with him. It didn't take much sense to figure out it was Willow Creek that he was really after. Word had got around town that some fellow from up North wanted to set up a logging operation in the South Carolina mountains and had enlisted Strother's help in finding suitable property. What could be more to his liking than three hundred acres of virgin timberland that the Union torches had somehow missed? Strothers found out in a hurry that his sweet talking did not work on the Tranters, for the Senator would rather die than part with his land, and Cam herself would prefer death to marrying that snake! However, whoever wanted to acquire

Willow Creek's forest had apparently lost interest, because they'd never heard anything else about it. No doubt Strothers had been deprived of a hefty commission, and knowing she was partly to blame did Cam's heart good.

Ludie Mae dropped a neatly pressed bundle of folded clothes into her lap. "Here. You looked like a ragamuffin last year. Seems like you could have at least taken the trouble to iron out the wrinkles before going out in public. Bad enough you have to run around in such a get-up!"

"You knew all along, didn't you? I had a feeling you did." Cam lifted up a pair of dark breeches and a crisp white shirt, both still warm from the iron. Her eyes came alive with a devilish gleam. "Were you shocked?"

The housekeeper headed to the door, her expression unchanged. "Trust me, gal, there is nothing you could possibly do that would shock me!"

"We'll see." Cam chuckled. "We'll see."

Scrambling out of her nightclothes and into her riding apparel, Cam ran to the mirror and surveyed her reflection. From whatever angle she viewed them, her curves and fleshy parts remained all too obvious. Even had she not already decided that this steeplechase would be the last, she knew only too well that her days of donning boy's dress were over. She'd be lucky if her identity was not given away even before the race began. No matter how tight the bandage around her chest, her breasts could no longer be concealed.

She sat down at her dressing table and began braiding her hair. A clipping she had torn out of last week's newspaper stared at her from the corner of the toilet mirror. There was no reason to read it. After reading and re-reading it a hundred times since it appeared in last Friday's *Gazette,* she knew it by heart. Up until a week ago, she had seriously considered not participating in the race and leaving everyone guessing just who the masked rider really was. But the announcement in the paper had made the temptation to ride one last time impossible to resist. In order to promote local business and inititate state-wide interest in the event, the winner of the steeplechase would not only receive the hundred-dollar purse, but would collect the three previous years' prize money as well. Never, at least not in any race she had ever heard about, had the stakes been so high. Four hundred dollars! That was all the money in the world. It would certainly cover all their harvesting expenses and tide them over a little longer besides.

Cam stopped downstairs long enough to stuff several ham biscuits into her pockets, then raced out to the barn. Traveller was already out of his stall. Tail and mane were braided and knotted, and his chestnut coat was wet and glistening in the early morning sun. The Senator was sitting on a turned-up crate painting the left hind leg of her horse.

Smiling softly, she slowed her stride and approached on tiptoes.

"Don't you swat that mangey tail at me, you no-account cuss, or I'll chop it off for you," she heard her father mumble. He loved that horse as much as she and nothing, not even his mumbled insults, would make her think otherwise.

"Regardless of what that daughter of mine thinks, you're nothing but a horse, and a mighty upitty one at that, so if you know what's good for you, you'd better start behaving."

"Morning, Cami, sugar," he called out then, without looking up from his work. "What's left of it, anyway. I was starting to think you had took sick on me."

She leaned down and kissed a spot on his head where the silvery blue strands were becoming thinner and fewer with each year that went by. "Never could sneak up on you," she said, offering him a biscuit. "Reckon us Tranters got a little Indian in us?"

He threatened her with the paint brush. "You just watch your tongue, young lady. I'm no mood to get riled. This damned horse of yours won't stand still long enough to get his leg painted."

"Looks to me like you're doing just fine." She kissed the tip of Traveller's nose, then held out her hand.

"Humph, sometimes I think you love that old plug more than you love your own poor pappy."

"What are you complaining for?" She gave her horse another kiss, then sat down on the ground beside her father. "I could have given you the sugar and him the biscuit."

She hungrily attacked her food and watched as he put on the finishing touches. His hand was much steadier than hers. No doubt he had been up since before daybreak readying her horse, and she doubted the reason had anything to do with his concern for Traveller's looks. He was worried. The anxiety was written all over his face.

"Since when did you hire on as groom around

here?" she asked finally.

His good-humored snort didn't offend her in the least. That was just one of his traits that she adored. He pretended to be a grumpy old bear when he was really just a pussycat.

She popped the last bite into her mouth, then leaned back and stared up through the drooping limbs of the willow. Not quite eight o'clock yet and the heat was already rising—today was going to be another scorcher. What little breeze there was couldn't begin to cool things down.

Patiently, she watched and waited. Sooner or later he'd let slip what was bothering him.

"You know, Cami, I hear tell there's twenty-five or thirty fellows signed up for the steeple-chase," he remarked finally. "Four hundred dollars is a lot of money, and I expect most of them'll do just about anything to win it."

"If you're looking to make a bet, I hear that fellow in the red mask is about as good as they come."

She could see immediately that her teasing had failed to soften his forlorn look and knitted brow. What with picking-time coming up, he had enough to worry about without having to concern himself with her getting trampled by some fool out to make his fortune at everyone else's expense. He had been troubled over the race ever since she showed him the announcement in the paper.

Sensing his anxiety, she reached out and took hold of his arm. "You just say the word and I won't race."

Her piece said, she wrapped her arms around her knees and waited for him to mull over her offer. The final decision rested with him, and she loved him enough to abide by it.

"What a shock those boys are in for when they find out who's behind that red mask," the Senator said, giving in to a chuckle. "You keep that up, though, and you'll be living out your days right here at Willow Creek, a little old maid."

"Nothing would please me more, I assure you." The matter settled, Cam jumped to her feet and began currying her horse. The Senator never said so, not in so many words, but she knew he worried a great deal over what would become of her once he passed on. He needn't concern himself, she had told him time and time again, but he paid no heed to her assurances. Why was it that everyone, her father and Ludie Mae included, thought a woman had to have a man to be secure in life? Husband or not, nobody was ever going to tame her. Not if she could help it.

Her gaze drifted to the dense stand of pines bordering the front lawn. Of course, if the right man did happen along, she could be mellowed a whole lot. He'd come to her tonight. She could feel it in her bones. Even the light breeze wafting through the willow branches overhead echoed his promise. I shall return when you are older. When you are older . . . when you are older . . . .

After a while, Cam put an end to the quiet reflectiveness of both their moods. "Tell you what I'll do, Senator. When I meet a man that can ride as well as I can, I'll snatch him up, and you won't ever have to worry about me dying an old maid."

The Senator stood up and stretched, then limped over to the pump for a drink of water. "You'll never meet your match, Cami Tranter," he announced with a proud smile.

I already have, she longed to tell him, but she kept her words to herself and went on about her grooming instead. Even though she knew absolutely nothing about her black-caped stranger, she had a feeling deep down that he would turn out to be the man of her expectations. No doubt the Senator would agree.

Recollections of what had happened two years ago to the day incited chaos within her. Absently, she reached for her necklace and, lifting the button to her lips, breathed the same whispered pledge of love she had vowed every night. *I love you, and I shall wait for you. No matter how long it may take.*

Cam dropped the pendant back inside her shirt. Last year, she had waited until well after midnight, and he never came. But he would this year—she just knew he would! He had to. She'd wait just as long as it took. A man like that was not easy to come by in a world of Frank Chambers and Strothers Bennetts. Another twelve hours and she'd be consumed by his love—except that tonight would be no fantasy.

Just thinking of what the night had in store made her cheeks crimson. Tonight she'd cross the threshold into womanhood. Tonight she'd be made a woman. His woman!

All her spine-tingling imaginings of the wonders the evening would bring disappeared the instant Cam sank into the saddle. There would be plenty of time later to dwell on him, but for the moment, she had something more urgent ot think about. If she were going to do her absolute best, all thoughts except those of the race must be erased from her mind. Racing cross-country was dangerous enough without having one's mind divided.

Late in the afternoon, hair tucked out of sight and mask secure over her nose, Cam took refuge in the woods surrounding the fairground. She had taken great pains to keep her whereabouts secret, and the reason had nothing to do with adding any drama to the already much anticipated entrance of the Masked Rider. Standing guard at the northern gate, from which she had entered last year and the year before, were some of Frank Chambers' cronies. No doubt the drunken ruffians were stationed there so they could jump the Masked Rider and try to unmask him before the race. She could see that the same worry must have crossed the Senator's mind as well, for he wasn't straying far from that corner. Good thing she had outsmarted them! Besides, there was no telling how Traveller would react to an ambush. He was already getting more nervous than was his nature, and she had to give him one comforting pat after another to keep his prancing under control. He seemed to sense that the stakes were higher than ever before.

From her vantage point, Cam could observe the flurry of activity without being detected. Everyone seemed to have caught the festive spirit. One would have thought the steeplechase was the social event of the year. Ladies were all done up in their frills and finery, each trying to outdo the others, while the gentlemen swapped tales over jugs of corn liquor. Younger children played games and bobbed for apples, and the older ones shimmied up greased poles after prizes. The air was filled with aromas so tantalizing that just smelling them made her mouth water. More booths than ever before had been erected, and inside was displayed everything from bright colored quilts with intricate designs to prize-winning jars of jam.

Judging from the hustle-bustle, this year's turnout was sure to be three times that of last year, and no one denied that the Masked Rider was what had drawn such a crowd. His reputation had spread even farther and wider than Cam had dreamed possible. The *Columbia Dispatch* devoted a full page to the Caesar's Head Steeplechase. Spectators came from all across the state, and a few had traveled great distances just to say they saw the race. Would their excitement ebb once the mask was removed and the famed equestrian turned out not to be a man after all? As far as Cam was concerned, what they thought really didn't matter, nor did their motives for being there. When she came right down to it, the money, though it was mighty tempting, wasn't really what made her reconsider donning the red mask one last time. It was high time folks realized that a woman's domain need not be limited to the home. A lot of women, herself included, were destined for better and greater things, and no one was going to tell her she couldn't accomplish anything she set her mind to just because of her sex!

Cam scanned the crowd slowly, her smile broadening when she saw the haphazardly shaven face she was looking for. Undoubtedly the Senator had realized that she intended to make her approach from a different direction, for he was busy making the rounds and talking politics en route. With his friend Wade Hampton in the governor's mansion for a second year, the conservative planter class was back in power. Last year's cotton crop had been the best ever, and this year's looked just as promising. Cotton mills were springing up all over the state, the lumber industry had increased with surprising speed, and gigantic steps had been taken to lure other businesses to the South. Yankee investors were coming down in droves.

As much as she despised the thought of Yankees making a dollar off the very same land they had tried to destroy, Cam had to admit that their presence was boosting the economy. Little by little, the North's opinion of the South was beginning to change for the best. President Hayes had encouraged a forgive-and-forget attitude by keeping his campaign promise of compromise. The last of the Federal troops had been removed last year, and the shackles of Reconstruction had at last been shed!

Cam paused for a moment and settled her gaze on Ludie Mae. She was too dear a friend to be regarded as merely a housekeeper. Lord knew how she or the Senator would ever have gotten along had Ludie Mae not taken it upon herself to set their lives in order. Her manner of dressing had changed very little since the days when she presided as mistress over the Academy for Young Ladies. She still wore the same style of dark poplin skirt and modest bustle and basque. A touch of lace at the throat and the cuffs was the only decoration allowed on her cream-white blouse.

Poor Ludie Mae! If Cam didn't love her old friend so much, she would have been tempted to giggle. There she stood, nervously shifting from one foot to the other, hands wringing and a look of impending doom written all over her face. She just couldn't understand why in heaven's name her young charge chose to behave in such a helter-skelter fashion.

Not too far away stood Abbey. She had always been the proper young lady, and look at what a fix she had gotten herself in because of it. How sad she looked. Except for a little plumpness around her middle, Abbey hardly presented the picture of motherhood-to-be. She looked as if all her energy had been drained right out of her. And there was no wondering why Cam's once robust, full-of-life-and-mischief friend had deteriorated into a frail form who looked a good ten years older. Marriage was not agreeing with her. All along, Cam had thought it no coincidence that Strothers took a sudden liking to Abbey right after Mr. Sullivan's death. Those three new cotton mills she had inherited made quite a handsome dowry. To this day, Cam regretted having told her old friend that if she married Strothers she deserved all the misery she got. Seeing her leaning against the fence looking so pitiful made her regret having said so all the more. No doubt Strothers had wasted no time in showing his true colors, but Cam knew Abbey would rather die than admit her misery. Soon, the two of them would have to have a heart-to-heart talk and try to salvage what was left of their friendship.

The closer it got to two o'clock, the more competitors began assembling in the arena. Cam studied each horse and rider, paying more attention to the ones she had never seen before, which easily numbered two dozen. From experience, she knew a horse's conformation usually revealed how good a jumper he would be, but evaluating the rider and his mount as one was the best way to determine their capabilities. Several of the horses were quite impressive with their high-stepping, fancy footwork, but only one looked as if it would pose any real threat. Huge and gray and every inch of eighteen hands, he was an exceptional creature, and he appeared as calm as her own horse. Astride him was a rider who, in his black riding breeches and billowing white shirt, looked every bit as regal and elegant as his mount. Heels, elbows and shoulders all in perfect alignment, he gave the impression of knowing exactly what he was doing.

While she couldn't quite make out all his features, Cam was certain she had never seen such a rider before, for if she had, she would have not forgotten him or his horse. Instinct told her that if anyone was going to give her a run for the money, it would be him.

At the sound of the bugle, a hush spread over the crowd, and the master of the race began reading off the names of the contestants. Straining to hear over the applause, Cam listened and watched for that one particular introduction to be made. The name Tate Carruth was called midway through the announcements, and when the gray capered into place, Cam knew her instinct was to be trusted. Tate Carruth was no mediocre rider out to make a name for himself; he was a skilled equestrian, and no doubt his mount was just as well trained.

Traveller pawed impatiently at the ground. Although he couldn't hear their snorts and neighs, he wasn't blind to the horses' bucking. Seeing them all gathered in the ring made him all the more anxious to join them.

Checking one last time to make sure everything was in its proper place, Cam gathered the reins in her hand. Then, legs clamped to his side, she spurred Traveller out of the pines.

Cheers reverberated from one side of the fairgrounds to the other the moment the Masked Rider's name was called. Unable to resist a few fancy moves of her own, she caproiled into place. If Mr. Carruth thought he was going to win hands-down, then he had another thought coming!

Frank Chambers greeted her entrance with a friendly wave of his hand, and she returned it with one just as affable.

Good old Frank! After the race, she must thank him personally for his help. He'd die when he found out he had unknowingly ended the rumor that the Masked Rider was from Caesar's Head. Always one to stretch the truth a mile, he had bragged to his cronies that the Masked Rider had invited him down to his home in Tryon to go coon hunting. If anyone had the least suspicion as to the identity of the mystery rider, Frank's tale had confused them completely.

Paying attention as Mr. Summer read the rules of the race proved an exercise in futility. The gray's rider was far more interesting than a list of regulations she knew by heart. His profile, rugged and somber, was more intriguing than handsome. Tall, lean and sinewy, he looked tough but was not without a certain amount of refined style. A perfectly erect posture made his thighs all the more forceful and his narrow hips even slimmer.

Cam forced her eyes ahead and locked her jaw in firm concentration midway through her perusal. Interesting as he might be, for the time being she must think of him only as a challenge to be met and an obstacle to be overcome.

The call for riders to prepare for the start of the race came none too soon. Thoughts other than those of what lay around the first bend were quickly forgotten as Cam assumed her racing position.

Pistol pointing skyward, Mr. Summer signaled the start of the race. Startled by the loud discharge, most of the horses stampeded out of line.

At the first turn, Cam felt a great surge of strength beneath her. Slowing Traveller into a canter had never been more difficult. At any moment, she was certain, her steed would sprout wings. He soared over the first hedge, then cleared both the water jump and a rider just thrown off his horse with room to spare. Nothing was going to slow him down, and he needed little urging through the muddy marsh a short distance later. It was as though he knew better than she what lay ahead, and he intended to execute his task the way he thought best.

Without breaking his stride, he leapt over the logs and plunged in and out of camouflaged ditches designed to trap horse and rider. His concentration was as deep as her own. A riderless horse galloping out of control past them was hardly given a blink of acknowledgement.

In and out of ditches, up and over walls nearly as tall as he was, Traveller somehow managed to land on the ground only long enough to collect himself before springing over the next hurdle. Cheers and applause from onlookers only encouraged him to gallop faster and jump higher.

Certain he could not be contained much longer, Cam decided it best to give him his head rather than struggle for control. Last year's strategy would simply not work in this year's race. He had trusted her judgment without question for the past four years, and now the time had come to put her faith in him.

All at once, they were accelerating past everything in sight. The horses they overtook seemed by comparison to be creeping along. At the tenth horse, Cam stopped counting, for staying in the saddle required her complete attention. To the amazed onlookers, she thought Traveller must look like an out-of-control runaway, and had she not known that the slightest tweak on the rein would bring him down, she would have believed the same herself.

Up until the moment they sailed over a pyramid of barrels and landed on all fours in the dirt on the other side, the gray had been all but forgotten. Then, dead ahead, Cam saw it and the bay battling for the lead. Traveller caught sight of them, too, and began pouring on the steam to catch up. The strength in his great limbs was inexhaustable.

Relieved that he offered no objection when she won the fight of control, Cam took charge of his gallop and paced his strides into a more controlled gait. They could, she felt confident, take on both the gray and the bay, but for safety's sake she decided against becoming overly greedy.

The echo of a rifle shot somewhere behind her served as a painful reminder of what could easily happen if a rider was careless. The sound reconfirmed her oath to take no risk, however small. Hanging back while the other riders fought for command of the final jump might cost a little time, but in the long run it would pay off. Besides, once they got into the stretch, not even the wind could catch up with her noble beast!

Content to approach the jump at a leisurely gallop from a wide, sweeping angle, Cam watched as the two leaders neared the stream. Already committed to the spot where he was going to take the jump, Frank suddenly jerked his horse around and rammed the gray's hindquarters. She could hardly believe what she was seeing. That was no accident—Frank was deliberatley trying to force his opponent off course! For one horrifying minute, she was certain both horses and riders would go down, one on top the other, but the mishap was miraculously avoided. The gray stumbled on the rocks, but righted himself almost as quickly. When its rider trotted him up the bank, she knew he was checking for injuries. His precaution demanded respect; he was a horseman in every sense of the word.

With a loud whoop, Frank whipped his horse past the gray.

More determined than ever that Frank would not finish the leader, Cam pointed Traveller ahead to the crossing she had selected. The turn was a bit tighter than she had calculated, but he had no trouble executing it.

Every tightly strung muscle straining, Traveller hurled himself over the creek bed and lunged up over the bank, completely missing the rocks. Hands high on his neck and seat far out of the saddle, Cam eased up on the reins. It was up to him now!

He needed no urging. He knew just what to do. Gaining momentum, he threw himself onto the logging trail. For one instant, Cam was certain she would be flung out of the saddle. She was nearly over his head before she managed to regain her balance.

The scenery went by so quickly, it made her dizzy.

Finally, Traveller and the gray were racing side by side. More than once, her opponent had the chance to edge her out at a turn, but he made no effort to crowd her. Not only was he a fine horseman, he was a true gentleman as well.

Ahead, Frank was having his share of trouble getting his horse to continue at top speed. No matter how hard he beat the mare, she refused to obey. She had been pushed to the limit and refused to do any more. No amount of whipping could rekindle that zeal once the spirit was broken.

The way Frank treated his animal infuriated Cam. If she were a man, she'd delight in taking the whip and giving him a dose of his own medicine. Maybe she'd do it anyway!

They closed in quickly, Traveller to the right of the bay and the gray to the left. All at once, they overtook and passed Frank as if he were standing still.

Down the stretch, the two were still running side by side, determined that the other would not get ahead. With long, fierce strides hammering the earth in unison, they charged across the finish, still neck and neck.

The crowd went wild. Whooping and hollering, hands clapping and hats tossing, they made it clear they had never seen a more exciting finish.

Giving him a chance to cool off slowly, Cam walked Traveller around on a loose rein. A few pats and whispered words of praise just weren't enough. She couldn't wait to throw her arms around him and give him the biggest hug ever.

The gray jogged up alongside them. "You couldn't pay me to call that one," its rider remarked.

Cam looked up, surprise written all over her face. His voice had a decided Yankee clip to it. She studied him closely, her eyes narrowed behind her mask.

Her opponent was grinning from ear to ear. His slicked-back hair fell in wet clumps below the collar of his full-sleeved white shirt. A single brown swath of hair falling carelessly over one eyebrow mellowed his harsh features considerably.

Cam found herself smiling in spite of herself. A Yankee! Good Lord! Who'd have ever thought a Yank could give her a run for the money? Why, he didn't look like a monster at all! In fact, he was rather intriguing. It wouldn't be hard to forget which side of the Mason-Dixon line he came from.

His eyes danced with matching delight. "Those three judges sure have their work cut out for them."

Cam nodded in agreement. The finish had been so close she doubted they'd be able to agree on a clear-cut winner. If one horse had beaten the other, it would have been by no more than a fraction of an inch.

"You are an excellent rider," Mr. Carruth observed. "One of the best I've ever competed against. Maybe even the best."

The longer his smile remained, the softer his rock-hard chin became, and the less Cam noticed his accent.

She started to speak, then decided against it. Instead, she returned his smile silently. He'd find out soon enough who she was. He was friendly now, but that would surely change once the truth was out.

Whip still lashing, a few minutes later Frank crossed the finish line in sixth place.

Cam watched, shocked, as he jumped off his horse and began flogging its backside even harder. For a moment, she thought for sure the poor mare was going to buckle under from the abuse, but to her delight, all at once she kicked out and caught Frank in the middle of his belly, then galloped off, leaving her master writhing in agony.

"Maybe next time he'll get his teeth kicked in," remarked Mr. Carruth, echoing her own thoughts.

Finally, after all the riders had checked back in, Mr. Summers stepped up onto the platform and motioned for quiet. "Ladies and gentlemen," he bellowed out, "looks like we got ourselves a draw."

The spectators heartily endorsed this decision.

"However," he continued, "because of the large amount of money at stake, Mr. Malone, Mr.

Jessup and I have agreed that a winner must be declared."

More cheers and shouts erupted.

Cam exchanged a worried glance with her rival.

Mr. Summers waved the crowd silent. "And to determine the outcome of the race, we have decided to have a—"

Cam's heart sank. A jump-off! Her worst dread had just been realized. That had been in the back of her mind ever since she and the other rider crossed the finish line together.

Her mind was made up. She would never ask Traveller to compete in a jumping contest until one horse dropped from exhaustion or was lamed. He had put his heart and his soul into the race, and she wasn't about to betray him. To hell with the money! She'd rather have her horse anytime!

Mr. Summer turned to them. "Gentlemen, is a jump-off agreeable to you?"

Cam glared at him. *Absolutely not!* replied her angry stare. She shook her head with firm conviction.

Her opponent's voice quieted the audience's displeasure. "As far as I am concerned, the race is over."

The crowd booed him, but he did not back down.

"These two animals have proven themselves champions. The very notion of subjecting them to further hardship is ridiculous, and I refuse to have any part in such cruelty."

With that, he swung out of the saddle and onto the ground.

Cam could have hugged him. Never in her life

had she expected to encounter a Northerner who was a gentleman!

She hopped down off her horse. A quick smile in Mr. Carruth's direction was met with a cheerful wink.

Disappointment rumbled through the crowd. Cam felt certain the spectators displeasure would be short-lived. The announcement she was about to make would liven things up quickly enough.

Mr. Summers threw up his hands as if to tell the crowd he could do nothing more.

"Ladies and gentlemen, the Fourth Annual Steeplechase has ended in a draw," he declared, sounding a little disappointed himself. "May I present the winners—Mr. Tate Carruth and—uh, the Masked Rider."

The crowd grudgingly applauded.

Mr. Summers presented Mr. Carruth with his share of the winnings, then turned to Cam.

The audience was so quiet she could hear a few people catching their breath in anticipation. She stole a quick look at her father. He looked as if he would burst his seams at any minute.

Cam lifted her mask at the same time that she jerked off her cap. Masses of imprisoned hair escaped, and she smiled. What sweet revenge!

Her name echoed through the crowd in disbelief. Camille Tranter. Camille Tranter? Camille Tranter!

Mr. Summers' mouth dropped open. His arm went limp before she could shake his hand. His two associates exchanged mute glances.

It was all she could do to keep from telling them just where they could shove their silly rules. "Thank you, Mr. Summers, Mr. Malone, Mr.

Jessup," she said with a sugar-coated smile.

The crowd roared their approval. Over it all, she could hear the Senator let out a booming "Ya-Hoooo!" and a proud "That's my gal!"

Taking off her gloves, Cam turned to her opponent and held out her hand. "Mr. Carruth, it was a pleasure competing against so fine a horseman. I can think of no more fitting finish."

"Tate, please." He clasped her hand between his. "I assure you, Miss Tranter, the pleasure was entirely mine."

Her eyes lifted, then dropped quickly, her glance consumed by his bolder stare. Her legs were trembling so, they felt as if they would surely collapse under her if he let go of her hand, and she knew mere exhaustion could hardly be blamed for her lack of strength. When he finally did let go, she was surprised to find she could still stand.

Regaining her balance, she left Traveller and ran to give her father a big hug. "We did it!"

"That you did, Cami, and I'm mighty proud of you." He gave her shoulders a rough squeeze. "Mighty proud, I am."

Ludie Mae hovered around her like a mother hen. "You're all right, aren't you? You're not hurt?"

"I'm fine, Ludie Mae. Never better."

One last kiss to each of them, and she returned to her horse.

Tate picked up the reins and handed them to her.

"Thank you," she mumbled, taking the bridle.

Even had she been able to, Cam wouldn't have broken the spell at that moment. There was something very familiar about the way his eyes caressed hers—too familiar—yet she knew that if she had ever looked into them before, she would surely have remembered. Was the gleam she saw intermingled with the green an acknowledgement that he, too, shared the odd sensation of having looked into her eyes before, or was the gleam only a reflection of her own?

"Tell me, Mr. Carruth—Tate—might we have been introduced before?"

Cam held her breath. If she sounded ridiculous, then so be it. She just had to know!

"I assure you, Camille, had we ever been introduced before I would most definitely not have forgotten."

Cam slipped deeper and deeper under his spell. No—neither would she!

3

"You can call me Cam," she suggested, as they tended to their horses later. "That is, if you want to. I mean, everyone else does."

Tate repeated her name softly. "You know, I believe I like it."

Cam went on with her grooming. If she were to look at him just then, she'd give herself away for sure. Already he had her tongue tied, and nobody had ever put her at a loss for words before!

Feeling his stare hot on her cheeks, she looked up, then back down just as quickly.

His smile was without a doubt the most engaging she had ever seen. And those eyes! Why she could just about lose herself in those jade depths.

It hadn't taken them long to become friends, and she was glad. Tate was such a nice man, so kind and considerate, and very, very charming as well. His having to share first-place honors with her didn't seem to bother him a bit. He didn't make any excuses for not coming out ahead, nor was he in the least patronizing. She could tell he respected her equestrian skill just as much as she did his, and that pleased her. He was older then she was—twenty-eight, maybe thirty—and his maturity was a refreshing change from the fellows closer her own age. They were mere boys in comparison. What she had earlier misinterpreted as arrogance was a polished refinement. Such gentility was hard enough to come by; coming from a Yankee, it was downright rare. His air of authority commanded respect, but his manner was completely unassuming.

"Where do you come from, Mr. Carruth . . . Tate?" she asked, conscious of a long pause in their conversation, a lull that resulted in a few surreptitious glances on both their parts.

"Baltimore," he answered solemnly. "But you mustn't hold that against me."

Red shadows crept across her cheeks. Something in his gaze told her he knew good and well the Tranters were die-hard Rebels.

"How you go on! Gracious, the War's been over for ten years." Cam gave a shy grin. She was the last person she would ever have expected to come out with a remark like that. Oddly enough, she meant it.

"I was hoping you'd feel that way." He started to reach for her, then changed his mind and gave her horse a pat instead. "Reckon that pig's done roasting yet?"

"I suspect so." She found herself wondering why he had pulled back his hand and wishing he had not. No doubt he'd be able to find somebody to share his supper with. Every girl in town who was not already spoken for, and a few who were, had been ogling him ever since the presentation of awards. No Yankee had ever been given a warmer welcome in Caesar's Head.

"I'd consider it a real honor, Cam, if you'd allow me the pleasure of your company at supper."

Cam looked up. She could hardly believe she had heard right. She tried not to look directly into his eyes, but she could not resist and found herself sinking deeper and deeper into those dazzling green pools. "I'd be delighted."

A worried frown suddenly replaced her smile as they made their way to the supper tent. Whatever had gotten into her? How on earth could she have accepted his invitation quickly? How could she have possibly forgotten that tonight, the love of her life would be sure to return. All her fantasies would cease being dreams and become reality. Nothing was going to keep her from her nine o'clock assignation. Nothing and no one—not even some Yank who had achieved the impossible by totally captivating her.

Cam started to speak, to decline his invitation and make up some excuse for doing so, but the words refused to come. She didn't want to say no, not really. And besides, what harm was there in having supper with him?

"Something wrong?"

His question caught her off guard.

"Wrong? Oh, no, of course not. Nothing's wrong. I—I suppose I really should have checked with the Senator first before accepting your invitation." She knew her words sounded as lame as her excuse. "You see, sometimes he makes plans that include me and forgets to tell me until we're already committed."

Tate looked puzzled. "The Senator?"

"My father. I call him the Senator. I started calling him that when I was a little girl," she rambled on nervously. Damn him, she thought. Nobody ever had her this rattled. "Everybody else did. Called him that, that is," she stumbled on. "And I guess it just stuck." She gave a nervous chuckle. "Lordy, he'd think I was trying to pull a fast one on him if I called him anything else."

Feeling as though her tongue were tied in knots, Cam paused, anxiously awaiting Tate's response.

His eyes dove deeper into hers. "I think I know what's bothering you."

"You do?"

He gave a grave nod. "Yes, I do, and I intend to put your mind completely at ease before we go one step farther." Ever so gently, he took her shoulders and turned her to face him. "We must clear the air right from the start. Otherwise, we're doomed from the beginning."

Doomed from the beginning? What on earth was he talking about? The way he was staring at her, right through her, made her heart beat wildly. She tried to avoid his eyes, but there was no place for hers to hide. Good heavens—he was talking about *them*, the two of them, him and her!

"I don't want anything to stand in the way of us."

"Of us?" she echoed softly. Just what kind of a spell was he weaving over her?

"Yes, of us," he repeated firmly. "Now, I know you can't help but wonder what I was doing ten years ago. It's only natural. So I'll satisfy your curiosity right off. Yes, I was in the Army, the Union Army, and yes, I did fight hard to stay alive. But I swear you on my mother's grave that I did not rape, plunder, or murder in cold blood. The War disgusted me," he said, brushing his palm gently over her cheek. "It turned my stomach inside out. Cruelties too horrible for words were committed by both sides. There were no winners, only losers. But I refuse to let us still be victims of those old hostilities. I beg you, Cam—let the past stay buried. We—you and I—must look to the future, for there our happiness lies."

Cam was at a loss for words. She could do little more than stand there with her mouth open. What could she say? What was there to say? Never before had she been so taken by a man. *I don't want anything to stand in the way of us,* he had said. Of us. What a warm, cozy ring that tiny word had to it. Us.

Smiling warmly, Cam took his arm. "You're right, Tate. Absolutely right. The time to put the past behind us is long overdue. We must look to the future."

For a moment, she lost herself in her own thoughts. The War was not the only past that should be put behind her. The man in the black cape should be put to rest once and for all. She had to get on with her life!

They walked on quietly. There was no need to talk. Mere words could never describe or explain what they were feeling. Being together, walking together, sharing the same thoughts were enough for the moment.

Cam caught her breath when she saw Frank and his friends blocking the entrance to the supper tent. She threw them a black look, but it went ignored.

Tate, however, waved them aside as if he were shooing away an annoying bug. "Excuse me, gentlemen."

The three glared at him for a minute, then grudgingly moved away when he met their stares with a look every bit as vicious as their own.

"I might have known you were the Masked Rider," mumbled Frank under his breath as Cam passed. "Think you're something, don't you?"

Cam held her tongue. Her escort would surely not think too kindly of a woman who spoke her mind. According to Ludie Mae, a man wanted a girl to act lady-like; when a girl stood up for herself, she scared the fellows away. For the time being, she'd just smile sweetly and go on about her business. There would be plenty of time later, when Tate wasn't around, to even the score with that bully. She could lick Frank any day of the week, and he knew it!

Once inside the tent, Cam helped herself to all the delicious food offered. She had missed all the fine eating for the past three years, and this year she was going to make up for it. Acting like a lady was one thing, but eating like one was an entirely different matter. Poor Ludie Mae would have a fit if she saw the man-sized portions of ham and sweet potato pie on her plate!

Relieved that Tate had not sat down at one of the crowded tables in the tent, she followed him outside. Other couples had spread their suppers on the ground away from prying eyes, but the grassy knoll that he chose was far removed from them as well.

After they had sat down on the ground and begun eating, Tate pointed at her necklace. "Your good-luck charm?" he asked.

"Sort of." Cam quickly stuffed it back inside her shirt. He'd think her crazy as a loon if she told him its history. "Mmmm. This sure is good. There's nothing like barbeque on a hot summer night."

"It's very unusual. Your necklace, that is."

She was anxious to change the subject. "You know, I have a feeling you knew all along I wasn't a man."

"No man rides with such natural elegance." Smiling sheepishly, he leaned closer. "Besides I heard you talking to Traveller before the race. That was a dead give-away."

For one fleeting instant, he was so close she thought he was going to reach over and kiss her.

"He's deaf," she said, "but that doesn't keep him from doing everything I ask."

"You're lucky to have him. Then again, he's just as lucky to have you." One light pat on her hand, and Tate resumed his meal.

Legs crossed Indian-style beneath her, Cam pretended to be completely absorbed in her supper. How empty her hand had felt when he took his away! She couldn't help but wonder if his kiss would have caused her insides to flutter the way the black-caped stranger's had.

Still pondering the answer to her question, she watched as the Senator made his way over to them. His sly grin brought to mind a pledge she had made earlier. Undoubtedly, that vow was still fresh on his mind as well. The day she found a man who could ride as well as she, she'd snatch him up.

A wink from him, and she knew he wasn't about to let her forget. What a surprise he had coming!

Tate was quick to rise to his feet.

Cam stood as well. "Senator, I'd like you meet Tate Carruth."

Tate's hand shot out. "Pleased to meet you, sir."

"Likewise, Mr. Carruth. Likewise." The sideways look the Senator sent to his daughter was one of amusement rather than displeasure. "Mighty fine race you ran, sir. Mighty fine, indeed. My daughter here is fierce in the saddle. You did better than most."

"I've never had a more masterful opponent. Nor a more beautiful one." Tate motioned to the spot where they had been sitting. "Won't you join us, sir? I'd be happy to go in and get you a plate."

"Don't believe so, but thank you all the same." Drawing hard on his pipe, the Senator gave Tate a last once-over. "I got a few things to tend to. You take good care of my little girl, you hear me?"

Tate stood tall and proud. "I intend to, sir. You can depend on that."

The Senator gave his daughter a kiss on her cheek. "Don't know when I've ever been prouder."

Her heart swelled with happiness. "You taught me everything I know, Pa," she said softly, her eyes starting to mist.

The Senator gave her another peck then backed away. "You young folks have a good time. Cami, don't stay out late. You know how Ludie Mae worries."

Cam watched a little sadly as her father limped away. The arthritis was stiffening his leg even more. Sometimes he hurt so bad of a morning, it took two swigs of 'shine to get him going. Seeing him in so much agony made her heart cry.

Cam eased back down onto the ground. Tate sat down beside her, this time edging a little closer to her. "Anybody can see you're his pride and joy."

"He's a wonderful man," she said softly. "One in a million."

"I look forward to getting to know him better," Tate told her, his soft but solemn words breaking her reverie. "Almost as much as getting to know his daughter."

Cam could do little more than smile. If she spoke, her quaking voice would surely give away her innermost thoughts. Yankee or not, she'd like to see a whole lot of him, too.

The wistful, almost longing way he was looking at her at that moment made her wish she had at least brought along a change of clothes. All the other girls her age were flitting about in afternoon frocks adorned with lace and ruffles, and here she was in the company of the handsomest man there wearing faded breeches and one of the Senator's cast-off shirts. Her attire had served its purpose, but there was nothing elegant about it at all. Being a tomboy had never made her any less a girl, but never before had she felt so compelled to flaunt her femininity. Maybe Ludie Mae really had been right all these years. Men liked girls to dress and act like girls!

Even as she surveyed the merrymaking around her, Cam was acutely aware of being the focal point of Tate's attention. Legs stretched out and her ankles crossed, she folded her hands primly in her lap and tried to project some semblance of a proper young lady.

His breathing was quick. She knew she was the reason for it, just as she knew he was he cause of hers. The fire of passion danced in his eyes. Could he read what was in her own gaze as accurately as she could his? What on earth was coming over her? One minute she was roasting, the next she was chilled. Why were her body's secret, hidden places suddenly starting to ache for his touch? Where would it all end? When would it begin?

"What brings you to Caesar's Head?" she asked, her words scarcely more than a whisper. She had to speak. Somehow she had to release the hot storm brewing inside her. Somehow, she had to get over the feeling of wanting to fling herself into his arms and grant him permission to take as many liberties with her as he dared.

"Tate? Are you all right?" she asked when he gave no indication of even having heard the question.

She felt herself sinking deeper and deeper under his spell. His eyes caressed her, held her tight. She didn't want them to ever let go. If only his hands would be so daring!

"Tate?" she whispered again.

He blinked abruptly. "I'm sorry . . . I don't know what came over me. You must forgive me, Cam."

His lips parted slowly into a wide smile. "What can I say? My head is filled with a thousand words, and yet I can't utter a single one," he told her quietly. "Do you understand? No, how could you when I don't understand myself."

Cam nodded. Her lips mouthed the words, I

do. She knew exactly what he meant. She, too, felt as though there were a flood of words waiting to gush out from her mouth. Yet, she could think of not one single clever word.

Their gazes locked and held. Yes, their paths had been destined to cross. It didn't matter why he was there, or where he had come from, or where he was going, for that matter. He was there, with her, and that was all that mattered.

"Ah, yes, you asked what brought me to Caesar's Head, did you not?"

Cam gave a reluctant nod. Whatever had passed between them had been put to rest for the time being. Should she be disappointed or relieved?

"Surely news of the Masked Rider didn't spread up North as well?" she asked.

"No, but had I known the Masked Rider's identity before now, wild horses couldn't have kept me away." His tone grew solemn, as did his smile. "Actually, I've come South on business."

"Oh? What kind of business?"

"Land." Tate swished his cider around in the glass, then downed it in one gulp. "I guess you could call me an investor of sorts."

Cam frowned. She wasn't sure exactly what reply she had wanted from him, but that certainly was not it. Over the past decade, South Carolina had been plagued with a multitude of so-called investors from the North. All they wanted to do was get their slimy hands on as much Southern property as they could, then sell it to the highest bidder. Money! That was all those Yankee investors cared about, and it didn't matter one little bit how they went about getting it.

She chanced a look at Tate. He seemed to know exactly what was on her mind. His eyes seemed to plead with her not to think the worst of him just because others who had come before had tricked and cheated and stole.

Cam took a deep breath. She mustn't be so quick to judge. What others had done didn't make Tate one of them. She knew people, knew how to figure them out and tell if they were lying or sincere. Deep down she knew that Tate Carruth really was a gentleman, and until her instinct was proven wrong, she'd go on thinking just that. Hell fire! Who'd ever believe they could raise gentlemen in the North! He had to have some Rebel blood in him somewhere.

She was about to inquire about his project, to put her own mind at ease if nothing else, when her eyes took the path his gaze had just taken.

How odd! He was looking right at Strothers Bennett.

Strothers waved and grinned his good-ole-boy smile, and when Tate returned his gesture, Cam felt her heart sink to her toes. It was bad enough Tate being from up North, but surely he couldn't be associated with that weasel as well?

"You know Strothers?" she asked casually.

His acknowledgement was somewhat strained. "Yes, I've—uh, I've known him for several years now. As a matter of fact, it was he who suggested I might find what I was looking for in the South Carolina mountains.

Exactly what is it you're looking for? she was dying to ask, but held her tongue.

"I get the feeling Bennett isn't one of your favorite people."

"That, sir, is putting it kindly."

"You mustn't judge me by the people I know." Tate cupped his hand gently over hers. "In business, certain associations are necessary."

Cam watched as his fingers slipped tenderly around hers. What a peculiar remark for him to make, and right out of the blue, as well. What he said made sense, though. Strothers had his greedy paws in just about everything. This wouldn't be the first time he had acted as middle man for the buyer and the seller. And just because Tate conducted business with the man didn't necessarily mean they were best friends. Tate was a gentleman. Strothers wouldn't even know the meaning of the word.

"Whatever your relationship with him," Cam began, feeling obliged to tell him, "if I were you, I wouldn't turn my back on that scoundrel for one minute."

She felt the absence of his touch the moment he unraveled his fingers from hers. "Believe me, Cam, I don't intend to."

His declaration surprised her. His look was as grave as his tone. Perhaps he already knew firsthand just what a scoundrel he was dealing with. Maybe Strothers' reputation was finally catching up with him.

Eyes narrowed in comtempt, Cam watched Strothers making his rounds. Poor Abbey was following close on his heels, like a devoted little puppy. Cam supposed it wasn't all that hard to see how her friend could have fallen prey to his charms. He was handsome, no doubt about that. He was blonde as a Norse god and had a devil-may-care air about him that most women found downright irresistible. If the truth were known, though, he had a lot more of Old Scratch in him than just his devilish look. Not even his overly friendly ways could disguise the calculating ruthlessness held in his icy blue eyes.

Seeing Abbey tagging along behind him changed Cam's mind about excusing herself when Strothers headed their way. How pathetic her old friend looked. Seeing her so defeated and forlorn was enough to make Cam cry. Most women looked all healthy and rosy when they were with child, but not Abbey.

"What that man's done to her is criminal," she thought aloud. "Absolutely criminal."

"You know Mrs. Bennett?" Tate asked.

Cam blinked quickly. No sense letting Strothers see she was unhappy. "We grew up together. We were closer than any sisters could be."

"Her getting married changed all that?"

"It ended it!"

How she despised Strothers. He knew Abbey was struggling to keep up, but he wouldn't even slow down, let alone give her his arm.

"Hell of a race, Tate!" exclaimed Strothers as he slapped him on the back. "Hell of a race! Sure didn't take you long to get in cahoots with the enemy, did it? Damn it, Cam, the way you ride and shoot, you ought to have been a man." Squatting down in front of her, he studied her closely. Not one part of her went unscrutinized by his blatant stare. "Naw, I take that back. You're fine just the way you are."

He edged a little closer, and when she realized he was about to give her a kiss, she leaned as far back as she could into the tree. The thought of any part of him coming into contact with her was enough to make her lose her supper!

Abbey finally caught up. "Hello Mr. Carruth," she panted, nearly out of breath.

Tate was on his feet at once. "I thought we decided on first names only."

"Yes, of course." Abbey's smile was sad. "Hello, Cam."

Cam mellowed instantly. Her heart went out to her old friend. Despite their differences, the time for them to be friend's again was long overdue. "It's good to see you, Abbey. Real good. How are you?"

"Fine, just fine." She nearly chuckled. "I do feel like an old sow, though."

"You look like one, too, sugar," her husband remarked.

What semblance of a smile there was on Abbey's face quickly disappeared.

"You know I'm just teasing, now, don't you darling?"

Even though he was smiling, Cam knew there was not one ounce of kindness in Strothers' words, and that made her hate him all the more. When he started to sit down beside her, the glare she shot back was all it took to encourage him to keep his distance.

"You want to sit down, honey?" he asked his wife.

Abbey looked as if she were about to burst into tears. "I—I don't see any chairs around."

"I can remedy that," offered Tate.

"Why thank you, Mr. Carruth . . . Tate. I'd appreciate that."

"Please don't get up, Strothers," Tate said, walking away. "I can manage."

Cam turned her head to keep from laughing aloud. She could have kissed Tate! Strothers hadn't made the least effort to rise. For the first time in a long while he had been put in his place—and it was no less than he deserved.

Paying no attention to the poisonous glares Strothers was sending her, Cam stood up and walked over to her old friend. For a moment, she thought Abbey was going to reach for her hand, but one smoldering look from her husband, and she drew back her arm. Cam ignored it and looped her arm through Abbey's. She could feel the tension draining at once. The distance separating them was immediately bridged. Six months of heartache was all forgotten.

A smile lit up Abbey's sad face, and the glow almost returned to her pale cheeks. "I'm so proud of you, Cam," she said softly. "I figured all along you were the Masked Rider. There's nobody, but nobody, who rides like you. Didn't I say that, Strothers?"

"You and old Tate sure looked cozy all snuggled up over her in the dark," Strothers said to Cam, as if he hadn't even heard his wife's remark. Cold eyes ran up and down her length. "What were you doing? Celebrating?"

Cam pretended not to hear him, treating him as he treated Abbey. Besides, acknowledging his remark would only give dignity to it. "Thank you, Abbey, that's real sweet of you to say so."

Tate's return was not a moment too soon. Strothers' open appraisal made her uncomfortable enough, but poor Abbey was downright miserable!

"Come out to Willow Creek next week for a visit," she suggested to Abbey when the two men became involved in a discussion about the up-and-coming textile industry. "Maybe you could even spend the night. Ludie Mae and the Senator would love to see you, and I . . ." Cam felt a lump rising in her throat. "You know I'd love to have you."

Abbey stared down at the ground. "I don't know, Cam."

She knew exactly what was on Abbey's mind. Damn Strothers! "It'll be just like old times," she promised. "Remember what fun we used to have?"

"Old times," Abbey echoed sadly, longingly. "What a shame we had to grow up."

"We cannot relive the past, but we can make sure we don't make the same mistakes in the future." Cam took hold of her friend's tiny hand and squeezed it tight. "Think about it, Abbey. Please."

Abbey stole a look at her husband, then sat up straight in her chair. She met Cam's questioning stare head on. "You just tell Ludie Mae I'll be expecting some of her chicken and dumplings."

Her voice was soft, but the flicker of defiance in her kittenish eyes was unmistakable.

"I'll pick out the hen myself!"

Cam felt better already. Maybe all was not lost, after all. Perhaps Abbey did have some of the Sullivan spunk left in her.

Strothers interupted Tate in mid-sentence. "What you ladies whispering about over there? Anything we ought to know about?"

Abbey stiffled a giggle. "Oh, nothing you'd be

interested in, dear."

Cam squeezed her hand again. Thank God they were going to put the past six months behind them once and for all. They shared so many wonderful memories! How silly they had been to let anyone spoil them! Strothers had nearly destroyed their friendship once, but he wasn't about to get a second chance. Abbey meant far too much to Cam for her to let that happen again. Any fool could tell Abbey needed someone to turn to, and from now on, she'd be there!

"So when does Widow Besley think you'll deliver?" Cam asked, as if nothing had ever interrupted their friendship.

"Sometime before the middle of October." Abbey sighed as she pushed an annoying blond curl out of her eye. "Lord knows how I'll make it through the dead of summer, though. Hot weather makes me miserable even when I'm healthy."

Cam heard little of what her friend had said after giving the date. Early October? That bastard certainly hadn't wasted any time making Abbey dependent on him. No doubt that was his little scheme to secure his hold on the Sullivan fortune and keep it for himself. Poor Abbey! She'd be lucky if she saw even a penny of her inheritance. Strothers was guilty of many things, but being a fool wasn't one of them. He would bleed the mills Henry Sullivan had put his heart into for all he could, then leave his wife and baby destitute.

Cam felt a hand take hers. She looked up, feigning a smile. "Tell you what let's do," she began as she gave Abbey's hand a squeeze. "We'll have us a baby party next week. I'll invite the Loudermilt sisters, Lindy Cord, Meggie Taylor and her husband's sister and—and whoever else we can think of. I'll see if Ludie Mae'll fix up some of that good peanut butter fudge that you like so much, and we'll all bring things for the baby. Doesn't that sound like fun?"

She could tell at once that the prospect of a party put Abbey in a better frame of mind. No doubt Strothers kept her isolated in that big mansion on Maple Street. Knowing him, he probably kept her under lock and key and only let her out when it suited his purpose.

"I wouldn't want to put you to any trouble," said Abbey, her voice nervous and excited. "I mean, after all, I've been a poor excuse for a friend lately."

Cam patted her knee affectionately. "Nonsense. You've been busy, that's all. Besides, all that's behind us now. From now on it'll be just like it used to be."

Her promise brought an unexpected glow to her friend's face, and a mischievous glimmer played in Abbey's eyes. "I know what your thinking, Cam Tranter, and you're wrong," she said quietly. "Nothing's going to come between us again." She glared at her husband. "I promise you that."

It was as though Abbey had read her mind. Perhaps Strothers didn't have as much influence over her friend as she thought. It was plain as day Abbey had a lot of fight left in her yet, and Cam was a little ashamed at not having given her the credit she deserved.

The way Tate kept Strothers so occupied talking about himself that he hadn't a chance to eavesdrop on their conversation made her wonder if perhaps he had done so deliberately. It didn't take long at all for the sparkle to return to Abbey's eye. Her dimples were dancing up a storm, and she was chatting away like a magpie. If Tate had manipulated it all, and she suspected he had, then she owed him one huge debt of gratitude.

Strothers stood up a little later and gave his wife an obligatory peck on the cheek. "Well, darling, guess we'd better be moseying on over to the tent. Don't want to miss any of that picking and singing, now, do we?"

Abbey refused his offer of assistance. "I'd just as soon get home. It's been a long day, and I'm worn out."

Cam could hardly believe she had heard right, and from the stunned look on Strothers' face, he was just as surprised as she that his wife had spoken her mind.

"Whatever you say, sugar." Arm wrapped tight around his wife's shoulders, he flashed a wide smile. "Talk to you folks later. Just as soon as I see the little lady home."

Abbey pulled away. "You're not coming back, are you?"

His arm wrapped back around her. "Course I am, sugar. You wouldn't want me to miss out on any of the fun just on account of you feeling poorly, now would you?"

Abbey shrank from his touch.

"I'll be in town on Tuesday," Cam told her friend. "I'll drop round to see you then if that's all right."

Strothers didn't give his wife a chance to respond.

"Why that sounds wonderful, just

wonderful!" he exclaimed, much too friendly for Cam's liking. "I was saying to Abbey just the other day that we don't see near enough of you and the Senator anymore." Grinning like a possum, he snapped his fingers. "Tell you what. Why don't you and your father come for Sunday supper? I know it'd make Abbey real happy."

Cam couldn't contain her smirk. She doubted he ever had his wife's happiness at heart in anything he did.

"Oh, please do, Cam. It'd be so much fun," Abbey piped up with an enthusiasm that lit up her face.

Cam nodded. How could she say no? "Sounds wonderful, Abbey. We'll be there."

"Good, good," Strothers said. "Nothing fancy, now, just me and Abbey, you and the Senator, of course our guest here."

Cam knew her astonished look gave her away, but she couldn't wipe away the surprise in time.

"Why, Tate did tell you he was staying with us for a few weeks, didn't he?" Strother's smile broadened. "Guess he must have forgot."

Cam couldn't contain her fury. It was bad enough that Tate was acquainted with the likes of Strothers Bennett, but staying with him as well? Their association had to be a lot more than a business one! The Senator always said that birds of the feather flocked together, and any friend of Strothers was definitely no friend of hers, no matter how intriguing he might be.

"Why don't we go listen to some of that music ourselves?" Tate said when they were alone again.

"I don't think so," Cam answered stiffly. "I need to be getting on home."

Tate's arm reached out and caught hold of her as she passed him. His grip was forceful, but it was not without a certain gentleness. "Just hold on here a minute. It's obvious my being a guest in the Bennett home riles you, but I can see no reason why you—"

Cam calmly pulled away. "It isn't the Bennett home, sir," she corrected him. "It's the Sullivan home, and the only reason Strothers has access to it is that he married it, just like he married the rest of Henry Sullivan's possessions."

She took a step back, half expecting him to reach out to her again, and when he made no attempt to close the distance between them, she felt sorely disappointed.

"And as far as your staying there goes," she continued, trying to mask her trembling with extra firmness in her tone, "that is none of my concern. Neither is who you chose to associate with. Why should I care? I hardly know you."

Cam took a deep breath to calm herself, while Tate stood there looking at her for a long time. Even in the dark, she could detect a glimmer of sincere regret. Her defenses slowly began to crumble. Perhaps she had been too quick to misjudge him. After all, he and Strothers were distinct opposites.

"Things are not always as they appear, Cam. You must believe me."

She couldn't bring herself to wrench her eyes from his. The effect he had on her was almost frightening.

"Trust me, Cam," he implored softly. "Trust me and believe me when I say that I will never do anything to make you regret having placed such a trust in me."

A moment later, after giving her a chance to mull over what he had just said, Tate offered her his arm. "Shall we go see if the dancing's about ready to start?"

Her slight hesitation disappeared the moment his fingers closed around her arm. Oddly enough, she did trust him, and womanly intuition assured her that trust was not misplaced. She felt as though she had known him far longer than a single afternoon. The instant he cupped his hand over hers in an unmistakeable act of possession, a familiarity passed between them, one she was certain he as just as aware of as she.

Laughing and chatting like old friends, they threaded their way through the crowd just as the first dance was about to be called. The envious looks the other girls were throwing her way came as no surprise. Tate was by far the best looking man in the place. She felt proud to be on his arm, and even prouder that their flirtatious smiles and subtle winks went unheeded.

"Like to dance?" he shouted in her ear above the hand-clapping and foot-stomping.

Head shaking, she shouted back, "My knees are still trembling from the race!"

Her gaze centered on the fiddler and Cam pretended to be concentrating solely on the music. Her legs were indeed quivering, but the race was hardly the reason why. So close was he to her that everything about her was quaking. Horseback riding had never caused such weakness!

She stole a look at him out of the corner of her eye. Her excuse seemed to satisfy him, for he, too, turned his attention to the promenade. What would be his reaction, she wondered, if he knew she was afraid to dance with him because she feared she would find herself so content in his embrace she'd think twice about keeping her rendezvous with her phantom lover? After two years, seeing the man in black once more had become almost an obsession, one she could not give up so quickly. For so long, her life had revolved around that promised reunion. Every waking minute had been spent in hopeful anticipation, while nights were reserved for creating passionate fantasies about what would be sure to happen once they were together. She couldn't forsake all her hopes and dreams—not yet. Anyway, she hardly knew the man beside her. He could have a sweetheart or a wife and family waiting for him up North. After all, marriage vows hadn't stopped his good friend Strothers from catting around.

Not only did she owe it to herself to be at the mine by nine o'clock, Cam reminded herself, she owed it to her dream-lover as well. If he did indeed keep his promise, the least she could do was be there to greet him. Once they were face to face, if she did not still feel the same way about him, then parting would not be so difficult. If she did feel the same—well, she dared not think about that—not right yet, anyway.

Seeing the Senator and Ludie Mae whirling around made her feel good all over. The two of them looked as if they were having the time of their lives. Ludie Mae's face had a girlish glow to it, and no one would ever have guessed the Senator had a bad leg and arthritis to boot! Why Ludie Mae had remained a spinster all these years was a mystery. She was a kind soul, pleasant looking, and had such polished manners one would have thought she was an aristocrat for sure. Any man that could have someone like her as his wife should thank his lucky stars. What a fool that man had been for ever letting her get away! What a shame another true love had never happened along for her!

After Cam had been watching them for a while, the sudden realization that she had an appointment to keep dawned on her. "What time is it?" she asked Tate.

He took out his watch and flipped it open. "Just a few minutes before nine. Why? You're not thinking of leaving, are you?"

Her heart sank. If only they could have had a little while longer . . . but no, she knew what had to be done.

The crestfallen look on his face when she replied to his question assured her that he shared her remorse at having to part company. It was even more obvious from the way he held on to her as they returned to where the horses were tied that he didn't want her to go anymore than she wanted to leave him.

"I'll see you home," he offered.

"Oh, no, please don't trouble yourself."

"What's wrong? Got another fellow waiting to take my place?" he teased.

"Heavens, no!" She couldn't help but wonder if he would be jealous if she did. "I don't live far. Besides, you'd get lost coming back into town."

He helped saddle her horse. "When can I see you again?"

Cam's heart skipped a beat. "I'm sure we'll

run into each other at Abbey's tomorrow night," she said lightly.

"But that's nearly a whole day away."

Her smile widened. He sounded just as anxious as she that they spend more time together, and alone. "I'll tell you what. If you find yourself over near Willow Creek way tomorrow, say about two o'clock, why don't you stop by for some apple cobbler? Ludie Mae makes the finest around."

Her invitation trailed off into a whisper. She stared ahead at the booth where wood carvings had been sold earlier.

Tate followed the path of her gaze. "Oh."

Fingers clenched around the reins, she watched in disgust as Strothers and the mill boss's wife groped and pawed at each other like a couple of dogs in heat.

"No-good bastard!" she spat. "He's nothing but an animal."

Tate shook his head in disbelief. "You'd think he' have more sense than to carry on like that here in the open."

"Oh, he's got plenty of sense." Cam's eyes were filled with as much hate and contempt as her words. "It's morals he's short on, and when it comes to them, he's worse than a tomcat. God, I hate that bastard! For what he's done to Abbey, he ought to be shot. I should have done it myself when I had the chance."

"Considering Abbey's condition, I don't think you should mention anything about this," Tate suggested when Strothers and his slut sneaked inside the booth. The disgust in his eyes at that moment convinced her he had about as much use for Strothers Bennett as she did. Nevertheless, her voice was cold as she jerked Traveller's reins from his hand.

"Believe me, I wouldn't give him the satisfaction of knowing he had caused her a moment of grief. You don't have to worry about me getting your friend into trouble, Mr Carruth. He's not worth Abbey's tears."

Tate gave her a leg up into the saddle. "You know, apple cobbler is my very favorite. Especially when it's drowned in fresh, thick cream."

Cam smiled in spite of herself. "I'll pass that on to Ludie Mae. See you tomorrow."

He gave her foot a squeeze, then stepped back. "Two o'clock. I'll be there."

4

Cam huddled closer to the giant oak across from the mine. Her eyes were as round as saucers, her ears strained and alert. The only sounds she heard were Traveller munching contentedly on a clump of brush. No one's eyes were on her. Anybody with any sense would be at the party, not waiting for a fairy tale prince to appear. So why did she feel so uneasy? she wondered, rubbing her cold, damp palms over her breeches. Perhaps what made her nervous was only the anticipation of what was to come—but what exactly would that be?

Her wait, Cam expected, was going to be a long one. She had half hoped to find him already there, and she didn't know whether to be relieved or disappointed when he wasn't. After all, she herself wasn't absolutely positive she had any business being there. Just how long was she going to live in hopes of a girlish fantasy coming true? One part of her still craved him every bit as passionately as she had two years ago that very night, but that little voice inside her still begged her to leave well enough alone!

To complicate matters even more, there was Tate. Tate Carruth! Perhaps he was the reason her feelings had suddenly become so complex. Just thinking about that jade stare of his and the way it searched deep into her soul made goose bumps jump up all over her. Tate Carruth! Even his name made her insides flutter. So disturbingly handsome he was, she couldn't erase his dark good looks from her mind for one minute. Thank goodness he had made no amorous overtures during the course of the evening, for had he done so, she wasn't at all sure she could have denied the desperate yearnings that played havoc with her usually calm heart. With so strong a feeling for him, what on earth was she doing keeping a rendezvous with a man who might well have forgotten all about her by now? What on earth would Tate think of her if he knew the real reason she had pleaded a hasty departure?

A deep whiff of the crisp balsam scent of the woods instantly cleared her senses. Taking all into consideration, she still owed it to herself to be there. If her phantom lover failed to appear, then perhaps the time had indeed come for her to abandon foolish dreams. How could she know if, after galloping off into the woods two years ago, he had given so much as a second thought to the silly child who had clung to him? Damn! She should never have allowed herself to get her hopes up. Never! Still, if he didn't show up, Tate Carruth could no doubt help ease any anxiety caused by a broken promise.

Cam kicked out at the ground, then slammed back against the tree. Good Lord! What was the matter with her, anyway? The longer she dwelled on such nonsense the angrier she got at herself. Here she was entertaining thoughts as wicked as any bad girl ever dared. Leaving one man's company to seek that of another, leaving the safety of crowds to venture into pitch-black woods where a woman was easy prey for any man—why, Ludie Mae would say she was just asking for trouble, and she would be right! Here she was acting no better than a whore! Surely, her mother's bad blood didn't flow through her veins as well!

That damned Strothers Bennett! He was the reason for all her confusion and turmoil! That no-account bastard made her so mad she could hardly see straight! How dare he carry on like that in public! Not even the pounding of Traveller's hooves had drowned out the animal-like noises coming from inside the booth. Such frenzied coupling could hardly be called making love, for surely that act would be sweet and wonderful, as it always was in her dreams.

Poor Abbey! If word of Strother's whoring around ever got back to her, she'd be the laughing-stock of the town. She'd be so humiliated, there was no telling what she might do. Cam had a good mind to tell Abbey herself, but doing so would cause more harm than good—she had learned that the hard way six months ago! Besides, even if Abbey wanted to leave her husband, she couldn't, not with a baby on the way. Strothers had no doubt tricked her into signing away the mill, as well as the rest of the Sullivan holdings. Dear, sweet Abbey. She had made her bed, and now she had to lie in it. What a mess she had made of her life.

What a mess I've made of mine! Cam thought

as she surveyed her bleak surroundings, wishing for Tate's warmth and goodness beside her. Here I am, totally without protection and waiting for a man I don't even know, one who could just as easily turn out to be a robber or a rapist, or even worse, a murderer! Out here all alone, with not even a gun for protection. If worse came to worst, a scream for help would be her only defense, but what with all the commotion from the fair-grounds, nobody'd even hear it.

It took but a minute to get a firm grip on herself. There were very few men in Greenville County she couldn't handle, and she wasn't about to start worrying about her safety now. Tonight, once and for all, she was either going to put an end to her fantasies or carry them out. She had come too far, waited too long, to back out now. If the black-garbed rider atop the magnificent white steed had any intention of keeping his promise, then tonight would have to be the night. If not—well, if not, the companionship of a man whose identity was no mystery would help remedy any heartache.

Tate . . . the stranger . . . Just thinking of them both spun her head around and around. So confused were her thoughts that it was Tate who appeared in her mind wearing a black cape and hood. Dwelling on one or the other was bad enough, but thinking of them both at the same time only compounded her confusion. From now on, she'd concentrate on only one at a time! Fate had caused the white stallion to bolt into her path that night, and fate must be allowed to link their destinies together again if they were meant to be. Tate should not be allowed to tamper with the outcome one way or another. After all, had he not shown up for steeplechase, there'd be no reason for the heartfelt dilemma facing her now.

Try as hard as she might, Cam could not oust Tate from her mind so easily. What was it about him that tempted her to forsake past dreams and promises? The spell he had cast over her was nearly as potent as that of her mysterious stranger. True, Tate was handsome, though not in the conventional way that Strothers Bennett was, for his features were stern and pronounced, but such harsh qualitites made his looks all the more striking. What a presence he had! He commanded respect and notice and instant obedience. No doubt he usually got them, too. Nevertheless, she knew absolutely nothing about him except that he was the finest horseman she had ever met. Granted, she knew just as little about the mystery man, but she'd wager her last nickel that he wouldn't associate himself with the likes of Strothers Bennett. Perhaps that unlikely friendship was what had held her back all along. Maybe that was the reason she had forsaken Tate and gone in search of the man of her dreams.

The cry of a nearby owl sliced the silence with its eerie screech and made Cam huddle closer to the tree. She didn't like to think of herself as being superstituous, but when it came right down to it, she reckoned she was, just a little. To mountain folk, the cry of an owl was a sure sign of bad luck to come. Whether or not it really could foretell impending doom remained to be seen, but if the whippoorwill answered with a shriek of its own, she certainly wasn't going to wait around to find out what would happen!

She was on her feet one minute and back on her knees the next as the rumble of approaching horses caused Cam to lower an ear to the ground. The longer she strained to hear the vibrations, the closer her dark brows knotted together. Just as she had feared, there was more than one horse coming towards her, and from the sound of the quakings inside the earth, they would be arriving very shortly. Most likely, the riders were late-night revelers en route to one party from another, but they could also be a couple of ruffians out looting. In either case, Cam was a sitting target for whatever mischief they might have in mind. It was too late to charge off on Traveller, for they would be certain to intercept her. All she could do was to hide and pray that Traveller stayed out of sight as well.

Stretched out in a saw-grass clump a good distance from the clearing, Cam pressed flat against the ground. Chin burrowed in the soft mire, she waited, scarcely breathing for fear of being discovered. If only Traveller would stay put! He might not be able to hear them, but that was no guarantee he couldn't sense the approaching horses.

Eyes leveled to the ground, Cam didn't dare lift them. The slightest twitch would be sure to give her away. Friend or foe, it didn't matter. If they were all liquored up—and from the way they were running their horses they probably were—there was no telling what they'd do if they found her there alone.

"That sure was the easiest money I ever did make!" roared a voice that was obviously made thick and husky by too much moonshine.

Unearthed sod showered Cam as the pair galloped past. It'd be a miracle if the flying hooves missed her head!

"Beats the hell out of sweating and slaving at that damn mill," shouted the other, his words slurred.

Even after the pounding of hooves became little more than fading echoes, Cam held her position. When she finally did rise, her legs were as wobbly as a newborn foal's.

It seemed like hours before she could breathe freely again. Thank God they had not discovered her! Just thinking of what might have been her fate had they flushed her out of her hiding place sent cold chills up and down her spine.

She hadn't gotten a good look at either of them, or at their horses. At the speed they'd come tearing across the clearing, they were hardly more than blurs. There was nothing familiar about either of the voices, but the nasty drawl one possessed would be hard to forget.

What had he meant about that being the easiest money he ever made? Cam wondered as she went to fetch her horse. Without a doubt, they had been up to no good. They both sounded as if they'd turned up the bottle a few times too many. One thing was for certain. She wasn't going to be anywhere near the mine if they did come back. If the mysterious stranger wanted to see her, he could come to Willow Creek. After all, he knew where to find her, which was a lot more than she knew about him.

The myriad of reds and purples exploding into the sky over the fairgrounds erased any second thoughts about staying that Cam might have entertained. It was midnight; the black-caped stranger was three hours late. If he had any intention of keeping his vow, he would have surely done so before now. He simply wasn't coming tonight, or any other night for that matter. How silly to think otherwise! The time had come to put her foolish fantasies to rest once and for all. From now on, she'd live in the present. The past would be forgotten.

Nostrils flaring and head held high, Traveller struck off toward home without waiting for her to give the command. Thank goodness for the full moon. The path couldn't have been better lit had it been illumined by a row of lanterns.

The faint scent of smoke drifted through the pines. What little breeze there was came from the north and carried on it was the unmistakeable smell of fire.

Cam reached down to give her horse a pat of assurance. No wonder Traveller was in such a head-tossing frenzy. The smell of smoke could drive a horse crazy, and his sense of smell was keener than most.

"It's all right, fellow. Everything's fine," she whispered.

Once his prancing was under control, she urged him on.

Fires were not uncommon at that time of year. There hadn't been any rain for weeks, and it would take hardly more than ash on a dry twig to send the whole forest up in flames. While Willow Creek was not immune to fires, the house was protected at the back by the Saluda River, and at the front by a wide pine break the Senator had cut just for that purpose.

Face screwed up, Cam squinted into the billowy clouds rising in front of her. Her eyes began to tear. From the looks of the smoke, the fire was dangerously close to the Winthrop property. If that was the case, then their old clapboard shack would just be kindling for the flames.

Clare Winthrop and her husband had been at the square dance when she left. Remembering a remark Marsh had made about sending the young'uns home with bellyaches made her spur Traveller on faster and faster, in case the children were alone at home. She prayed she was wrong and that she was making the trip for nothing, but if she were right . . . the thought made her shudder.

The closer they got to the fire, the less Traveller acted up. A tight hold on the reins kept him under control. It was as though he knew they were going straight into the heart of the fire and had resigned himself to trust his mistress's judgment.

The sight she found when she charged onto Winthrop land was even worse than she had expected. The property was not being threatened by the blaze—it was being consumed by it! The base of the ramshackled dwelling was encircled by a ring of fire. From the looks of the bright orange demons leaping around the ground floor, the house would not stand much longer. Another few minutes and it would be nothing more than a few sticks of wood feeding the fire.

The Winthrop twins were running back and forth in front of the house, arms waving and frantic cries for their sissy piercing the crackle of the fire. Seeing the little girl standing at the open window, her doll clutched to her chest, made Cam break out in a cold sweat.

"Jump, Sari, Jump!" shouted the boys. "We'll catch you."

Cam didn't wait for Traveller to halt before she jumped off.

"Jump, Sari, you must," she called up to the frightened child. "Come on, let's play a game. Catch Sari, Catch Sari." She motioned for the boys to join in.

"Catch Sari!" they all shouted in unison.

The little girl uttered no sound, not even the least sob. She just stood there, her little face showing no more emotion than that of her rag doll.

It was no use. The child as too afraid to move. Even if she could see them, chances were she hadn't heard a word they had said. Her mind was as numb as her little body. Soon she would be so overcome with smoke, she would pass out. A state of unconsciousness seemed most kind, for once the fire spread to the top floor, the rafters would collapse, and little Sari would plunge into the inferno below.

No! Cam couldn't just stand there and watch the little girl die. Regardless the risk, she had to go in after her.

"Matthew, hop on Traveller and go for help!" she shouted to one of the boys. "Mark, you start filling up water buckets."

"But what about—"

"Quick! Just do as you're told."

Without waiting to see if her orders were carried out, Cam ran around to the back of the house. So far the blaze was confined to the front.

If only her luck would last another few minutes!

Hot smoke stinging her cheeks, Cam ran past the tiny sitting room where near ceiling-high flames had devoured what little bit of shabby furniture there was.

Chin tucked close to her chest, she dashed up the stairs. Rickety boards moaned beneath her feet. She could feel their heat clear through the soles of her boots. Somewhere beneath the frayed carpet and pine steps, fire was dancing at her feet. She dared not look down.

Tripping halfway up, Cam grabbed hold of the bannister, then jerked back her hand all in the same movement. The railing was as hot as the end of a poker.

"Sari! Where are you?" she called out as she threw open each upstairs door and peered inside.

When she finally found her and took hold of the tiny hand, the child refused to budge. "Come on, Sari. Let's go. Your brothers are waiting," Cam told her, trying to stay calm. "Traveller's going to take all of you for a ride. Doesn't that sound like fun?"

Eyes glazed, the little girl stared out the window. She hadn't heard a word.

Cam jerked her around. The little face of void of any expression.

She shook her tiny shoulders. "It's me. Cam. Can you hear me, honey?"

She tried to pick the child up, but she was dead weight in her arms.

"Come on, sweetie. Hop on my back, and I'll take you for a piggyback ride."

Smoke seeping up from the cracks in the floor curled around her feet and rose slowly around them, shrouding them both in a veil of haze. Unless she acted fast, neither of them was going to get out alive.

As a last resort, Cam slapped the little face and, the instant Sari began sobbing, drew her close to her breast.

"I'm so sorry, baby. I didn't mean to hurt you."

"I'm scared," whimpered the little girl as she burrowed her tiny body as far into Cam as she could. "The bogeyman's come to get me. I'm sorry I ate so many cookies. I won't do it again. Just don't let him get me."

"I won't let that mean old bogeyman get you." Cam swung Sari up onto a chair. "You just do as I tell you, and everything will be just fine."

Thumb in mouth, the little girl nodded.

"Hop on my back, and hug tight around my neck. All right?"

Sari did as she was told.

"That's my girl."

Cam leaned out the window to have a look below before lifting her foot onto the ledge. Her heart sank. There was no way she could jump into that lake of fire without one or both of them being consumed alive. The only way out was the way she came in. She prayed the stairs would not give way beneath her.

Holding tight to the little arms dangling around her shoulders, Cam made her way into the hall. The fumes were suffocating, and she dared not risk the least cough for fear of inhaling more of the deadly vapors. The temperature must have risen a good twenty degrees in the past few minutes.

She descended the stairs slowly, cautiously, testing each step before putting down her foot. More than one felt as if it were about to give way under her weight, but miraculously, none did.

A few strides past the bottom landing, and Cam thought for certain she had gone blind. Dense clouds of smoke billowed all around her, setting up invisible barriers. She reached out, desperately hoping to latch onto something that would help her feel her way to safety, but there was nothing but heat and smoke to hold onto. Hot air stung her cheeks more sharply than any slap. Heat seared through her breeches, burning the flesh underneath,

Still she was determined not to panic, for that would certainly result in both their deaths. If she couldn't retrace the path she had taken in, then she'd just have to find another passage to safety!

The room began spinning round and round, taking her with it. Her head grew heavier and heavier. Sari's whimpering coughs turned to choking bursts. Cam gasped for air. Her chest felt as though it were about to explode. Her legs were about to give way beneath her. Slowly, ever so slowly, she began sinking to the ground, and she was powerless to halt her descent. Soon, very soon, she would be at the mercy of those very devils that were dancing only a few yards away. For Sari's sake, she hoped the end would be painless.

Then, out of nowhere, something—someone—took a firm hold of her hand just as she had given up all hope. Thank God! Matthew had brought help just in time!

Sputtering and coughing, Cam stumbled out

of the house. Half crawling, half walking, she managed to drag herself back from the blaze. At last she could breathe! The night air was cooling to her face. They were safe. Thank God! Thank whoever it was that led them to safety!

Mark came running up behind them. "You okay, Cam? Sari?"

Cam nodded and motioned for him to tend to his sister. Then she collapsed onto the ground.

As soon as her fit of coughing ended, she looked around to thank the person responsible for saving them. There was no one, save for the three of them, anywhere around.

"The man who came in after us—where is he?" she asked, puzzled.

Astonishment was written all over the boy's face. "Wuzn't nobody went in there after you."

Cam managed to sit up. "But there was. Sari and I would have died had it not been for him."

No sooner were the words out of her mouth than the upper floor of the house toppled down to the ground. Flames leapt higher and higher amid the crackling timbers. The raging reminder of what would most certainly have been their fate had their rescuer not reached them in time caused convulsions in the pit of her stomach. Had the smoke not rendered them unconscious, they would surely have been burned alive like human sacrifices.

Huddled together with the children, Cam watched speechlessly until all that was left of the house was the flame itself.

"You're certain no one else was in the house with us?" she questioned him at last.

Mark looked at her as if she were crazy. "I

swear it, Cam. I swear it! Maybe you just imagined it."

Imagined it! No, she couldn't have! A hand had reached out for her. She had never been more positive of anything in her life. Her rescuer was real, not imagined. He was no trick played on her by her smoke-dulled senses. He had been right there in the burning house beside her! Just as he had been at the mining camp earlier when she had felt someone's eyes on her. He—her black-caped stranger—had been with her all along.

He had kept his promise and returned to her. Just as he had said he would. Perhaps the two men who came tearing across the clearing on horseback had prevented him from making his presence known. Perhaps, he trusted no one but her. Only he knew the reason for not revealing himself once the two of them were alone. No doubt he had followed her to insure her safe return to Willow Creek. He had seen her go into the burning house. He had known she was in danger and had braved the blazing flames at risk of losing his own life to save her. He did love her! The two-year wait had not been in vain!

Sari crawled up into her lap and snuggled close. "I saw somebody in there, too," she whispered so her brother couldn't hear. "Was that the bogeyman?"

Cam snuggled her closer. "The bogeyman? Heavens, no. That man was our friend. Our very, very good friend. He saved our lives."

"Where is he now?" she asked, clutching her doll tight.

"I don't know, sweetheart. I just don't know."

With a sad sigh, Cam swept the surrounding

woods with as thorough a gaze as her tired eyes would allow. There was no sign of him anywhere. But he was out there, somewhere, watching her that very minute. She knew it! She could feel it!

"Will he be back?"

Cam began rocking the little girl. Sari's question echoed her own thoughts. "I hope so, honey bunch. I really do hope so."

Sleep had not been quick in coming. It was nearly daylight before Willow Creek came into view. The pillow was a welcome luxury, but eyes that couldn't have been propped open on the way home refused to close. Instead, they focused on blurred images inside her head, images of her mysterious hero. Try as hard as she could to dismiss them, all of the night's events teemed in her mind.

Matthew had finally returned with a good many of the townsfolk in tow. The Senator had arrived as white as a sheet, fearing the worst had befallen his daughter. Ludie Mae had rushed to her side, and seeing the burn caused by taking hold of the hot bannister, had quoted a verse or two from the Bible, then rubbed her lips across it so it would not blister. Blowing out the fire, she called it, and no one doubted for an instant her ability to do just that.

Cam had looked everywhere for Tate, but he was nowhere to be found. Just as well. She was having enough problems coping with the emotional turmoil caused by her mysterious rescue from the fire.

Firefighters—men, women and children alike—were powerless to defeat the blaze. All anyone could do was watch helplessly as all a family's earthly possessions went up in smoke. Only a stone fireplace remained of a house that once stood there. Nobody could figure out how the fire got started, but as dry as it had been the past month, everyone reckoned it could have taken something as tiny as a cigar butt to ignite the flames.

And poor Marsh Winthrop. Only his pride kept him from breaking down and crying like his wife and children. He was a hard-working man, but it seemed his labor never paid off. Unlike his pappy and his before him, he was just not cut out to till the soil. He could take anything apart and put it back together again blindfolded, but tinkerers and inventors never got much ahead, not in the South Carolina hills. He could have sold his land to one of the outsider investors who were always passing through, but had refused numerous offers. Instead he had held out, figuring that parting with family ground would be the final insult to his manhood. He'd been determined to see it through the hard times until the very end, but no one had expected the end to be so bitter.

At least the children escaped uninjured. Their futures looked bleak, but at least they were all alive and healthy. Marsh would probably have to go to work at the mill and move his family into one of the cramped box houses up on Mill Hill. He'd most likely have to sell off his property now to pay off his debts, and they'd have to make do as best as they could. But like all mountain people, they were survivors. They'd get by.

When sleep finally did come, it was a peaceful repose but filled with such dreams as never dared play in her subconscious before. Cam knew she was dreaming, and knew just as well that she had the power to remove herself from her trance at any time. But she couldn't bring herself to do so, not until she could taste those appetizing delicacies once more.

In her dream, she traveled back to the mining camp. Her handsome stranger was waiting for her, beckoning her to join him as quickly as she could. Arms outstretched, she moved toward him slowly, very slowly, feet off the ground. Clad only in long wisps of silk, she floated toward him on a plump, puffy cloud.

Whipping off his cape, he had spread it onto the ground. Then, taking her in his arms, he had laid her ever so gently down on the cape. He undressed her slowly, worshipfully, paying homage to each satiny expanse of flesh revealed. The hood still hid his face from view, but his eyes—those big, wide-awake orbs as brilliant as a cat's—beheld her in unquestionable adoration. There was no need to speak. Each knew what the other was thinking, what was in the other's mind and soul, and nothing else mattered save the voices of their hearts.

Kisses breathless and explosive tantalized with hot promises of ecstasy still to come. Taunting, teasing caresses more scorching than any flame plunged her to the brink of madness, then back to sanity again. Sacred territory, which she had sworn would never be violated by any man, was anxiously relinquished. Her phantom lover had returned to claim what rightfully belonged to him, and she possessed neither the strength nor the desire to stop him. No longer was she her own woman. She was his, and she would deny him nothing.

Hands made frantic by desire tore at his shirt, popping button after button until the strength of his chest merged with the softness of her own. Only when her flesh was his flesh would she find true fulfillment.

He entered with a gentle force and drove himself deeper and deeper into her very essence until they truly were as one. Each breath, each heartbeat was shared. And when it had ended, and she felt his lips raining tiny kisses all up and down her tired body, her eyes came drowsily awake. Surely heaven could be no more wonderful.

Wait! Something was different. The black hood no longer concealed his face from view. She could see him! She could distinguish each and every feature. She knew him! His identity was no longer a mystery.

It was Tate Carruth!

Tate! She still couldn't believe it when she dragged her weary limbs out of bed several hours later. Tate! How strange that thoughts of him should infringe on a time reserved for another.

Tate! Had she known it was Tate all along, would she have offered any resistance to lips that roved across the most secret of places and inflamed caresses that made her feel wonderfully alive? No, she thought not. If anything, she would have welcomed him with an ardor even more fervent.

She could have awakened herself at any time after making such an astounding discovery, but she had elected not to, and there was no use deceiving herself about the reason. Not only was she enjoying herself far too much to bring her fantasies to an end, she was curious, very curious, to see if Tate were as amazing a lover as her dark stranger. She was certain the answer would cause her to erupt in smiles the rest of the month, maybe even the year. Yes, yes, yes, yes! He had proven himself to be every bit as magnificent!

5

"Why don't you let me in on your little secret?"

Tate grinned as he dug into his second helping of hot cobbler and cream. "That way we both can enjoy it."

Shy lashes swept across her cheeks. Let him in on her secret? She wouldn't dare! Just thinking of last night's ecstasy shadowed her face with a dozen shades of red.

"Secret? What secret?" Cam wiped the smile, which she was certain must be a silly one indeed, from her lips. Extinguishing the bright blue sparkles that danced in her eyes would not be nearly so easy.

Her wide-eyed innocence made his own smile broaden all the more. "The one you're keeping from me," he replied.

"Why, Tate Carruth! I haven't the slightest notion what you're going on about." Ever so daintily, Cam spooned a bite of cobbler into her mouth.

Just how practiced was he in the arts of love? she wondered. After experiencing his many talents last night in her dreams, she could believe that most women made themselves easy conquests. The temptation to join him in the swing had been difficult enough to resist. Considering the imagined intimacy they had shared only a dozen hours before, positioning herself so close to the source of her bliss would surely cause a stir inside her that he would be sure to sense.

Instead, she was sitting in the old cane rocker an arm's length away, but that did nothing to dissuade his bold glances. Even without looking at him, she could tell Tate couldn't keep his eyes off her. Sparks were flying inside him as well. The way his eyes boldly swept across her shoulders sent her heart racing.

The jade glimmer that had greeted her when she stepped out on the porch to welcome him a little while ago was all it took to convince her that she had been a fool to worry over the absence of feminine finery from her wardrobe, a condition that was of her own chosing rather than that of necessity. The only distraction from her crisp, cool, white afternoon frock was a pale blue sash adorning the waist. A ribbon the same shade kept the dark cascade of waves off her neck and from around her face. Her first glance in the mirror had assured her that elegance could truly be found in simplicity, and the Senator's addressing her as Camille rather than his pet name of Cami had brought home the realization that the days of girlish frolic were gone forever. She truly was a woman, a woman who was ready to love and be loved.

"You sure you're not going to share your secret with me?" Tate's eyes were as persistent as his query. "Not even if I threaten to stay put right here in this swing until you do?"

Warm sensations similar to the ones she had experienced in her bath after dwelling too long on him gushed through her.

"Trust me, even if I did have a secret, which I assure you I do not, I doubt you'd find it very amusing."

His eyes wouldn't let go. "Why don't you let me be the judge of that?"

Cam crushed her urge to do just that. Heaven forbid that she should tell him what was really on her mind! Satisfying her own curiosity as to whether or not he'd be easily shocked was one thing, but embarrassing him was an entirely different matter. And embarrassing him would surely be what would happen! How horrible he'd think her if he knew such lusting thoughts passed through her mind. After all, he had been the perfect gentleman at the picnic—almost too perfect! Not once had he tried to steal a kiss, even though she had willed him to do just that! A squeeze of her ankle when he guided her foot into the stirrup could hardly be misconstrued as an amorous advance. Nevertheless, if her instinct proved right, and it did more often than not, Tate Carruth was just as accomplished a lover as he was an equestrian!

Tate reached down to scratch her dog's belly. "Good-looking hound. What's his name?"

Cam breathed a sigh of relief. Thank heavens the topic of conversation had changed before she said anything she might regret later.

"Beggin'," she said with a grin. "He was named for his favorite pastime."

A little surprised, she watched as the dog drifted deeper and deeper into contentment. His sad-eyed frown was deceitful. "You know, he usually doesn't cotton to strangers so quickly."

"No doubt he can recognize a true friend when he sees one." He gave a floppy ear a gentle tug. "Right, fellow?"

Cam rocked slowly. The attention he was paying Beggin' made it all the easier to study him without being detected. He might have directed his comment to the dog, but something in his tone told her he had meant it for her. She certainly had no objection to their being friends. As a matter of fact, the prospect was a very pleasant one indeed. His stay in Caesar's Head might be indefinite, but while he was there, she had no objection at all to seeing as much of him as possible. After all, she might not share her secrets with him, but they did share their love of horses.

The longer she watched him play with Beggin', the wider her smile became. Tate sure had a way with animals. Beggin' had been known to grab hold of a visitor, stranger or not, and hang on until commanded to let go. He hardly ever let anybody walk up to the house without alerting the whole county, but he had let Tate ride right up to the door without making a fuss. The only other time he had shirked his duty was the night the black-caped stranger brought her home. She hadn't heard a peep from him then, either. He hadn't even come round to investigate. At the time, she really hadn't given it much thought. There had been more pressing matters to concern herself with, but now she found it to be more than just a little puzzling. It was downright odd!

Tate stretched his long, firm legs out in front of him and sank back into the swing. Starched gray cuffs rolled up to his elbows, the bottom buttons of his waistcoat unsnapped, and his jacket draped carelessly over the back of the swing, he had made himself right at home.

"I thought the Senator and Ludie Mae would be joining us," he remarked, one brow raised. "Reckon they decided I was harmless?"

Cam said nothing. Her father was conspicuous by his absence. After gobbling down his dessert, he had mumbled something about helping Ludie Mae with some chores, then disappeared. Every now and then, the drawing room drapes gave a slight flutter, and Cam was certain the breeze was not to blame. Knowing those two, there was undoubtedly a conspiracy going on inside the house that very minute. Cam had lost count of how many times the Senator had reminded her of her promise to snatch up the first man who proved himself as good in the saddle as she. The riding breeches she had traded for something more feminine had started him going, and he'd not likely shut up any time soon. Not that she needed any reminding of the promise she had made him. More than once since yesterday that same vow had crossed her mind as well. The problem was, what if Mr. Tate Carruth didn't want to be snatched up? Maybe somebody else had beat her to it.

"And are you?" she asked, anxious to tune back into their conversation. "Harmless, that is?"

He closed his eyes with a lazy grin. "I have a feeling that even if I did pose some kind of a threat, you'd have no trouble putting me in my place."

"Between me and Beggin', I believe we could fend for ourselves."

Cam settled back into her chair and began a slow, steady rocking. She was perfectly content to watch him while he took a little catnap. At first she hadn't thought him to be exceptionally handsome, but the more she studied him, the more she realized it was the strength and prominence of his dark features that made mere good looks insignificant. His firmly set features warned of a stubborn, aggressive strength, the kind that made character.

Even more important, she felt comfortable with him, more at ease than she'd ever been with any other man but the Senator. Yesterday's competition had taught her a lot about him. He viewed her as an equal and respected her as an opponent. Without a doubt the only threat he posed was to her heart. A man like Tate could almost make her think twice about swearing eternal devotion to her mystery man. After last night's ecstasy, divorcing Tate in her imagination from the man in black would be a near impossible task.

His eyes came open instantly, as if he had sensed he was the target of her intense perusal, and settled questioningly on hers.

Cam made no effort to look away. Eyes unflinching, she kept them fixed to the tiny half-moon scar on his cheek and pretended to be waiting for the answer to the imaginary question she had just asked.

"I am sorry. Please forgive me." Looking embarrassed, Tate drew in his legs and sat up straight. "Truth is, I was so comfortable I couldn't resist grabbing a few winks. What a bore you must think me."

"Oh, no. I think I must be the bore," Cam teased. "Why else would you have gone to sleep?"

"Never, not in a thousand years would I think you a bore. Quite the contrary, I assure you." His smile was the only trait that hinted of a boyish side to his nature. "Now, what were you saying?"

Fast thinking wasn't necessary. There had been a question on the tip of her tongue that she had been dying to ask ever since he arrived.

"I was just curious about what happened to you last night," she answered without blinking. "Most of the town turned out to fight the fire, and I sort of expected you'd come along as well."

"Ah, yes. Well, you see, after you left, the party became very dull, so I decided to call it a night. By the time the alarm was raised, I must have been dead to the world." His gaze did not veer from hers. "Not very gallant of me, I must admit. I regret not being there to help out. Lord knows, you could have been killed."

For one second, she was tempted to tell him about her rescuer, if for no other reason than to see if he showed the slightest hint of jealousy. But she could not. He'd surely think her crazy!

"Of course, you did have your good-luck charm," continued Tate, with an nod to her pendant. "I fear I could never compete with the power it possesses."

For a moment, she was at a loss for words. It was almost as though he knew far more than he let on.

"I'm certain that had you been there, I would have had no need for my good-luck charm."

It wasn't until she said the words that Cam believed them herself. Tate was every bit as much of a man as her hooded stranger, and it would be unfair to slight him merely because she could see his face.

"I promise, from now on, any time you need me, I'll be there." A look that was deep and searching and seemed to reach far down into her soul took her captive. Finally his smile released her. "Now what about that tour of Willow Creek you promised?"

Tate took up and offered her his arm. Cam took hold without a moment's hesitation. It seemed only natural her arm be looped around his.

Arm in arm, his hand resting atop hers, they strolled across the grounds. She couldn't think of anyone she'd rather be with, not even her mystery man, and with each passing minute, she became more certain of it. After last night, she did indeed owe the man in the black cape and hood a tremendous debt of gratitude. From time to time, he might even steal into her dreams and make love to her, but not even he could evoke such palm-sweating sensations as the flesh-and-blood man at her side. She had a feeling that Tate Carruth was soon to become more than a fantasy involvement, and that was just fine by her!

Tate pointed out across the pasture where Traveller and Tristram were kicking up their heels. "Didn't take those two long to become better acquainted." He gave her hand a squeeze. "I sure hope the same holds true for their owners."

The firmness of his fingers woven around hers sent her heart somersaulting all the way down to her toes. Better acquainted, did he say? Nothing would please her more.

They stood at the fence laughing as the two stallions played catch-me-if-you-can as if for their masters' entertainment. The delight Tate and Cam shared at their horses' frolics drew them even closer together.

Just when it seemed Tate could get no nearer, his rock-hard thigh pressed into her hip. The pressure created by his change of position left her feeling completely at his beck and call, and she honestly could not say she minded.

"I haven't seen Traveller enjoying himself so much since Apollo used to jump his fence and come over to play," Cam remarked, anxious to break the silence lest he guess exactly what thoughts were on her mind.

"Apollo?"

At last the skittering inside her chest was subdued, and she was able to lean into his hold and fully enjoy the wonderful sensations flooding her.

"Apollo was an Arabian that lived down the road at Hunter's Glen. Talk about a spectacular creature! White as snow, but a bit too high strung for my liking. Of course, Clayton Griffin liked his horses with lots of spirit." Frowning, Cam shook her head. "Poor fellow."

"Who? Griffin or Apollo?"

"Both," she replied sadly as they walked on. "A couple of years back, Apollo turned mean. Lots of people say he went plain crazy. He trampled poor Clayton to death."

Tate gave a sympathetic nod. "If you don't know how to handle them, horses, particularly strong ones, can be mighty dangerous."

Cam frowned. Why Apollo should suddenly have turned on Clayton was every bit a mystery now as it had been two years ago when it happened.

"That's what was so strange. Clayton knew more about horses than anybody in the county put together. He had a way with the worst of them. Why, I've watched as he turned more than one rogue into as well-mannered a horse as you could ever hope for." Remembering the days she had sat on the fence mesmerized by Clayton's horsemanship brought a sad smile. "He had quite a way with them. The Senator said it was because he had more patience with them than he did for people."

"Sounds like your friend was a lonely man."

"That he was. He kept to himself and encouraged everybody else to keep their distance, too."

Strong fingers laced themselves even tighter around hers. She tried not to react to the turmoil hammering at her chest, but ignoring it proved just as hard.

"If you ask me, though, I'd say his bark was much worse than his bite. Deep down, I suspect he was real unhappy. The person he was closest to was his houseboy. In fact, it was Jackson who found him dead in Apollo's stall. That poor darkie! He's never been quite right since."

Excitement raged inside her as she tried to go on. She had to keep talking. Otherwise, Tate would guess the reason for her quickness of breath. Her fingers were on fire. Never had she felt so out of control!

"Jackson still lives there," she said matter of

factly. "And the way he fusses around Hunter's Glen, you'd think Clayton was going to come galloping up the drive any minute."

"And the family? Do they still live there?"

"If there is a family somewhere, nobody around here knows about it. Clayton lived here all his life, some fifty years, I believe, and if he ever did have any kin, he never spoke of them." Cam paused. Thank goodness the beat of her heart had slowed to a canter! "Sooner or later, I suspect someone will show up claiming to be a long lost-cousin, and if they can prove it, they'd sure come into a mighty nice inheritance."

"You know, if I could find a place up here that I liked, I might just consider buying it," Tate remarked out of the blue. "There's a solitude and contentment you can't find any place but in the mountains."

His stare, penetrating and probing, flamed her cheeks. She dare not look up at him for fear of revealing thoughts and desires that were best left hidden. The prospect of Tate moving to Caesar's Head was a very pleasant one indeed! Perhaps last night's dream was a premonition of wonderous events to come.

"If it's peace and quiet you're interested in, Hunter's Glen sounds like just the place you have in mind. Talk to Strothers about it," she suggested.

"Strothers? Why him?"

Cam swallowed hard. He was so close, she could feel his breath hot in her ear. How much more of it she could take she didn't know.

"At one time, he was interested in Hunter's Glen himself, but he's since moved on to bigger projects. He tried to track down the heirs but didn't have any success at all. Just as well. Had he found them he'd surely have come up with a way to swindle them out of their inheritance!"

Chuckling, Tate bent down and picked up a rock. "You don't think much of Strothers, do you?"

"I don't like to think about him at all." She replied to Tate's questioning glance with one just as frank. "Something wrong?"

His puzzled frown remained, even when he sent the stone skipping over the river's surface. "Strothers led me to believe the two of you were quite friendly at one time. I guess he was wrong."

"You're damn right he was wrong!" Cam stopped dead in her tracks. Her blood was so hot it was boiling. What kind of filthy tales had that bastard been spreading about her? She'd fix him! One way or another, she'd fix him good!

"If he considers me ramming my knee between his legs as being friendly, then I reckon we were downright intimate!"

Tate leaned down and kissed her cheek. His lips were but a whisper brushing across her skin.

Her anger gave way to contentment. "What was that for?"

"I figured he was lying. I'm glad I was right." He took her hand again with unmistakeable possessiveness. "I never could picture the two of you together."

"I could say the same about the two of you," she blurted without thinking. "He's no gentleman, Tate," she went on, figuring the damage was already done. "He'd knife his best friend, then pour salt in the wound if he thought he had something to gain from doing it."

His stubborn mouth might have been set in a smile, but the grave, almost hostile glare reflected in those bottomless pools of green gave her reason to believe that Tate, too, knew what lurked beneath Strothers' facade. The urge to press the matter was great, but she resisted it. That snake in the grass had ruined enough of her life as it was. He wasn't going to ruin her friendship with Tate as well.

Chatting and laughing with the familiarity of old friends, they went on with their stroll. Strothers Bennett was the thought furthest from both their minds.

After a tour of the property, they winded their way back down along the river. As if he could tell exactly what was on her mind, Tate headed to a lone willow tree standing guard at the river's edge. The shade of its weeping branches created a welcome oasis. This was where she had hoped their walk would end all along.

Sitting on the ground beside him, only inches separating her from the cause of last night's ecstasy, brought to mind a scene from an English novel she had just read. She was the lady of the estate, he her lord. Such an idyllic setting existed in real life after all.

Tate appraised the scenery, taking it all in with an appreciative eye.

Cam followed his gaze up to the house. The history of Willow Creek was the one project the Senator always made a point of explaining to their guests. A century before, the two-story structure had been built for Captain Billy Young, the Revolution's boy hero who had been nicknamed

"Terror of the Tories."

Surely Captain Young could have loved Willow Creek no more then than Cam did now! Built from native rock dug from the Saluda River, the house sat amid a jungle of greenery. So dense was the foliage surrounding it that little more than the twin gables was visible from afar. With its deep-recessed windows, enormous granite fire-places in each room, and the wide piazza where one could wile away the days sitting and rocking, her home could have been lifted right off the pages of a fairy tale picture book.

"No wonder the Senator's so adamant about not wanting to part with a single acre of this place," said Tate. "Paradise could be no lovelier."

Cam smiled. His sentiments echoed her own. "My father would as soon sell me."

"If that's the case, I'd better get my bid in right away."

Her heart soared high past the tree top. The sentiments they shared went far beyond an appreciation of Willow Creek.

But then her smile began to fade. How odd! The Senator had said nothing to Tate about selling off any of the property, at least not in her presence. Perhaps the subject had been brought up when she went into the house to help Ludie Mae carry out the coffee.

The demanding pressure from the rock-hard thigh pressing hers soon made her forget all else. She could hardly remember her name, much less the topic of a conversation that took place over an hour ago.

Scooting a few inches to the left was all she had to do to escape from the power he wielded over her, but she didn't want to escape from it, not really. If anything, she wanted it to push against her even harder!

"Caesar's Head," remarked Tate.

"I beg your pardon?"

"Caesar's Head," he repeated. "It's an unusual name for a town. Where might one find the head of the great Roman here?"

Cam relaxed. Thank heaven he was too intent on the view to pay much mind to the storm brewing inside her.

She pointed across the river to a large rock jutting out from the mountainside. "That's the head of Caesar. To those with a creative imagination, it bears a striking resemblance to Caesar's profile."

Tate studied the rock for a moment, then shook his head. "Guess I don't have much of a creative imagination."

"No? Perhaps if you look hard enough you can make out the shape of a nose and a mouth," she suggested. His concentration gave her just the chance she wanted to make a more detailed study of his profile. It was far more interesting than that of any rock. Nothing about him showed any sign of weakness. Yet, even in his strength, there was a kindness to be detected, a kindness that told her he was a very gentle man.

Tate shook his head again. "Looks like a dog to me."

"Bravo," she applauded. "That's another version of how the rock got its name. Some hunters took their dogs tracking up there, and one of the hounds got lost."

"And that dog's name just happened to be

Caesar, right?"

Cam laughed. "That's right." Realizing that she, not the rock, had become his point of focus, she hurriedly continued. "The explanation that seems the most reasonable, however, is that the name Caesar's Head came from someone mispronouncing the Indian word for chief. Saechame. Or something like that."

Tate lifted her hand from its resting spot atop her knee. "By Indians, do you mean the Cherokees?" One by one, each finger in his grasp was kissed.

Cam could do no more than nod. The words were there, somewhere stuck inside her throat, but they would not come out. If she forced them, she'd start stuttering for sure. What havoc he caused inside her! Catching a good breath had never been so difficult.

"Legend has it the chief of the Cherokees promised his people that the mountain would always belong to them," she continued as soon as she once again had control of her senses. "He married his only child, a daughter, to the valiant warrior he had chosen to succeed him. But no sooner was the old chief buried than the new one sold their mountain to the white man for a few beads. His wife killed him for breaking the vow to her father and to their people."

"So what became of the girl?"

Cam smiled. How often she, herself, had wondered the same thing!

"I hope she was made the new chief."

Tate brushed his cheek with her hand. "Ah, do I detect a bit of admiration for the brave maiden?"

"Land can become so important a part of your

life, you would kill for it if need be."

His eyes pierced hers in a penetrating stare. "Would you?"

"If someone tried to take Willow Creek, I'd do whatever had to be done." She received his stare with the same directness with which he cast it. "And not think twice about it."

"You sound like a lady after my own heart."

Oh, I am, I am, she wanted to cry out. His heart. Was that truly what she wanted? Yes, she thought so.

Little by little, she felt herself slipping under the spell of that hypnotic green stare. She knew what was coming but denying it was the furthest thought from her mind. It came as no surprise to find her face in his hands, their noses touching. Nor was it any surprise when his smile blended with her own in a tender little kiss that promised more of the same to come.

She would remember that kiss forever, even when she was old and gray. It wasn't the fumbling peck of an awkward boy groping in the dark. Nor was it brutal, like Strothers' kiss when he tried to force her into submission. Tate's kiss was everything a kiss should be. Everything and so, so much more. Not even those delivered by the man in black could compare with the potency of the one she had just experienced. Nor had they filled her with such a sense of urgency!

One kiss grew into another, and still another, each more fiery than the rest. His lips asked no questions. They made no demands, but merely affirmed the unspoken declaration of what they had both suspected all along. She was to be his, and he hers.

Steam rose quickly inside her, its vapors clouding her mind. She supposed she should get up and leave. Any self-respecting, decent girl would . . . wouldn't she?

One more kiss was all it took to convince her to stay.

"I've been wanting to do that since yesterday." Tate pressed his cheek to hers with a soft moan. "If you're angry, I won't blame you."

His attempt at an apology made her smile. Funny, but her initial impression of Tate Carruth was that he was a man who took what he wanted without apologies or regrets.

"How can I be angry when you've done only what I had hoped you'd do all along?"

Her eyes remained hidden in the curve of his neck. She dared not look at him. He'd think her shameless for sure!

She could sense his relief, and she, too, released a long-pent-up sigh.

"You've no idea how pleased I am to hear you say that."

Strong arms tightened around her, forming a protective barrier from the outside world. For the longest time, they just sat there, locked in each other's embrace, gently rocking together and reveling in their shared moment of intimacy. Though neither wanted to break the spell by speaking, both knew the time would come when holding each other could no longer contain the storehouse of emotions inside them.

When Tate finally did let go, he turned his attention to the woods across the river. "What's over there?"

"Five hundred acres of the state's finest pineland," Cam replied proudly. "That was one of the few forests in the South to escape the Yankee torch. We could row over there if you'd like," she added, trying to keep her offer matter of fact.

His nod was solemn. "Yes, I believe I'd like that."

Her heart stopped in mid-beat. It seemed forever before it started up again. Yes, she believed she'd like that herself. There, they would be perfectly alone, two people, a man and a woman, swallowed up by row after row of giant pines as far as the eye could see.

The skiff was tied up at the boathouse right where she had left it last week after an excursion to her place of refuge among the pines.

The Saluda River was as calm and peaceful as a millpond, the boat but a ripple on its surface. Even had the river been riddled with enormous waves and swells to toss the little boat from side to side, she wouldn't have wanted to return to shore. She'd come too far to turn back now. Watching Tate effortlessly stroking the water with the oars, she could think of little but the thick cords of muscles that looked about to burst through the thin cotton covering his oak-hard chest. He truly was a magnificent man to behold. At first, she hadn't thought so, but now, if she could assign physical attributes to the man in black, the two men would be remarkably similar.

"You're smiling," remarked Tate as they glided into shore. "You must hold this spot very dear to your heart."

Cam quelled her urge to hop out and tie up the boat. Instead, she waited for him to give her a hand out. "These woods hold some very special memories. As a little girl I used to come over here and sit for hours listening to the birds."

Memories. What kind of memories would the woods hold for her after today? she wondered as she held onto Tate's hand and stepped out of the boat. There was something in his touch that assured her she would look back on this moment with a special happiness.

"Any reason why this has never been logged? Your father has a gold mine in these trees."

The feel of his arm tight around her waist sent her head spinning and her senses reeling. What an effect he had on her! Was he as aware of it as she? Could he possibly know her legs turned to jelly each time he reached for her? If it weren't for his holding her tight against him, she'd have already crumbled to the ground.

"I'm sorry, what did you ask me?"

How could he possibly expect her to concentrate on conversing under such circumstances?

If he sensed the reason for her lack of attention, he gave no indication, and for that she was grateful.

"I asked why the Senator hasn't logged these woods. There's a small fortune to be made in lumbering."

Cam gazed up at the sylvan giants. Their tops were so thick, she could hardly make out the patches of blue beyond then. Even in the summer, a pine hammock was the coolest spot to be found. The sun seldomly cast its shadow on the needle-strewn ground. And that crisp, clean scent of evergreen! If a fortune were to be made from the trees, then finding a way to package such a heavenly smell would surely make one very wealthy indeed.

But log it? He must be mad. One moment he saw Willow Creek as a paradise, the next, a money making opportunity. Then again, he was a businessman, and they always placed economics above nature. No doubt Strothers had made some mention of the struggle they had endured the past year just to get by.

"Cutting down one tree in this forest would be like raping the land of its dignity. No amount of money can justify that humiliation." She was still disappointed that he would even ask such a question, but not enough to move out of his reach. "The land's been good to us. The least we can do is return the favor.

Tate kissed the top of her head. "Good land is like a kind, beautiful woman. It should be loved and cherished forever."

Indigo pools merged into a sea of green. Past fantasies danced in front of her, and she wasn't at all sure from whose eyes they were playing.

Another moment and the closeness was more than she could endure. Each part of his body was in communication with hers. Even the tips of their toes touched through their shoes. When their lips came together, it was as though the breath had been snatched right out of her!

When his hands began their oh-so-adventurous climb up from her waist, she knew right where they were headed, but it seemed forever before they reached their destination. Plump summits rose to greet him. The instant his finger tips brushed against the inviting peaks, a cry went up inside her for him to rip away the cloth keeping them imprisoned.

All too soon, he ceased his exploration. The solemn glint in his stare encouraged her, pleaded with her, to voice her protests now before the situation became even more out of hand.

Arms wound tight around him, Cam pulled his head down to her breast in reply. All afternoon she had hoped their meeting would end just this way. He wanted her. There was no doubt about that. Soon, very soon, he would know just how much she shared in his desires. If the storm inside her were ever to be quieted, then he must take possession of her then and there.

"Love me. Please love me," she whispered, between little moans of delight.

His reply was interspersed with the little kisses he dropped all up and down her throat. "I do . . .I will. Now and always. I swear."

With that, he swept her off her feet and carried her deep into the woods, stopping only when the dense canopy above made it impossible to distinguish the time of day. There he lay her down ever so gently onto a bed of cool earth.

She could hardly believe what was happening. Her fantasies were about to become reality. One moment she was afraid she wouldn't know what to do when the time finally did come, and the next, she was certain her woman's intuition would direct her.

She could sense a frantic urgency building in his hands as he tugged at her frock, and that eagerness made the palpitations inside her chest quicken even more. With each button they plucked, his fingers grew more and more bold, pushing and probing, kneading and caressing their way to the secret joys held within until at last they were massaging her bare flesh with a force that rivaled her heart's beating.

Taking a lesson from him, Cam began unbuttoning his shirt, but the more hurriedly she approached her task, the more bumbling her hands became. Tate came to her rescue not a moment too soon, for if she didn't soon feel his crushing chest upon her she would certainly die.

Her dreams had been more bedtime stories in comparison to the desperate desire now flooding her. He brought out the animal in her. She felt like a jungle cat just wakening from a long nap. All she wanted to do was to stretch and claw and pounce. She was a tiger, his tiger. The passions he unleased were his to do with as he wished.

Her lips devoured his. How thirsty she was! Only he could reach so parching a thirst. Never had she thought she would ever want to give a man total possession of her body and soul, but now, now it was all she could do to keep from crying out at the top of her voice, *Take me. I'm yours. Do with me as you will!* Her pleas would not come. She was too tired. She lacked the strength to do more than hold on tight as he explored territory that had been off limits to any man before him.

His need was great. She could feel it pressing hard against her, probing as far as it could into the spot he would soon lay his claim to. Desire spread from one to the other like a fire in dry twigs. God, but she wanted him! Fantasizing about some mysterious black-caped man seemed childish now, for she had possession of a real man, a real flesh-and-blood man who could make any dream she dared dream come true!

Had he not tugged off her dress and all the

trappings underneath, she would have done it for him. She was on fire and there was only one way to extinguish the enormous blaze he had ignited inside her.

Free of all save her natural covering, Cam lay there, hot and proud, looking up at him with an eagerness which matched his own. She felt no shame, no regret. He feasted on her nakedness with the deliberate greed of an epicure about to indulge himself with the most delectable of culinary delights. He was hungry, as hungry as she, and he wanted it all!

Tate stripped quickly, leaving her no time to brace herself for the awesome surprise revealed to her. He was strong and hard, a legend come true. No artist, no matter how talented, could ever do justice to his body's magnificence. He was art itself!

She couldn't keep her hands off him. Even had she wanted to stop, there was no way she could stop her hands from darting in and out of rock-hard contours that begged to be explored. The tight muscles of a chest as smooth as her own were made just to dig her fingers into. She wanted to know all there was to know about him, to feel all there was to feel, and if that took an eternity, then so be it!

For the longest time, he hovered above her, watching, smiling, taking in all the exotic wonders laid before him. Then he began kissing her, his lips teasing and caressing parts of her body she could see and those she could not. What sweet, sweet torture!

Her skin crawled inside his, his flesh becoming her own. Starvation could never cause such a desperate hunger. Her lips craved more, demanded so much more, but how much more of the marvelous torment she could take?

Was that her own voice she heard pleading for him to go on, to search deeper still?

"Yes, oh, yes, more, more. Please make love to me, Tate. Now. Don't make me suffer another second. Teach me, show me. I want all of you."

He swallowed her in his reply.

How natural it felt to draw up her legs and guide him in to the very core of her being. So knowing were her body's responses, she almost forgot she had never before been with a man. Her dreams were the only experience she'd ever had in such matters. The feel of flesh tearing flesh was the only reminder that this was where the dream must end and reality begin. What little pain there was faded into the honeyed warmth it had created. Come morning, she'd ache for sure, but the soreness would be but a way of keeping alive so cherished a memory of the joy she had known.

Desire coursed through her veins with a vigor she hadn't dreamed she could possibly possess. His hard, thrusting passion, forceful and purposeful, but not without gentleness, lead her to paradise and back. She caressed and was caressed, trembled and made to tremble, and each time she felt certain she was about to expire from the very exhaustion that brought her back to life time and again. How long such ecstasy would last she did not know, but if lasted the next hundred years, it would end much, much too soon.

Later, Cam awakened to find him staring down at her, a smile on his lips and a look of satisfied contentment glazing his eyes.

"You're mine now," Tate whispered as he brushed his lips over her damp brows. "No one is ever going to take you away from me. I love you, Camille Tranter. And don't you ever forget it. I've loved you from the first moment I laid eyes on you."

Her arms reached out to him and pulled him down onto her once more. His words were but echoes of her own sentiments. She loved him! And she'd tell him. But first, she'd show him. The tiger he had awakened inside her was about to spring to life once again.

6

Keeping her attention on the dinner conversation was becoming more and more difficult. Talk of the newly emerging textile industry held little interest, nor did predictions of economic growth for the South brought on by forced industralization. Who cared about the advantages of wool mills over cotton mills, anyway?

How could she possibly devote her complete, undivided attention to anything but the wonderfully charming, handsome man sitting across the table from her—so close, yet so far away! No aristocratic hero from the latest English novel could even begin to compare with so elegant and so debonair a gentleman.

Tate Carruth. No subject could be more intriguing, no topic more worthy of her attention. He was everything a man should be and more, so much more! How could her mind ever dwell on anything else?

Cam couldn't keep her eyes off him. Where her eyes were, her hands and lips longed to be. Recollections of that afternoon of loving sent her heart into a frenzy. He was all she could think about. She could still feel his wonderfully wicked hands as they awakened her most secret parts; she could still smell the husky, male aroma that enveloped her, all of her, with its magic, and still taste all the delicious sweetness his lips had to offer. The roses he had painted on her cheeks were there to stay. No scrubbing would ever take away their glow. She would have gladly spent a lifetime with him in the pine hammock, in their pine hammock. Had it not been for Abbey's dinner party, they might well have stayed hidden in their cozy little bower until dark. She had arrived there a girl, but she left it a woman, a woman whose most hidden longings had been fulfilled.

It had been written all over her face, Cam felt for sure, the moment she emerged from the forest. She dared not look at anyone for fear of giving herself away. If the Senator noticed any difference, he said nothing, merely asked if she and Tate had a pleasant visit and let it go at that. Ludie Mae had been particularly chatty, but even if she did suspect anything, she'd never let on, and that was just as well!

Just thinking about what had happened between them made Cam's flesh go all hot and sweaty. She belonged to Tate now. Funny, but never in a hundred years would she have said that about any man before him. But she belonged to him, just as he now belonged to her. What they had shared, no one could ever take away. Even though there had been no talk of the future, he had declared his love, and she hers in return. He was in her blood, and there was no question that she was in his as well. Regardless of what tomorrow or the next day held, their destiny had been sealed. What a twist of fate for one who had always sworn a man would never be so important a part of her life suddenly to be unable to comprehend the possibility of an existence without him! He had said he loved her, and she believed him with all her heart.

Nodding her head in agreement, Cam smiled politely at an observation the Senator had just made to Tate that slaves had never comprised the bulk of wealth in the South, nor had plantation owners depended solely on them for labor. She was relieved when Tate offered no objection but readily admitted slavery had not been the main issue of the war, contrary to what Mr. Lincoln professed.

So far, the evening could not have been more perfect. The pheasant was the finest she had ever tasted. Conversation flowed as smoothly as the claret, and everyone was so pleasant—even Strothers. Abbey had fussed and fretted with every detail, so determined was she that the evening be enjoyable for all. A more gracious hostess there could not be. Being in the family way had obviously taken its toll on her, but there was an unmistakeable glow to her cheeks, one that could only be attributed to her forthcoming motherhood. Strothers had surely spent all day rehearsing for his role as doting husband and host, for he could not have been any more considerate and attentive a spouse toward his wife, or a more charming and witty host toward his guests. Either he had something up his sleeve, or he had undergone a drastic metamorphosis in the last twenty-four hours. Somehow, Cam was certain there was more behind that congenial pearl-toothed smile than met the eye.

Still, not even Strothers could ruin her evening. Had the dinner party been a complete disaster, all would not have been lost, for the man sitting opposite her would make up for any discomfort. Just thinking of the afternoon's delights caused soundless cries to erupt in her throat. Her fingertips were still aquiver from the hidden places they had so brazenly explored. She was surprised she had gotten this far in the meal without dropping her fork or knocking over her wine glass. Her mind was simply on far more important matters!

Once again, Cam tried to follow the flow of conversation. The Senator was now explaining to Tate why tobacco grown in the high country had a better flavor and aroma than that grown in the lowlands even though the production in their area was considerably less. Tate's questions regarding profit and productivity spurred the Senator into a lengthy dissertation about quality, not quantity, being a true farmer's objective.

When Strothers changed the topic to politics and the inflationist groups in both the Republican and Democratic parties, as well as the new Greenback party, which was demanding an even larger circulation of paper money, Cam allowed her thoughts once again to drift back to the pine hammock and to the sensual joys she had experienced there. Just as she was reliving that instant when she and Tate had become as one, the embroidered linen napkin slid off her lap. She quickly leaned over to retrieve it, nearly bumping heads with Strothers on the way down. One bold leer as he tried to sneak a peek beyond the dusty rose ruffle shaping a V between her breasts told her that he was up to his old tricks.

His breath was hot in her face. "I see you're still wearing that gold trinket you found in the woods."

Cam sat up quickly.

"You're not still sweet on that dark stranger, are you?" he asked, needling her. "Goodness gracious me. I can see from that blush that you still are. It must be a very frustrating search indeed, for a man who can compete with your dashing hero," he remarked with a wink to everyone else. "All done up in black, was he?"

Cam was determined not to let him know he could rile her so easily. A stolen glance at Tate revealed his ears had been quick to perk up.

She smoothed the napkin onto her lap, her smile fixed to her face while all the time thinking how she'd love to strangle her dearest friend's husband.

"That's right, Strothers. Black cape, black hood, black boots—and in the dead of the summer, too. Fancy that."

Abbey paled a shade lighter than her cream-colored gown. "Really, Strothers, must you tease her so?"

Cam smiled in spite of herself. No doubt Abbey had let slip what she had been told two years before in the strictest of confidence. It didn't really matter. Not anymore. All that was behind her. After this afternoon, she could only belong to one man and his identity was by no means secret.

"I'm sure Strothers meant no harm, did you

dear?" Abbey stammered.

His smile was lethal. "Lordy, no. Cami knows I was just joshing her. Why, me and her's great friends."

Cam took a sip of the wine. The cool liquid did not sooth the lump in her throat. Great friends, did he say?

Goblet to his lips, Tate viewed the exchange with a puzzled frown. "A man in black, did you say? That certainly sounds very intriguing!"

Once again, Strothers directed his attention to the swell of Cam's breasts. "Perhaps you'd care to share your experience with us," he suggested smoothly. "I can't speak for the others, but I know I'm just dying to hear about that romance of yours with the mystery man."

"Heavens, no. I wouldn't dream of boring you all with something as dull as a childhood infatuation."

He was not going to get her goat—not without a fight anyway!

"However, speaking of romances," she began in a hushed voice, "does anyone know what happened with the Coopers last night at the dance?"

It was all she could do to keep from laughing when Strothers began to fidget. She paused, drawing out the suspense as long as she could. Strothers was in the hot seat now, and she wanted to keep him there as long as possible.

Abbey urged her to continue. "No, tell us what happened."

"Well, when I was fixing to leave," she continued slowly, "Bud came tearing up on his horse, swearing at the top of his lungs and threatening to kill whoever it was messing around with his Nellie."

All the color drained out of Strother's face. His smile looked as if it were glued to his lips.

Cam shot him a triumphant glare that dared him to press her any further.

"Poor man," remarked Abbey sympathetically. "You know, when Bud's sober, you couldn't find a friendlier fellow. But let him get a drink in him, and he's terrible. I guess that wife of his just brings out the devil in him."

Cam enjoyed watching Strothers sweat. While she had the upper hand, she was going to enjoy it.

"From what I hear, Nellie Cooper brings out the devil in most men. Isn't that right, Strothers?"

He tugged at his collar.

"I mean, haven't there been lots of fights down at the mill over her?"

"I'm afraid I'm too busy running the mill. I don't have time for such nonsense." He downed the wine that was left in his goblet and called for another bottle.

Cam stole a look at Abbey, then, satisfied that all was well, breathed a sigh of relief. As much as she enjoyed putting Strothers on the spot, she wouldn't hurt her old friend for anything in the world. Thank heavens Abbey was oblivious to the goings-on behind her back. From now on, she'd have to take extra precautions to see to it that Abbey was not caught in the crossfire in the war between her and Strothers.

While Strothers continued to squirm and Abbey kept fussing over her guests, the Senator filled the strained silence with more questions directed at Tate.

"So tell me, my boy, what line of work are you in? I can tell by your hands you're no farmer, and you're much too polite to be a lawyer, so I assume that you're in some kind of business or another."

"He's what you would call an entrepreneur," interrupted Strothers as he made his way around the table filling everyone's wine glass. "Ain't that right, Tate? Why, he's got his hands in just about every kind of business there is."

"Oh, is that so?" The Senator leaned back in his chair and took another sip of the claret.

"I'm afraid Strothers does tend to exaggerate." Smiling, Tate sipped his wine. "Actually, my business interests are quite diversified. My family has holdings in real estate, construction, shipbuilding . . . I believe there might even be a bank or two in there somewhere."

Cam cut into her piece of pear pie, but left it suspended on the end of her fork. Was it her imagination, or was Tate hedging? Just what exactly was it he did for a living anyway?

If the Senator shared her feelings, he said nothing. "Seems to me your father is a pretty lucky man to have you overseeing his interests. You said his name was Philip, didn't you?"

"Yes, sir."

"He come South very much? I'd like to meet him."

"I'm afraid my father's dead, sir," Tate told the Senator. "He passed on several years back."

"Oh, I'm sorry, my boy. So sorry." The chair's front legs returned to the oak floor with a dull thump.

With a sad smile, Tate raised his wine glass. "So am I, sir. A son could never have had a finer father."

Cam lifted her own glass in a silent toast. She could say the same of Cameron Tranter.

Strothers rose from his seat. "Gentlemen, how about joining me in the drawing room for a cigar and a brandy?"

Tate's eyes drifted across the table and held Cam's there. His smile was so disarming, she could hardly remember what it was that had her so puzzled a moment before.

"Only if the two most beautiful ladies in South Carolina be permitted to join us."

Strothers' smile remained, but it was plain to see Tate's suggestion did not set too well with him. And as far as Cam was concerned, that was all the more reason to accompany them.

"You know, the more I hear about this fellow in black, the more intrigued I am with him," Tate remarked as he seated Cam on the curved-back sofa, then positioned himself a respectable distance away. "It all sounds so fascinating. Just like something out of a novel."

Cam wondered if he were jealous. "Oh, it wasn't nearly so fascinating as Strothers makes it out to be, I assure you."

Even though there was enough room between them for another person or two, she could still feel the tremendous pressure of his body. How she longed to have him on top of her once more, to have her breasts crushed by the wonderful force of his powerful chest. If only they could sneak away tonight—just for a little while—just so they could rekindle their inferno of love.

"I understand some fellow fitting that description was seen out near the Winthrops last night," Tate continued after Strothers had poured him a brandy. "Can't be too many fellows running around in a black cape and hood this time of year."

Cam's ears pricked up, but she tried to hide her interest. So she had been right after all. She should have known better than to doubt her instincts. They seldomly led her astray. The mystery man had been right there with her last night after all. Considering the events of the afternoon, it would have been better had his presence been a figment of her imagination. Her man in black might well be the substance of a young girl's fantasies, but Tate was there in the flesh, and he had fulfilled all the longings of a woman and so much more!

"Oh, and who did you hear that from?" she asked, suddenly aware that all eyes, Strothers' especially, were boring right into her.

Tate thought for a moment, then shook his head. "I don't remember now. Must have heard it when I was in town this morning."

"In the wee hours of morning, I might add," broke in Strothers with an exaggerated wink. "You were out so late last night yourself I figured you must have been helping fight it. Terrible thing, fires. What a shame to have your whole life go up in smoke. Sure wish there was a way I could help those poor Winthrops along."

Cam couldn't imagine Strothers helping anyone along but himself, but she was too confused to dwell on what he had said about the Winthrops. His remark about Tate was what was so baffling.

She looked to Tate for an explanation, but he

said nothing. Could it be she had misunderstood him earelier? Had he not said he had gone back to the Sullivan house and gone directly to bed after she left the party? Perhaps she had indeed heard wrong. Of course, that was it. Strothers and Nellie had her so shaken up she just hadn't heard right. That was all. Tate had nothing to gain by lying to her.

"If you ask me," offered Strothers on his way to the big oak sideboard where he filled his snifter a second time. "My guess is that those young'uns of Marsh Winthrop's got a little careless and set the fire themselves."

"Don't reckon we'll ever know for sure. Will we?" The Senator drew slowly on his pipe. "That's the bad thing about fires. You never know if they were intentional or accidental. Poor cuss," he continued, shaking his white head. "Marsh sure has had his share of bad luck. Seems like he's been doomed to failure from the start. He could never eke out a living from that soil. 'Bout all that rock and scrub grass is fit for is raising sheep. I tried to get him to go into the sheep business, but you know how stubborn those Winthrops can be."

"Seems to me like this whole town's had a run of bad luck these last couple of years," Abbey piped up as she carried in a silver tray. "Seems like it all started with Clayton Griffin's accident. Remember, Strothers?"

Strothers rushed over to take the tray away from her. "Now, darling, you know you shouldn't be lifting heavy things like that in your delicate condition. Why, what would Doc Benton say? Here, let me. You just sit down and look pretty."

Cam rolled back her eyes. Since when did

Strothers worry about his wife's frailty? From the look on Abbey's face, she was wondering the same thing.

When Strothers brought the tray around to her, Cam pretended not to notice as his eyes boldly swept the top of her gown. The man was an animal. No two ways about it! All he could think about was satisfying his own carnal cravings. Even though her dress was only slightly off the shoulder, and the cut in a line far too modest to be fashionable, she felt for a moment as though she were indecently attired, and that she was somehow responsible for him looking at her with such lust. If it weren't for poor Tate being so close to the danger zone, she'd accidentally tip the tray over and show Mr. Bennett what it really felt like to have his manhood on fire.

Cam chuckled to herself a moment later. No doubt Strothers had known exactly what was on her mind, for he stepped back quickly as soon as she had taken one of the dainty Wedgewood teacups.

"Why don't you play something for us, Abbey?" Cam suggested as she sipped her tea, which was a blend of orange and spice. "Didn't you tell me your aunt just sent you down some new pieces from New York?"

"Well, yes, but . . ." Abbey looked to Strothers for a word of encouragement but found none. "I really haven't had much of a chance to practice."

"Nonsense," Tate spoke up as he returned an empty snifter to the tray and took a teacup when Strothers passed by. "Why, I heard you playing this morning, and believe you me, no sweeter sounds could have come out of the finest concert halls in New York."

Tate stood up, walked over to his hostess and offered her his arm. "Madame, allow me."

"Oh, Tate, you're just much too kind." With a flushed smile, Abbey took his arm and allowed him to escort her to the big grand piano that was her pride and joy.

"Who says Yankee boys ain't gentlemen?" remarked Strothers, his hint of sarcasm going unnoticed.

Cam kept her eyes on Abbey the entire time. She could feel Strothers' eyes glaring at her with unmistakeable hatred. No doubt he had decided a long time ago she wasn't worth his wasting his time on. He may have been amused by that incident in the barn before his wedding, but now there was no doubt that he loathed her, probably just as much as she despised him, and that was just fine by her. There was no better reason than mutual contempt to encourage someone to keep his distance.

Cam listened to the music. The sweet harmony lulled her into an uncharacteristic mellowness as Abbey's fingers danced across the ivory keys, producing sounds that brought to mind a crisp spring day with dogwoods in bloom and bees and butterflies flitting around them.

Abbey really is very talented, she thought to herself. Her friend could have easily been one of those concert pianists Tate was talking about earlier, who played in the finest concert halls in New York. That's what Abbey had been studying hard to become before she became trapped in a loveless marriage. No doubt the only solace she received from a troubled union with Strothers came from her music.

Strothers sprawled out onto the armchair, looking like a spoiled child who wasn't getting his way. His impatience for his wife to finish the concerto was difficult to ignore. When he was miserable, he wanted everybody to know it.

"I don't suppose you've ever reconsidered selling off any of those woods across the river, have you, Senator?" he asked, raising his voice over the music. "I know for a fact you could get a mighty pretty penny out of it."

Cam could see her father's smile was very strained, but she knew he would bite his tongue for their hostess' sake.

Abbey stopped in mid-tune and threw her husband an angry glare. "Don't you pay him any mind," she apologized to the Senator. "Strothers thinks everybody ought to be as money hungry as him."

The Senator waved away her concern. "That's all right, my dear. No harm done. Your husband just likes to get my dander up. He knows it would be a cold day in hell before I sell off one stick of those woods."

Cam watched as her father stared down Strothers, his eyes as unflinching as the smile hewn to his face. She glanced over to Tate, whose gaze was intent on her. There was something troubling in his look. She couldn't quite figure out what.

"Can't fault me for trying, sir. Just checking to see if you'd changed your mind." Strothers saluted the Senator with his brandy snifter, then took a long gulp, followed by an even longer one.

Over the crystal rim, he followed the path Tate's eyes had taken.

"Oh, by the way, remember when I told you about a fellow who was interested in obtaining the logging rights to Willow Creek? Well, that fellow's still interested in case you change your mind." His stare was stone cold as it settled on Cam and stayed fixed to her as he dealt his final blow. "Yes, siree. Mr. Carruth here has big plans to expand that timber business of his, ain't that right, Tate?" You did tell them you were in sawmills, too, didn't you?"

Strothers went on like nothing was wrong, completely ignoring the shocked discomfort of his wife and guests. "Yes, siree. Carruth Lumber is one of the largest in the nation, and they're looking to expand down here. Ain't that right, Tate?"

A dead stillness encompassed the room. No one dared to move, much less speak.

Cam felt the sick lump rising to her throat again, but she'd be damned if she gave Strothers the pleasure of knowing how he had unnerved her. What he had been waiting to happen all evening finally had. He was the one with the upper hand now, and he wasn't about to let her forget it. How he loved dealing such cruel blows! No doubt as a child, if he ever was one, he had taken great delight in pulling the wings off flies and watching as they wiggled helplessly about before he squished them!

She hoped, prayed, that he was lying, that it was all just another of his tricks, but when Tate made no effort to defend himself, she knew

Strothers had masterminded the whole evening just for that purpose. She should have suspected something like that all along! No wonder Tate had been so evasive about his business dealings. Damn! She should have been able to put two and two together before having her face rubbed in it!

One last time, she looked to Tate for some sign that Strothers was wrong but was met instead with a stone-cold expression. His eyes betrayed nothing.

Cam raised her chin with a cool stare in his direction. Her mind was spinning with uncertainties. What a fool she had been! How easily she had played right into his hands. Birds of a father did flock together, and no doubt Tate's soul was as coal-black as Strothers'. Otherwise, he would have told her himself about his interest in Willow Creek rather than have her find out from Strothers. What an absolute idiot she was! She might make her share of mistakes, but one thing was for certain: she never made the same one twice. She should have stayed loyal to her black-caped hero! At least, he hadn't lied to her. He had promised to return when she was older, and he had kept his word.

"Do play us another song, sweetheart," entreated Strothers with a cat-that-ate-the-canary grin on his mouth. "Something cheerful."

Cam glued a smile to her mouth and kept it there. "Oh, yes, Abbey, do play something again. The one about the girl named Dixie was always my favorite. Remember the girl who put the knife through her lover's heart?"

Abbey, who looked like all she wanted was for the door to open up and swallow her, obliged

Cam's request. Her hands moved gracefully across the keyboard, but her heart just wasn't in her music.

Cam patted her foot in rhythm. Those bastards! They weren't going to get the best of her. She'd show them. So Tate Carruth had been after Willow Creek all along, had he? And what about that afternoon? Had that little interlude in the woods been intended to soften her up for the kill? Perhaps he had hoped to use her as a pawn against her father. Ha! He and Strothers must have had a good laugh over that. Well, damn them both! They'd regret the day they ever crossed her. She'd like nothing better than to tell them right where they could go and in no uncertain terms, but she couldn't do that to Abbey.

Poor Abbey! The minute Strothers opened his mouth about selling off Willow Creek, she looked as if she were having to fight to keep from bursting into tears. Besides, storming out of the house would prove to Strothers that he had managed to unnerve her, and she wasn't about to give him that pleasure.

Instead, she would put a smile on her face and feign an air of cool indifference. Outwardly she'd be the poised and well-mannered lady Ludie Mae had brought her up to be. Little would they know that on the inside lurked a wildcat just waiting to sink her claws into those conniving sons of bitches! If only that afternoon's memories could be erased from her thoughts! If only she could keep herself from wanting more of Tate, even after knowing just how low down he really was!

Not a minute too soon, the mantel clock struck ten, and the Senator slowly raised himself from the plump cushioned chair where he had sat nodding.

"Well, my dear," he said as he limped over to his daughter. "I do believe it's time we take our leave and let these good people get to bed."

Cam rose, her body as stiff as her smile. "We wouldn't want to wear out our welcome, would we?"

She forced herself to address Strothers as well as Abbey. He had hurt her badly, but hell would freeze over before he knew just how devastating an effect his revelation had on her.

"Thank you for such a lovely evening."

Strothers flashed his most charming smile. "It was our pleasure, dear Cam. Our pleasure, indeed."

For a moment, Cam thought he was going to have the gall to kiss her, but at the last moment he backed off, and she was certain the poison-dart glare she shot him had done just what she had intended.

Abbey kissed the Senator's cheek, then reached for Cam and clasped her hand tightly. "I am so sorry." Then in a bit louder voice, she added, "You're still coming round for tea on Tuesday, aren't you?"

"Why, of course." Cam's smile remained fixed to her face. Just how much longer she could keep up that facade she didn't know. "You just start making up your guest list for your party, you hear?"

Abbey apologized once again when the men walked out onto the porch ahead of them. "I am truly sorry, Cam. I just don't know what gets into Strothers sometimes. I seem to spend most of my time lately making apologies for him. He never used to be that way."

Cam gave the frail shoulder a reassuring squeeze. Poor Abbey. She was blind to the fact that her husband had been low-down all along. What a superb job he had done of pulling the wool over her eyes!

"No harm done. Really." She tried to sound convincing. "Please don't worry."

Tate's searching glances made her all the more hell-bent to carry out the little charade until the end, no matter how bitter.

"I certainly hope your stay in Caesar's Head is a pleasant one," she told him, ignoring his outstretched hand as she brushed past.

One look from those mesmerizing eyes of his, and he'd have her locked into his spell once more. She simply would not allow that to happen. Not again! Not ever!

"Allow me, please." Tate stepped in front of the Senator just as he was about to help his daughter into the buggy.

"I must talk to you soon—alone," he whispered into her ear as he took a firm hold on her elbow.

Smiling, Cam waved good-bye to Abbey. Her gaze stayed fixed straight ahead. She must not allow her eyes to meet his, no matter how great the temptation. Being locked into that spell of his would have devastating results. Once had been tragic; twice would be fatal. She must be strong. Strong!

"I have nothing to say to you, Mr. Carruth. Not now, not ever."

7

Only when the buggy came to end of Maple Street did Cam permit her eyes to blink, and when she did, tiny wet drops slid down her lashes onto her cheeks.

Damn him! Damn him to hell! He and Strothers were two of a kind. Why had she been so blinded by love? Love? Ha! He didn't love her. He just wanted to use her. Well, she'd show him. No man was going to get the best of her. The bastard!

The mile-long ride out to Willow Creek seemed like ten. Thank heavens the Senator didn't notice her silence. If he did, he said nothing about it. Instead, he just kept talking a mile a minute about the time Henry Sullivan convinced a Yankee captain sent out to round up Confederates that the Senator had slipped through their lines and was probably halfway to Mexico while all the time he was hiding out in the wine cellar right under their noses.

"Ain't that something about that fellow in black showing up at the Winthrops the other night? And I thought you had just imagined it," the Senator remarked as he pulled off his boots inside the front door. "I can't for the life of me figure out who that could be. Can you?"

Cam slumped down into the nearest chair and pretended to stifle a yawn. "Sure can't. But whoever it is must get mighty hot in that get-up." She tried her best to sound cheerful, but knew she was falling short. From the look on the Senator's face, he knew it, too.

"Something bothering you, Cami?"

"Oh, no, nothing at all." She faked another yawn. "Just tired, I guess." Tired of being taken for a fool, she thought angrily.

The Senator dropped a kiss on her forehead on his way to the stairs. "I reckon I'll turn in. Five o'clock comes mighty early, and I ain't the spring chicken I used to be."

"Can't prove it by me," she returned teasingly. There was no point in letting her father spend all night worrying about her being in the doldrums. He had enough on his mind as it was, with tobacco harvest being so close at hand and no money in the till to cover cutting costs. "I saw you out on the dance floor last night shaking your leg with Ludie Mae."

"Ah, Cami, you imagine things." He chuckled over his shoulder. "Good night, darlin'."

"Good night." She could have sworn those apple-plump cheeks of his actually blushed.

A moment later, after turning down the light, Cam trudged up the stairs. Her legs felt as burdened as her heart. What a fool Tate had made of her! How could she have been so naive as to stand by and let it happen? What a fool he had made of her! And the worst part was that she had been a willing victim! Victim? She had been a sucker! She had all but begged him to make a fool of her. Well, there was not much she could do about the past, she decided as she turned down her bed. But one thing was for certain. Mr. Carruth's future in Caesar's Head was not going to be very promising, not if she got her way.

Sleep refused to come no matter how hard she willed it to numb her weary body so that her senses would be dulled as well.

Tate! Tate! Tate! Even the crickets chirped his name. The shadows on the wall formed his outline. His scent still clung to the dress she had worn that afternoon and left carelessly draped across the foot of her bed. Tomorrow, she'd burn it. But although the dress might go up in flames, the memories wouldn't. They'd linger for a long time to come, constantly serving as a reminder of just how easily she had been duped. Damn! How could she ever hope to get him out of her system if everywhere she turned there was something of him to remind her? Surely there had to be a way to exorcise him from her heart and from her soul!

Unable to stand the torment building inside her, Cam hurled herself from the bed and threw on a sleepcoat made of white eyelet cotton. Somehow, she had to escape from the haunting memories. Somehow, she had to get away from Tate, from herself, and clear her mind. Come tomorrow, she didn't want the name Tate Carruth to stir any hidden feeling inside her. What happened between them couldn't be undone. She'd bear the scar of that humiliation forever. Granted, she couldn't pretend never knowing the potency of his lips, his hands, that rock-hard chest.

No, she could never forget the details. But surely, surely there was some way she could convince herself that the time they shared together in the pine hammock had meant no more to her than it had to him.

She left her room by the window rather than the stairs, where she ran the risk of waking Ludie Mae or her father, and shimmied down the big willow tree outside her room just the way she had done as a little girl. Too bad she still wasn't the same little girl sneaking out to spend the night with a sick animal! Too bad she was a woman whose first real experience of love had left a bitter taste in her mouth that no doubt would linger for many years to come.

No sooner had her slippered feet hit the ground than her legs bolted out in front of her. She had no idea where they were taking her, nor did she care. She loped into the woods like a pursued animal fighting for its very survival, running until she could run no more, but still running deeper and deeper into the wooded darkness.

Her breathing unable to keep pace with the violent throbbing in her heart, Cam crumbled to the ground, her head between her knees. Catching her breath a moment later, she looked up. The surroundings there were all too familiar. It came as no surprise where her flight had directed her. It seemed quite natural that the spot where she would seek refuge from her trouble be the site of the old mine. There, far removed from outside influences, she could think and find a solution to the mess she had gotten herself into. If only she had waited for her mystery man to come to her again as he had promised he would. If only she had not gotten sidetracked by someone who had little regard for either her or her feelings. If only . . .

"I figured I'd find you here."

Her heart stopped beating. For a moment, she feared it would never start up again. It was him! Her phantom lover! He had returned, just as he had promised! He would ease all the pain Tate had so callously inflicted.

She jumped up and whirled around. The smile froze on her face.

"Oh. It's you. Leave me alone."

Tate Carruth was the last person she wanted to see, and she hadn't prepared herself for meeting him. She needed more time to let her anger boil, more time to let the hurt give way to hate.

She turned her back to him, praying that he would go away. Maybe he would just leave her alone if she ignored him. She wouldn't listen to a word he had to say. She'd not look at him or even acknowledge his presence. Oh, make him go away, she prayed silently as she held tight to her necklace. Make him go far, far away. Why was he there anyway? To pour salt into her wounds? He was not so unlike Strothers after all!

Cam leaned agaisnt a tree, giving him no more notice than she would any other annoying pest. But why were her legs so weak? Why did she feel as if they would give away on her any minute? Damn Strothers to hell! If he hadn't brought that up about the necklace, then Tate would have never known where to come looking for her.

Once again, she reached for her necklace and pressed the gold disc tight between her thumb and forefinger. Give me strength, she pleaded silently. Give me strength! Don't let me be taken in by him again!

Tate walked toward her, but stopped at arm's length. Hands dug deep into his pockets, he stared right at her. He said nothing. He just stood there, watching her and waiting.

Waiting for what, she hadn't a clue. But hell could freeze over before he'd get one word out of her!

She could feel that old, too-familiar ache coming over her just as it had that afternoon. He was so close that she had only to reach out for him, and he'd be within her grasp. But she wasn't about to, even though she ached to feel the power of his arms around her, and his hands roving and discovering sweet, never-before-traveled places that gave him so welcome a greeting.

Stop it! she cautioned herself. Such thoughts served no purpose but to make matters worse. She must be strong. Strong! Strong enough to say no and mean it. Heaven help her if she could not.

"I know what you are thinking, Camille Tranter, and you are wrong."

At last he spoke. His declaration was strong, yet not without gentleness. "I did not come to Caesar's Head with the purpose of swindling the Senator out of his land. You must believe me."

Oh? Then exactly why did you come here? To take advantage of some poor female fool, then flaunt it in her face? She was dying to ask him these things, but the words would not come. She couldn't bring herself to believe that Tate could be that rotten. She couldn't be so poor a judge of people. But why had he kept his desire to obtain the logging rights to Willow Creek secret if he were truly innocent?

Tate placed his lantern on a slab of granite, then lay his hands ever so lightly on her shoulders. "And what happened between us this afternoon had nothing to do with my being here. I meant every word I said." His voice dropped to barely a whisper. His words were so soft that even the woods stopped to listen. "I do love you, Cam. Truly, I do. I've loved you from the very first."

Cam shrugged out of his hold. His breath was hot on her neck. She could feel his palms burning through her cotton sleepcoat. She couldn't take much more! Love her, indeed. How naive, how foolish did he think she was?

"Cam, darling, say something. Anything. Cuss me out if it would make you feel better. Just don't shut me out like this. Not after all the joys we've shared."

His cheek nuzzled hers. For a moment, she almost allowed herself the luxury of enjoying it, then just in time, she caught hold of herself and stepped away. She could not listen any longer. If she did, she'd start believing his empty words. She'd done that once already today, and what a fine mess she had gotten herself in because of it.

Her mind was a maze of confusion. How sincere he sounded, how genuine his words. But she knew better. He had shown his true colors, and he could not undo the damage already done, or soothe the pain he had inflicted.

Cam reached for her necklace, once again seeking the comfort she always found in the little gold disc. Please make him go away while I am still strong, she pleaded silently to whatever force might be listening. Please make him go away before I start listening to the voices of my heart.

Tate followed her when she walked away, but this time he kept his hands to himself. "You know as well as I that Strothers will do anything in his power to come between us."

Cam couldn't keep her back to him another instant. The urge to see for herself whether a truth or a lie was reflected in those hypnotic green eyes proved too hard to resist. She took a deep breath. She must be strong, for only through that inner strength would she find the courage to send him away and out of her life forever.

"Come between us, you say? Goodness, Tate, how you go on. Why, if I didn't know better I'd think that little romp in the bushes meant something to you after all."

The light-hearted smile she had ordered onto her lips felt as if it would shatter her face into a thousand little cracks. Damn him! Why couldn't he have just left well enough alone and never laid eyes on her again! Why must he continue tormenting her with words he did not mean?

"A little romp in the bushes?" His shock was evident in his tightly drawn features and in his words, slow and deliberate and disbelieving. "Is that how you view the beauty that we shared this afternoon? A little romp in the bushes?"

Her smile died, then came to life again. For a moment there, he had actually sounded hurt. He was good. No doubt about that. What a pity the stage was deprived of so fine an actor!

"Granted, that was a rather poor choice of words, and I do apologize for that, but you know what I mean nevertheless."

His upper lip stiffened. "No, I do not. Perhaps you had best explain."

"Well, gracious alive, Tate, must I draw you a picture?" Cam took a firm rein on her feelings and forced still another set smile. Now was not the time to weaken. The sooner it was over the better. "I certainly wouldn't want to hurt your feelings, Tate, not for anything in the world, but Strothers can't come between us. Nobody can, for that matter. You see, there's absolutely nothing for anybody to come between."

"Go on."

The light from the lantern caught more than just a flicker of dismay in his eyes. If she didn't know better, she'd swear he was stunned. She couldn't think about it. She must not! Searching for a spark of truth in such finely polished jade would only worsen the pain.

"You must understand," she began, taking a few steps to the left, then to the right so she wouldn't have to subject herself to his melting stare. "The men around here are all so boring. Why, I've known them all my life. When you came to Caesar's Head, well, silly as it may sound, I just figured that . . ." The words became harder to get out. Still they had to be said if she were going to be left with any pride or dignity at all. "I figured you'd be here today and gone tomorrow, so what harm would there be in having a little bit of fun with no strings attached?"

"Here today? Gone tomorrow? No strings attached?"

It was impossible to tell if the solemn tone in his voice reflected sarcasm or dismay.

All at once, she was at a loss for words. At first

she had wanted so desperately to hurt him, to make him just as miserable as he had her, but now that she had done what she had set out to do, now that the lies had been told, she regretted even the tiniest one. How could she ever hope to convince him she didn't care when she couldn't even convince herself?

"You mean there were others? Perhaps even other strangers who just happened to be passing through? Here today, gone tomorrow?"

Cam swallowed hard. She had come this far. There was no turning back. "Oh, my. You didn't think you were the first, did you? Gracious, I must be a better actress than I thought."

For a moment, she was certain she had gone too far. His look was so severe, she feared he was going to strike her. But suddenly, each rough feature hardening his face softened with the tenderness of his smile.

"Darling Cam, I know for a fact there was no one before me. And we both know no man will ever succeed me in your arms."

His arms opened wide, beckoning to her, but she stood her ground.

"What an arrogant Yankee bastard you are!"

Her whole body was trembling, not from anger so much as from his nearness. "You don't own me, Tate Carruth! No man does! And don't you think for one minute that what happened between us gives you the right to me. I am not some property that can be bought or sold or traded!"

He closed the distance between them with slow, determined steps. His nostrils flared with deep, heavy breaths. There was no mistaking the thoughts going on inside his head.

"Don't you come one step closer. I'm warning you, Tate. You take another step, and I'll make you regret it. I swear I will."

"Shut up, Cam!" His hands locked against her spine. Reclaiming her lips with savage intensity, he crushed her to him. His tongue was cruel and hungry and unyielding.

Her protest stuck in her throat. All resolve was shattered with the hunger of his kisses. Instinctively, her body arched towards his. Her hands moved from her side to his cheek, then wound around his neck, rubbing the warm flesh between her palms.

One more moment, just one more, and I'll push him away forever, she swore silently as he kissed the pulsing hollow of her throat while rogue hands explored the soft line of her back, then her waist, then her hips.

The magnitude of her own desire amazed her. He had wronged her. He had deceived her, made her the butt of his cruel joke, yet she wanted him, wanted him just as desperately as she had that afternoon. Her whole body ached for him. She had been branded, and his mark would stay on her forever.

Arms that a moment before had hurled themselves around him suddenly began pounding his chest.

No! She would not let herself be humiliated a second time. She had her pride. She had her dignity, and that would not be stolen from her again. Not by him! Not by any man!

"No! You let me go! Do you hear me? Let me go!"

Her protests were smothered by a mouth that was ravaging and unyielding.

Tate held on tight, his grip all but cutting off the flow of blood. "If I let you go you now, you'll be lost to me forever, and I won't have that! I couldn't bear it!"

His lips breathed fire into her ear and down her throat. His hot breath drifted in through the cotton and seared the bare flesh beneath. All the inner strength she could muster cried out for him to stop, please stop, but the mute pleas went unheeded.

Once again, his demanding mouth hunted hers. She clamped her teeth together. Still, they parted willingly at his command, giving him easy passage. His kiss was even harder and more barbaric than before. He was starving, she his first taste of food. It numbed even her toes. Still, he would not let up, not even when she collapsed against him. His tongue searched deeper and deeper.

Everything about him, his lips, his hands, his legs, bruised her. He was as one possessed, possessed with an uncontrollable longing, a passion that would not be satisfied. He held onto her for dear life, yet she knew she was not being held prisoner against her will. Her limbs were free to push and kick and shove. She could claw at him, punch him in the gut, then take off running as fast and as far as her legs would carry her. But all she wanted to do was draw him closer. There were a hundred ways she might escape—if she truly wanted to.

She couldn't make up her mind. Did she or didn't she want him to leave her alone? The hardness pressing into her midsection was making it even more difficult to decide. Her excitement was growing with his. Deep down, she knew all she had to do was ask and he'd leave her be. But no, that wasn't what she wanted, not really, for in denying his need she would be denying her own as well.

Crazed fingers searched for the swell of muscles bunching inside his collar. Yes, yes, oh yes, she had to have him just once more, just this time, then it would be over, good-bye forever. She would show him she could be just as insensitive and as emotionless as he!

Cam attacked his mouth with a hunger matching his own, but she did not merely surrender to the domination of his lips. She, too, became as one possessed, obsessed, taking what she wanted with just as savage an intensity.

Desire blazing to an even higher peak, Tate lowered her down onto the cool ground. Limbs entangled together, she felt for sure they'd both topple over and hit the ground full force, but somehow he managed to maneuver them so that his knees took the brunt of the impact.

One hand remained clamped around her waist, so tight she could hardly breathe, while the other parted the sleepcoat without bothering to undo the buttons or ties. She heard the material rip, the buttons pop off, but did not care. Had he not set her free, she would have done so herself. She could feel him growing to even larger proportions upon his discovery that she was wearing none of her lacey finery underneath.

With breaths as labored as a stallion's, Tate wedged his leg between her thighs, his knee digging deeper and deeper into the territory he would soon lay claim to once again. Cupping one in each hand, he tasted first one, then the other of the firm, swollen breasts that rose eagerly to his command. His teeth closed tight around each nipple, flicking them with his tongue until they became as hard as pebbles.

Roving hands moved down her length, reminding her that where his hands traveled, his lips would not be far behind. Round and round the full, dark summits that grew even fuller with each sweep of his tongue, up to her throat and down an imaginery line dividing her in half, in and out of her navel and across the rise of her belly roamed his hands, unmercifully teasing and tormenting until she could endure no more. Soon, she had lost count of just how many times she had faded in and out of reality only to be revived time and again. She wasn't even aware of his breaking free of his trousers and shirt, and as he stood there proud and erect with the moon's shadows bathing his glorious body in the splendors of midnight, she knew she could never deny him anything.

Opening herself up to him, reaching for his arms and pulling them to her, Cam beckoned him closer. Back arched, she guided him to her, receiving him with a passion even more intense than that of the afternoon. They came together in a frenzy, their bodies grinding and writhing and fitting together as if the two were one, had always been one, and would forever remain joined that way.

Her legs wrapped tight around him, entrapping him, preventing even the least disjoining. Each thrust was met with an urgency that made her wild, and that she could tell aroused his cravings all the more. The deeper he plunged, the sweeter his movements became. She was lost in him, and she really didn't care if she ever found her way out again.

A tremendous quaking shot through her. Every bone, every muscle, each tiny trembling inside her knew that he had released the joyous pressure that had been mounting inside her all evening.

Cam closed her eyes and reveled in the sweet ecstasy taking over her most secret of places. How wonderful it felt having him atop her and feeling the magnificent pressure of his form crushing hers.

He started to ease off, murmuring something about his weight being too much of a burden for her to bear, but she tightened her hold around him. She wanted him there. She wanted to feel him inside her as long as she could, for when they were like that she could pretend he truly did love her.

Her eyes came awake from their dreamy slumber. He was still there, his legs astride her, looking down at her in a sad, almost longing way.

Cam smiled.

The smile he returned was one of pleasure mixed with relief. He dropped a kiss onto her nose, then sprinkled more under her chin and down the satiny expanse of cool, soft flesh to the curve of her hip.

Her smile faded. She knew she should hate him, but God help her, she could not. He wasn't like Strothers. He was good and decent and honest. He wouldn't deceive her in spite of what Strothers might lead her to believe. Still, she had to know for certain one way or another, and there was only one way to find out for sure. She had to speak her mind!

"Why didn't you tell me right off the real reason you had come to Caesar's Head?" she asked, her eyes defiant and penetrating. "Why did you let me find out from Strothers, of all people?"

Please don't let him lie to me, she pleaded silently. Don't let my trust in him be misplaced.

Tate expelled a troubled sigh. "Granted, I recognize my mistake now, but had I told you from the start, I doubt you would have had anything to do with me."

"Then what Strothers said this evening, it's true?"

"Some of it, yes."

"Oh," Knowing he was telling the truth didn't make the hurt any less severe.

He rolled off her and stretched out beside her, but kept a tight hold on her arm as though he were afraid she'd bolt into the woods.

"I admit to enlisting Strothers' aid in finding suitable timber acreage, and yes, I did come here hoping to acquire the logging rights to Willow Creek."

Every muscle in her body tightened.

"Please hear me out," he softly ordered as he pinned her even tighter to the ground. "When I learned that the Senator had no intention of selling those rights, I let it go at that and instructed Strothers to look elsewhere."

Cam did not want to relax in his grasp, but her body failed to heed her warning. "Why didn't you tell me?" she asked again.

"Oh, Cam, I was afraid to. Can't you see that?

I was afraid you'd refuse to have anything to do with me. I was afraid you'd think my only interest in you was in your land."

She tried to pull away, but his arm held her secure. "But you knew I would find out sooner or later."

"I know it was wrong to keep it from you. It was stupid, I admit, and I truly am sorry. You must believe me when I say I would have told you myself when the time was right."

"And when would that have been? After the damage was already done?"

"Oh, Cam, darling Cam. Surely you know me better than that."

A brush of a kiss across her forehead did nothing to soothe her. If anything, the maddening touch of his lips urged her on.

"And what about now and this afternoon? Was seducing me part of your plan to get those logging rights?"

His jaw tensed. There was no mistaking the hurt in his voice.

"How can you even think such nonsense? What we shared were the most beautiful experiences of my life. You are a part of me now. Surely you cannot deny that I am a part of you as well."

Cam said nothing. Even when she had sworn vengeance against him, she could not have denied him that.

"As soon as I learned just how strongly both you and your father felt about Willow Creek, I decided against even making an offer. Why as special as those woods are to you, I could not cut one tree in clear conscience. I swear it. Please, you must believe me."

"But what Strothers said tonight about . . .

"No doubt it was meant to drive a wedge between us. Good Lord, the man would have had to be blind not to see the sparks flying between us. Surely you're not going to play right into his hands, are you?" His query was a gentle breeze filtering through her hair. "Darling Camille, I give you my word as a gentleman, I would rather die than do anything to hurt you."

His word as a gentleman . . . What a wonderful echo that had to it. His word as a gentleman. Someone else had given his word as a gentleman, too, and that someone was long gone. But Tate was there. He was there in the flesh, not some phantom lover.

"Tate, if you're lying to me, I swear . . ."

"I'm not, my darling. I am not." Once again, he rolled over on top of her. Taking her face in his hands, he covered it with kisses, leaving no spot untouched. "Trust me, sweetheart, you will not regret it. In your heart you know that I will never hurt you. Never, I swear. You have become my life. To lose you would be to destroy myself."

Her legs wrapped around him, pulling him still closer. They could have fit together no more perfectly had they been created that way. That was where he belonged. That was where he should remain for always. Of course she believed him. How could she not?

Slowly, ever so slowly, he slipped inside her once again. His lean, powerful form took charge, guiding and directing each flutter inside her.

A moan of pleasure escaped from her lips. His lovemaking was not rushed, but she wished it were. Even if they had an eternity of love together, that would not be enough. She wanted all of him now! Tomorrow she might well hate him as well as herself, but at that every instant, she wanted their hot, fiery passion to last forever!

8

Cam hurried into the alcove behind the stairs and closed the door tight behind her, determined not to budge from her little office until her work was completed. Today would be the perfect day to catch up with her bookkeeping. There would be no distractions. The Senator was out in the tobacco with the new foreman he had just hired. Ludie Mae was busy doing her gardening, and Tate was in Greenville tending to some business.

The last few days without him had been pure torture. Thank heavens he was due back that evening. His absence had been a constant reminder of just how much she loved him. She was worse off than she thought for someone who had long ago vowed never to belong to any man! Why, lately she had even been toying with the idea of what it would be like to spend the rest of her life with him!

Still, the time apart would be good for them. She had spent every waking moment for the last two weeks in Tate's company. That was the only place she really longed to be. A lot of questions had gone unanswered since that night at Abbey's and later on the woods at the old mine, but she trusted him. She believed him and believed in him. He would never wrong her or her father. He was too much of a gentleman for that.

Still, now was not the time to dwell on their romance. There were far more crucial matters at hand. Her accounting chores had been all but neglected, and no matter how long it took, she had to catch them up. She had a responsibility, one which she had always prided herself on doing well. That obligation had taken second place for too often during the past few weeks. So tight was their budget, they could ill afford to lose track of even a penny, and by the time Cam left that room, every cent would be accounted for.

Sitting down behind the old walnut secretary that had once stood in the front hall and served as a mail drop for the entire county, Cam opened the black-bound ledger and began thumbing through the pages until she found her place. Even then, it was Tate's face, not the row upon row of figures that stared back at her. Her heart wasn't in her work, but that was no excuse not to do her best, and she began the tedious task of transferring figures from loose bits of papers to the columns where they belonged.

The deeper she sank into the thick leather cushions of the armchair, the more depressed she became. The Senator was a farmer and a politician. He simply did not have a head for numbers. Thank heavens Ludie Mae had seen to it that accounting had been just as important a part of her education as needlepoint and etiquette. She should have kept a closer watch on her father. He had far outspent their budget. Just the amount charged at Chambers' General Store for farm supplies was staggering!

She could kick herself for being so irresponsible. How could she have neglected the farm so? Tate was to blame. There was no doubt about that. But he had hardly twisted her arm and forced her to spend every waking moment of the day in his company. She had done that all on her own. She would have been all too willing to spend the nights with him as well, but she dared not be so bold. She was taking enough risk just by sneaking out after midnight and meeting him in the woods.

Once again forgetting the task at hand, Cam laid her head back against the chair's plump back. How heavenly the past fourteen days had been! There was nothing she hadn't shared with Tate. If he wasn't with her in body, he was there in spirit. During the time he did spend away from her, looking at other suitable properties for his sawmilling projects, she was so miserable she could only dwell on how sweet the reunion would be when he did return. Tristram had traveled the road from town to Willow Creek so frequently, he could do so now without a rider on his back.

Never had she dreamed a whole lifetime of happiness could be squeezed into so short a time. Two weeks, and she felt as though she had known him all her life. Daily pastimes that she had come to take for granted over the years suddenly came alive with excitement and new meaning in his company. Hardly a day had passed without an early-morning gallop through the woods, a picnic on the ridge, or a hot afternoon visit to a deserted cove where they could go skinny-dipping and later bask in the sun, reveling in the delights each other's flesh had to offer.

She could have known him no better had she known him a lifetime. Even when they first met, it had been hard to view him as a total stranger. He had a way about him that made him seem very familiar. It hadn't taken long at all for him to make himself right at home at Willow Creek once he convinced the Senator his daughter was the reason he came courting, not the land rights. Tate had fit right in, just as if he belonged there and always had.

The Senator couldn't have agreed more. He had even made the remark that having found a worthy opponent at checkers, he wasn't about to let him get away. Her own feelings echoed the same sentiment. Now that she had found the real man of her dreams, she was going to do everything in her power to make sure that he stayed.

Sooner or later, of course, he'd have to go back up North to take care of whatever business interests he had left behind, but he had promised never to stay away long, and the anticipation of how sweet the reunion would be when he did return somehow got her through his absences.

She wondered what he was doing now, at that very moment, in Greenville. No doubt he'd have his share of offers to keep him company in the big city, probably more than the other men all put together. Though he had never said so, she had suspected right from the start that their love affair was not his first. How could it be? After all, he was nearly ten years older than she, and a man of the world who could hardly be expected to have lived the life of a monk. Their love affair might not be his first, but if she had her say, it would definitely be his last. The fact that he had known the pleasures of more than one woman was hardly cause for jealousy or distrust. She could live with the notion of countless beautiful women having given him a loose rein on their passions, but whatever had happened before her was history, ancient history. She was his present. She was his future!

Frowning, Cam forced her eyes open and fixed them on the page in front of her. Unless she sorted out their finances, the future of Willow Creek and its inhabitants would be rather grim. Her first allegiance always was and always would be to her home and family. Perhaps soon, Tate would be part of that. The prospect made her go all warm and tingly inside.

She straightened up in her seat. She'd dwell on that subject later. Right now, there were more important tasks at hand, namely how to survive until their tobacco was harvested, cured and marketed.

A long while later, Cam closed the ledger and pushed back from the desk. Her eyes ached and the crink in her neck had long since turned into a nagging cramp. What she had suspected after the first hour of poring over the books, she feared would soon come to pass after the second hour and had confirmed by the end of the third hour. Willow Creek's financial dilemma was even more bleak than she had initially thought. Perhaps it was a blessing in disguise after all that the Senator never cracked the cover of the big, black book. The figures in the minus columns would be sure to bring on chest pains more terrible than ever before. But there was no sense in burdening him when there wasn't much anybody could do about it anyway. She'd just go on letting him think they were getting by.

If only the forecast for the future looked more promising, but it didn't, not by a long shot. It was no longer a question of making it through until the tobacco went to market in the fall. They'd be lucky to pay next week's wages for the few men who tended the fields part-time. And there was no place to turn. Considering last year's disaster with root rot, the bank wouldn't look too kindly on lending them money, and the Grange no longer supported the struggling farmers as it once had. She supposed they could seek financial aid from the big national bank down in Greenville, but Willow Creek would have to be put up as collateral, and the only thing worse than losing their home would be losing it to one of those damned Yankees.

Damned Yankees, she thought to herself with wry amusement. When it boiled right down to it, that's what Tate was. A damned Yankee. But he was different. He wasn't like those scoundrels who came South to cash in on somebody else's misery and misfortune no matter what that damned Strothers made him out to be.

What were they going to do? she asked herself over and over as she flopped down onto the rose velveteen love seat that was squeezed in between the desk and the wall. Many, many times during the past week, she had been so certain these were the happiest days of her life. How could she have been so selfish to think only for herself when the very future of Willow Creek was at stake?

A light tap sounded at the door.

"Cami, you in there?" called out Ludie Mae. "I've brought you some cookies and lemonade. Chocolate peanut. Your favorite."

Cam let out a troubled sigh. Not even Ludie Mae's recipe for happiness could ease her troubles. "Come in," she called out.

"Lord sakes alive, child!" exclaimed the housekeeper as she set down the tray on the desk. "You look like you've just lost your best friend."

Cam's face remained downcast. "I have. At least I will if I don't do something quick."

"You and that nice young man of yours have a spat?" Ludie Mae sat down on the love seat beside her. "Tell old Ludie Mae all about it, you hear?"

"I wish it were that simple."

"Then what is it? Go on, honey, you know you can tell me." Seeing the opened ledger on the desk, she gave a knowing nod. "Oh, I see."

Cam sighed. There was no point in holding back from Ludie Mae. "We're in bad shape. Down to our last dime, and I just don't know what to do." Cam took another deep breath. She might as well know, After all, Ludie Mae was family, too, and where their next meal was coming from would matter just as much to her as it did to Cam and her father.

"It doesn't look good at all, Ludie Mae. We owe more money than we've got coming in, even if this year's harvest is as good as the Senator swears it's going to be."

"Why, is that all? Lordy mercy, I thought somebody was going to . . . now you just wait right here. I'll be right back." She threw a smile over her shoulder on her way to the door. "And wipe that frown off that pretty face. It's going to stay there permanently if you don't."

Puzzled, Cam watched as her old friend left the room with steps far spryer than when she entered.

A few minutes later, when she returned carrying a leather packet, Cam was even more perplexed.

Ludie Mae dropped the pouch into her lap. "I believe I have a solution to your problems. Well, don't just look at it. Open it."

Cam did as she was told. Inside were so many greenbacks she couldn't even begin to count them.

"Where did you get all this money?" She hurriedly flipped through the bills. "Why, there must be a thousand dollars in here. Maybe more." She handed the pouch back to her friend. "What did you do? Rob the First National?"

"Oh, Cami, how you go on!" Ludie Mae sat with her hands folded primly in her lap. "You keep it. It's yours now."

Cam stared at her in disbelief. "Are you all right? You haven't been nipping at the Senator's rheumatism medicine, have you?"

Ludie Mae rolled back her eyes. "Why, you ought to be ashamed of yourself, young lady, for even thinking such." Her tone grew more solemn. "Now I want you to take that money and pay off some of Willow Creek's debts, you hear me? Whatever's left over, you just put under your mattress and save for a rainy day. Land sakes alive, child. Don't look at me like I'm off my rocker. Willow Creek is my home, too. You and your daddy have been all the family I've ever had these past eighteen years. It's high time I showed my appreciation." She lowered her voice. "The only condition is that I don't want Cameron—I mean, the Senator—to ever know anything about it, all right?"

Cam couldn't believe her ears, or her eyes for that matter. With that kind of cash, Ludie Mae hadn't needed to work for them or anybody else.

She tried to give back the money, but her old friend shooed it away.

"I can't take this, Ludie Mae. You're mighty sweet to offer it, and I love you for it, but . . .

Cam stopped in mid-sentence. Wait a minute! What had Ludie Mae said a minute before? She didn't want Cameron finding out about it. Cameron. Ludie Mae had never called the Senator by his given name before. And the tender way she said it, hanging on to each syllable . . . Surely she couldn't be . . . could she? But why not? Why couldn't Ludie Mae be in love with the Senator?

Ludie Mae dropped her head. Her cheeks became flushed. She knew exactly what Cam was thinking.

Visions of Ludie Mae and the Senator dancing at the Fourth of July party flashed in front of her. How happy and how young Ludie Mae had looked whirling around on the Senator's arm. Her blush had been that of a shy school girl.

"Ludie Mae, are you— Good Lord, you are!" Cam flung her arms around her friend's neck. "You're in love with him, aren't you?"

She nodded. "Guilty, I confess."

Cam kissed the gray waves framing the pert little face. It all made sense now why Ludie Mae had left her post as headmistress at the Academy to come to work for the Senator and tend to his baby girl, why she had chosen to stay on even after his daughter was grown to look after the family like a mother, even though she had more than enough money of her own to live comfortably and never have to work again. It all made sense now. Why hadn't Cam seen it earlier? How could she have been so blind all those years?

"For twenty years I've loved that man, but he's not once suspected," said Ludie Mae softly.

"Twenty years? But what about your fiance? The man who left you to marry someone else?"

Ludie Mae shook her head. Her look was one of timid embarrassment. "I lied, Cami. There was no fiance, only Cameron."

"Poor thing. It must have killed you when he married Mama."

"I was crushed." She tried smiling through pale blue tears. "Half the time he didn't even know I was alive, but I loved him all the same. I knew she would hurt him, but all I could do was bite my tongue and wait."

"And be there to pick up the pieces when she did," remarked Cam sympathetically. "Well, do you know what, Ludie Mae? I'm glad she ran off with that turpentine merchant, and we got you in her place. I couldn't have got a finer mother than you had I hand-picked her myself."

Cam studied her closely, for once seeing Ludie Mae in a totally different light. She wasn't that old. In fact, she was quite a bit younger than the Senator. She had a lovely face, one that shone with gentility and refinement. Why, a man would be proud to have her for his wife. What that dear, sweet soul must have given up to take care of a man whose short but nevertheless painful experience with marriage had left him swearing never to walk down the aisle again! Well, something just had to be done. They deserved each other. The time was long overdue for someone to have a heart-to-heart talk with that father of hers, and that was just exactly what Cam intended to do as soon as he came in from the fields.

"All right, Ludie Mae. I'll take the money, but only if it's understood right from the start that this is no gift. We're not charity cases—at least, not yet," Cam told her after thinking the situation over. "I'll see to it that every cent is paid back and with interest."

"But . . ."

"There are no ifs, ands, or buts about it, Ludie Mae." Cam reached for her friend's hand and gave it a firm shake. "Congratulations, madam, you have just gone into the tobacco business."

"Papa, can I talk to you for a minute?" Cam asked after the noon dishes had been cleared and Ludie Mae had retired for a little cat nap.

The Senator stopped rocking. One eye came open and stared at her suspiciously. "Lord help me, now I know I'm in trouble. The last time you called me Papa was when Mrs. Jenkins had you by the ear and came dragging you home after you punched her little Sonny-boy in the gut. All right, let's have it. What have you got yourself into now?"

"Oh, Papa. Sonny deserved it. He always was such a bully. I just gave him a dose of his own medicine."

Chuckling at the recollection, Cam sat down on the porch at her father's feet and curled her legs up under her. "You are a wonderful father, sir. No daughter, or son for that matter, could be any luckier than I am. However, wonderful as you are, sometimes you can be mighty thick-headed."

"Thick-headed, huh? And here I was thinking you had gone and got all sentimental on me. All right, gal, let's have it. How else do you plan on insulting me?" he asked with gruff tenderness. "Thick-headed, indeed. I ought to turn you over my knee for that."

"Yes, thick-headed." Cam scooted around and folded her arms over his knees. "Ludie Mae has been in love with you for years, and you haven't had the sense to see it. Now, I'd call that pretty thick-headed, wouldn't you?"

"Ludie Mae? In love with an ornery old cuss like me? How do you know that? You're joshing me, ain't you? Well, tell me, gal, and be quick about it."

"I have never been so certain about anything, Papa. She told me so herself this very afternoon, but if you dare say I told you so, I'll deny it."

"Ludie Mae in love with an old fool like me?" he repeated slowly as if he couldn't believe it. "Well, how do you like that? How do you like that?"

Cam smiled. He liked the notion, she could tell. Ludie Mae had asked her to say nothing about the money to him, and she'd abide by her wishes, but her old friend had said nothing about her playing matchmaker!

Much later in the afternoon, Cam was on her way to town. Rounding Schoolhouse Corner at a gallop, she slowed down to a trot in front of the little red-steepled building. She couldn't help but chuckle thinking of the fit Ludie Mae would be sure to have if she saw her all helter-skelter now. Raven black tresses that not more than an hour ago had been combed and ribboned in lilac streamers were now tangled from her gallop. The crisp white blouse with its puffy sleeves and fancy lace collar was now wrinkled, and the lavender skirt with its fashionably nipped-in waist that had been so flattering now bore more than one mud splatter from a quick charge across the river. Poor Ludie Mae just never did understand that only sissies rode side-saddle. Nor did she understand that Traveller was far too noble to be hitched to a buggy.

Granted, for two weeks she had been trying her damnest to be the kind of refined Southern girl Ludie Mae had tried to bring her up to be, but there was a limit to the lengths she'd go for her old friend—or for Tate! Besides, Tate himself had said time and time again that what most attracted him about her in the first place was her skill as a rider, and it didn't seem quite right to change too much about herself all at once.

The mill whistle blew three times. It seemed like the entire town was regimented by that whistle, for no sooner had it sounded than the schoolhouse doors were flung open and children scattered into the streets anxious to get as much playtime in as they could before being summoned home to do their chores. A little way out of town, first-shift workers would be trudging home after putting in ten long, grueling hours at the sweat box, their name for the mill, while the evening workers would be assembling out front ready to begin their shift.

Cam halted at the water trough in front of the livery stables and let Traveller drink his fill, then proceeded on down the oak-lined street on a loose rein waving and returning greetings from folks she had known all her life.

Caesar's Head had changed very little from when she was a child. Some faces had gotten older, some younger, and a few new buildings had sprung up at the end of Main Street, but for the most part, the town looked just as it always had. In the summer, the streets were a bit more crowded with visitors from the low country who came to escape the heat of the flatlands and lounge in the cool mountain breezes. The natives complained, but no one could deny the boost the tourists gave to the town's economy.

Cam rode on to the next block, where a well-kept square abloom with azaleas and rhododendrons formed the center of town. Prominently situated on one end of the square was the white-columned courthouse with the big copper dome that had long since turned green. Flanking it was Chambers General Store, which sold everything from dry goods to fertilizers, Widow Cates' and Widow Warlick's rooming houses, and a few shops like Millie Dean's that catered to the whims of the town's womenfolk. Further down was the bank, the hotel, and the Baptist Church.

Cam halted in front of Chambers' and didn't bother tying her horse to the hitching post when she jumped off. There was no need to tie him. Traveller always stayed right where she left him, patiently awaiting his mistress' return.

Even though winter was still a long time away,

several of the town's old-timers were gathered in the corner of the store around the big, black pot-bellied stove that got hot enough in December to heat up the whole town. A checkerboard was spread out atop the pickle barrel, and two of the old fellows were quietly contemplating their next move. Whatever the topic of conversation among the rest of the group, it had that corner of the store buzzing like a swarm of yellow jackets. Old Man Crump's outraged insistence that he had seen some man in black galloping over Graveyard Hill atop a white steed caught Cam's attention, and she strolled over to check out the yard goods so she could hear more.

"You damn fool," she heard one of the whiskered old men exclaim. "If'n it wuz midnight, just how could you tell what color his cape wuz?"

"Yeah, Crump," offered another, "sounds to me like you've been nipping some of your private stock."

"Say what you will, boys," drawled the story-teller, unperturbed by their jesting. "I saw him with my own two eyes, I did, and I wasn't all likered up neither. Came riding across the cemetery plain as day he did just like some demon let loose from hell."

"Can I cut some of that gingham for you, Cam?"

Cam looked up suddenly to see the store's owner standing in front of her.

"That would make a mighty pretty dress for you," he said, peering over his spectacles. "Why, I bet Ludie Mae could whip something up out of that in no time."

"Can't afford to do much else but look," she

said smiling.

"Take your time. Don't cost a penny to browse," he told her as he wiped his hands over the front of his apron. "Oh, good morning, Miss Battle," he called out to the old maid who had just walked in. Excusing himself, he rushed to help her.

By the time Cam's attention had returned to the group in the corner, their talk had already changed to a different subject. She felt a twinge of disappointment, not that she believed all of Mr. Crump's tale about a devil on horseback, but even the best liars had to take a little from the truth. Most likely, he had indeed seen for himself her mystery man in black. Without a doubt, he had returned to Caesar's Head after all, but why had he not made his presence known to her if the vow he had made two years before was indeed the real reason for his return? After all, he did know her name, and he did know where to find her. Was he waiting for her to seek him out?

A flutter of excitement raced through her. How could she even think such thoughts when she had already pledged herself to another! Besides, just who did that man in black think he was anyway, to expect her to wait for him to come back. She wasn't a child any longer! She had outgrown those kinds of games a long time ago.

"Nice race, Cami. The Senator must be awfully proud of you."

Old man Crump jolted her back from her reverie.

"Yes, siree bud." piped up his friend. "You looked mighty good. That horse of yours is some animal."

"Why, thank you, gentlemen." Cam flashed the group her most charming smile. "Now tell me, what was that I was hearing a minute ago about some man in black galloping across the cemetery."

"Don't pay that old fool no mind, missy," advised one of the old timers. "Crump can't tell what's real and what ain't when he's sober, much less after he's paid a visit to that still of his."

"Yeah," chimed in another without looking up from his next checker move. "Next thing you know, he'll be trying to get us to believe the horse sprouted wings and just spirited the rider away."

"You boys just laugh all you want. Don't bother me none." With a smile, Crump settled back in his chair and began rocking slowly. "He who laughs first always laughs last. You just remember that, you hear?"

Cam waited until Mr. Chambers finished sacking up supplies for Miss Battle before approaching the long pine counter.

"I've come to settle up our account," She told him, opening the leather pouch hanging from her shoulder and pulling out a folded piece of paper. "As best I can figure, this is what's due you. I've listed farm supplies and personal supplies separately."

Mr. Chambers scanned the figures with a frown. "Yep, it's all down here, all right." He lowered his voice and leaned over the counter. "But listen, Cam, I don't mind keeping you on the books a little while longer. Me and the Senator, we go way back, and I know he's good for it just as soon as that 'baccy of his goes to market."

"We appreciate your patience, and your

credit, Mr. Chambers, but I insist on paying you the full amount now. All nine hundred and thirty five dollars of it." She handed him a roll of bills that had already been counted and separated. "Is something wrong? You look a little flushed."

"No, no, no, I'm fine. Fine. It's just that . . ." Once again Mr. Chambers wiped his palms over his apron in a nervous gesture. "It's just that, well, a couple of months back, Mr. Bennett said . . ."

Cam felt her blood begin to boil. "And just what does Strothers Bennett have to do with Willow Creek's accounts?"

The scrawny chicken neck poking out from the stiff collar turned beet red. "He just asked what was owing on your account and assured me that . . ."

"You told him?"

"Oh, no, no. Of course not. I'd never do that. I told him that was between me and my customer." Mr. Chambers ran his thumb under his collar. "Anyways, he told me to go ahead and let you folks charge whatever you needed, and he'd stand good for the money. Plus a half a percent for my patience," he added sheepishly.

"I didn't know you were in the banking business, Mr. Chambers."

Cam tried to keep her voice quiet. The poor man already looked as if he were about to have a heart attack. Besides, it wasn't his fault Strothers had approached him with such a good proposition. Smarter men than Mr. Chambers had been taken in by Caesar's Head's fast-talking lawyer.

"Do me a favor, Mr. Chambers. The next time Bennett comes in here nosing into my business, you just tell him to make his inquiries to my face.

That is, if he's man enough. All right?"

Mr. Chambers nodded. His Adam's apple was still pumping frantically. "I am truly sorry if I've offended you, Cam, but it ain't no secret how hard your daddy's been struggling to make ends meet, and I just thought Mr. Bennett was trying to help out. That's all, I swear."

"Believe me, Strothers Bennett helps out only if he has something to gain by doing so, and at someone else's expense. You'd do well to watch out for the likes of him, Mr. Chambers, or he'll have this store before you know what hit you."

Before she left, Cam handed him another list and a few more bills. "I'd like these delivered this afternoon, if possible." She turned to go, then turned back again. Perhaps she had been a little harsh with him. After all, he could hardly be blamed for Strothers' tricks. "And thanks again for being so patient with us. I know you've got bills to pay like everybody else."

The shop owner gave her a weak smile, then took his duster out of his hip pocket and began dusting the counter top.

Waving her good-byes over her shoulder to old man Crump and his cronies, Cam hurried towards the door and bumped right into Clare Winthrop.

"Oh, dear, Mrs. Winthrop, are you all right? I didn't hurt you, did I?" she asked as she held on to the woman's arm. "How careless of me not to watch where I was going. My mind was some place up in the clouds, I guess."

"Lawdy no, child. I am fine. Just fine." A look of certain doom shadowed her pale features even when she smiled. "I been meaning to get out to Willow Creek and tell you again just how grateful

I am for you saving my girl's life. If you can think of anyway I can repay you, you just let me know."

Cam gave the slightly stooped shoulder a gentle pat. "I told you before, Mrs. Winthrop, you don't have to repay me. I'm just glad I came along when I did and was able to help out."

"I'd have never been able to forgive myself had little Sari perished in those awful flames." Mrs. Winthrop took a tattered handkerchief from her sleeve and dabbed at her eyes. "I should have gone home with them myself that night, but Marsh said they'd be fine. Those young'uns had et till they was sick, and well, Marsh, he was having such a good time for a change, I thought maybe if we stayed on . . ."

"Shh. Don't blame yourself, Mrs. Winthrop. You had no way of knowing what was going to happen."

"You know, Deputy Barlowe says it looks like the fire might have been set, but I know my boys wouldn't be so careless. They wouldn't lie to me neither. They said they weren't playing with matches, and I believe them." Mrs. Winthrop dabbed at her eyes once more. "Thank the good Lord for folks like you and that nice Mr. Bennett."

Cam felt the hairs on the back of her neck bristle at the mention of his name. Seemed like everybody was singing his praises today. Was she the only one in all of Caesar's Head who knew him for the low-down, rotten cheat he really was?

"Why, had it not been for that kind man, we'd be sleeping out in the streets. A real fine gentleman, that Strothers Bennett. Real fine. Why, do you know what all he did for us?"

Cam shook her head. Strothers Bennett never

in his life helped anyone out of the goodness of his heart. You could bet your bottom dollar there was something in it for him if he did!

"Why as soon as that man heard about our troubles, he came over to see Marsh hisself and offered him a job as a machinist over at the mill. And you know how my Marsh loves to tinker. But that ain't all. He gave my oldest a job, too, and moved us into one of the mill houses right away and told me to charge anything I wanted here at the store, and he'd take care of it until we was on our feet again. And do you know what else?"

Cam shook her head. There was no way she could muster the same enthusiasm as Mrs. Winthrop. Strothers had obviously manipulated the Winthrops into the position where he wanted them, along with everybody else—right in his debt.

"He bought our land from us, too, and for the same exact price he offered us before, even though the house burned to the ground. And he . . ."

"You say he made you an offer for your farm before?"

"That's right. Said the offer still stood. Said he wasn't about to take advantage of us just because we had fallen on hard times. Real gentlemanly of him, don't you think?"

"Oh yes, real gentlemanly, indeed." Cam didn't even attempt to hide the bitterness in her tone. Strothers Bennett, a gentleman? Ha!

"Could be that fire was a blessing in disguise," Mrs. Winthrop went on after singing more of Strothers' praises. "Lord knows I've been after Marsh long enough to sell out and move into town. The only thing you can grow in that soil is hard times." She gave a quick smile. "I reckon I'd best get on about my business. Thank you again, Cam, for everything."

"Give Marsh and the children my best." A half hearted smile was all Cam could manage to accompany her farewell.

Those poor Winthrops sure had fallen on hard times now that they were in Strothers' debt, she mused as she threw a leg over the saddle. Little did they realize that their problems were just beginning.

A blessing in disguise . . . A blessing in disguise. Mrs. Winthrop's words kept ringing in her ears as she road back down the street toward Abbey's. Strothers was anything but a blessing. Satan in disguise she could certainly believe, but a blessing? Never! Why, she wouldn't put it past him to have set the fire himself, considering how badly he had wanted that land in the first place, though heaven only knew what he wanted it for.

A moment later, she all but stopped Traveller in his tracks. If he didn't set the fire himself, you could bet your last dollar he had somebody do it for him! Yes, now that was more like it. Strothers never liked to soil those lily-white hands of his when there was dirty work to be done.

She thought back to the night of the Fourth of July celebration. What was it those fellows had said when they came galloping past the old mine? Ah, yes. One of them had bragged about just making the easiest money of his life. Then the other had made the remark about whatever it was they had done being a lot easier than slaving away in the mill.

Of course. It all fit together now. Whatever

Strothers wanted, he bought, and if it weren't for sale, he'd see to it that it soon was. You could bet he already had a buyer lined up for that old homestead. Nobody or nothing ever stood in his way of getting what he wanted!

Cam had a good mind to go to the sheriff herself, but what good would that do? Sheriff Thomas was as decent a man as they came, but Strothers had him fooled the same way he did everybody else. The Senator always said, if you gave a crook enough rope, he'd hang himself. Well, Strothers' lynching was one event she wouldn't miss for the world. One day he would meet his match, and something told her that day wasn't very far away!

9

By far the grandest residence in the county, perhaps in the whole state, was the Sullivan home, which most people referred to as the Sullivan mansion. There, with Abbey, Cam had spent a great deal of her childhood. Built in the ornate, Victorian style, the large brick house had a mansard roof, gabled windows and a tall cupola in front. The porch extended all around the house except right in front where long, high steps led up to a double oak door that had been imported all the way from England.

Moses, the colored boy who had been the Sullivans' houseboy for as long as she could remember, appeared out of nowhere to help her off her horse. He always seemed to know she was coming long before she ever got there.

Thanking him, she flashed him a grin as big as his own. "You take real good care of my fellow. You hear?"

"Yes, m'am. I do just that."

Cam watched as he led the big chestnut around back. Moses was one of the few people she did trust with her horse. He always gave him a good vinegar rubdown, then turned him out back to graze until she was ready to get on her way.

Moses' sister, a stocky, dark girl named Jasmine, opened the door before she knocked.

"Afternoon, Jasmine. Mrs. Bennett up and about?"

Jasmine's smile lacked its usual cheerfulness. "I's real glad you's here, Miss Cam. I's worried sick about the mistress. She's been feeling mighty poorly." Her shrill voice lowered to barely a whisper when they stepped inside the great foyer. "And it ain't jes the babe either. Mr. Bennett, he be real mean. Always yellin' and makin' her cry."

Cam's fists clenched by her side. "Does he hit her?"

"Oh, no, m'am. I ain't never seen him lay a hand to her, I swear. She jes cries all the time. Why, she be in bed right now boohooing her eyes out." Jasmine lowered her head. "I knows what goes on inside these walls stays here, and you know I ain't proned to gossip, but I jes had to tell you, Miss Cam. You's gots to help her afore she does some injury to herself or that child."

"You did right by telling me, Jasmine." She gave the red checkered shoulder a reassuring pat. "I'll tell you what. I'll go on up and see if I can't cheer her up. Maybe in a little bit, you can bring us a pot of that orange spice tea that she likes so much."

"Yes, m'am. I do jes that."

Cam ran up the winding staircase taking two steps at a time, her toes barely touching the hardwood. What a happy house this used to be, she mused. But if these walls could talk, what tales they might tell about the time since Strothers moved in and took over!

Cam knocked softly on the door to the master suite, then walked in without waiting for an invitation. The sight that greeted her was enough to bring tears to her eyes, but she took extra care to keep her shock to herself.

Abbey was pale and lying all crumpled up in the big, four-postered bed, looking like some long-neglected rag doll. Her hair hung in limp, blonde strands. There wasn't a trace of color to her cheeks; her whole face was as white as her bed jacket. Her eyes were puffed, from too many tears no doubt, and shadowed by deep, dark circles.

Guilt tugged at Cam. She couldn't help but feel partially responsible for what had become of her best friend. What a fool she had been to let pride stand in the way of a reconcilliation for all those months! When Abbey needed her the most, she had abandoned her, and all because of one of Strothers' out-and-out lies. Well, that was not going to happen again. From now on, she'd be the tower of strength Abbey so desperately needed in her time of despair, and there wasn't a damn thing Strothers Bennett could do about it!

"Good afternoon, Abbey, darling," she greeted her friend cheerfully as she pulled the drapes and flung open the windows. "What a beautiful day it is! There's no rain in sight, so get on up and get dressed. I've got a big afternoon all planned for us, starting with a nice long walk and a little shopping."

Abbey retreated under the covers. "Please, Cam, that sun is blinding."

"Nonsense, a little fresh air and sunshine will

do you the world of good. Up and Adam!" Cam pulled back the covers. Except for a rounded middle, her friend was nothing but skin and bones. She tried hard not to voice her concern. "Come on, Abbey. You're not under the weather?"

"Well, no.

"Worn out?"

"Not exactly."

"Then whatever it is that's ailing you, I've got the cure." She gently pulled her friend up and helped her to her feet.

Jasmine entered a short while later. Cam took the tray from her, then dismissed her with a wink.

"Here you go, Abbey. A cup of strong tea is just what you need to get you moving."

"Oh, Cam, I don't know if I'm up to this or not. Maybe we'd better go on this outing of yours tomorrow or the next day." Abbey slumped down into the nearest chair. "Oh, Cam, I'm so miserable, sometimes I just want to die. I've gotten myself into such a mess. Strothers doesn't love me. He never did. He'd be the first to say so. I feel like such a fool."

Cam pulled up the velveteen dressing stool and sat down beside Abbey. She took her friend's hands into her own. What could she say that would comfort her? That Strothers did in fact love her? That everything would be fine once the baby came? Abbey was telling her nothing she didn't already know, but there was little Cam could say or do to make her realization any less painful.

"Oh, Abbey. I do love you dearly, and I so hate seeing you all torn up like this. Believe me, if there was anything I could do to help, I would, but I just don't know what it would be." She gave the frail hand a tight squeeze. "But you've got to understand. Right now, that little baby inside of you needs all your love and attention and strength, and you must pull yourself together for its sake."

Abbey waited the longest time before speaking. Finally, she nodded. "You're right, Cam. Sometimes I get so caught up in my troubles, I forget just who is most important in my life." Smiling a weak smile, she patted her stomach. "My poor little babe. With Strothers for a father, I pity him. Lord knows how he'll turn out."

"But it's got you for a mama, and you're sweet and kind and caring. Your goodness will surely make up for all of Strothers' bad," Cam assured her. "Now you hurry and go put on something real pretty, because after we finish our stroll around town, I'm taking you to the hotel for supper."

Abbey rolled back her eyes. "When are you ever going to stop telling me what to do? Do you realize you've been bossing me around since we were little?"

"You didn't listen then, and you don't listen now."

They giggled like a couple of schoolgirls. It did Cam's heart good to hear Abbey's voice ring with laughter.

But her friend's features resumed their solemn cast much too quickly. "I should have listened to you when you told me Strothers was no good. Oh, well, I've made my bed. Guess I'll have to lie in it."

Cam couldn't stand the thought of Abbey being locked into a loveless marriage forever with a monster like Strothers. Abbey needed to enjoy the rewards of real love, the kind she shared with

Tate. She was tempted to tell her that if she really wanted to be free of Strothers, the Senator was the one to help her. But she decided against it. That was a decision Abbey herself had to make with no interference from anyone.

A while later, sitting in the dining room of the Caesar's Head Hotel after an early supper of catfish and fried potatoes, and stuffing themselves with chocolate peanut twirls, Abbey looked like a totally different person. Gone from her eyes were the dark circles and wrinkle lines that had been etched across her face from day after day of worrying. The carefree girl she had once been was lost forever, but the young woman remaining looked poised and surprisingly in control.

Abbey leaned over the white-linened table and touched Cam's elbow. "Oh, look," she whispered. "There's Bud Cooper's wife. Did you ever see such a vulgar get-up?"

Cam gave a quick glance over her shoulder at the woman who had just entered the room with a large, sweeping gesture. Wearing a Sunday-best bombazine with orange silk warp and worsted fillings that clashed with her burnt copper curls, a stylish hat with curled-up sides and orange streamers, and carrying a matching lace parasol, Nellie Cooper looked far too grand to be the wife of a mill worker, even if that mill worker was the foreman.

Cam had no doubt where the money had come from to support such extravagant tastes. If word of Strothers' infidelities with that floozy ever got out, it would just kill poor Abbey. What humiliation!

"I hardly think the mill's paying Bud that kind

of money, do you?" Abbey remarked, her bitterness unmistakeable. "If it is, then our finances are a whole lot worse off than I thought."

Cam kept quiet. There was no mistaking the anger in her friend's tone. Could it be that Abbey knew about Nellie already?

"Why, good afternoon, Miss Tranter, Missus Bennett," Nellie said as she sashayed by on her way to meet the black-haired woman who had just waved to her from across the room. "I must say, Missus Bennett, you are looking very lovely these days. Being in the family way certainly becomes you."

Cam watched as Abbey's jaw tightened.

"Why, thank you, Nellie. How sweet of you to say so." Abbey flashed her sweetest smile. "But you're the one who's looking so lovely. Why, you are just a sight to behold. Orange is most becoming to you, especially with your lovely red hair."

Smiling, Nellie patted the big pile of curls underneath her hat.

Cam held her breath. She could almost see Abbey sharpening her claws on the table. She hardly had time to blink before Abbey's hand moved slowly to her cup. The next thing she knew, the full cup of tea had been spilled in Nellie's direction, staining the coral frills with ugly, brown streaks.

"Oh, dear. How careless of me."

Cam could hardly keep from laughing. In Abbey's rush to wipe away the stains, she had turned the whole pot of tea over onto the dress.

"Oh, I do apologize, Nellie. I am just so clumsy these days. Being in the family way, you know."

Nellie's face turned several shades redder than her hair. Mumbling something under her breath, she forced a strained smile, then walked away with considerably less hip movement than when she had approached them.

"Why, Abbey Sullivan, if I didn't know better, I'd swear you did that on purpose."

It was all Abbey could do to keep from laughing aloud. "I reckon that husband of mine will just have to buy his lady friend another orange frock. Lord, what a hideous color. Oh, Cam, I wish you could have seen your face. Hers was surprised enough, but yours was downright astounded. Oh, did that do my heart good!"

Abbey reached for another sticky peanut twirl. "Now, don't tell me you don't know about Strothers and her catting around. Just about everybody in town does—except her husband, it seems I pity the two of them if Bud ever catches on." Her eyes showed a lively sparkle as she licked her fingers clean. "Now don't you look so shocked, Cam. I don't care who he's bedding. Not anymore. He's worthless and no good, and as soon as I have this baby of mine, I'm going to find a way to get myself out of the mess I got myself into."

For once in her life, Cam was at at a complete loss for words. Apparently her old chum had more spunk than she gave her credit for. What a shame she had to endure such agony and heartache before she found such strength.

"Lands alive. Would you look at the time," Cam exclaimed when the grandfather clock chimed six. "I was having such a good time, I forgot I told Ludie Mae I'd be home by five. I'm surprised she hasn't sent the sheriff out looking for me."

"Strothers is going to think I've left home for sure. Not that I really give a hoot what he thinks anyway. Cam, why don't you just stay with me tonight?" Abbey suggested as they walked back to her house. "It's getting so late now, you'll never make it back to Willow Creek before dark. I can send Moses to tell them not to worry."

Cam shook her head. The prospect of spending the night under the same roof as Strothers was far from inviting. She'd just as soon take her chances alone in the dark.

"That's awful sweet of you, but I'd best be heading on home. Tate said if he came back tonight, he'd come out to Willow Creek if it wasn't too late, and I'd sort of like to be there in case he does."

"You're in love with him, aren't you, Cam?"

"I never thought I'd feel that way about any man, but yes, I am. I am in love with him."

Cam linked her arm through Abbey's, and they walked down the street, heads together and chatting the way they had done for all their lives until Strothers came along.

"I am so happy for you. Tate is such a wonderful man. So unlike that husband of mine. For the life of me, I can't figure out how Tate ever got hooked in with him."

Cam said nothing. Countless were the times she had wondered the same thing.

"Abbey, do you know why Strothers was so interested in the Winthrop property?" she asked suddenly. "I saw Mrs. Winthrop at the store, and she couldn't stop singing his praises. She was really grateful to him for buying them out."

"I don't know why he'd be interested in their land, but I do know what you're thinking, and I wouldn't put that past Strothers for one minute."

Cam nodded, understanding what Abbey meant. Strothers was rotten to the core. She'd lay odds he had that fire set deliberately so he could come in and buy them out. Living with a man like him must be pure hell. Thank God Tate was good and kind and honest.

A fancy black carriage was parked in front of the Sullivan house.

"Isn't that just the most obscene contraption you ever did see?" Abbey said, laughing. "Strothers had it delivered from Columbia yesterday. He thinks he's real aristocratic tooling around in that thing."

Moses came out to greet them, and Abbey sent him around back to tack up Traveller.

"I would ask you in, but it is nearly dark, and if you're going home, you'd best get on your way." Abbey threw an annoyed glance over her shoulder to the shadow standing in the doorway. "Besides, I'm sure you have better things to do than pay your respects to Strothers."

Cam's laugh was anything but cheerful. The less she saw of that man the better! At least, she could leave. Poor Abbey had no way of escaping. Not yet anyway. But at least, for what Abbey had said at the hotel, there was hope."

"Evening, ladies," Strothers drawled a moment later as he stepped out onto the porch, cigar in hand. "I was getting real worried about you, sugar. A lady in your condition shouldn't be gallavanting all over town."

Abbey ignored him. "Maybe Moses should go along with you just to make sure you get home safe."

Cam chuckled. "Now, don't you go worrying about me. I doubt anyone in this county is brave enough to tangle with me."

"These woods around here get mighty dark at night. No place for a lady," Strothers remarked smugly as he came sauntering towards them in long, easy strides. "Ask me real nice, and I might take you home in style," he said as he motioned to his new carriage with an elaborate sweep of his arms.

"No thank you. I can manage on my own."

"I reckon you're looking to meet up with that fellow in black, are you?" he asked, drawing long and hard on his cigar. "I hear those woods by the old mine is one of his favorite haunts."

"Guess who we ran into at the hotel this afternoon?" Abbey piped up before Cam had a chance to say exactly what was on her mind. "Nellie Cooper. You know her, don't you? Bud Cooper's wife. Well, you never seen such finery in your life as she was wearing. I do declare that mill must be paying exorbitant wages these days—either that or Sally Rose has taken her in part-time."

Cam chuckled. Sally Rose ran the local whorehouse.

Strothers closed his mouth tight around his cigar and said nothing. Puffing angrily, he blew the smoke in Cam's direction.

Not a moment too soon, Moses appeared with

Traveller.

"You sure you'll be all right?" Cam whispered after Strothers had stomped back up onto the porch.

"That husband of mine is many things, but a fool isn't one of them. He knows better than to lay a hand on me. Why, Jasmine and Moses would make mush out of him if he did."

Abbey's voice lowered to barely a whisper. "He doesn't know it yet, but just because he's my husband doesn't give him free rein over my mill. My daddy made certain in his will that only a Sullivan by birth would ever profit from it. You tell the Senator I'll be needing his expert legal advice soon, will you, Cam? The sooner I undo this, the better."

"You better hurry, sugar. You don't want to overexert yourself."

Cam hugged her friend close and kissed her cheek. "If you need me, just send Moses to fetch me."

A strange feeling of doom assailed her when she swung herself into the saddle. Something told her she shouldn't be going, but she knew she couldn't stay either, not with Strothers around. That would just be asking for trouble.

Dusk had settled in over the mountain, but darkness had not yet fallen when Cam reached the fork. If she stuck to the road, nightfall would beat her home, but if she took the short cut through the woods, she could race it and win.

Making up her mind, she nudged Traveller into the bushes. As she had told Abbey, no one would tangle with her, and even if anyone was fool enough to try, she had already proven she and her horse could outdistance anybody in the county.

Darkness had all but fallen inside the woods. The trees were but shadows against a background of haze. The air was hot and sticky, and even the noises of the insects and animals were lazy and tired.

There no reason to worry, Cam told herself. The ride home would be quick. Traveller knew the trail by heart. All she had to do was hold onto the reins and stay in the saddle, and he'd get her to Willow Creek safe and sound.

But one thought intruded on her mind over and over. Would this be the night she'd once again encounter her mysterious stranger? Had that been hidden in her thoughts all evening, and had she purposely delayed her trip home thinking she might run into him?

No! She must not let herself even think about him or a chance meeting. And he wasn't *her* mysterious stranger, either. He wasn't anything to her. Not anymore. Anyone so determined to keep his identity secret could only be a fugitive from the law, and she shouldn't get involved up with someone who came and left at whim. Besides, not for the world would she risk losing Tate. He was all a man should be and much, much more.

The wanderings of her mind refused to be quieted. Could it be he had been trying to see her, but she had been too busy with Tate to pay him any mind? Maybe he had come back to keep that promise he had made. How many times during the past week had he been right behind her, and she hadn't even known it? After all, he had saved her life that night of the fire. Who knows how many times he had waited for her in those very woods she had been avoiding?

She could feel her defenses begin to crumble. What harm was there in seeing him, in talking to him, and explaining she was no longer the young girl who had been so infatuated and fascinated by a man who was just like a character out of some romantic tale? What harm, indeed? If he had in fact returned to Caesar's Head on her account, the least she could do would be to see him. She owed him that much. Perhaps, deep down, she owed herself that much as well.

Cam checked her horse to a walk and listened, scarcely daring to breathe. There was no mistaking the sound of hooves pounding the trail behind her. It was not her imagination. It was almost as if thoughts of the man on the white steed had actually willed him to come to her.

She reached up and squeezed the gold disc for good luck. She should be afraid, but she wasn't. There was no reason to fear him. He would never harm her. They were friends.

A twinge of sadness nagged at her. Friends, but never lovers. Nor would they ever enjoy the intimate bliss of her dreams. Why should that make her feel a little sad?

"Cam—wait up."

Her smile was quick to vanish. She knew that voice all too well.

Somewhere not too far ahead, a tree limb snapped.

She jerked around. Strothers was coming up behind her, but the mystery man was near, too. She could feel it. Whenever he was near, a little flutter of excitement always came over her even before she saw him. He was close, probably just around the bend. She could sense him. She had to get rid of Strothers. She could outrun him, but that would lead him right to the man in black, and she couldn't jeopardize her friend's safety.

"Go away, Strothers. I'm warning you. Leave me alone," she yelled over her shoulder.

Strothers charged past her, then stopped his horse suddenly in front of her, whirling it around so that he was blocking her passage.

"I thought I'd best make the gallant gesture and see you home, Cam, darling, even though you are ruder than hell to me."

It didn't have to be daylight to know that smile of his was just as sinister as ever. Ice blue eyes leered at her through the darkness. He was up to no good, no doubt about that.

"I am more than capable of seeing myself home. Now if you will just move aside, I'll be on about my business, and I suggest you do the same."

Strothers yanked the reins from her hands. Traveller pulled back.

"Not so fast there, honey. You and me are long overdue for a little loving, and I intend to get me some right now."

She spat in his face. "Go away, Strothers. You disgust me."

His reply was a suggestive laugh.

"You let me pass, or I'll make sure you regret it," she warned him. "So help me I will."

He edged even closer. His free hand rubbed at the bulge in his crotch. "What you going to do if I don't, honey? Yell for that fellow in black? Why, I bet you'd be all too happy to spread those pretty little legs for him. Come on, sugar, you know you want it as bad as I do. There's no use pretending you don't. I seen the way you look at me."

"Don't flatter yourself. I'm not one of your mill whores."

He grabbed hold of her hair and tangled it between his fingers.

"Let . . . me . . . go!"

His breathing grew even more labored. "I'll bet you could be a real little hellion in bed if you set your mind to it. Come on, give me a little bit of what we've both been waiting for a long time. After I'm through with you, you'll be begging me to poke you again. You won't have to go panting after no Yankee or that made-up lover of yours when I'm through with you. Hell, no. I'll show you what a real man can be."

He leaned over the saddle. Teeth as white as a wolf's grinned hungrily at her.

Cam heard none of his incoherent mutterings. Obviously she had been wrong. If her phantom lover was in the woods, he had no intention of helping her out. No matter. She could manage on her own. All Strothers had to do was get a little bit closer and she could make her move.

"That's it, baby. No use fighting me. Just relax. Me and you will be real good together, I promise."

His lips touched hers.

Hers parted with slow, deliberate motion.

His tongue probed its way inside. Animal noises growled deep from within his throat. "Oh, sugar, we are going to be so good together."

His taste revolted her. Her stomach was churning, and it was all she could do to keep her sickness from erupting. But she waited until he was relaxed. His right hand let go of her hair while fingers that had been tight around the reins a moment before now made their way to her breast.

Finally, she could stand no more. Her teeth clamped down on his lip and didn't let go until she had tasted blood.

"Why you little bitch! I'll fix you. Damn you!"

She heard his curses behind her. Traveller had already lunged forward, and they were well out of his reach.

She heard the pounding of hooves behind her and glanced quickly over her shoulder. Strothers was right where she had left him. The noise was coming from *him*—the man in black atop a white mount. He was there!

"Why you miserable son of a bitch," she heard Strothers shout out. "Who the hell are you? What do you want?"

Cam whirled Traveller back around. The mysterious stranger was circling Strothers, his horse pawing nervously at the ground.

"You get that white bastard away from me. You hear me?"

Obviously Strothers couldn't decide whether to make a run for it, or risk waiting it out.

"So you don't talk, do you?" he asked, trying to sound brave. "I'll fix you, you bastard."

Cam saw Strothers reach inside his vest pocket. She knew he was going after the tiny, pearl-handled pistol he kept there.

"Watch out!" she yelled to her rescuer. "He's got a gun."

A split second later, she heard the crack of a whip, then the sound of something else—the pistol, she assumed—hitting the ground.

Strothers' hand shot to his face. "I'll see you in hell, you bastard. You'll pay for this!" he exclaimed as he went thundering off down the trail.

Cam sat perfectly still atop her horse. She couldn't move even if she wanted to. She wanted desperately to go to him, to her mysterious saviour, but her legs were too numb to nudge Traveller forward. So she had been right! He had been with her in the woods all along!

Their eyes reached through the darkness and locked together. Words were not needed to communicate the conversation of their hearts.

"You came back. I knew you would."

He nodded.

Her voice was quiet and full of awe. "You were there the night of the fire, weren't you?"

Once again, she could sense he was nodding.

"Please talk to me," she begged him. "Tell me who you are. Let me see your face."

There was something almost sad in the way he shook his head.

"At least, tell me your name. Just tell me that much."

She could hear him backing his horse away. "Don't go. Stay just a little while. Talk to me."

He hesitated, but only for a moment. Then he dug his heels into his horse, and the white creature spirited him away into the woods.

Cam waited and watched and listened long after the leaves had ceased their rustling and the ground had stopped quaking, hoping and praying that he would return, but knowing down deep he would not, at least not that night.

Somewhere out there, he was watching her at that very moment, and he would be watching over her like a guardian angel until she reached the safety of Willow Creek. The time just wasn't right yet for him to make himself known, but soon, very soon, he would reveal himself to her, and she would know the truth at last. After waiting two years, what was another day or week or month? Besides, all she had to do was think of him, and he would appear!

10

Cam kicked out at the covers, fighting the quilts and fighting sleep just as she had done for most of the night. Her thin cotton nightgown, damp from her endless tossing and turning, had long since been discarded. Still there was no relief to be found, not even in her bareness. All the windows in the room were raised high and the drapes pulled back, but there was no breeze to wander in. The room was still and thick with heat, just like the outside air. Not a sound could be heard for miles around. Even the bullfrogs and crickets, usually wide awake and in loud harmony in the few hours before dawn, refused to utter their songs.

Cam stared up at the rafters, eyes wide open. There was no point in keeping the lids closed any longer. Sleep would not come, and it wasn't going to. Was it the heat or the chaos going on inside her mind that made rest impossible? So many nights during the past two years had she lain in that very bed dreaming the same dream over and over about the return of her man in black. Would thoughts of him occupy her mind forever? He had captured her heart that long-ago night. How long would she be destined to remain his prisoner. His presence lulled her into fantasies of the intimacies they had shared only in her imaginings, yet his absence no longer troubled her, for Tate had come to fill that vast emptiness her heart had not long ago known. How silly she must have sounded earlier, pleading with the stranger to show his face and reveal his name! What on earth had come over her? How would she ever explain such brazen behavior to Tate?

For a moment she allowed her thoughts to run wild. Suppose he had taken her into his confidence as she had pleaded with him to do—would she have so willingly given herself to him as once she had imagined? Surely she would have come to her senses before it was too late. Wouldn't she have? Now, she had far more to lose—the love and devotion of a good, decent man—if she dared allow a silly infatuation of her youth to become more than just that. Perhaps it would have been easier had the man in black never come back into her life.

Well, no more. Enough was enough. From now on, she mustn't let him occupy her thoughts even for a moment. Granted she was indebted to him, but that debt need not wreck her life. It was certainly no cause for her to be reduced to nothing but a trembling mass any time he was around. How hurt Tate would be if he knew what went on inside her head whenever the stranger was near! How disappointed he would be in her if he ever suspected she had been in such close contact with him. She loved Tate! He was her life! There were no two ways about that. There was no room in her life for the man in black, not any longer. Tate was as much of a man as he, and just because there was little about him she did not know was no reason not to be in awe of him. If she weren't careful, this ridiculous infatuation of hers was going to cost more than she ever dreamed possible.

Cam gave the covers a final kick, then sprang to her feet, all in one quick motion. Damn! Why couldn't she just tell herself the man in black was no longer an important part of her life and let it go at that? Why did she have to keep trying to convince herself of that? Was he truly not out of her system, even though she had done all she could to exorcise him from her soul? What a tangled mess of confusion inside her head! How could she sleep, much less sort out her life, under such condition? And the heat had very little to do with it!

She leaned out the window. Not the slightest breath of air stirred. Oh, why couldn't she think straight? What she needed was a long soak in a tub of cold water. Perhaps then she could understand the turbulence inside her.

Another hour and the sun would be up, and it would be time to rise. Already it was starting to peek up from the horizon. A few clounds had begun gathering over the river. Perhaps there'd be some rain today. Just what was needed to settle the hot dust! Maybe it would even wash away her confusion and cleanse the ambivalence from her system. Yes, rain! That was her one salvation.

Thanks heavens Tate would be back today! When she was in his arms, she didn't think of the mysterious stranger. He'd make everything all right again! But if Strothers told him about the incident in the woods? If he did, all details of any wrong-doing on his part would of course be omitted, and by the time he finished the story, he would be the one who turned out to be the hero, not the man in black. How would Tate react? Would he be jealous? Would he feel threatened? Would their relationship suffer because of a girlish infatuation? All that was certain was that she would be sure to drive herself crazy if she didn't dismiss the man on the white horse from her mind once and for all!

There was only one thing to do. Rather than risk Strothers getting to Tate first, Cam would have to tell him what had happened in the woods. He would understand. He would realize that was a part of her life before she met him, and having known him, there could never, would never, be any man for her but him. He would understand—wouldn't he?

She gazed longingly out the window. If only he were there at that very moment so she could explain that to him and show him he was the only man she desired. If only . . .

The neigh of a horse somewhere out in the distance broke her reverie. Tate was all but forgotten. The man in black was out there, watching her, at that very moment! She just knew he was. Could he somehow read her mind and know of the turmoil inside her heart? Yes, of course. That was it! He was beckoning her to come to him. He wanted her to meet with him soon—now! He had had a change of heart from earlier. He wanted to see her. She could feel him pleading with her to come closer, closer. Invisible arms were pulling at her. Come. Come. Come!

No! No! No! She must not even think of him. She had promised herself she wouldn't. It was Tate she loved! Tate was the man who had claim to her heart. She would be faithful to him.

Oh, why couldn't she think straight? If such frenzied thoughts persisted, they'd drive her mad for sure. The man in black was nowhere near Willow Creek! It was all in her mind. He was all in her mind! Oh, God, the heat was making her crazy. If only she could cool down! If only she could think straight. The river! Yes! A swim in the river was just what she needed to put her mind back on track. The Saluda was always cool, no matter what time of year. Yes, a swim would do her the world of good! It might even make her forget how close she had come to destroying what she had shared with Tate!

Grabbing her nightdress from the floor, she hurriedly slipped it over her head and headed toward the door, then decided to bolt the lock instead. The Senator and Ludie Mae were both light sleepers. She couldn't take the chance of waking them by sneaking down stairs that creaked with each step, when she could just as easily climb out the window and shimmy down the big willow.

It took no time to scamper down the tree. The talent had not dulled with age. She could still jump to the ground with the agility of a cat. Beggin' was there to meet her, just as he had always been there any time she decided on a late-night adventure.

No sooner had her feet touched the ground

than her legs bolted right out from under her, and she ran as quickly as she could to the river's edge with her dog on her heels. The sense of such freedom gave her a feeling of exhilaration such as she had never known before. It was as though she had truly escaped her worries and left them in the room to do battle among themselves. Only once did she halt from her fleeing pace and look back behind her. For that single instant, she could have sworn she was not alone. Seeing that she was indeed, she laughed aloud at herself, then ran on, spurred even faster with thoughts of plunging her body into the cool mountain water.

By the time she reached the river, her gown was back over her head and hanging from a tree limb. When she dove into the water, her breath was stolen by the much welcomed coldness of the rush of water that enveloped her. She felt better already. It was almost as though she were being cleansed of all her troubles and of her obsession. No worry seemed unsolvable now. No problem was insurmountable.

With long, easy strokes, she glided over the water, turning effortlessly from her stomach to her back and back again as she kicked across the river. She swam until she was exhausted, until all strength had been drained from her limbs, then floated on her back for a while, drifting aimlessly with the current, eyes closed and arms fluttering ever so slightly to keep herself afloat.

The whinny of a horse, this time even closer than the last, caused her eyes to open suddenly and brought her head out of the water. Had she only imagined it, or was there someone out there? No, there really was someone out there, and it could only be one man. She knew already that he would be on a white steed. Since their earlier parting, he had been watching the house waiting for the chance to speak to her. He had beckoned to her with his gentle and invisible caresses. At long last, he had decided to reveal himself to her and answer those questions that had been burning inside her since their first meeting.

Her eyes searched the woods. She could see nothing, yet she knew he was there. She had that feeling, just like all those other times when he had come to her. Yes, once more he had come to her. At any moment she would see him galloping out from inside the pine hammock. Was there no way to quiet the pounding inside her chest? She felt her heart was about to run away from her. He was there! Yes, he had come to her at last!

Heart racing wildly, she attacked the water with furious strokes, swimming to the other side of the river as fast as she could. She had to get to him before it was too late, before he changed his mind and went galloping back into the darkness, perhaps never to again be seen. She must get to him!

Lifting her head out of the water and taking a quick look around, she took a deep breath, then put her head back under. He was there, on the other side. He was there, waiting for her to come to him, willing her to come to him. His silent command shouted through the darkness. Come . . . come . . . come . . . .

Only a few more yards to go, yet it seemed as if the entire length of the Saluda were separating them! Come . . . come . . . come . . . .

Struggling for air, she surfaced one final time.

Yes, he was there! She could see him now. His back was to her, but soon, very soon, she would see his face. Would it be the kind, handsome face of her dreams, or would it be scarred and disfigured? Or would it be the face of a hardened criminal fleeing justice? It didn't matter. She just wanted to see him, to look into his eyes. Only then could she be released from the spell he had cast on her two years before!

She could feel his stare on her even when she was under water. Why had Beggin' not barked? Why was he sitting so calmly on the river bank? Was the mystery man a spirit from the other world? Had he mesmerized her hound dog, too? Once she saw his face, would she really be free of him, or would he still haunt her mind every minute of the day? She had to know for sure one way or the other, and there was only one way to do that, and that was to come face to face with him once and for all!

As soon as she hit the shallows, she sprang up out of the water and waded the rest of the way to shore. With each passing moment, she was getting closer and closer to the man of her dreams, yet it seemed as though her legs were moving in slow motion. She was drifting to him, just as she had done so often in her dreams. Another few feet and she could reach out and touch him. Another step or two and she would be able to distinguish his every feature. Only a little farther and she could reach out and touch him!

Slowly, very slowly, Cam stepped out of the water as though she were in a trance, guided by some force other than herself, and obeying the silent command of his thoughts. She moved toward him proudly, making no effort to cover herself. Her hair hung in wet curls down the valley between her breasts. She was his. She had always been his, ever since that first meeting. What was the point in denying it? At long last, the hour she had waited for was upon her. That act of possession was about to be completed.

Her smile froze suddenly on her face. Her feet stopped in their tracks as her heart ceased beating.

"Tate!"

The figure turned around. What light there was from the approach of day settled on his face, revealing an expression that was strangely absent of any emotion.

"You sound disappointed." His remark was flat. "Were you expecting someone else?"

His words were harsh and cold, much colder than the river.

Cam was quick to compose herself. He must never know! Never!

"Disappointed? Expecting someone else? Don't be ridiculous. I knew that was you. When did you get back?"

She tried to speak and act as if there was nothing wrong. Still, she could hear the tremors in her own voice and see the quivering in her limbs that she was trying so desperately to conceal.

Slowly reaching for her gown, she slipped it over herself. Never before had she been so modest in Tate's presence. Why now did she feel that she had to cover herself? Why did she suddenly feel blemished by her thoughts and ashamed of her actions? Ashamed of him seeing her with nothing on? There was no way he could have heard what was going on inside her head as she stepped out of the water. Nor could he have suspected that she was coming to greet someone else. Still, something was wrong. Something was very, very wrong. She could see it in his eyes, tell it in his voice.

He made no effort to come to her, to wrap her in his arms in a loving homecoming embrace. Could it be he knew? No, he could not know! That was impossible. There was no way he could even suspect.

"I've missed you." Her words were soft. How desperately she wanted to run to him, but she could not. Not until he gave her some sign.

"Have you now?"

Cam nodded. How odd! He sounded as if he doubted her.

For the longest while, they stood facing each other, eyes intent on each other but no words passing between them.

Finally, after what seemed to be forever, he shook his head, then smiled at her and opened up his arms.

She ran into the comfort inside.

"I've missed you, too, Cam. You will never know just how much," he mumbled before a kiss that was long and hard. "Never did I think I could ever love so deeply."

She could feel herself sinking deeper and deeper into his embrace, drowning in his scent, his touch, his taste. What a fool she was! How could she even think of another man when he was all the man a woman could possibly want or need. How close she had come to losing it all! Well, not again. Never again! She'd spend the rest of her life proving to him that he was indeed the man she expected to find when she stepped out of the river.

"What are you doing out here alone dressed like that, or should I say, undressed?" he asked when they had finally parted and settled comfortably beneath a willow tree.

"It was so hot, I couldn't sleep. I thought a cool dip would help me relax."

"And did it?"

"I feel comfortable now, but that's because you're here." She lifted her head from his shoulder. "What are you doing here?"

"I just this minute rode in from Traveller's Rest," he replied. "I know it sounds silly, but I couldn't wait to see you, so I thought I'd come on out and wait for you to get up."

"I'm so glad you did." She snuggled back down beside him. "These past few days have been horrible without you. I didn't think you were ever coming back!"

"Anything exciting happen while I was gone? Any more sightings of that fellow in black?"

Her heart stopped beating. No, there was no way he could know. She must be careful lest she give herself away and lose him forever.

"Rumor has it in town that somebody on a white horse was seen galloping across Grave Yard Hill the other night. Of course, when some of those fellows get all likkered up, there's no telling what they'll see."

Should she tell him or not, she wondered, trying her best to quiet the dilemma playing havoc inside her. Should she risk him hearing about it from Strothers? Strothers wouldn't tell. He wouldn't be so stupid. Nor would he be so ready to admit he was the one who came out on the bottom. No, she wouldn't tell him. The sooner their talk changed from a topic other than the stranger in black, the better!

Cam kissed his cheek. "I am so glad you're back. Why, I might never let you out of my sight again!"

"You mean that, don't you?"

"Why, Tate Carruth, you sound like you don't believe me. Of course I mean it. I told you I love you, and I have never said that to any man before."

"Your heart belongs only to me?" His jade stare settled on her necklace. "To me and no one else?"

A sharp shiver ran up her spine. Damn. It was almost as though he could see inside her head, but how could he possibly know anything about her most recent encounter with the stranger? Why did he suddenly have doubts about her feelings towards him? Curse Strothers! Why did he ever have to go and mention anything about that in the first place? At least he had finally gotten his just reward. It was going to take some doing explaining that whip mark across his face. No, Tate would never hear from him what had happened during his absence. Strothers wasn't eager for anyone to know he'd been made a fool of!

"You know, Tate, I'll let you in on a little secret if you promise not to laugh."

"Promise."

She snuggled closer, pressing herself tighter to him. "I made the Senator a promise not too long ago that if I ever found a man who could outride me, I'd hang on to him, and I just thought I'd give you fair warning that I intend to do everything in my power to make good on that oath."

Finally, Take broke into a grin. His hardened features relaxed. Whatever was troubling him earlier had disappeared at last. "Why, Camille Tranter, I do believe you mean that."

She wrapped her wet body around him and tucked her curves still closer. "I don't mean to ever let you get away."

Laughing, they fell back onto the ground, lips fused, kissing, hands touching and exploring and working wonderful magic such as they had never known before, unable to get their fill.

Tate's kisses had the intensity of a year's separation, not a mere two days'. His tongue dove deep into the sweetness it had missed as he raised her gown over her head without taking his lips off hers.

In no time, she had lost all count of the kisses. All she knew was that she never wanted them to stop.

Her eyes came open once more and searched the nearby trees. He had been there, but he was gone now. Just as well. She could belong to only one man, and that man was beside her at that moment. There was no place in her heart for another, no matter how sentimental the bond binding them. She was Tate's, and she wouldn't change that for anything in the world.

Certain she could not wait another moment to satisfy her ravenous hunger, she watched anxiously as Tate stripped off his clothes, her eager hands teasing him with hints of the vast pleasures which lay ahead.

As soon as he was above her, she flung her legs around him, her silken thighs inviting, welcoming the sweet invasion that would in a little while send her soaring to distant summits.

He moved slowly against her, teasing and tormenting with his mouth in ways she had never dreamed possible. Her whole body shuddered upon his command; her insides quaked with a need so intense she thought she would burst into flames at any moment, but still he refused to be hurried.

"There is no rush, my darling," he whispered into her ear over and over. "No rush at all."

Hungry lips feasted on desire-swollen breasts, which rose and fell in fevered response to the delicious torture.

His lips moved downward, his tongue gliding slowly and wickedly down the creamy expanse of flesh to the soft roundness of her belly and beyond, while nimble fingers followed closely behind, calming flesh that quivered and shuddered with passionate desire.

She could not contain her screams of delight. He had not yet laid his claim, and already she had been sent soaring high into the mountain. What bursts of sensations he had set free inside her! Hot blood pounded through her. Bodies merged. They were as one, their needs and wants interwoven.

One more kiss, and he drove himself hard and deep into her most secret of chasms, sending her from beyond all earthly limits and back again until she could stand it no longer. His thrusts grew more and more powerful, more intense, and it was all she could do to meet them while one explosion after another ripped through her. Still she cried out for more until they had both erupted one final time in their shared need.

Cam closed her eyes with a sigh and a smile as she sank deeper into the cool earth. How could she possibly waste a moment's thought on the man in black. Her dream lover could not even begin to compare with the one in real life.

Afterwards they lay, not speaking but still joined, both finally giving in to the love-sated fatigue of their frenzied coupling.

When Tate finally rolled off her and over onto his side, he carried her with him, holding on tight as if he were afraid she might be snatched from his arms.

Cam awakened first, the sun's rays nearly blinding her. Smiling contentedly, she snuggled closer to her lover. How lucky she was to have Tate as her teacher in the sweet lessons of love. How childish her girlhood fantasies were in comparison. She loved Tate more than she had ever thought it possible to love any man. He was her life, her love. Nothing was ever going to jeopardize their relationship again, not a war that had been fought two decades before, not Strothers Bennett, and certainly not some man parading about in a black cape.

Tate kissed open her eyes. "What a serious look you have, my love. No troubling afterthoughts, I hope?"

She flung her arms tight around his neck. Her legs gripped at his buttocks, her toes digging playfully into the taut flesh.

"After that homecoming, how could any thoughts possibly be troubling to either of us?"

Kisses fluttered through her hair. "I was afraid that fellow in black would have taken my place while I was gone."

Her smile faded out only for a moment. "No one will ever take your place. No one. Not ever. You have my word on that."

Never would he know of last night's moments of weakness, Cam swore silently. Would she have given in to the two-year-old fantasy had the mysterious stranger not galloped away, or would her love for Tate have been strong enough to help her resist the temptation? If only she could know the answer for sure. No matter. That decision was one that would never have to be made anyway. Never again would she get herself in so precarious a situation. Never.

Tate lifted the gold disc from between her breasts, then dropped it.

It felt very cold against her flesh. Why did she have the feeling that he could read her thoughts when her mind was on the other man?

"Tell me, Cam, why do you still wear that thing after all this time if he means nothing to you?"

"It's a good-luck charm," she answered quickly. "Nothing else. And believe me, the way I go tearing through these woods on horseback, I need all the good luck I can get."

Could she part with it if he asked her to? she wondered. She wasn't quite sure. It would be like severing her one last tie with the man whose face she had never seen. Was that what she really and truly wanted? When, if ever, would she be able to answer that question truthfully to herself?

"Do you want me to take it off?" She reached for the clasp. It would be a lot easier coping with the loss of a love she had never truly had than with one that had become so important a part of her life.

"No, no!" Tate gently grabbed her hands and kissed each finger. "I'd not have a moment's peace if I thought my jealousy had brought you bad luck. You wear it, just as long as it's superstition and not loyalty to a past love that keeps it around your neck."

"If it makes you feel any better, I also keep a horseshoe tacked above my door."

"And a rabbit's foot in your pocket?"

"Don't laugh," she cautioned him, her words teasing and suggestive.

Her hand slid down his stomach, her fingers dancing over the taunt flesh that tightened even more at her touch. What hunger he incited within her! Would she never have her fill of him? Would she always long for more and more and still more?

"I do believe I know a way that I can prove to you that you are the one I love and not some crazy fool who goes around dressed for winter in the middle of the summer."

"Oh? And how do you propose to do that?"

Her fingers crept to the inside of his thighs. Flesh that had been soft and relaxed a moment earlier leapt to rigid attention.

"Oh, Cam, Cam," he moaned over and over as she gently caressed the source of her great pleasure.

He tried to roll her over, but she threw one leg over his hips and held firm. "No, my darling. It is my time to love you."

She quickly guided him inside her and, amid his moans of ecstasy, moved slowly on top of him, grinding herself deeper and deeper into him, all the while keeping his arms pinned to his sides.

"Please, let me touch you," he mumbled. "Let me feel you. This is driving me mad."

"Patience, my darling. Patience."

His mouth soon did what his hands could not as he lifted himself up and hungrily devoured first one breast then the other, his teeth nipping playfully at each rosy peak.

Passion rose inside her like the hottest inferno, clouding her senses, and making her a slave to the wonders so recently discovered. Waves of ecstasy throbbed through her once again, and she melted closer to him, losing herself to her body's awakenings.

"As much as I would love to stay here locked in this wonderfully wicked embrace," began Tate softly, "I fear I would be placing my life in grave danger if by chance the Senator happens along on his early-morning walk."

"Oh, but my father never walks before breakfast," she told him, not budging from where she was. Chin resting on his chest, she stretched out her legs onto his. "And considering our present position, I hardly think you could be accused of taking advantage of me." Chuckling, she rolled off. "However, to protect your reputation and keep your honor as a Yankee gentleman intact . . ."

"Not to mention keeping my neck intact."

"That, too," she said, grinning. "I shall concede to your wishes. Why don't you come up to the house for breakfast? That trip must have worn you out."

"It wasn't the journey that exhausted me, my sweet."

Cam smiled with satisfaction as she picked up her nightgown and backed away slowly as she slipped it over her head, aware that he was watching her every move, just as she was watching his, already anticipating with great pleasure their next session in love.

Keeping her hands to herself as he dressed was a near-impossible task. Would she never stop wanting him? She hoped not. What fires he ignited inside her. Surely this was the man destiny had intended for her! He had to be!

"By the way, you had me so preoccupied, I nearly forgot to tell you my good news," Tate announced as he buttoned the wide cuffs of his loose-sleeved shirt. "While I was in Greenville, I was able to track down Clayton Griffin's lawyer. It seems that a long-lost cousin turned up after all, and he's willing to let me lease Hunter's Glen for a while until he makes up his mind what he's going to do with it."

"Oh, Tate. That's wonderful." Cam threw her arms around him. "So that means you won't be going back to Baltimore any time soon?"

"Not right away. Think you can make a Southern gentleman out of me, or do you reckon I'm beyond hope?"

"I am certain there has to be a little rebel blood in you somewhere," she said with a laugh. "I'd be willing to take my life on that!"

"And what makes you so certain?"

"Because a pure-blooded Yank could never do to me what you do and live to tell about it."

One last kiss, and Tate whistled for Tristram. The big gray trotted up beside him from his grazing spot a few yards away. "I would offer to take you up to the house, but considering the way you're dressed, I think it in both our best interests if you go on ahead. I'll be on along after a respectable time."

"Hurry!" Cam ran on ahead, blowing him kisses over her shoulder until he had disappeared from sight.

She could hardly believe her good fortune. If Tate had made arrangements to lease Hunter's Glen, that could mean only one thing. He intended to spend as much time with her as possible, and that was just fine with her. By the time she got through with him, he wouldn't even know where to find Baltimore on the map, much less make his way back up there!

11

"Why, good morning, Tate. What a lovely surprise," Cam greeted him as she descended the stairs a short while later.

After leaving Tate, she had run all the way home. Certain her escapades had gone undetected, she had scurried up the same tree she had made her escape by and swung herself in through the open window. Humming to herself, she had dressed quickly in a pale rose day dress trimmed in crimson stitches, then waited until she heard Tate's voice downstairs before leaving her room.

She could hardly keep a straight face as she said, "I thought you were in Greenville. When did you get back?"

"I arrived not more than ten minutes ago," he answered with a remarkably straight face.

"Welcome back." Cam turned to her father and gave him a quick kiss. "Good morning, sir."

"Morning, dear."

"Senator Tranter has been kind enough to ask me to stay for breakfast," Tate told her, his smile not flinching. "I hope I'm not imposing."

"Imposing? Why, heavens no. We're delighted," she returned lightly. "Just delighted."

The Senator cleared his throat. "I'll just go tell Ludie Mae to throw another slab of ham in the frying pan." As he limped passed his daughter, he mumbled softly, "You could give him a little encouragement, you know. A peck on the cheek, maybe. Poor fellow must have rode all night to get here, and it don't take much smarts to figure out why."

"My father says I should give you a little encouragement." She mouthed the words to Tate when the Senator's back was to them.

It was all she could do to keep her giggles to herself, but a stern look from Tate cautioned her to keep quiet. She gave him the little peck her father had suggested while the Senator watched from the doorway of the next room nodding his approval.

As soon as her father had disappeared around the corner, however, Cam attacked his lips with considerably more passion.

"You are going to get us both in serious trouble," he warned her, laughing. "Or one of us killed, and I think I know which one of us that would be."

"Oh, he'd never do that," she assured him, her hands pressed against his chest.

"Oh yes he would and there's no court in the land that would convict him, either." Keeping one eye open and peeled to the door leading to the back, Tate gave her a quick kiss on the mouth, then pushed her to arm's length. "Oh, yes," he said in a voice loud enough to be heard throughout the house. "Luckily, I was able to see everyone I needed to see with a minimum of difficulty and get my business conducted as quickly as possible."

A little while later, they were all settled at the big oak dining table, which was piled high with platters of ham and eggs, biscuits, gravy, grits and fried potatoes. Cam could hardly keep her eyes from Tate, or her feet from wandering up his leg as he told them of his intention to move into Hunter's Glen that very day.

Ludie Mae beamed as she poured him more coffee. "So that means you'll be staying around these parts for a spell, does it?"

He stole a look at Cam. "Yes, m'am, it most certainly does."

"Why, that's just wonderful, isn't it?" Ludie Mae gave Cam a gentle pinch as she passed by. "Isn't it, Cam?"

"Oh, yes m'am. It most certainly is," she replied solemnly.

The Senator gave much thought to chewing the ham he had just put in his mouth. "You know, I can't for the life of me place this cousin of Clayton's. I thought I knew everything about that man there was to know, and I would have remembered if he ever mentioned any family. Then again, Clayton never did strike me as being much of a family man. What did you say this cousin's name is?"

"Mr. Jonas Syler," Tate replied. "S-Y-L-E-R. I'm not quite sure how he's related. Quite a distant cousin, I believe. From what I understand, Mr. Odom, the lawyer who handled Mr. Griffin's affairs, had quite a time tracking him down."

"Jonas Syler." The Senator repeated the name again. "Can't say as that rings a bell. No matter. I am surprised, though, that this Mr. Odom hasn't found somebody before now to look after Hunter's Glen. There's been plenty of folks inquiring about it."

Tate reached for another biscuit. "Maybe the right person hadn't come along."

"Good thing Strothers didn't find out about this Syler fellow," Cam remarked as she helped herself to some more potatoes. "Otherwise, the railroad might have ended up with that land."

"The railroad?" Tate stopped chewing.

The Senator hungrily attacked his breakfast once again. "Couple years back," he explained, "Strothers got some fool notion about Coastal Mountain Railway cutting through the mountain. He talked Clayton into selling off some of his land to them with him acting as middleman."

"No doubt for a hefty commission," Cam interjected.

The Senator nodded. "No doubt. Anyway, Clayton seemed to think it was a pretty good idea at first, then he backed out. Don't rightly know why. He told me he didn't like sleeping with the devil. I took that to mean Strothers, not Coastal Mountain."

"I guess old Strothers was pretty upset about that," Tate said.

"If he was, he didn't show it. Probably had another scheme in the making by then anyway. Course, it wasn't too long after that Griffin got killed. Never could understand that horse turning on him," said the Senator, shaking his head. "Why, Clayton had brought that stallion up from a foal. He could whistle, and that horse would tear through hell and high water to get to him."

"From what Cam has told me, it is hard to believe an expert horseman like Griffin would fall victim to such an accident," Tate mused aloud. "Still, I suppose stranger things have been known to happen." He looked right at Cam.

"Oh, absolutely." Her gaze wandered across the room. Strange things always seemed to happen when Strothers was involved. The Winthrop fire, for instance, was just a little too convenient. Could the same be said about Clayton Griffin's death?

"Something wrong, Cami?" inquired the Senator. "You're not eating."

"Oh, no. Just thinking." She rearranged her eggs. There was no point in revealing her thoughts now. After all, her hatred for Strothers was no secret. Tate might just think her a bit too eager to get the noose around Strothers' neck, but she was certain that was one job that husband of Abbey's could do all on his own. "Were any provisions made in the will for Jackson?"

"Jackson? Oh, yes, Griffin's houseboy. Indeed, yes. Griffin provided quite handsomely for him," Tate answered. "He left him with enough money to live out his days quite comfortably. As a matter of fact, I'm surprised he's stayed on at Hunter's Glen these past two years."

"That old darkie worshiped the ground Clayton walked on." The Senator pushed back from the table and crossed his arms over his stomach. "He couldn't be run off with a stick."

"Hunter's Glen is the only home Jackson has ever known," Cam remarked a little sadly. "I hope you'll let him stay on, Tate, in spite of what Strothers might have said about him."

"What does Strothers have to do with it?" Tate asked.

"After Griffin died, Strothers tried to have Jackson run off the place," answered the Senator. "I have a feeling Strothers was out here nosing around, and Jackson run him off, but in any case, nobody else had the heart to make him leave. Then when word came up from Clayton's lawyer that Jackson could stay on until the heirs decided what to do with the property, there wasn't anything Strothers could do about it.

"Jackson told me he had made a promise to his master and was honor-bound to keep it," the Senator added. "Always called him Master Griffin, he did. Anyway, you just ask Jackson, and he'll tell you that "Massah" Griffin is going to come back to Hunter's Glen any day. Why, I saw him not too long ago, and he was all smiles and told me in all seriousness that Massah Griffin had indeed come back."

"Interesting," Tate mumbled.

"In spite of his little quirks," Cam interupted, "Jackson is a good man. You'd do well to keep him on. Besides, he'd be lost without Hunter's Glen, and heavens knows that place couldn't function without him."

"I have no intention of asking him to leave. As a matter of fact, I'll do my best to get him to stay on." Tate gave Cam a broad wink. "I find that I am strangely drawn to anyone who has an axe to grind with Strothers Bennett. Do you think I might trouble you to ride over to Hunter's Glen with me after breakfast and introduce me to Jackson?"

"Why, of course," she replied. "I'd be pleased to help out. Seeing as how we're going to be neighbors and all. You don't mind, do you, Senator?"

The Senator rolled back his eyes. "Since when have you asked my permission for anything, young lady. No, of course I don't mind. Besides, we need to take every chance we can to show our Northern citizens what Southern hospitality is all about."

Tate smiled. "Yes, sir. There's a lot to be said for Southern hospitality, that's for sure." He turned to Ludie Mae. "And speaking of such, that was a mighty fine breakfast, m'am. You Southern gentlemen sure are lucky, Senator. We don't get cooking nearly that fine up where I come from."

"Why, thank you, sir," said Ludie Mae, blushing at the attention. "It's always a pleasure cooking for a man with a hearty appetite."

"You know, Tate, I couldn't agree more about me being lucky," remarked the Senator thoughtfully some time later. "Yes, siree. I am one lucky cuss." His eyes latched onto Ludie Mae's flushed face. "Problem is, along with being a lucky cuss, I'm also a blind one. I reckon I'm about twenty years too late, Ludie Mae, and I'd be the first to admit to being an old, half-blind fool. Most days my rheumatism has got me down so bad I can't get out of bed without a nip or two of corn liquor. But just out of curiosity, Ludie Mae—what would you say if I was to ask you to marry me, faults and all?"

"I'd say, what took you so long?" Her reply was quick, as she went on about her business of clearing the table.

"Then that's a yea?" the Senator asked, his face all smiles.

"That's a yea," she replied.

"Hurray!" Cam exclaimed with a shout of delight. "It certainly took you long enough, Senator, but I do believe we're going to have ourselves a wedding."

Tate kissed Ludie Mae on the cheek, then gave the Senator a slap on the back. "Congratulations, sir. When's the big day?"

"Don't rightly know yet," he replied. "I thought I'd take my fiancee on a picnic up to the ridge this afternoon, and we can discuss all the details. That all right with you, Ludie Mae?"

"Whatever you say, Cameron."

Cam followed her old friend out into the kitchen and nearly choked her with bear hugs. "Finally—after all these years! I can't believe it!"

Ludie Mae sank into one of the cane-back chairs and fanned herself with her handkerchief. "Lord-a-mercy. I can't believe it either. The way my heart's pounding, you'd think I was on the verge of an attack. Pinch me, Cam, so I'll know for sure I'm not dreaming."

Cam gave her arm a playful slap. "You're not dreaming. I heard it with my own two ears. You've got two witnesses. So there's no way he can back out of it."

Ludie Mae held her chest.

"Now don't you go having a heart attack, Ludie Mae. At least, not before your honeymoon," Cam teased her.

One gray brow shot up instantly. "And what would you know about honeymoons and the like, young lady?"

"Why, I've known lots of girls who've gotten married, and according to them, that's the best part of the wedding," Cam replied without a blink.

"Too bad you and I can't both tie the knot at the same time and save the preacher another trip out here later on."

"And just who would you have me marry?"

Ludie Mae nodded in the direction of the dining room. "You might fool your pappy, honey, but don't you think you've pulled the wool over my eyes for one minute. He might be blind to the goings on around here, but I'm not."

"But Ludie Mae . . . You mean to say you'd have me marry a Yank!" Cam exclaimed in mock horror. "Why, I'm shocked!"

Ludie Mae put her arm around Cam and gave her a motherly hug. "Honey, did you see how he put away those grits? Believe you me, he's got some rebel blood in him somewhere."

Cam smiled. Not too long ago, she had made that very same observation herself!

"Well?"

"Well, what?"

"You going to marry Mr. Carruth or not?"

"And just what makes you think he's going to ask me?"

"Has he?"

"No. He hasn't. So there." Cam could hardly keep her smiles inside her. "But I'll tell you this much. If he ever does, I'd be a fool to say no."

"Penny for your thoughts," Tate said as they rode side by side down the narrow, oak-lined drive leading up to Hunter's Glen.

Cam smiled but said nothing. How could she

tell him of the little chat she just had had with Ludie Mae? Who'd have thought that she, Camille Tranter, sworn to a carefree life, would jump at the chance to walk down the aisle, and with a Yankee to boot? Who, indeed? She could hardly believe it herself. But as she had told her old friend, if he asked her, she would be a fool to say no. And the Senator didn't raise her to be a fool.

"So are you going to let me in on that little secret of yours or not?"

"No, sir. I am most certainly not." Standing up in the stirrups, Cam leaned over the saddle and kissed his cheek. "I believe I'll just keep you guessing. After all, we girls have to keep some things to ourselves."

He pulled her closer, nearly unseating her, and kissed her long and hard. "I do have my ways of persuasion, my darling."

Her fingers danced teasingly across the top of his thigh as soon as she had regained her balance in the saddle. "As do I."

"Touche!" With a great roar of laughter, Tate shot out in front. "Race you to the top of the hill."

"Cheat! You're getting a head start."

"But you're supposed to be the best rider in the county. Catch me if you can!" he yelled over his shoulder.

Cam nudged Traveller into a canter, and he lunged forward to catch up.

Her smile suddenly faded, and her mouth dropped open. Her hands went limp and she lost the rein contact. She was left balancing herself in the saddle as her horse went charging on ahead.

For a moment there, as Tate had surged on in front of her, she could have sworn that Tristram bore a startling resemblance to the horse belonging to the mysterious stranger. But it couldn't be. What a ridiculous notion. Just a coincidence. That was all!

Tate slowed down and let her catch up; then, just as they had done on the Fourth of July, they galloped neck-and-neck the rest of the way.

"You didn't have to slow down," Cam remarked, catching her breath. "We'd have caught up with you on our own."

Tate gave his horse a pat and a loose rein, then grinned sheepishly at her. "I know. You did that the first time I ever laid eyes on you."

Before she could respond, an old black man with cottonlike hair came running up the drive to meet them.

Cam waved and called out his name. "Hello, Jackson!"

His dark face was one toothy smile when he met them. "Massah Griffin. Massah Griffin. I shore is glad to see you. Figured it was 'bout time, I did."

Tate exchanged querying looks with Cam.

"That's not Mr. Griffin, Jackson," she said gently. "This is Mr. Carruth. He's going to be living at Hunter's Glen now. Do you understand?"

"Why, course he be living here. He belong here. This be his home!"

Tate offered his hand to the old darkie. "It's a pleasure seeing you, Jackson. I've been hearing nothing but good things about you."

"Why, thank you, sir." Jackson stared at Tate for the longest while, then his squinting puzzlement vanished and he was once again all smiles. "I's take real good care of this place, sir. Nobody loves it likes I do." He gave Traveller a big pat, then Tristram an even bigger one.

Taking hold of the reins, Jackson led the horses and their riders the rest of the way while bellowing "Swing Low Sweet Chariot" at the top of his lungs.

"He truly is a wonderful old man," said Cam softly. "With him around, you wouldn't have to worry about a thing."

Tate took her hand. "You don't have to convince me of that. Why, I wouldn't let him leave if he wanted to."

"Good. I thought that maybe Strothers had . . ."

"Hell will freeze over the day I let Strothers Bennett make my decisions." He lifted her hand to his lips and nibbled on her fingers. "Besides, if Strothers hates him, that's all the more reason for me to keep Jackson on."

Cam met his broad smile with an inquisitive one, but he offered no explanation. Sometimes she simply could not figure him out. If she didn't know better, she'd think he had no more use for Mr. Strothers Bennett than she did!

Hunter's Glen had changed very little since Clayton Griffin's death. The pastures were lush and green and stretched as far as the eye could see. The white fence enclosing the property had recently been given a fresh coat of paint. The only difference in the fields was that no horses frolicked there, and when Griffin was alive there had never been less than a dozen. The granite and timber house with its great stone-pillared portico stood proud and erect atop a grassy knoll surrounded by giant oaks dripping with Spanish moss. Yet, despite its rustic charm, the house had never really had a happy look about it, not like Willow Creek. Perhaps once Tate took up residence, Cam hoped, all that would change.

The closer she got to the house, the eerier the feeling enveloping her. Her heat-ridden body was quick to cool. At any moment, she almost expected the big oak doors to swing open wide and Clayton Griffin, attired in jodphurs and spit-polished black riding boots, to march out onto the porch, his riding crop tapping impatiently at his knee, demanding to know immediately the purpose of their visit.

Griffin hadn't been the friendly sort. He was a loner who didn't bother anyone and wanted the same consideration in return. Yet, unsociable as he was, Cam could not help but remember what great delight he seemed to take when she rode over to his place and sat on his fence as he schooled his horses in all those fancy dressage moves of classical riding. He didn't just ride the horses, he danced with them. Not once had she ever heard him raise his voice at his pupils or seen him take the whip to them. When he talked to them, his voice was soft and gentle and coaxing, his tone the kind one would use with a child. His love of horses said a lot about him, no matter how gruff and ornery the folks around Caesar's Head made him out to be.

Once at the house, they took off the saddles and rested them on the split-post railing out front.

"I'll jes turn these big fellows out in the field and let them chomp grass for a spell," Jackson said cheerfully. "You foks jes go on in and make yoreselves right at home. I'll be in directly."

"You're going to love it here," Cam told Tate, taking his arm. "I just know you are. Why, with a little love and elbow grease, this place could be just like it was in the old days. I'd be glad to help out if you want."

"With what? The love or the elbow grease?"

"Whichever you like."

His big hand covered hers. "I wouldn't have anybody else but you."

Her heart skipped a beat. Could she be reading more into his words and the way he said them than he intended? She really must not let her imagination run wild!

But the kiss he gave her as they stepped over the threshold was all the answer she needed.

The parlor looked just the way she remembered it from two years before when she and the Senator had come to pay their last respects. Just inside the archway was a long, maroon velvet-covered table that served as a catch-all for hurriedly discarded objects. Several sober-looking, black-bound volumes taken from the glass-doored bookcase rested there, as did a riding crop and a pair of leather gloves. A large granite fireplace occupied an entire wall of the parlor. On the mantel were some of the wooden carvings of wild animals that Griffin collected, and above it hung a painting of a magnificent white stallion pawing at the sky. In front of the fireplace were a pair of plump, deeply tufted arm-chairs covered in the same gold broche as the draperies hanging from the tall, arched windows. A long, sloping-arm sofa stood against the opposite wall and on either side were green velvet love seats separated by a striped moquette rug.

"It looks as if he never left," Cam remarked softly.

"Yes, as if it's waiting for him to return," Tate agreed. "I wish I could have met him. In spite of what most people think, I am sure he was as fine a man as they come."

"The Senator certainly thought the world of him, and he's an excellent judge of character." Cam led him on into the dining room. "What a pity he never confided in anyone. He was content to live in his own little world, sadness and all."

"What makes you think he was sad?"

"He was. You could just tell it. He needed a family. Many times, he told my father how he envied him."

"Some people make tragic mistakes and are forced to live with them the rest of their lives."

Cam let his remark pass without comment, no matter how puzzled she was by it. Perhaps the lawyer had gone into even more detail with him about Griffin's life.

Ceiling-to-floor tapestries depicting scenes from fox hunts, with red-jacketed riders atop high spirited mounts jumping hedges in pursuit of the hounds, covered the dining hall walls. In the center of the huge room was a mahogany table with enough red velvet-cushioned chairs around it to serve two dozen guests. Hanging from above was a magnificent gold-and-crystal chandelier.

"The Senator told me that Clayton used to have the finest parties in the state in this house," Cam said as she surveyed the great room. "Folks would come all the way up from the coast just to go to one of his hunt breakfasts. But that was before the war, when the Senator was a much younger man. Something happened, no one knows quite what, and Clayton withdrew into his own world. For some reason, he became bitter. Strange, isn't it?"

Tate said nothing.

One glance and she could see he was lost in his own private reverie. A peculiar look, as if of deep-felt sorrow, shadowed his face.

"Tate? Is something wrong?"

He became his old self almost immediately. "No, nothing at all. I was just thinking of all the grand parties that must have gone on here." He wrapped his arm around her waist. "Maybe I'll just have one myself in a week or two. It will give me a chance to thank all the folks who have been so kind to me and to meet the rest of my neighbors. What do you think?"

"I think that's a splendid idea." How she loved the feel of his fingers pressing tight into her flesh. There was something almost possessive in his touch, and she'd be the last to complain!

"I take that to mean you'll consent to being my hostess?"

Her heart fluttered once again. "Why, I'd be most honored, of course."

Jackson cleared his throat behind them, and they turned to see him standing the hallway. His face was still aglow with his big-toothed grin.

"I jes picked out the plumpest hen you ever did see for your dinner, suh," he said with a curt bow to Tate. "You ain't tasted nothing, suh, until you've had a mess of my chicken and dumplings. They was always Massah Griffin's favorite, and I suspect they be yours, too."

"Thank you, Jackson. I can hardly wait until noon."

"Yum," agreed Cam. "Neither can I."

Beaming happily, Jackson excused himself.

Tate offered his arm to Cam. "Lead on, madame. I am most anxious to see where the master of the house sleeps."

After a quick inspection of the library and the kitchen, they climbed the stairs. The gray stone walls rang with their laughter.

Six smaller chambers, all readied for guests, occupied the second floor.

"I've been meaning to ask you—where did you get Tristram?" Cam asked as they climbed the stairs to the loft that was given over to the master suite. "He did come from around here, didn't he? I mean, surely you didn't bring him down from Baltimore."

"Actually I bought him down in Travellers Rest. A high spirited cuss, he was. The fellow that used to own him had plenty of scars and broken bones to prove it. Why, we came all the way up that mountain bucking and rearing. It's a wonder I didn't get my neck broken. Anyway, by the time we got to the top, we had developed quite an understanding. He knew I was the boss, and I knew he'd let me keep thinking that until he got another wild hair in him."

Tate turned the brass doorknob and waved her in ahead. "What a shame this room cannot be graced with your presence each and every night."

Once again, Cam kept her thoughts to herself, but something told her he was hinting about what turn their relationship might eventually take.

Never before did she think she'd be chaffing at the bit to get tied down to any man, much less to a Yankee.

She tried to listen as Tate discussed the merits of so large a room and of the changes he intended to make, but her mind was on other, more important things—such as whether the day would ever come when she would be mistress of Hunter's Glen.

Forcing her thoughts back to the present, she surveyed the master suite, nodding her head at some of Tate's ideas and shaking it at others.

How inviting the bed looked with its high carved-walnut head and plump pillows with starched shams! It faced a large bay window that opened out onto a spectacular view of Caesar's Head ridge. She couldn't wait to see her first sunrise from that spot!

A bureau with an oval glass door and a marble top was pushed against one wall, and beside it was a tall wardrobe. A big, comfortable armchair and footstool were positioned in front of the fireplace, and beside the chair was a small table on which lay a pair of gold spectacles and an opened book, the reader's stopping place marked with a strip of satin. The neat arrangments of papers and files atop the mahogany desk made one think the room's occupant would return at any moment and continue his work right where he had left off.

"Looks rather cozy as it is, don't you agree?" asked Tate as he sat down on the bed and gazed out the window. "What a magnificent view to wake up to every morning."

"Yes, I was just thinking that very same thing myself." Cam walked slowly around the room.

"Everything is so neat and tidy. Why, there's not a speck of dust to be found anywhere. Poor Jackson, I believe he really does expect Clayton to come back any day now."

Tate patted the space beside him. "Jackson isn't exactly who I was thinking about right then."

"Oh, and just who were you thinking about? Should I start sharpening my claws so I can scratch her eyes out?"

"Come here."

She did as she was told.

"Don't you think we should at least rest for a spell before exploring the rest of the grounds? I wouldn't want to tire you out. You might never come back."

Cam walked slowly towards him, her eyes mesmerized by his. "Why, Mr. Carruth, don't tell me you're already worn out. Why, it isn't even noon yet."

He pulled her down beside him. "Sleep isn't exactly what I had in mind."

Tate kissed open each button of her day dress, then slid the dusty rose cotton down around her shoulders, his teeth nipping at the soft flesh revealed. One hand undid the ribbon holding back her hair, then fanned the dark curls around her shoulders while the other hand explored and searched beneath the lacy underthings.

Her flesh was already all atremble from the want of his touch.

Smiling, Cam melted into him. Sleep was the furtherest thing from her mind as well.

12

Cam waved good-night to the last of the guests. The day had been a long one, but while she was worn to the bone, she wasn't the least bit sleepy. Finally, after all those years, Ludie Mae and the Senator had tied the knot at last. How pretty Ludie Mae had looked in her violet organza, and the Senator—why, no groom could have been prouder. The way he stared adoringly at his bride in spite of her blushing glances, one would have thought the newlyweds were many years younger.

Guests and well-wishers had come from miles around to hear the exchange of vows and feast on the suckling pigs that had been three days smoldering in the ground. She and Tate had stood side by side, so close the preacher could have been directing his words at them, and every time "love" was mentioned or an "I do" whispered, he would squeeze her hand. Could it be that he, too, was thinking of the day when the exchange of vows might be their own?

She had been so sure that he was about to propose when they were waltzing out under the stars far away from the others. Gazing deep into her eyes, he had very softly told her that there was something he had been meaning to get off his chest, and the sooner it was done, the better. But no sooner were his words out than who should appear to ruin the moment but Strothers Bennett. Strothers! He hadn't even been invited to the wedding, but, typically, he had showed up anyway. No doubt he had been lurking in the shadows spying on them all evening, just waiting to spoil such a perfectly blissful moment. Once Strothers had finally left them alone, she had hoped Tate would continue, but when she tactfully encouraged him to go on and tell her what had been so burdening his heart, he dismissed her sweet inquiry with a shrug of his shoulders and a quick peck on her cheek before whirling her into the square-dance circle. Damn Strothers! What a knack he had for showing up at the most inopportune times!

Though somewhat disappointed, Cam knew it was only a question of time before Tate revealed his intentions. So close had they become, it was as if they had both been waiting all their days for the other to come into their lives. Why, Tate himself had sworn he never knew what it was like to be in love until he met her, and she had certainly never experienced such overwhelming emotion before. What she had felt for the mystery man could hardly be interpreted as love. After all, if she met him on the street, she wouldn't know him from anyone else.

No, any romantic notion she had entertained about the mysterious stranger had finally been put to rest after that last encounter in the woods nearly a month before, when Strothers had finally been put in his place by the crack of the whip. It was strange that no one ever mentioned of that incident, and when Strothers was asked about the nasty scar that marred an otherwise flawless face, he laughed it off as a careless accident incurred while driving his fancy new carriage a bit too recklessly!

During the time since that night in the woods, Cam had hardly given a moment's thought to the man in black. So busy had she been helping Tate get settled into the old hunting lodge and restoring it to the same grandeur it possessed in Clayton Griffin's better days, that she hardly had time to ride through the fields as she did each year while the tobacco was being harvested, much less to dwell on some man who just rode in and out of her life at whim on his white steed.

At first, she had tried hard not to think of the stranger, not to dwell on what might have happened between them had it been he and not Tate who had been waiting for her that night as she stepped naked out of the water. She had been so ashamed of those wanton feelings for a man whose face she had only imagined! But now, having come to terms with those feelings once and for all, she was certain that the next time their paths crossed—and she was confident they would—no tears would be shed, nor regrets felt when she told him he no longer wielded such power over her. What had begun two years before would remain in the past. There was no room in the present for him, and the only future she could envision would be one shared with Tate.

If only Tate could be convinced of that. Sometimes, she would catch him staring sadly at the gold pendant. Nothing she could say would convince him that it meant nothing more than a good-luck piece, just like the horseshoe tacked above her bedroom door or the rabbit's foot she kept tucked in her saddle bag. Still, any time she offered to take it from around her neck, he would insist it remain there to protect her when he wasn't around.

If only she could be with him right now, right at that very moment, she wished as she sat down in the old cane rocker where she had wiled away many hours deep in thought. She would show him just how much she loved him, and that no matter what, he would always be the only man for her. Always.

She turned her chair in the direction of Hunter's Glen and rocked slowly, lost in her recollections.

Every night since Tate had moved into the lodge, she had shimmied down the weeping willow and crept off into the woods where he was waiting, and Tristram would spirit them both off to their little love nest. But tonight, when Tate left, he had seemed somewhat preoccupied, distant, and she had been too proud to ask if he would be waiting for her in the hammock at midnight, for she suspected his answer would be an excuse. He just hadn't been the same the remainder of the evening after Strothers' interruption. No wonder she hated Strothers so! He seemed hell-bent on destroying her life and her family.

After the Virginia reel, when Strothers had cornered him a second time and insisted on speaking to him alone regarding some kind of business venture or another, Tate's mood had undergone a serious change for the worst. After that he had seemed despondent, lost in his own thoughts, and when she made mention of it, he neither denied it nor offered any explanation.

Once again she cursed Strothers. No doubt he took great delight in doing all he could to make her miserable. He had come to the party alone, uninvited, and making apologies for Abbey, who he said was too fatigued for festivities. Then, he proceeded to flirt shamelessly with every woman there, married or not. No decent man would have left his wife under such conditions, but Strothers could never be mistaken for a decent man, and to refer to him as a "husband" was to make a mockery of the word!

Poor Abbey! Cam could hardly stop thinking about her friend. Having to go through such agony all alone was really taking its toll on her. Yesterday, when she had paid her a visit, Abbey had been as white as a bedsheet and was so wracked with cramps she could hardly move. Doc Benton had assured her the pain was normal, a sort of preparation for childbirth, but that hadn't made the hurt any less severe. Poor Abbey. So frail was she that Cam often wondered if she would be able to hold up once the real pains began. And that husband of hers was doing nothing to make the ordeal any less painful. According to Jasmine, his late night absences were becoming more and more frequent. Some nights he didn't even bother coming home, and when he did, he avoided his wife as if she had the plague. Some comfort he was!

In spite of everything, though, Abbey seemed

to be holding up rather well and sticking to her guns about throwing Strothers out as soon as the baby was born. And Strothers was too blind to see he was treading on such thin ice. Not only did Abbey intend to kick him out of the house, she wanted him out of the mill too, and that was not going to set well by him at all!

Thank goodness Henry Sullivan had indeed made provisions in his will to protect his only child from the likes of opportunists such as Strothers. What a surprise Strothers had in store for him when he found out that Abbey had the final say in the mill's management in spite of his claims, and that from now on she was going to exercise those rights, and there was nothing he could do about it regardless of what the law said about husbands' privileges! Abbey suspected he might already know what was going on, for not too long ago she had caught him nosing through her personal papers, which included her father's will and an unfinished letter from her to her Uncle Thurman in Asheville requesting recommendations for a mill manager. Strothers had made some feeble excuse about searching for a misplaced contract, but she had known he was lying all along.

Cam whistled for Beggin' and gave him a hug when he appeared at her feet. How unfair it was that Abbey suffered so when it was her husband who should be going through such anguish. But at least through her weakness, Abbey had found she possessed the strength to take control of her own life for a change. Now she, too, knew the sooner she was rid of Strothers the better! He had beaten her into the ground long enough.

Cam gazed longingly into the woods. No amount of wishing was going to make Tate suddenly reappear and sweep her up onto his horse. Perhaps that was just one of those times when he wanted to be alone. There was nothing she could do about it. Had she pushed for an explanation, he might have thought she was smothering him, and no man liked that, especially one who so cherished his independence.

One more wistful sigh in the direction of the hammock, and Cam rose from the rocker and went into the house. There was no use crying tonight. Tomorrow was going to be a busy day. More tobacco was to be cut, and she didn't want to disappoint her father by not being by his side. And later in the day, she had to get back into town to see her dear friend. Somebody had to help her pull through this!

A few minutes later, Cam fell across the bed and closed her eyes. Sleep would be much easier coming than she had thought.

She settled her head into her pillow with a sigh and a smile. Even if she couldn't be with Tate right then, she could think about him all the same, and they would meet in her dreams.

It seemed her eyes had only just fallen shut when they came open again suddenly. She hadn't woken up afraid in many, many years—not since she was a little girl. She looked around the room in startled dismay. If she had just had a nightmare, she certainly couldn't remember it, but something had caused her to break out in a cold sweat. Her body shivered despite the heat. Something was wrong. Something was very wrong!

Abbey! She was her first thought.

Abbey was in bad trouble. She hadn't just dreamed it! She could feel it. Abbey needed her desperately. She had to go to her now. There wasn't a moment to lose.

Cam leapt from her bed and threw on an old housedress. She hesitated at the Senator's door but did not knock. There was no point in waking them up. They'd just worry, and she was already doing enough of that for all of them!

She ran down the stairs, pausing at the bottom to step into her slippers, then rushed on out the door and into the night.

Traveller's soft whinny broke the stillness. No time wasted with a saddle, she slipped a halter over his head and jumped on his back, then charged out of the stable yard at a gallop.

Abbey's life was in grave danger. She just knew it. Her feelings were rarely mistaken, and right at that moment all she could think of was death and dying!

Damn Strothers! He had been pretty drunk when he left the party. If he laid one hand on her and jeopardized her life or that of the baby, Cam would kill him and not blink twice about it. Or better yet, she'd tell Bud Cooper what had been going on behind his back and let him do it for her!

Only once as she cantered through the dark woods did she think of the man in black. When she passed by the mine, she could have sworn someone was watching her, but she didn't have time to waste on such foolishness. Abbey needed her. She was the only real family her friend had left. She could only pray she was not too late!

"Who be out there? Who that be?" demanded

a timid voice not too far away.

"Moses? Moses, is that you?"

Abbey's houseboy stepped out from the trees, his hand holding tight to his chest.

"You done scared the life plum out of me, Miss Cam." He was panting so hard he could hardly get out his words. "Dey say Clayton Griffin's ghost haints these woods. Lot of people seen him."

"What are you doing out here?"

He dropped down onto a stump to catch his breath. "I was coming to fetch you."

"It's Abbey, isn't it! Good Lord, what's wrong?"

"She's having a terrible time birthin' that young' un, m'am. The doc, he says he doan know if she gonna make it or not."

Cam said a silent prayer. Her fears had been well-founded.

She held out her arm. "Come on, Moses, hop on. He can carry both of us back to town."

Moses shook his head. "No, m'am. I'd jes slow you down. You go on. I still gotta find Mr. Strothers. You ain't seen him, have you? No? I reckon I'll get on out to Hunter's Glen, then, and see if he's with Mr. Carruth."

"Damn him! Why isn't he at home when she needs him!" exclaimed Cam, certain that if he were there she'd wring his neck herself!

Moses shook his head. "He ain't never home no more, Miss Cam. Poor Miz Abbey, she's had to go through this all alone, ceptin' for you."

Cam had a good idea where Strothers could be found but kept her thoughts to herself. Abbey would be better off without him there. She was in enough pain as it was.

Traveller charged on into the darkness as if he were running a race. His hooves hardly touched the ground. Still, it seemed forever before they reached the Sullivan house. She was off his back even before he had time to halt.

Jasmine was waiting at the door, her big doe-eyes all red and puffy. "The pain, Miss Cam. The pain is awful. It's gonna kill her. I jes know it is." She wrung her hands in desperation. "What is we gonna do? I jus know Miss Abbey's gonna die. I can feel it in my bones. I jus know it."

Cam took her by the shoulders and gave them a firm shaking. "Now, hush up, Jasmine. You hear me. I'll have no more talk like that."

It was hard to keep her own voice calm and reassuring when she, too, had that same feeling in her bones. "We've got to be strong for Abbey's sake. You understand me?"

Jasmine took a deep breath and tried her best to smother her sobs. "Yes, m'am.

An agonizing scream pierced the floor above them, followed by a deathly stillness. The next thing Cam heard was Doc Benton's soothing voice encouraging his patient to hold on a little longer, that it would all be over soon, and she'd have her little babe in her arms.

"You'd better tear up some bedsheets and start them boiling," she told the negress. "No telling how many Doc's going to need. And while you're at it, boil some coins and brew up some silber tea in case there's a lot of bleeding."

"Oh, yes, m'am. Anything you say, Miss Cam. Jes don't let my Miss Abbey die."

Cam tried to settle her fears with a gentle pat.

"She's not going to die, Jasmine. Not if I can help it. Now you do what I told you, you hear? I'll go on up and see what I can do to help out."

She's not going to die . . . she's not going to die. . . .

Cam's words echoed inside her head.

Please, Lord, don't let her die!

Cam ran up the stairs as fast as she could go, taking two at a time and tripping more than once. Another scream made her stop cold, too numb to move, but then she collected herself and charged on ahead even faster.

The door to Abbey's room was cracked. She opened it the rest of the way and tiptoed inside.

"Cam? Cam, is that you?" a weak voice called out. "Thank God you're here."

"Shh, Abbey. Everything's going to be fine."

A pair of oil lanterns, one on either side of the bed, shed the only light in the room. Not a window was raised, yet the air was still and cool. The room smelled of sickness. Worse still, it smelled of death.

A cold shiver ran down Cam's spine. Death! Please, just this once let my feelings be wrong, she prayed silently.

Abbey lifted her arm, and with considerable strain motioned her closer.

Cam tiptoed across the room, fearful that even the slightest noise would bring on more agony. She was afraid to take hold of her friend's hand, afraid that the least pressure would squeeze out what little life remained in her feeble bones.

Abbey was half-lying, half-sitting in bed. A mountain of pillows cushioned her back and kept her propped up. Her face was a ghostly white.

There were corpses that looked more alive.

"Hold my hand, Cam. No, tighter. Tighter. I need to feel your strength." Her face contorted in an awful grimace. "The pain! My God, the pain!" she gasped. "Will it never end? It's so bad, Cam. I can't go on. It takes everything out of me. I am so afraid I'm going to die. I just know I am."

Cam looked to Doc Benton for some encouragement but received none. His expression was grave. She knew that he, too, feared the worst.

"Just breathe through the pain, Abbey," the kindly old doctor told her. "Just breathe through the pain. That's it. Deep, deep breaths. You've got to help your babe out. It needs its mama real bad, Abbey. You've got to be strong for it."

Cam dipped a washcloth in the basin of cool water beside the bed and sponged the perspiration from her friend's cold forehead. "Do you remember when we were little, Abbey, and you didn't want to jump in the river because you were afraid you'd drown? Remember what I told you?"

Abbey managed a weak nod as she sipped the whiskey Doc Benton put to her lips. "You told me not be scared. That you were right beside me and you'd not let anything happen to me."

"That's right. I am beside you now, too. And I won't let anything happen to you, Abbey. I swear it."

Abbey's respite lasted but a moment before more screams, each louder and more powerful than the last, shook the room.

"Can't you give her anything for the pain?" she pleaded with the doctor.

He shook his head. "I dare not. The baby's

weak enough as it is. A dose of laudanum or bromide would surely kill it. Poor babe, fighting for its very life!"

Doc Benton lifted the sheet from the foot of the bed and examined Abbey. "It can't go on much longer, or I'll lose them both." Scratching at his thick sideburns, he contemplated his next move. "All right, Abbey. Take a real deep breath. Now, push, sweetheart. Push with all your might."

Abbey held on tight, her fingers gripping Cam's knuckles. Her face was so twisted with misery it was hardly recognizeable.

"That's it, Abbey my girl, you're doing fine. Just fine. Now push. Push!"

Cam echoed the doctor's instructions. Hot tears stung Cam's cheeks. Abbey wasn't strong enough to endure such torture. Each breath her friend struggled to draw, she feared would be the last.

"There. That's good, Abbey. That's real good," the doctor said encouragingly. "I can see the baby's head coming. It's almost over."

One last, great groan and Abbey's head went limp on the pillows. All struggle, all movement disappeared from her body. She let go of Cam's hand.

"Abbey, Abbey—can you hear me?" Panic rose in Cam's throat. "Abbey, you can't die. Not now."

"She's not dead, Cam," he said softly, his voice strangely solemn. "She's just passed out. The pain was too great. It took everything out of her."

Cam was puzzled. If Abbey was not dead, why

did Doc sound so distraught?

She turned around to see him wrapping a blanket around the tiny form. The babe made no sound. Nor did it move. Weren't babies supposed to come into the world kicking and screaming?

"It was a little girl," he said softly, staring at the bundle in his arms. "A little girl."

"Was?"

Doc nodded. "Was. The cord got wrapped around her little neck. Cut off all the air."

"My, God, No!" Cam dropped down into the nearest chair. After all that, the baby was dead? It couldn't be. "No, it can't be dead. Not after all that hell Abbey just went through. It can't be dead. It isn't fair! It just isn't fair!"

She buried her head in her lap and sobbed for the friend who was closer than a sister and for the child who would never know life.

Doc gently laid the baby in the cradle.

Cam reached over and absently rocked the cradle very slowly as she sang a soft lullaby. The little girl was beautiful—fair-skinned and blonde, just like Abbey. No doubt her eyes were the same pale sky blue. Poor child. She looked so peaceful now. So serene and content, as if she were just sleeping. What a brave little girl! What a struggle she had put up, only to lose in the final moments. If there truly were angels in heaven, then surely she must have joined their ranks.

Cam felt a strong hand on her shoulder.

"Childbirth is a wonderful, gratifying experience, Cam," the doctor told her softly as if he knew just what she was thinking. "Only in rare cases does the mother experience such devastating pain or are the results so tragic."

Cam nodded. "What hell it's going to be for Abbey to wake up wanting to hold her babe to her breast only to find out the child has no more life in it than a rag doll."

"That's why her husband needs to be here," Doc said, his voice not without a trace of anger. "Where the devil can he be? I sent Moses to fetch him hours ago. There's not many places in Caesar's Head where a respectable man can go at this hour."

"No, but there are a lot of places to go that aren't respectable." In spite of the doctor's questioning look, Cam let it go at that. She stood up slowly. "I think I know where to find him."

She hesitated, then moved closer to the bed.

Abbey was sleeping, her breathing steady but labored. The real pain would not begin until she had awakened.

"Will she wake up soon, Doc?"

"Oh, no. Not for a long time yet," he said as he rolled his sleeves back down and buttoned them. "You go on and bring home that husband of hers. I'll be here all night."

Cam leaned down and kissed Abbey's cheek. It was cold, so cold, and the color of plaster.

The cradle was still rocking as she walked passed, but she just couldn't bring herself to look inside again.

Jasmine came running up the stairs to meet her. "How is she? How's my Abbey girl? What's wrong? She ain't dead?"

Cam shook her head. "No, she's not dead."

"Praise be to God!" Jasmine shouted. "And

the baby—how's the chile? When does Doc think it'll be borned?"

Tears welled up in Cam's eyes once more. "It was a little girl. She tried hard, but she didn't have a chance. Somehow the cord got wrapped around her neck."

Jasmine sank down onto the step and covered her face with her apron.

"Is Moses back yet?" Cam asked when the sobs quieted.

The colored girl nodded. "He's out in the kitchen, plum tuckered out. He couldn't find Mr. Strothers nowhere. "He went to the mill, to the tavern, even over to Sally Rose's, but none of her gals had seen him."

Cam gritted her teeth. It came as no surprise that Jasmine would suggest Moses look for him there. After all, at Sally Rose's run-down shack down by the river, a man could buy as much whiskey and as many women as he wanted to last him through the night.

"He even went out to Mister Carruth's but there weren't nobody home."

Her news took Cam by surprise.

"You mean Mr. Carruth wasn't home?"

"Yes, m'am. That's right. Jackson said he hadn't seen him since he left to go to your party."

How odd, thought Cam. Tate not home. Where could he be?

But she had no time to think about that now. As much as she despised the task at hand, she had to find Strothers. And there was only one place left to look for him. Mill Hill. That was where Bud Cooper lived, or rather where Nellie Cooper lived! He'd be there. Something told her he would be.

She had no choice but go and break up his little party. If only Tate could go with her—he'd know how to handle the matter.

Traveller was waiting out front, right where Cam had left him. His hooves ominously clip-clip-clopping over the cobblestones, he trotted down the quiet street into unfamiliar and what she was certain would be hostile territory.

13

Sullivan Mills was situated by the river, where the force to run its spindles and looms was generated by the huge waterfall behind it. Beyond the mill sat Mill Hill, which wasn't a hill at all. The ground was flat and bald, the earth red clay. Two dozen or more clapboard houses, all the same size and crackerbox shape, paint peeling and in dire need of repair, stood four to a row.

Catcalls and whistles greeted Cam when she turned Traveller down the first row.

"Where does Bud Cooper live?" she asked the group of men sitting on one of the porches drinking from a jug and shooting dice by candle-light.

Any other time she would have told them in no uncertain terms just what they could do with their obscene gestures and remarks, but tonight she just didn't have the time to spare.

"I asked you a question," she shouted down from her horse. "Bud Cooper. Where can I find his house?"

"You don't want anything to do with old Bud,

honey," said one as he came struggling towards her, his breeches riding low on his hips and his chest shirtless. "Not when you can have me."

He took hold of Cam's foot. "What do you say about that, pretty lady?"

Cam jerked back her leg and kicked him in the stomach as hard as she could, sending him sprawling backwards onto the ground. His friends howled with laughter.

"I asked you a question, mister," she said as she encouraged Traveller to dance around him so that his hooves came dangerously close to the spot where the man lay rolling around and holding his stomach.

"Bud don't live on Mill Hill no more," another man piped up. "He's moved over to Cedar Street."

"Yeah," joined in one of the others. "Ever since his old lady started . . ."

"You just hush up there, Ben Mabry," cautioned a third. "You want to lose your job, or maybe get that dumb neck of yours twisted in two by Bud?"

Without another word, Cam whirled her horse around and headed back into town.

It didn't take long to figure out which house on Cedar Street belonged to Bud Cooper, not when Strothers' fancy new carriage was parked right out front for the whole town to see. The bastard didn't even have the decency to try to conceal his catting around, Cam thought with contempt. But his day was coming and she sure hoped she was around then to see him get just what he deserved!

The house was all lit up, and laughter came from inside. Strothers' voice came through loud and clear. At least she'd be saved the embarrassment of getting them out of bed, Cam decided as she jumped off her horse.

She glanced inside the front door window before knocking. Through half-drawn curtains, she could see Nellie sitting on Strothers' lap, his head buried somewhere inside the ruffles of her dress.

Lounging on the sofa was the same black-haired girl Nellie had met at the hotel. Her skirt was hiked up to her knees and a lacy camisole was showing beneath a half-buttoned blouse.

Sitting at the table, his back to the window, was a second man. Like Strothers, he was in his shirtsleeves and waistcoat, but unlike his friend, he looked bored and miserable.

The man turned his head to say something to Strothers. He looked anything but pleased.

Cam could hardly believe her eyes. That man was Tate! What on earth was he doing there?

She could feel her blood begin to boil. What a stupid question! Obviously, he was doing the same thing Strothers was, the only difference being he hadn't made himself quite at home yet.

That bastard! Why, she had a good mind to—

Cam quickly calmed herself. No, now was not the time to pick a quarrel with Tate. She'd do what she had come there to do. She owed Abbey that much, though God in heaven knew she'd be better off if Strothers never showed his face to her again.

And Tate? She was not about to give him the benefit of knowing how hurt and humilated she was. As the Senator had always said, birds of a feather flocked together. What a pity it had taken Cam so long to find out the truth of that!

She rapped quickly on the door, then stepped

back, mustering all the grit she could as she listened to the shuffling commotion inside.

Nellie came to the door giggling. "Yes?"

She cracked the door just enough to peek outside, then opened itider upon recognizing the visitor. "Well, well, well, would you lookie here?" she said, all smiles. "Come to pay me a social call, have you?"

"I'd like a word with Strothers," said Cam flatly.

"With Strothers? Why, honey, I am surprised. I figured you'd be wanting to see his friend. Maybe drag him back to Willow Creek with you."

"Who's out there, Nellie?" Strothers called from inside.

"Somebody to see you, darling."

Nellie backed away, her smile anything but friendly. When Strothers squeezed passed her, she gave him a possessive pinch on the backside, her eyes not straying from Cam's for a minute.

"Hurry up, will you, darling?" she whispered loud enough for Cam to hear. "You know you can't get a gal all worked up and then run out on her."

Strothers' mouth dropped open when he saw who was standing there. "What are you doing here?" His frown turned into a thin-lipped smile, and he opened the door wider so she could see who else was there. "Never expected you to come looking for me, darling." Smile still intact, he made a big display of tucking in his shirt. "Course I knew you would sooner or later."

Her eyes glared hate. "Shut up, Strothers!"

Tate came to the door and pushed Strothers out of the way. "Cam, what is it? Are you all right?"

No, I am not all right, you bastard, but what concern of yours is it anyway? she wanted to shout at him. Instead, she took a deep breath to calm her temper. Fists clenched at her sides, she directed her words to Strothers, ignoring Tate as if he weren't there. Damn him! Why did his eyes look so pleading?

"Doc Benton sent me to get you, though God in heaven only knows what good you'll be."

Strothers snickered. "What's the matter? My old lady about to drop the young-un? Hell, I reckon she can manage to do that without me. I was there for the important part."

It was all Cam could do to keep from hitting him. "The baby's dead, Strothers, and Abbey's not much better off. Not that you care."

She turned to go, leaving Strothers standing there with his mouth hanging down.

Tate called out after her. "Cam, wait! Wait for me."

She walked away quickly, determined not to run as she heard her name repeated. The sooner she got away from that voice the better. What was he caling her back for anyway? To add salt to her wounds?

Only when she had swung onto her horse and was trotting away into the darkness away from Strothers and his floozies and away from Tate—most of all away from Tate—could she take a firm rein on her feelings.

The tears streaming down her cheeks made her feel guilty. They should be shed for Abbey, for her little girl who would never be bounced on her Mama's knee, not for some no-account Yankee bastard who had the morals of a tomcat! Damn him! Damn Strothers! Damn them all to hell!

When she returned to Abbey's room, Doc Benton was sitting on the edge of the bed, one hand holding Abbey's hand, the other nursing a glass of whiskey.

"You find him?" he asked without looking up.

"I found him." Her voice all but broke. She could not bear looking at the tiny cradle, yet her eyes refused to direct themselves anywhere else. "He'll be along shortly."

Not long afterward, the downstairs door slammed shut, and footsteps could be heard shuffling up the stairs and down the corridor.

Strothers stomped into the room. Behind him, Cam could see Tate waiting in the hallway.

"I'd like to speak to the doc alone, if you don't mind," Strothers told her. His glare was as icy as his words and cut right through her like a razor-sharp icicle.

Without speaking, Cam left the room and walked by Tate as though he wasn't even there.

"I can't tell you how it grieves me about Abbey losing that baby," Tate said as he fell into step with her. "Poor Abbey! Thank God she has you. She sure as hell doesn't have much in that no-good bastard she's married to."

Cam could hardly believe her ears. Why, he was behaving as if the incident back at the Coopers' had never even occurred.

"I could have sworn you and that 'no-good bastard,' as you call him, were the best of friends." She made no attempt to hide her bitterness. "After all, you share in the most intimate of associations."

"I think the world of Abbey—you know that, Cam."

"Save your sympathies, Tate. She doesn't need them. Not from Strothers and certainly not from you!"

Tate followed her on down the stairs and into the parlor. "We're going to have to talk. I know this isn't the most opportune of times, but what I have to say has to be said."

Cam poured herself a stiff drink from the crystal decanter on the sideboard, not even caring exactly what it was she was about to swallow.

"I really don't see that we have all that much to talk about."

"What you think you saw back at the Coopers' place wasn't what you saw at all."

He took hold of her arm; she shook herself free and walked over to the window and stared out onto the empty street. No doubt he was going to try to worm his way out of it, but she had seen him there with her own two eyes. Let him deny that! Not what she had seen at all? What did he think she was anyway? Blind? Stupid? Or both?

"I love you, Cam. You know I do. I'd never cause you one moment of regret. You do believe that, don't you?"

She shrugged her shoulders indifferently, then belted down the liquor as she had seen her father do many times. Whatever it was burned all the way from her mouth down to her toes. Thank heavens her back was to Tate, and he couldn't see the face she was making.

"Cam, look at me."

She refused to turn around.

"You're acting like a child."

She was tempted to throw her drink right into his face, then decided against it. She was going to keep her composure if it killed her!

"All right, have it your way, then. I'd prefer to look in your eyes when I give you my explanation so you'll know for sure I'm telling the truth, but if you refuse to face me, I am left with no other alternative but to address my words to your back." He hesitated. "Just turn around, Cam. It won't take but a minute to say what I have to say, then if you still want to throw that drink in my face, I'll take a step closer so you can get a better aim."

"My aim is just as good as yours." Reluctantly, she turned around and walked over to the fireplace and sat down in one of the wing chairs.

"All right, Tate, I'm listening." One hand gripped the arm of the chair, the other her glass. "Say whatever it is you feel you must say, then please get out of this room." And out of my life, she very nearly added, but something kept her from doing so. "I want to be alone."

Tate pulled the matching chair closer to hers. There was no way she could avoid his eyes. His closeness was smothering her. She could hardly breathe. The sooner it was over the better!

"When I left Willow Creek tonight, I had every intention of going home and going to bed. I've had a lot on my mind these last few days, and I just wanted a chance to collect my thoughts."

He looked to her for encouragement to go on but received none. Instead, she stared at him with a blank look on her face, wishing he'd get on with his lies and leave!

"Strothers was waiting for me when I got there. He said he had valuable information for me, proof that . . .

"Proof that what?"

"Proof of something I have been investigating. Something I am not at liberty to discuss. Not right now anyway."

"How convenient."

"Believe me, darling, if I could tell you of my involvement in certain affairs, I would, but I cannot. I just cannot. Not yet."

He certainly sounded convincing enough. Perhaps he was a better actor than she thought.

Cam allowed herself a quick glance into his eyes. He could even look her in the eye without backing down! Of course, any good liar could look you right in the eye and never blink.

"Would you care to explain how you ended up at Bud Cooper's? Not that you owe me any explanation, of course. I don't really care. I'm just curious."

She waited, taking a pretend sip of her drink and wondering how he was going to get out of that one.

Tate gave his head a rather disgusted shake. "That was Strothers' doing, I'm afraid. I wanted nothing to do with it, or with them. But it seems that he had arranged a little party in my honor without the guest of honor even knowing about it, and the only way I could get the information on certain business dealings that he knew I was seeking was to go with him."

"The dealings you're not at liberty to discuss?"

He started to reach out to her, then pulled

back his hand. "Please, Cam, I know this all sounds very cryptic, but you must believe me. My God, what kind of a man do you think I am to seek the company of that kind of woman."

Cam thought long and hard over what he had just told her. True, Tate had looked pretty miserable sitting at the table while the others went about their little party. She had noticed that right off, before she even realized it was Tate she was looking at. And that certainly sounded like Strothers' tactics. Knowing him, he'd stop at nothing to stir up trouble between them.

"Well, do you believe me? Am I forgiven?"

"Had that been Bud Cooper and not me, you'd be dead now, Mr. Carruth."

"Strothers sent him down to Columbia to look at some new looms. Otherwise, I'm sure that if he had come home about then, he would most definitely have shot first and asked questions later." Once again, pleading eyes searched her face. "Am I forgiven?"

"If it all happened the way you say it did, then there's nothing to forgive, is there?"

Tate smiled his relief.

Try as she might, she could not help returning his smile, weak though her own was.

"Good. I'm glad." His smile widened.

Cam let out a heavy sigh. Perhaps she had jumped to conclusions. That wasn't the first time, and it probably wouldn't be the last. In spite of the "certain business dealings which he was not at liberty to discuss," she supposed she did trust him. After all, until she heard to the contrary with her own two ears, she had no reason to doubt his honesty.

She chanced another look at him, this time allowing her eyes to be taken captive by his intense green stare. "When I saw you at Nellie's with Strothers and that other woman—well, I must confess, all kinds of horrible thoughts ran through my head."

"I know. I know, darling, and I couldn't blame you at all. It must have looked very incriminating indeed. You thought me no better than Strothers, but you must believe me when I say we are two completely different men."

"But knowing what you know about him, how can you continue associating with him? Why, he'd cut you dead if he thought he had something to gain from it."

Tate nodded in agreement but volunteered no answers.

"I know." She said and repeated his words, "But in business, certain associations are necessary, no matter how unsavory."

"Trust me, Cam. Just trust me."

He pulled her to her feet, then put both arms around her waist and pulled her close. She offered no resistance. Instead, she sank into the comfort of his hold, welcoming his strength. The events of the past few hours had certainly taken their toll.

She began to sob. "It was horrible, Tate. Much too horrible to describe." Tears flowed down her cheeks. "Poor Abbey! What agony, what suffering she had to endure, and then after all that for the baby to be born dead. It just isn't fair. Abbey has known nothing but grief and sorrow this past year. First she lost her father, then she got trapped in that awful marriage, and now this. It's just not fair!"

"No, it isn't, dearest. Not fair at all." He pulled her even closer and kissed away her tears. "But no one ever said life is supposed to be fair."

She felt his body stiffen.

"Damn Strothers," he said with undisguised disgust. "You'd think he could have shown a little more compassion and understanding when she needed him. Maybe this will give him cause to mend his ways. God knows, Abbey is going to need him now more than ever."

"Hell would freeze over before that man ever thought of anybody but himself," Cam said bitterly. "The only reason he married her was because of the mill, and the only reason he wanted that baby was to secure his position at the mill."

"Hard to believe any human can be so cold, isn't it?"

"He's hardly human." She noticed he made no effort to defend Strothers. Tate knew just how underhanded he was, no doubt, and something told her he had found out from past experience—but what? What could possibly have persuaded him to stay friendly with a man who would stop at nothing short of murder to get what he wanted? Revenge? Perhaps.

Strothers walked into the room just as she was about to put that very question to him. He said nothing to either of them, nor did he acknowledge their presence. Instead, he walked over to the sideboard and poured himself a drink. After downing the first, he poured himself a second, then a third.

Finally he turned around, the glass shaking in his hand.

"I'm glad you're not mad at my friend here,"

he said to Cam. "We were just having ourselves some fun. Right, partner?"

"She knows what went on there."

"Does she now?" Strothers gave a low chuckle before taking another long sip.

"Is Abbey still sleeping?" asked Cam quietly.

"Hell, yes." His gaze was anything but that of a rational man. "She'll be dead to the world for a day or two. Oops, poor choice of words. Sorry about that." He downed the rest of his drink, then slammed the glass down onto the marble-topped sideboard. "See you good folks later. Moses will take you home when you're ready," he told Tate. "Until then, make yourselves right at home. You don't have to do your smooching down here when there's plenty of beds upstairs."

Tate rushed over to him. For a moment, Cam thought he was going to hit him. Instead, he stood with his fists clenched by his side. "You shouldn't be going back out Strothers. Abbey needs you. Stay here with her.'

Strothers whirled around, nearly losing his balance, and brushed Tate's hand from his shoulder. "Why should I hang around this old mausoleum? She'll be out for quite a while, and I got my own needs to tend to. Besides, what I do ain't none of your business, old man."

Tate grabbed hold of his arm once more, this time making him wince. "I think you'd better stay."

Strothers gave a drunken laugh. "And who's going to make me. You?" He sobered up quickly. "Hell, Tate, there ain't nothing I can do around here. The young-un's dead. I can't bring her back, and Abbey—well, she won't even know I'm gone."

He gave Tate a little nudge in the ribs. "If it'd make you feel better, why don't you come along and watch over me. The night's not gone yet, and I know where there's a whole lot more fun just begging to be had. Why Sally Rose has some girls who'll . . ."

"You are revolting." Cam's eyes spat fire. "You are lower than low!"

Strothers' eyes spit the flames right back. "Tell you what, darling, you mourn your way, and I'll mourn mine. 'Night, all!" With a click of his heels and a curt nod to them both, he left the room without so much as a glance behind him.

Cam looked up at the dueling pistols hanging above the fireplace. She could very easily shoot him in the back and not think twice about it.

"That bastard! Mourn, did he say? Hell, he doesn't know the meaning of the word. The only tears he'll ever shed will be for himself. He doesn't give a damn about Abbey or that little girl."

She was so angry she was trembling and had to sit back down before her legs gave way.

"One day all this will come back to him. I just hope I'm around to see him suffer!"

"Oh, he'll get what he's got coming to him. You don't have to worry about that." Tate's bitterness matched her own. "If my hunch is right, Bud Cooper's not the only one who's out for blood."

"What hunch is that?" Cam was curious. Could it be he knew more about Strothers than he was letting on?

"Mind you, I can't prove it, but I wouldn't put it past him to have been involved one way or another in that Winthrop fire, seeing as how he was the only one who stood to gain from those poor folks' misfortune," Tate remarked, arms crossed behind him as he paced the floor. "From what I understand, Lennox Stone out of Besley has had their eye on that land for quite some time. They want to dig a quarry here, and there's no rockier land in all these hills than that. Strothers bought the land for peanuts and stands to make a mint if the deal goes through."

"Who told you that?"

"I have my sources."

She waited, eager for him to explain, but it was apparent he had no intention of doing so.

"I'm sure your sources are accurate," she said finally. "That sounds just like Strothers. Everything always seems to happen much too conveniently to suit his plans."

She then told him of the conversation she had at Chambers' store with Mrs. Winthrop some days before.

"And you know something else," she continued, about to reveal something she had not yet discussed with anyone, not even her father. "I've had this funny feeling all along about Clayton Griffin's death, too."

"What do you mean? You don't think it was an accident?"

She shook her head. "You ask anyone in the county, and they'll tell you if there was one man who could handle horses, it was Clayton. And that white stallion of his would have rolled over and played dead if he told him to."

"But how does Strothers fit in?"

"Remember what the Senator was telling you the other day about the railroad that went sour when Clayton backed out at the last minute?"

Tate nodded. "I see what you're getting at. Strothers did have something to gain from that partnership. A lot. But didn't Griffin end the partnership before his death?"

"It wouldn't matter. With him dead, Strothers could have bought Hunter's Glen himself, as he tried to do, and see the railroad deal through without splitting the profits with anyone. Of course he hadn't counted on not being able to find the heirs to sell it to him." She thought long and hard over what she had just said. The more she thought about it, the more sense it made. "Of course, I don't have any proof, mind you. It's just a feeling."

He kissed her cheek. "And your feelings are seldom wrong, are they?"

She remembered her feelings about Abbey earlier. "No, they're not, though God knows I wish they were sometimes."

"You know, Strothers is still hounding me to get rid of Jackson. It may be that he's afraid that old darkie knows something that will point the finger at him."

"You're not, are you?"

"Believe it or not, I like watching Strothers squirm."

"You are a most difficult man to figure out, Mr. Carruth. If I live to be a hundred, I don't think I'll ever be able to."

"At least I know you're planning on keeping me in your life that long." He squeezed her shoulders as he walked by to pour himself a brandy. "Tell me, what kind of feelings do you have concerning me? Not bad, I hope."

Cam looked him right in the eye. "I have a

feeling that you are keeping an awful lot from me, and I have a feeling, too, that you're not going to tell me what it is until you are good and ready."

Tate grinned. "Does that make you mad?"

"Just curious."

He took his watch out of his waistcoat pocket and flipped it open. "It's nearly two o'clock. I think it's time I was seeing you home."

Cam shook her head. "No, I'll spend the night in Abbey's room. If she wakes up frightened, I want her to know there's somebody there who loves her."

Tate caressed her cheek. "In that case, I reckon I'll just stay here, too. If she has two people here who love her, maybe she'll get better twice as fast."

His sweet sincerity touched her. The offer made her wonder how she could have ever doubted him. There was so much she wished she understood about him. In some ways, he was just as mysterious as that stranger on the white horse.

14

Stifling a yawn, Cam turned a page of the novel in her hands. Usually she could entertain herself for hours with a good book, but the characters held little life, and their romances and adventures seemed incredible in the cold light of reality.

It wasn't even midnight yet, and already she could hardly keep her eyes open. The strain of the last several weeks was definitely taking its toll. She had lost her rosy complexion and a couple of pounds in weight, too. She was wearing herself thin trying to be too many places at once, and there was little she could do to remedy the situation. During the day, her time was divided between Tate and her father, in the fields where the tobacco was being cut, then hauled to the curing barn back at Willow Creek where it would dry and cure for sixty days before being sent to market in the fall. If there were time before supper, she would try to snatch a catnap, but more often than not, she barely had time to wolf down a bite of supper before heading back to the Sullivan house to keep her nighttime vigil by Abbey's bed.

If Strothers objected to her being there, he kept his mouth shut—not that he was there to say much about it anyway. He came home of a morning just long enough to change his clothes and shout his breakfast order to Jasmine. Then he was out again. According to Tate, he had sent Bud Cooper off on another trip so there wasn't much doubt about where he was spending his nights. He had managed to make an appearance at the funeral, but although he might have fooled most of the folks there, he hadn't deceived Cam for a minute. What a master of deception! Grief? Why, that was merely the means of getting everything his way. Even Doc Benton was convinced of Strothers' sincerity.

Abbey moaned in her sleep, and Cam rushed to the bed to comfort her as she had so many times during the night. As a child, Abbey had been scared to death of the dark, and even as a young woman, she had slept with the lantern dimmed. That fear of being alone in the dark must have had a lot to do with her marrying Strothers so soon after her father's death—that and the fact that he had made sure he got her in the family way before the wedding so there was no chance of her backing out.

The one time Abbey had regained consciousness that awful night, she had made Cam promise not to leave her alone in the dark. And that was one promise she intended on keeping for however long she could.

How wonderful and understanding Tate had been through it all. He had sat up with her that first night, and more than once she had seen unshed tears glinting in his eyes as he stared into the empty cradle. Later, during their hours alone at Hunter's Glen, she could feel his urgency tensing every muscle in his body as he pulled her close and held her tight, but not once had he suggested making love. For many such hours, he had been content just to hold her close and give her solace. In the end, she had been the one who initiated their making love, and the torrid rush of desire that flooded them both drove them to hour after hour of unbridled passion, and as they succumbed at last to exhaustion in that big maple bed, Tate had sworn love and devotion for the rest of his days and made her promise the same.

"Maggie! Maggie!"

Abbey tossed her head violently from side to side. "Maggie . . . I can't find you. Where are you . . . come to Mama, darling."

"Shhh. Everything is just fine." Ever so gently, Cam smoothed back the damp blonde curls from her friend's forehead.

Maggie. Margaret Elizabeth. That was the name Abbey had chosen for her little daughter, in honor of her mother who had died many years before. Maggie. How many times during the night had she mumbled that name over and over again. Just hearing her call it out made Cam go all shivery. To Abbey, little Maggie was not dead. She was just sleeping.

After the laudanum had worn off the day after that night of agonizing screams and pain, Doc Benton had tried as gently as he could to break the news to her, but Abbey turned a deaf ear. Her eyes glazed over, and she rambled on and on about the big plans she had for her baby girl. There had been no point in trying to reason with her then or now.

In her mind, her little baby was happy and healthy. If she suspected otherwise, she never let on. Only at night would she be plagued with troubling dreams of not being able to find her baby. Only when it was dark did she realize something was wrong.

When the painful wails were reduced to sobs, then to silence once more, and Abbey had again slipped into a deep sleep, Cam returned to the chair. On her way, she passed the little cradle where six generations of Sullivans had slept. There would not be a seventh. Doc Benton had told Strothers that birthing another child would be sure to kill Abbey. Now, inside the cradle, snuggled in pink blankets embroidered with kittens and puppies and rabbits was an old rag doll, Abbey's favorite as a child.

To Abbey, that doll was her little Maggie. She cuddled her, cooed to her and made such a fuss over her, a person would have had to look twice to make sure it was no flesh-and-blood baby.

Even during her more lucid moments when the effects of the drug had worn off, Abbey refused to believe the little thing she was holding in her arms would never, could never, draw a breath of life. And as long as she was under the influence of a drug that left her wandering in a fantasy land, she would go on believing it. Eventually she would have to face the truth, but Doc insisted that the depression resulting from such a shock might well cause a complete mental collapse. As for Strothers, he had left instructions with Jasmine to administer her mistress a fresh dose of laudanum as soon as the old one began to wear off. Cam was certain that if he had his way about it, he would keep her groggy and bedridden the rest of her days. At least that way he could go stealing from her and the mill without anyone ever finding out about it or trying to stop him.

Tate had as much as he could take from him, too. Strothers had told him that if the baby had to die, he was glad it was a girl and not a boy. A son was what he had wanted. A son to carry on the Bennett line.

The Bennett line, Cam thought with disgust. What did Strothers want? Someone to carry on his tradition of whoring and gambling and shady business dealings? God have mercy on any child sired by that no-account bastard.

Why Tate still bothered with him, knowing all the things he did, would always be a mystery. Tate said he needed to keep a friendly relationship going because of valuable information pertaining to certain business ventures in which he was involved. When she pressed him to explain, he'd tell her the same thing he always did, that when the time was right she'd have all the answers she wanted. And just when would that time be right? she wondered for the hundredth time.

Cam closed her book. It was no use going on. The tiny black print was just making her sleepier.

She massaged her temples, but the throbbing persisted. Perhaps if she could close her eyes for just one minute . . .

Cam opened her eyes some time later, not knowing how long they had been closed. She heard the downstairs door open and close, then voices in the foyer and muffled laughter coming up the stairs. The voices were those of a man and a woman. She could hardly believe what—who—she was hearing. Strothers was bringing his whore home, to Abbey's home! Was there no end to the wickedness of that man? It was bad enough that he flaunted her in public, but to wallow in his filth under the same room where his child had died and his wife had all but given up her will to live—why, it was not only inexcusable. It was deplorable!

"My, my, my. Ain't this just the biggest house I ever did see," Nellie whispered. The softer she tried to make her voice the louder it became.

The chuckling stopped. Then came the rustle of satin and the smacking of lips.

"Mmmm . . . that ain't all that's big. Goodness me, he is plum monstrous. You must have some horse in you somewhere down the line, lover boy."

"You wait till you start riding that sucker, sugar. I'll show you just what kind of a stud I am."

Cam tried to close her ears to the moans and groans and animal-like grunts that followed, but it was useless. What was he going to do? Take her right there in the hall?

"Them love juices of yours as hot as hell, darling. I believe you've done gone and blistered my fingers."

"Reckon you'll just have to use your tongue, big boy."

Cam felt sick to her stomach. How vile, how depraved they could make something so beautiful as a man and woman making love. That was the difference. They didn't make love. They coupled like two animals in heat.

"Not here. Not in the hall, Strothers." Nellie's

hushed shrieks of delight echoed through the room. "Strothers, look! Somebody's in there."

"Just my old lady, but don't worry none about her, sugar. She's so doped up she don't know if she's coming or going. Wouldn't matter much even if she did."

Nellie's voice got lower and more serious. "No, stop it. There is somebody else in there. Look, sitting in the chair."

Cam heard footsteps coming up behind her. She closed her eyes, pretending to be asleep, not even flinching at the smell of a liquored breath hot on her face.

Strothers strode back out into the hallway making no attempt to lighten his heavy footsteps. His chuckle was deep and husky. "That's just Cam Tranter. Hell, she's probably dreaming about doing what we're going to do."

"Shhh. She might hear us."

"Hell! Who gives a damn? We could teach her a thing or two about what to do with that fluff between her legs."

A long silence, then another squeal of delight from Nellie. "Oh, Strothers, you know what that does to me. I can't stand it much longer, sugar. I got to have it now. I am on fire!"

"Well, darling, you have come to the right place to get that fire put out."

The door across the hall opened, then closed, sealing inside the animal grunts and loud laughter coming.

The sun came up slowly, inching its way from inside the horizon some hours later. Wide-eyed and awake, Cam followed its journey to the treetops. As tired as she had been hours before, she could not sleep now, not with the disgusting sounds and noises coming from across the way. Why, the way Nellie screamed and Strothers carried on like he was in some contest, it was a wonder the whole town hadn't been awakened. Many times during the night she had wanted desperately to just get up and leave, but she couldn't leave Abbey there alone, not with them. She had to protect her from such sordid surroundings. Thank heavens the laudanum spared her any more grief than she already had.

Cam stood up and stretched. She had so much to do during the day, but what she really wanted to do was go home and sleep. Maybe it would be best for all if Abbey recuperated at Willow Creek for a while. Perhaps she would go by Doc Benton's on the way home and see what he thought about the idea.

She met Jasmine coming up the stairs. The colored girl was fuming.

"Why, that man. He ain't got no decency at all, Miss Cam. Why it's a shame and a disgrace the way he carries on right under his poor wife's nose."

Cam motioned for her to lower her voice, then pulled her into one of the guests chambers. "Shhh, now Jasmine, you got to watch what you say. If you make Strothers mad, he's liable to fire you and Moses, and think how bad off Abbey would be then."

"He makes me so mad I want to take the butcher knife to him, and I will if he messes with me. Why, him and that slut is in the dining room 'specting me to wait on dem hand and foot. An' you ort to hear some o' the things they talkin' about. Why, dem two's gonna split hell wide open. They are."

"I'm not so sure the devil would have them." Cam tried her best to calm Jasmine. "Tell you what. You just go on back down and go about your business. Miss Abbey is going to be up and about soon, and when she is, I suspect she'll throw him out on his ear."

Jasmine crossed her arms defiantly. "Humph. Not if'n he has any say 'bout it. Why, to hear him tell it, he can have her put in a home for the addlewitted if'n she keeps claimin' that doll is her baby."

Cam felt her blood boil. "Oh, he can, can he? Well, we'll just see about that."

Leaving Jasmine to check in on Abbey, Cam tiptoed down the stairs and ducked in behind the big Chinese screen in the library, where she could listen to what was going on in the dining room without anybody knowing she was there.

"I swear, Strothers darling, this is just the most magnificent mansion I ever did see," Nellie gushed. "All this pretty china and crystal and furniture. Why, I'd give anything to live in a house just like this."

"Anything, huh? What you got left, darling, that you ain't already given away?"

"Now you just hush up, Strothers Bennett. Bud Cooper got my cherry, and before you came along, I never did step out on him once. Do you hear me?"

"Yes, darling, I hear you. Hey, what do you

reckon your old man would do if he knew we were having a tumble behind his back?"

"There's no reckoning about it. He'd cut out your heart and feed it to the buzzards."

Strothers' laugh had a twinge of nervousness to it.

"Then I better make sure we don't get found out. Maybe I'll send him up to Asheville next week to look at some more looms."

"Oh, yes. You do that. He's started fancying himself as one of those big-shot businessmen now that he's living it up in those highfalutin hotels in those big cities. Why, he's too stupid to even suspect the real reason you're sending him off."

"Lucky for us, eh, sugar? So you think you'd like to live here in this old house of mine?"

Cam wanted to shout out just whose house it was, but she restrained herself.

"Your old lady don't know how lucky she is to have all these gorgeous things, and you to keep the bed hopping to boot."

"Why the long face?" he asked a little later.

"Oh, I was just thinking. No matter how many more raises you give Bud, we ain't never going to afford anything so grand."

"You think the only way you're going to get to live in a place like this is with Bud?"

"Considering he is my old man, what else am I supposed to think?"

"Sugar, there ain't nobody that says you have to stay with him the rest of your life."

Nellie expelled a long sigh. "Only till one of us dies. Believe you me, if'n I ever did try to leave him, he'd break my neck in two, and I ain't joshing, either."

"Not if he was dead first, darling."

Nellie gave a nervous laugh. "And just what are you talking about? Bud's as healthy as a mule. He's liable to live to be a hundred, God forbid!"

"Healthy men have accidents, too."

"Accidents? What kind of accidents?"

"Oh, whatever kind best suits the purpose. He could get in a drunken brawl up in Asheville and get shot, or he could get cut up when somebody tried to rob him. Or maybe one of those heavy pieces of machinery he's bringing in could fall on him. Hell, sugar, that mill's a dangerous place. Accidents happen there every day. Some more fatal than others."

"I look real pretty in black." There was a hint of excitement in her voice. "My mama always told me I'd make a beautiful widow."

"I don't doubt your mama for one minute, darling. Now how about passing me some more of them eggs? If that nigger wasn't so uppity, she could be down here waiting on us. What she needs is the razor strap taken to that black ass of hers. And if'n she messes with me, I'm liable to do it, too."

"You might like it too much, Strothers." Nellie's voice became low and husky. "Remember how excited you got that night you took the switch to me?"

"I remember, honey. I remember."

"Well, if you ask me, I'm just as happy she ain't here," giggled Nellie. "If'n she was, I'd have to get my hand out of there, and it feels so nice and warm in your drawers."

"Better watch out, woman, or I'll throw you 'cross this table and ram it so far up in you, you won't ever see daylight again."

"Promises. Promises. Mmmmm. This is much better than fatback and eggs."

Cam held her hands over her ears. She had heard more than enough already. Still, she owed it to Abbey to find out exactly what it was that so-called husband of hers had planned for her!

"You know, sugar, getting rid of my old man is one thing," Nellie remarked a while later. "But the way I see it, even if you do cause him to be in an accident, we still got problems. I mean, you'd still have yourself a wife."

"Not for long, Nellie, my gal. Not for long. Ohh. Damn you. You sure know how to pleasure a man, don't you?"

Cam gritted her teeth. She could think of no words to describe those two. They were lower than low!

"So what you got planned for your old lady? Maybe an accident for her, too?"

"Nope, won't be no cause for no accident, least not if she keeps on being crazy as a bedbug." He lowered his voice. "You see, like I told you earlier, I can have her committed to the crazy house in Columbia, and if she ain't crazy when she gets there, she will be when she gets out after being around all them loons."

"But what about her family? They won't let you do that."

"What family? Hell, I'm the only kin she has. Down here, anyways. Seems like she got an uncle up in Hendersonville, or maybe it's Asheville. I can handle him, though. I turn on my charm and I'll have him swayed to my side in no time." He chuckled softly. "And to insure everything going my way, I've been seeing to it she gets three—hell, sometimes four—times the dose of laudanum that Doc prescribed. If I take it away from her all at once, she's sure to go crazy."

"You are so smart, Strothers. I do declare you have to be the smartest man I ever did know." Nellie's voice suddenly lost its delight. "Wait a minute. Even if you did put her away somewhere, she'd still be your wife, and all me and you would be is shacked up. Why, we'd be no better off then we are now."

"Better to be shacked up here in this magnificent mansion than over on Mill Hill, which is exactly where we would end up if my plan fails. However, if she is declared incompetent to handle her own affairs, then I'll be her guardian over all the money. Understand?"

Nellie sighed long and hard. "I reckon so. But if she was to die, wouldn't all that money be yours anyway, seeing as how you are her husband and all?"

"Believe me, if something was to happen to her, those cussed Tranters would have me lynched whether I had anything to do with it or not. No, to save my own skin, it's best she be kept alive. Now why the long face?"

"Sometimes I get the feeling that you're still a little sweet on Cam Tranter."

Strothers laughed. "That little tease? She might still be sweet on me, but I don't give a doodley damn. Hell fire, she might know how to get it up, but she don't know what to do with it once it's there. Believe me, I know. Poor old son-of-a-bitching Tate. He's in for one big surprise when he figures out somebody done beat him to it."

"You sure you still don't like her? Just a bit, maybe?"

"I prefer an experienced woman. Why, they know just what to do without me telling them."

Nellie giggled. "You mean, like this, sugar breeches? And this . . . ?"

"Mmmmm."

"Sugar . . ."

"Yeah . . . ?"

"You didn't mean it about me getting that slut to play around with us in bed, did you?"

"Now, darling, just how many times do I have to tell you there ain't no other woman for me but you. Here. See how you like these. I wouldn't give nothing like them to Mary Lou."

Nellie squealed with pleasure. "Oh, Strothers, emerald earbobs! Why, they're beautiful."

Cam felt a volcano seething inside her. Abbey used to have a pair of emerald earbobs that belonged to her mother. She'd bet her life that was the same pair. The day they had gone into town for a stroll and early supper at the hotel, Abbey had tried frantically to find them, but they were missing from the ivory jewelry chest she kept hidden in her wardrobe. Obviously, they weren't missing any longer. Was there no end to the depth Strothers would stoop?

"You 'bout finished with breakfast, sugar?"

"Why, I do believe you're trying to get rid of me."

"Don't forget, I got work to do down at the mill."

"Too bad," Nellie said. "I was hoping me and

you might go back upstairs for another tumble. Maybe try out a few of those funny positions from that book of yours."

"As much as I'd love to, darling, we better wait until tonight. Oh, one more thing, you better leave by the back door. Wouldn't want tongues to start wagging, now would we? Aw, come here, wipe that sour puss from off those pretty lips."

The sound of their kisses could be heard throughout the house.

"Tell you what, I'll try to stop by at noon—and say, sugar, how 'bout seeing if Molly Lou's free tonight?"

"Damn you, Strothers."

Cam could almost hear the tears swelling up in Nellie's eyes.

"You can be so cruel. You know I love you so much it hurts," she sniffed, "and still you're wanting other women. Ain't I enough for you? Don't I do everything and anything you ask me to?"

"Course you do, darling. Course you do. Come here. Let me give you a big hug. Say, remember that pretty lace shawl you were admiring in Millie Dean's dress shop? The one with the pink roses embroidered on it? Well, I'll tell you what. I'll bring it with me tonight when I come, just to show you that no other woman means to me what you do. Maybe you can strut around with nothing on but that. All right?" He smacked her on the backside. "See you later, darling."

A few minutes later, Cam was sitting on the floral settee closest to the door in plain view of the foyer. She wanted to be right where Strothers couldn't help but see her on his way out the door.

"How long you been down here?" His pale brows pulled tight together as he impatiently awaited her reply. "How long, I asked."

"Long enough." Hands folded in her lap, Cam glared him long and hard. If looks could kill, she knew he'd already be ten feet under. "You know something, Strothers Bennett? You are revolting. Absolutely revolting. I used to think you were an animal, but now I realize how wrong I was. Animals don't go round wallowing in their own filth. You do."

He took a step toward her, but the hate burning in her eyes sent him back two. "What's wrong, darling? That little scene last night get you all hot and bothered? Or maybe what you heard over breakfast got you all worked up. Hell, you know you could get a little bit of what Nellie's been getting a whole lot if you'd just ask me real nice."

Cam stood up and stared him right in the eye. He was the one who finally dropped his eyes to the Oriental rug, not she.

"Don't make me sick, Strothers. The only females who get all hot and bothered by you are the whores who get paid for it."

"Why, Cami Tranter, I do believe you're jealous."

Eyes leering and lips all but smacking, he made a grab for her arm, then backed off when she lifted it against him.

Her smile was venemous. "You lay one hand on me, and I swear you'll wake up dead tomorrow."

"What you gonna do? Sic that crazy man with the white horse on me?"

She laughed. "I noticed you didn't stay around him too long. Nasty scar you got there, Strothers. Nasty, indeed. How would you like to have one on the other side to match?"

His hand dropped back down to his side. "So just what is all this about? Surely you're not going to start sermonizing to me, are you? If you are, I ain't in the mood."

"Your soul isn't worth saving."

Strothers made his way to the sideboard, his strides cocky and deliberately slowed, and poured himself a drink. "Just get to the point. I'm a busy man. Say what you got to say and get out."

"Busy? Busy doing what? Stealing and spending the Sullivan fortune?"

"Stealing? Spending? How you go on! Why I'm just looking after the interests of my poor, troubled wife. A husband's got rights, don't you know that?"

"And do those rights give you permission to bring your whores into your wife's home and bed them right under her nose?"

Laughing, Strothers downed his first drink and poured another. "I'll bet you had your pretty little ear to the door all night, didn't you? Learn anything, darling? Or maybe you'd like special lessons from the teacher?"

Cam said nothing. Her poison glare quickly made his good humor vanish.

"So I brought some tramp here last night. What's it to you, anyway?"

"Frankly, I couldn't care less where you go or

what you do, but since my dearest friend is involved, I've taken it upon myself to make it my business." She looked him square in the eye, but he refused to look back. "Abbey has been subjected to more grief in one year than most people have in a lifetime, and you are to blame for most of it. I do not want her hurt any more. Do you understand?"

"I'm touched."

She ignored his sarcasm and continued. "I know all about your plans to have her committed, and let me give you one word of advice. Don't!"

He turned white but said nothing.

"And as far as any accidents you might have planned, I suggest you forget all about those, too."

Strothers flashed his most charming smile. "What do you take me for? Some kind of monster? Hell, sometimes a man's got to brag a little and make a lot of promises if he wants to get his way. Why, I was just shooting my mouth off to Nellie. That's all."

"I'm sure you wouldn't want anybody to go shooting off their mouth to that husband of hers, now would you?"

"There's no need for that." For once, his voice was without its usual cockiness. "No need for that at all. I think you've made yourself clear."

"Good. I was hoping you'd see things my way."

Cam knew that for once, she had the upper hand, but there was no time to gloat over it, as Strothers had proven so many times before. She didn't trust him, no matter how much he sweated at the mention of Bud Cooper. Strothers was dangerous. He struck fast and when his victim least expected it. She could not afford to let her guard down for one minute. She'd just be asking for trouble if she did.

15

An hour later, Cam was on her way back to Willow Creek after having received little satisfaction from Doc Benton. He, like so many other folks in Caesar's Head, had been taken in by Strothers' smooth talk and sincere manner. Very few recognized him for the sneaking, underhanded scoundrel he really was. Her suggestion that Abbey would recuperate best at Willow Creek was met with complete disapproval. She was better off at home, Doc had told her, in familiar surroundings with the security of a loving family.

Cam had also learned that a round-the-clock nurse would be arriving from Greenville to look after Abbey. The fact that Strothers had picked her himself made Cam all the more suspicious. It came as no surprise that Strothers had discussed with the doctor the possibility of sending Abbey away to a sanitarium, where physicians specially trained in emotional disorders would help her separate fantasy from reality. A greater shock had been that Doc Benton seemed to think such measures, drastic though they were, would prove beneficial to his patient in her present condition, and there was no way that Cam could convince him that Strothers was anything less than a caring, wonderful husband who loved his wife dearly and would do all in his power to make her well again.

Cam could barely keep her eyes open as she rode home through the woods. Traveller knew the way, and he was trotting along on a loose rein with little guidance from her.

Something made her drooping head lift quickly. Her eyes came open abruptly. She stared ahead in disbelief, then rubbed her eyes to make sure she wasn't dreaming. Standing untethered at the entrance to the old mine not more than fifty feet away was the big white steed belonging to the mysterious stranger. What was he doing in the woods in broad daylight? No doubt his rider wouldn't be far away. Perhaps she should turn around and head back into town. No, she had no reason to hide from him. Now was as good a time as any to put to rest once and for all any doubts she might still have. Running away would solve nothing.

A rush of excitement surged through her, and she nudged Traveller on. Finally, after all this time she was going to meet him. The thought of looking him square in the eye made her come alive. Would he be sporting that black cape of his? Surely not. It wasn't even eight o'clock yet and already the heat was oppressive.

Her heart skittered wildly. Finally, at long last, she was going to come face to face with the man who had for so long occupied her girlhood fantasies. She could hardly contain the excitement inside her. What would he look like? What would he think of her? Would telling him what she must about Tate be any more difficult after she laid eyes on him?

The white horse gave a low whinny.

Traveller broke stride.

Cam's mouth fell open. What a cruel trick her tired senses had played on her. What a cruel trick, indeed! That horse wasn't white; it was gray, and its identity was no more of a mystery than its owner's.

But her disappointment was short-lived. The man who was there in the flesh was far more desirable than the one who occupied only her fantasies.

Tate stepped out into the clearing.

"Good morning. I was starting to think you had taken the long way home."

She gave him a weak smile, then slid down out of the saddle and returned his kiss with as much ardor as her weary body could muster. As glad as she was to see him, his surprise had left her a little disappointed. After all, she had gotten her hopes up to meet, at last, her—no, not her, *the*—mystery man.

Disappointment fled, to be replaced by guilt, then shame. Tate was a far sight better than some phantom who haunted the woods and made silly promises to lovesick girls. When would she ever get that through her head?

"I got held up in town." She caught a whiff of food frying. "Mmmm. What is that?"

Tate offered her his arm. "Come, madame, allow me to show you to your table."

She clapped her hands in delight at what she

saw. A red-and-white-checked tablecloth covered the sump of what had once been a giant oak, and atop it were china, crystal, silver and linens all bearing the Hunter's Glen crest of horse and hound. Beyond it was a circle of rocks, and on top a low-burning fire was a skillet. Inside were huge slabs of ham and a dozen eggs.

"Well, what do you think?"

Strong hands encircled her waist, and she leaned back into his hold resting her head on his massively strong chest. "If I didn't know better, Mr. Carruth, I'd say you were an incurable romantic."

"Shh. Not so loud. I don't want the whole town knowing what a sucker I am for a pretty face."

With great decorum, he spread a blanket around the 'table,' seated her, then served her breakfast. From a wicker hamper nearby, he took out a pitcher of milk and poured her a glass.

"Credit for the hoecake goes to Jackson," he said as he cut her a piece of brown crust. "And the strawberry jam, too. My talents go only so far."

"Mmmmm. It's delicious!" Cam attacked her food with hungry vigor, forgetting all about the ladylike bites she should be taking. "Sorry. I hadn't realized how hungry I was."

"I like my women to have big appetites." Tate leaned across the stump and kissed her. "It keeps their strength up."

Smiling, she bit into more of the hoecake. Once again she could not help wondering just how many other women there had been. Not that she had any reason to be jealous of any one who came before her. It was only the ones who came after that mattered. Tate was too experienced a lover not to have had his share of women. One thing was for sure, though, he was never anything less than a gentleman with any of them. Of that she could be certain!

"So how was Abbey doing when you left her?" asked Tate between bites. "Any better?"

"She would be if Doc would put an end to all that laudanum she's been getting. Why, half the time, she doesn't know if she's coming or going." Cam shook her head sadly. The worst part of it was that she was totally helpless to anything to help Abbey. "I suggested to Doc that she stay out at Willow Creek for a while, but he wouldn't hear of it. He said she needed to be at home with her loving husband. Ha! The only person Strothers loves is himself."

She then told him about last night's dalliances right under Abbey's nose, but was careful to omit the most embarrassing details.

"I don't doubt for one minute that Strothers would stoop that low," Tate remarked after learning of the plans to bleed his wife dry of the rest of her inheritance and have her committed. "But perhaps now that you've found him out, he'll be reluctant to go through with it. If you ask me, he'd be stupid to do anything but walk the straight and narrow now."

"Oh, he'll keep walking just as crooked as ever. You can count on that," Cam said with total confidence. "Maybe it'll take him a little longer than he anticipated to get his hands on all that money, but he'll find some way to get what he wants. I'd stake my life on that."

"I know it's easy to say and damn near

impossible to do, but try not to worry so much about it," Tate told her as he traced the troubled lines on her forehead with his gentle lips. "Strothers would be crazy to harm her now that we're on to him. He's caused too much pain and suffering already to too many people. God only knows how many poor, unsuspecting souls have fallen victim to his lust for money, but Abbey will not be one of them. I give you my word on that."

Even Tate's promise wasn't enough to keep her from being upset. "But how can you stop him? How can anybody stop Strothers from doing as he damn well pleases?"

"Rest assured, darling Cam, I have my ways."

The sincerity in his words, and the kind compassion reflected in his stare did away with any doubt she might have had that he could do as he said. She wished she knew what his "ways" were, but there was no point in questioning him. So much about him still remained a mystery, nearly as much so as the man in the black cape.

She studied him in a totally different light, a little surprised at noticing certain things she had not paid much attention to before. He, too, was tall and slim and powerfully built. His caresses were strong and promising. Desire currented through him to her just as it had between her and the . . .

Cam stopped chewing in mid bite. The eggs lumped in her throat. What if . . . Could it be that . . . ? No, it wasn't possible! Tate and the mystery man? Could they be one and the same?

She remembered the dream she had after meeting Tate at steeplechase, the one in which the black-caped stranger turned out to be Tate. At first she had dismissed it as purely coincidental, but perhaps her heart was trying to tell her something even then, something her mind was too rational to let her believe.

Tate? The same man as the stranger in black? Could it be dismissed as mere chance that Tate's arrival in town coincided with the return of the mystery man nearly two years to the day? Had it been Tate who rescued her from the burning house, and all those times in the woods late at night had it been Tate whose eyes were secretly watching her all along? Had he been the one who left his whip's mark on Strother's face? That same night when she had felt the presence of her phantom friend so near, it was Tate who showed up in his place. Tate had been the one who made her fantasies of the man in black come alive. He had been the one who fulfilled her every need and desire as only one very special someone could do. Was he her fantasy lover as well as her real one? She seriously considered that possibility. Did it make sense? Perhaps such a notion was not so far fetched after all.

"You look like you're a million miles away." Tate brought her back from her deep reverie with a kiss. "Still troubled over Abbey, I know. I can't say as I much blame you."

Cam nodded. Abbey . . . among other things.

If only she could talk to him about it. Perhaps he would put her mind at ease. Still, she knew better than to mention it to him. If she were wrong, and they were two separate people, then Tate would be annoyed that she still thought of the man whose button cover she wore around her neck for good luck. Then again, if Tate were indeed the man who wore the black cape, he might just as easily deny it. After all, if he had wanted her to know, he wouldn't have kept it a secret for all that time.

No, perhaps it were best she did keep such thoughts to herself, at least for the time being, at least until she could gather the information she needed either to prove her suspicions or disprove them.

Once again, Tate interupted her deep thoughts. "Why are you looking at me like that?"

Her smile broadened. He was the man who had swept her up onto his horse that night two years ago. She just had that feeling, and her feelings seldomly led her astray. Why hadn't she allowed herself to see the truth before now? Of course, they were one and the same! The events surrounding both their arrivals were no coincidences.

"Cam! You're still looking at me with that funny little sparkle," Tate accused her, laughing. "If you don't tell me what's going on inside that pretty little head of yours, I might just be forced to pin you to the ground and find out for myself."

"I can't say I'd put up much of a resistance."

"Well?"

"Oh, all right then. Can't a girl ever have any private thoughts?" She leaned over the stump and kissed his nose. "If you must know I was just thinking how kind and wonderful and handsome you are, and how lucky I am that you took a shine to me when you could have your pick of girls. Now are you satisfied?"

"Very. But tell me, just out of curiosity, how do I compare with your other beaux? Say, the fellow in black?"

"There is no comparison, my darling. None whatsoever!"

Tate pulled her to her feet. "That is just what I wanted to hear." His lips sought hers, their power taking from her what little strength the food had just replenished.

"We'd best get moving," he mumbled, but his lips did not cease trailing kisses down the creamy expanse of her neck. "Or else this little breakfast could get out of hand."

She could feel the want pulsating through her. "Spoilsport! You know, I was always taught one should not eat and run. It's neither healthy nor polite."

His mouth found its way to her shoulders, and she prayed it would not stop there. "But you're so tired, my darling," he teased.

"Was tired. Was, as in then, not now." Cam nibbled on his ear lobe, her tongue darting in and out of his ear in slow, teasing little movements. "But I'm suddenly starting to feel very much revived. Undoubtedly that hoecake of Jackson's did the trick."

His hand moved inside her blouse, tantalizing the rosy peaks that greeted him, then slipped under the band of her skirt and skimmed over her belly to the silkiness beyond.

The slow, gentle massage sent tremors vibrating between her thighs.

She moaned softly. He knew every inch of her body, as familiarly as he did his own, as if he had devoted years, not a few months to studying it. Yet his touch never failed to elicit intense erotic excitement inside her. Would it always be as wonderful between them? Yes, she did believe it would!

"What a shame this shortcut is traveled by practically everyone in town," Tate whispered against her bare flesh.

The huksy warmth of his breath against her breasts made the burning sweetness flowing inside her still hotter.

Cam molded herself even closer, tucking her curves into the granite contours of his body. His need grew harder and harder, pulsing against her with its rigid arousal, and proving once again that the power she wielded over him was great as the power he had over her.

"You know, Tate, a Southerner believes one should never start what can't be finished, but I suppose that was one lesson in etiquette your Yankee teachers neglected."

"Don't underestimate us Yanks, my sweet."

Before she had a chance to reply, he had scooped the blanket from the ground and swept her off her feet in one swift movement.

"Just where do you think you're taking me?"

"To a Yankee's den of iniquity."

She held tight to his neck. Molten tenderness rose inside her.

"Oh, I've heard about such places," she exclaimed in mock shock. "That's where us poor, helpless Southern belles have our virtues violated. Alas, poor me, I am at your mercy. Yours to do with as you wish. Please be gentle, kind sir. I beg you."

He silenced her with more kisses.

It took but a moment to realize where he was heading. It had been years since she had been inside the cave that served as entrance into the old mine. At one time, she had known that mine shaft like the back of her hand, when she had explored all the tunnels and corridors that had long since caved in.

His strides were full of purpose and knowing. Could it be that spot was not totally unfamiliar to him? Had he explored there before, and if so, why?

Daylight had not yet found its way past the cave's arch. The air was musty, but a pleasant coolness lingered there.

"And just how do you know of the existence of such places?" Her tone was teasing, but her question was anything but. Just how *did* he know?

"This is where I dishonor all of Caesar's Head's delectable lovelies."

He set her on the ground, and she struck a provocative pose. "Then be on about your business, if you must," she said with a irrepressible giggle.

Tate undressed her slowly, almost worshipfully, his eyes savoring every luscious curve and mound revealed. Then he jerked off his own clothes so quickly that her exploration of his inviting flesh had ended almost as soon as it was begun.

He pulled her to him, not at all gently. The hysteria of desire rose inside her. He could do with her as he wished. She did not care, for only in his satisfaction could she find her own fulfillment.

His mouth not leaving hers for an instant, he lifted her into his arms, then dropped down onto his knees and laid her down upon the blanket, his rock-hard body capturing her in its prison of arousal.

There was no time for sweet words or gentle kisses. Their need was far too great, the fire flaming inside already burning out of control.

Flesh to flesh, man to woman, lover to lover, their passion shattering the last shred of self-control, they both took what they wanted. Their need was explosive, their pleasure raw and filled with a lust that knew no shame.

And afterwards, they lay drowned in a flood-tide of exhaustion as they slipped into the numbed silence of satisfied lovers.

All too soon, a shower of tiny kisses across her cheeks forced her once again to enter the world of reality.

"Mmmm," was all she could utter.

"As much as I hate to disturb so lovely a sleeping beauty, I fear I am left with no other alternative. I did promise I would meet your father out in the fields as soon as I had tended to my . . . shall we say, my personal affairs in town."

Her arms reached around his neck, and she brought his face down to hers. She could tell from the growing thickness probing into her thigh that with little effort, she could easily coerce him into staying a while longer. Still, she too needed to be out in the fields.

One last kiss, and he helped her to her feet. Clothes that had been discarded in a frenzy of passionate haste a little while earlier were now returned very, very slowly.

"Ready to go?" he asked softly.

She sighed, she could tell he hated leaving as much as she. "If we must."

A black bundle stuffed in behind some rocks

in the corner of the cave caught her eye as she headed toward opening.

Tate saw right where her curious gaze was directed. "What do you suppose that is?"

"I don't know."

But she did know, even as she mumbled her reply. She knew just as well as he what was there.

And even before she had retrieved it from its hiding place and held it up, allowing it to fall to its full length, she knew, too, that it would be the black cape and that somewhere on it would be a button missing its gold cover. The pieces of the puzzle were starting to fall into place, slowly but surely. But why had he waited so long to come back into her life? What had happened in those years? Would she ever know?

"Ah, could that be the infamous black cape?"

Cam rolled it back up and dropped it back behind the rocks. That slight twinge of sarcasm in his question had not gone undetected.

"Who knows? It might be."

Feigning indifference and disinterest, she looped her arm through his.

"Aren't you just the least bit curious about its owner?" he queried as they walked out into the light. "Don't you care just a tiny bit?"

She met his probing gaze head on. "Not at all. I only have room in my life for one man at a time, and whether you like it or not, my darling, that man is you."

Even though his smile widened and the hand on her shoulder tightened with possessive intimacy, Cam could sense that he still did not quite believe her. And she knew, too, that until she could convince him that the man in black was part of her past and nothing more, he would never reveal the reasons behind his masquarade. Somehow, there had to be a way she could convince him. Somehow, there just had to be!

16

Just as she had done for the last four Wednesday mornings, Cam sat on a bench in the town square, her shopping bag beside her. Occasionally, she would exchange small talk with one of the many passersby who frequented the town green at the same time every day, but polite chit-chat about the cooling weather, or new preacher at First Baptist, or the raid on Sally Rose's which turned out to be the old one's undoing, held little interest. With one eye peeled to the street, she watched and waited for the large, white-uniformed frame of Nurse Eliza Barnes to come waddling out of the Sullivan home and make her way to her first stop, Chambers' General Store. Jasmine had Moses follow her the first time or two and reported back that the nurse always followed the same Wednesday routine. Out of the house at ten, then to Chambers' where she collected mail and posted letters and browsed at the yard goods but seldom bought anything but peppermint sticks, then on to the bakery, Doc Benton's, and Millie Dean's Dress Shop, where she would gaze longingly at dresses much too small for her. At noon, she'd stop by the hotel for their blue-plate special, then at one sharp she would start her long walk back home.

Cam despised Nurse Barnes in spite of Doc Benton's insistence that the woman was a strict professional. Strothers called her a jewel, an indespensible jewel, and if he thought that highly of her, then Cam had all the more reason to dislike the fat, bossy nurse who took charge of the house as if it were her own and ran the staff with an iron fist. Cam suspected that she was even a bit of a nipper, for more than once during Cam's visits to Abbey she had smelled whiskey on the nurse's peppermint breath, and Jasmine swore on a stack of Bibles that the dainty little teacup she always carried around with her contained something far more potent than tea.

But her ungainly appearance, domineering nature and penchant for strong drink were not the main reasons that Cam took so instant a dislike of her. The woman refused to let her visit alone for five minutes with the "poor, darling sick child," as she called Abbey. Once or twice, she had left the room on the pretense of letting them have a nice long chat, but one quick glance into the dressing-table mirror only confirmed what Cam had suspected all along—that she was hiding in the hallway eavesdropping on them. Abbey had known it, too, and she made sure she gave gushing words of praise of Nurse Barnes' many virtues and made a fuss over how wonderful Strothers had been to see her through so difficult a period, since the "jewel" was undoubtedly reporting back to her employer every word said.

Finally, Cam saw the bulky white form ambling down the street. She waited until the nurse had disappeared inside the store before leaving the bench and hurrying in the other direction on the opposite side of the street.

Moses was standing at his post in front of the livery stable talking to his cousin, who was the blacksmith's apprentice. There, he had a good view of any place Nurse Barnes might be headed. When Cam passed, he tipped the brim of his straw hat and gave her a big smile. His job was to keep an eye on the nurse and hurry back to the house as fast as he could if she finished her errands earlier than usual.

Jasmine met her at the door. "Whew, I sure am glad that old busybody is out of this house. She's been so ornery lately. Why, I can'ts do nothin' right what without her yellin' and screamin' at me."

"We'll be rid of her soon," Cam said hopefully as she dropped her parcels on the table inside the foyer. "How's Miss Abbey doing today?"

"She'd be a whole sight better if that woman would give her a little breathing room. Why, she can't even go into her mama's sewing room lessen that nurse goes in snoopin' right behind her." Jasmine pulled a chair up to the window and took her post as sentry. "I took up some lemonade and little cakes. You two have a real nice, long visit. I'll fetch you if the old ogre comes back."

Abbey was sitting at the dressing table brushing her hair when Cam walked in. She was still weak and pale from her ordeal, as was to be expected, but each day she showed more of an improvement. There was a bit of color back in her cheeks, even though her flesh was still a bit gray. All in all, Abbey was doing well. In time, perhaps, the hurt would ease.

"I didn't think that old battleaxe was ever going to get out of here this morning." Abbey reached for her dear friend's hand and gave it a squeeze. "If Doc doesn't send her on her way soon, I swear I'm going to pick her up and throw her out the window myself."

"I'm afraid that's a job for the whole town." Laughing, Cam took the gilded brush and began brushing Abbey's pale blonde locks.

Many were the times during the past month that she had thought Abbey was lost for good. Emotionally, she hadn't recovered from the strain of losing her babe and probably never would, but at least she had begun to accept the fact that she could have done nothing to prevent it, nor could she have changed events. No longer did she sit for hours at a time rocking her rag doll and cooing to it as if it were a real baby. Now, when Nurse Barnes gave her a dose of laudanum to help her sleep and forget, Abbey didn't reach out eagerly for it but rather spit it out into a small glass she kept hidden behind her night table just for that purpose, for she had figured out for herself the drug was doing more to dull her senses than to keep her in control of her faculties.

"Did you tell Doc you want her out of the house?" Cam asked as she arranged the blonde tresses into a fashionable chignon at the nape of Abbey's neck.

"Oh, that old fool hemmed and hawed and said he was afraid I'd overexert myself, but that I should do whatever would make me feel better."

"Actually it's Strothers who insists she stay," Abbey said, making a sour face at the mention of her husband. "He's afraid I'll have a relapse, or so he says. Knowing him, he's wishing I'd have one so he could justify sending me to that crazy house. Why, he told the nurse and the doctor that he's afraid I'm going to kill myself in a fit of depression. Can you imagine that? Even as distraught as I get sometimes when I dwell on my little Maggie, why in heaven's name would I want to kill myself? That would just make it all too easy for him to take charge of everything, and I have no intention of making life a bed of roses for him. He's going to sweat it out just the way he's made me suffer. You mark my word. That bastard is going to pay dearly for what he's done to me."

Cam wanted to shout a big "hurrah!" that could be heard all the way to Willow Creek, but she kept silent. Instead, she only smiled and gave her friend an understanding nod and let her go on talking without interruption. There was so much Abbey had to get off her chest, and the best thing Cam could do would be just to listen and offer opinions and advice when asked.

"Do you know what that low down swine told me yesterday?" Abbey asked, not expecting an answer. "He got all lovey-dovey and told me right in front of that lard bucket that he wanted me to get all better real soon so we could commence work on making us another baby. What does he take me for anyway? I'm no fool. I may have been once, but I've got a lot more sense now. Doc said trying to have another baby would kill me. Kill me, mind you. Of course, I reckon that's what

Strothers has in mind. If he can't prove I'm crazy enough to be locked away, he'll just see to it I die in childbirth."

Abbey's voice began to lose its strength. When she gazed at Cam's reflection in the mirror a moment later, there was a scared-rabbit expression on her face. "To be honest with you, Cam, I wouldn't be the least surprised if he tried to do away with me himself, or pay somebody else to do it. Strothers doesn't like dirtying his own hands when he can pay somebody else."

Cam gave her friend's shoulder an affectionate squeeze and tried to make her words as reassuring as possible. "He wouldn't dare, so don't you even let such thoughts trouble you. Why, we're all on to him, and if there's one thing that husband of yours loves above all else, it's his neck. He knows the Senator and I would have it in a noose so fast it would make his head spin."

"I wish a thousand times over that I'd listened to you and never married him." Abbey braved a smile. "But there's no use crying over the past, is there? Did the Senator have a chance to look over my daddy's will?"

Cam gave her a big wink. Thank heavens she had some good news for her about that. "According to him, it doesn't matter what anybody says about husbands' rights. Your daddy left specific instructions regarding his legacy and those wishes cannot be ignored."

"Thank God!" Abbey breathed a sigh of relief. "I thought I was right, but with all that legal language I just didn't know for sure."

"You were also right about the beneficiary

being blood kin in the event you passed away. Not next of kin, but blood kin."

Abbey gave a satisfied nod. "So that knocks Strothers right out of the running. Good. At least he doesn't stand to gain anything from doing away with me. And what did the Senator say about my getting a divorce? Will that be possible?"

Cam pulled up the rocking chair and sat down beside her friend. "Now there's where we run into a snag or two. It can be done, mind you," she added hurriedly when her friend's face fell, "but it will take time to come up with sufficient cause and proof to substantiate our claims."

"No doubt they don't see adultery as just cause," Abbey remarked bitterly. "Not with the men writing the laws."

Cam tried to continue on a cheery note. "I'm sure if that weren't the case, a good many of the wives in this country would be lining up on the courthouse steps."

Would Tate be faithful? she wondered to herself. In her heart she knew the answer was yes. He was too much of a gentleman to be otherwise.

"There's one more problem the Senator can foresee. And that is . . ." Cam hesitated, not knowing quite how to broach the subject of Abbey's emotional stability.

"I believe I know what that problem is," Abbey said, frowning. "Strothers will claim that I'm emotionally overwrought because of my baby, and that I don't know what I'm doing. As good an actor as he is, he'd convince the court, but we'll find a way around that," she said a little more enthusiastically. "I have all the confidence in the world in your daddy. He'll figure out something. You just wait until I tell Strothers to pack his bags. He'll be fit to be tied!"

Cam smiled. She'd love to see the look on that bastard's face when he found out the good news.

"Why, I bet he drops down on his knees and repents and swears on his dead mama's grave that he's going to turn over a new leaf," Abbey said, chuckling.

"And do you know what else I'm going to do?" she asked as soon as they had stopped rolling with laughter. "I've decided that just as soon as I'm back on my feet, I'm going down to the mill myself and take over sitting in my daddy's big leather chair. I might not have much of a head for business, but I can damn well learn. That mill is mine and nobody can keep me from taking my rightful place there. Since Strothers took charge, all that mill's done is take, take take from the poor folks of this town. Well, it's time it started giving back a little. We do that and our profit will increase tenfold. You mark my words."

"You know, you're beginning to sound just like Henry Sullivan!" Cam hugged her old friend as tightly as she could. It had been a long time since Abbey had been so enthusastic about anything. Why, Abbey had more guts and backbone than she had ever thought possible.

"I am sick and tired of kowtowing to him," Abbey said, thoroughly heated up now. "He's not going to run over me any more. No more bedding his sluts under my nose and giving them little baubles he's stolen from me. No, m'am. If he doesn't leave this house—*my* house—of his own accord, I'll make his life in Caesar's Head so miserable he'll wish he never heard my name."

She gave Cam a defiant wink. "And don't think I can't do it, too. He thinks he's married to some puppet who dances on command, but he's got another thought coming. This puppet has danced her last jig for Mr. Strothers Bennett."

Abbey gave a quick glance toward the cradle where her rag doll lay. For a moment, her smile vanished, and Cam was certain she was about to burst into tears. Then she walked over to the wardrobe in steady, determined steps. Her eyes were watering when she turned back around after taking a dress from the closet. "You know something, Cam? I'd have made a real good mama. A real good mama."

Abbey walked into Cam's open arms. She rested her head on her shoulder and left it there for a long time.

"I know you would have, Abbey I know that."

Some time later, Jasmine burst into the room.

"You'd best be leaving, Miss Cam. Dat nurse, she's comin' up the walk, and she looks fit to be tied."

Abbey quickly wiped the tears from her eyes. "Don't you dare budge from that spot," she instructed Cam with remarkable calm. "Jasmine, when that old battleaxe arrives, you tell her I want to see her right now. Immediately. This is my house, and I do not want her in it a moment longer than is necessary for her to get her things together."

Jasmine's face lit up. "Oh, yes'm. Yes'm, Miz Abbey. I takes care of that right this minute."

Abbey winked at her friend. "I do believe this

is going to do me a world of good!"

Cam threw back her head and roared with laughter. "If I'd known you had this much piss and vinegar in you, Abbey Sullivan, I'd have never bossed you around so when we were little."

"And you should have seen the look on that nurse's face when Abbey told her if she weren't out of the house in five minutes, she was going to call the sheriff and have her dragged out by the hair on her head."

Cam was still laughing that evening as she recounted the story to Tate over supper at Hunter's Glen. "Why, I thought her teeth were going to drop out. After she left, Doc Benton came in trying to give Abbey medicine to soothe her troubled nerves, and she lit in on him, too, telling him he was a poor excuse for a doctor if all he could do was feed her medicine that kept her in a daze."

Tate shared her amusement. "And what did old Doc say to that?"

"Why, what could he say? He just looked at her like she was crazy. She set him down and gave him a piece of her mind, and by the time he left that house, he was convinced Abbey had more sense than all of us put together."

"Sweet little Abbey? I swear I didn't think she had it in her. I guess I had her pegged all wrong."

"Wait until you've heard the rest of it," Cam told him as she cut a slice of Jackson's pecan pie. "Nurse Barnes must have gone straight to the mill, because not more than half an hour after she went storming out of the house, Strothers came strolling into the bedroom sporting a big smile and carrying a huge bouquet of lillies, Abbey's favorite, in one hand and a box of chocolates in the other. He was so full of sugar this and darling that! Lord, it was sickening! Why, he was even bending over backwards to be nice to me."

"You've got to give that devil his due. When he wants to, he can charm a snake. I know. I've seen him in action more than once." Tate poured them both more wine. "I just hope Abbey doesn't give in to that charm."

"Give in? Why, by the time he got there, she was just getting started. She gave him hell up one side and down the other. You should have seen the look on his face when she told him in no uncertain terms that she wanted him out of the house, out of the mill and out of her life. No ifs, ands or buts about it! Why, you'd have thought the floor had come up and hit him in the face."

Cam stopped laughing when she realized she was laughing alone. "What's the matter? You don't think it's funny?"

Tate shook his head. "Don't get me wrong, now. I'm glad that Abbey's finally sticking up for herself, but I'm not so sure it was a good idea to let Strothers see her hand so early in the game."

Cam pushed back the pie. Suddenly, she wasn't very hungry for sweets. "What are you getting at?"

"Just that Strothers is a very clever man, and once he knows what's on Abbey's mind, he can go to work against her. Why, I don't doubt for one minute that he's at Doc Benton's right now trying to convince him that Abbey's ranting and raving is proof positive that she's a very disturbed young woman, and the sooner she gets help the better!"

"Oh, Abbey's in full control of her senses. Anybody can see that. As a matter of fact, this is probably the first time in a long while that she has been." Cam sighed long and hard. "You don't think he's going to try to cause more trouble for her, do you?"

"Strothers knows what he wants, and he's not going to stop until he gets it. He'll play the concerned, caring husband part to the hilt. You just wait and see. Before he's through, he'll have half the town feeling sorry for him and not for Abbey."

"Well, at least he'll be plotting his strategy someplace else," Cam said. "He packed up his clothes and left without a fuss. There's no doubt that he'll be trying his best to figure out a way to make Abbey take him back, but she won't relent. She sent Moses for a locksmith as soon as he was out the door and said she'd shoot him herself if he tried to break back in. She even said she'd swear to the sheriff she thought she was shooting a burglar. Oh, Lord, I hope he doesn't try to get even. I wouldn't put anything past him. You don't think he'll hurt her, do you?"

Tate took hold of her hand and brought it to his lips. Not one finger was left unkissed. "Don't worry, darling. Whatever move he makes won't be a sudden one. Strothers is very meticulous in that respect. He likes to consider all the possibilities and weigh each one very carefully before making a move. And as I told you before, I won't let him get away with anything else. Not any more. I can stop him, and I won't hesitate to do it if he starts to get out of line." His kisses lingered up her arm. "So you see, my darling, there's no point worrying over it tonight. With Moses and Jasmine standing guard, Abbey couldn't be safer. Strothers is many things, but a fool isn't one of them. He knows who'll come out on the bottom if he tangles with those two."

"Yes, I suppose you are right." Cam's smile was one of relief, her sigh one of mounting desire. "Those two would be as vicious as pit bulls if they thought for a minute that their mistress was in any danger."

He stared into her eyes with unhidden adoration. "God but you are beautiful. And to think, tonight I have you all to myself—not for just an hour or two, but all night. I can hardly believe my good fortune."

Her lashes swept across her cheeks. His voice was thick with desire. There was no wondering just what the night had in store. No wondering at all.

The night, the entire night, was theirs to do with as they wished, and what wonderful hours of endless love that quiet darkness would bring. Just thinking about it made goose bumps rise all over her. The Senator thought she was spending the night at Abbey's, and he'd never be the wiser. She didn't like deceiving him, but he probably knew what was going on anyway. She'd never been able to get much past him.

All night long! She still couldn't believe it. Why, Tate hadn't kissed her once through supper, but she could tell what had been on his mind all the same. Her thoughts were echoes of his own, she was sure. They were wasting precious time dilly-dallying over the supper table; the sooner they climbed those stairs the better.

"Would you like some coffee? Brandy?"

"No, thank you." She didn't want her senses dulled one bit tonight. She wanted to remember everything, so she could relive it all time and time again those nights she had to spend alone in her own bed.

Tate pulled her chair out from the table.

"That certainly was a delicious supper. Jackson outdid himself, I must say," Cam said casually.

"He'll be pleased to hear that." Tate brushed a kiss over her shoulder.

"Where is he? I just realized I haven't seen him once all night, and usually he's hovering about like a mother hen."

"I gave him the night off."

"Oh. He isn't sick, is he?"

"Jackson, sick? I don't think he knows what that word means. He's just been working so hard helping me fix the place up, I thought I'd let him have a little time to do as he wants."

Tate took her arm, but instead of escorting her up the staircase, he led her out onto the porch.

He inhaled a deep breath. "Hmmm. Smell that good mountain air. So fresh and clean! I can't think of anything more invigorating than the scent of balsam."

Cam wound her arms around his neck and pulled his head down to hers. "Nothing? Think real hard."

"Come to think of it, you're pretty invigorating yourself." He held her at arm's length and studied her from head to toe. "Why, I do believe you are just the most invigorating sight I ever did see, or taste." He reeled her back in, and his teeth nipped playfully at her neck while heat-filled palms smoothed her bare shoulders. "Or feel. Damn, but you are gorgeous."

Cam smiled to herself as she pressed her eager body still closer. Tate always knew just the right thing to say and do. She had set out that evening with nothing else in mind but to make an impression on him such that no other woman had ever done, and impress him she had.

Not a single remnant remained from the not-too-long-ago day when she considered feminity a curse. Many hours had been spent primping at the dressing table, but the effort had not been in vain, for she knew she had never looked lovelier or more desirable. Beautiful, he had called her. She could never quite think of herself in that light, but it made her feel good all the same that he did. Tonight she felt beautiful. Maybe she really was!

Her hair hung in loose curls around her face and down her back. Tate liked it that way, especially when they were making love, because as he had told her once after taking the pins from her hair, he loved getting his fingers all tangled up in that lush thickness.

Not too long ago, she could have cared less about her clothes, just as long as they were loose and comfortable and allowed her to jump on and off Traveller without getting caught up in the hems. Tonight, she must have tried on everything in her wardrobe trying to decide on just the perfect attire for an evening that could not be anything less than perfect as long as she was in his company. Finally, she had settled on a cornflower-blue gown with a skirt that hugged tight to her hips and a wide satin sash that made her waist look even smaller than it was. The color brought out the blue-black sheen in her hair, and the off-the-shoulder bodice with its ruffles and bows accentuated the ripe fullness contained within.

With a smile and a soft sigh, she sank back into his embrace. What pains she had taken with her toilet, only to hang her pretties on the bedpost for the night!

She nearly laughed aloud. Right at that moment, that was the only place she wanted them—on the bed post. Tate's bare flesh was all she wanted covering her.

Hot blood pounded through every vein. She could feel his excitement growing and throbbing against her. In the two, nearly three months, that they had known each other, they must have made love a hundred, maybe two hundred, times, yet each time was filled with more passion and desire than the first. He knew each intimate little detail of her body, just as she knew his. Not one part of either of them had gone unexplored by the other. No man and woman could know each other so intimately, so intensely.

Would he ever ask her to marry him? At one time she would have made a horrible face at such a suggestion, but with Tate it was different. She desperately wanted to be his wife, and if he didn't ask her soon, she'd have to do the proposing. After all, it was a leap year. But what if Yankees did not adhere to the same customs as Southern mountain folk? Or worse still, what if he said no?

"You're shivering, my darling," he whispered. "Is it too cold out here for you?"

Cam shook her head. How could she tell him the real reason for her sudden chill when her body was on fire? What if he were as opposed to marriage as she had once been? What then? Just because they were lovers was no reason to assume they'd one day be man and wife. But there was no use crying over lost maidenhood now, she reminded herself. She would rather die unmarried, without her virtue, than have missed all the passion and excitement she had enjoyed with Tate.

Even if she had it to do all over again, she would still have given herself to him. All she had to do now was to convince him that he could not possibly get along without her. There were plenty of women in the world, as he most likely knew all too well—women who, like Nellie, were all too willing to provide a little love for a trinket or two. But there was only one woman who could return his passion with the same ardor because she loved him more than she loved anything else in the world. And she was that woman!

Lips upturned in a mischievous curve, she turned around slowly. Her eyes sought his and dove into those pools of jade. She'd have him. Destiny had decreed it long before they met. It was out of her hands now.

"If I am shivering, my darling Tate, it is with the anticipation of the wonders the night has in store."

Then why are we standing out here wasting precious minutes?" His words were low and throaty.

"My sentiments exactly."

Arms wrapped tight around his middle, she peered over his shoulder and out into the darkness in confused dismay. What kind of trick was her imagination playing on her? One goblet of wine had never affected her so before. There could not possibly be a rider on a white horse at the end of the drive. No, there couldn't be!

Still, there was no denying what she was seeing with her own two eyes. He was there, out there watching and waiting.

No, she wouldn't let herself think of such nonsense. Why, Tate had been the man in black all along, hadn't he? Could she have been wrong? Perhaps they were two separate men after all.

"What's wrong, Cam? You look like you've seen a ghost."

She shook her head slowly and tried to regain her composure. A ghost was exactly what she had seen, a ghost straight out of her past. But how could she tell him that? She simply could not!

"Are you all right?" he asked again.

Her arms tightened around him. "When I'm in your embrace, I feel better than just all right."

She blinked rapidly, then looked back down the drive. There was no one there. But there had been. She was certain of that.

"Are we going to spend all night out here?" she asked him, trying to make her question light and airy.

"Not on your life." Tate swept her up into his arms. "I've got big plans for us."

Cam laid her head on his shoulder, glorying in his wonderful embrace. The black-caped stranger was all but forgotten. "Who am I to argue with the lord of the manor?"

In an Oriental vase on the bedside table was a

bouquet of prize yellow roses from Jackson's flower garden, their sweet scent dispersed on the ever-so-gentle breeze. Beside it, in a fancy silver bucket, was a bottle of champagne and two fluted crystal glasses. The bed was already turned down, and on one satin cased pillow lay a single rose. Low-burning candles scattered around the room created a soft, rose-hued atmosphere. The setting could have been no more romantic!

Cam smiled with pleasure and gave Tate an enormous bear hug when he set her down onto the rug. Their courtship had been far from traditional, but he had wooed her all the same. Tonight was no exception.

"I wanted everything to be just perfect," Tate told her upon seeing her delight.

"Oh, it is. It could not be any more so."

He uncorked the bottle and poured them each a glass of champagne. "I tried to find some violinists to serenade us with romantic love songs, but all Caesar's Head had to offer was the Kagle boys, and I don't think their fiddles know much beside toe-stomping, clogging music. It's just as well, though. If the Senator ever caught wind of what you and I have been up to, my toe wouldn't be all that got stomped."

"Oh, I don't know. The Senator thinks pretty highly of you. There aren't many Yanks he'd let on his property, much less come calling on his daughter, without filling their backsides full of buckshot."

She was tempted to tell him the truth about the promise she had made to the Senator that time about marrying—not just snatch him up as she had told him earlier—the first man she could find who could ride as well as she, but decided against it. If his reaction were anything but encouraging, the evening would be spoiled, and she certainly did not want that, not when the promise of endless hours of love had already been sealed.

Tate clinked his glass against hers. "To us, my darling Camille."

"To us." Smiling softly, she sipped the cool wine. To us. Those two words had the ring of a very promising future.

Tate rested his glass on the table, then took hers out of her hand and placed it alongside his.

Cam caught a quick breath and waited. Hours seemed to pass before he closed the distance separating them.

Arms entwined tight around her waist, he drew her to him, gently at first, then with more power until the crushing force of his chest stole what strength she had in reserve. His mouth entrapped hers, and she said a silent prayer that his lips never set hers free. Soundless cries erupted in her throat. His tongue touched and played, then probed deeper and deeper, taunting her with promises of what still lay ahead. Oh, how she ached to feel the delicious power of those muscular cords strapped to her. What hunger he awakened inside her! What reckless abandon! There was nothing she could not, would not, do—nothing at all.

His fingers did not fumble as they began unfastening her pearl buttons, but Cam stopped his hand in mid-course.

"No, my darling. You have given me so much

pleasure, it is time I returned the favor."

Candlelight danced in his eyes. "And just what do you have in mind?"

"Let me show you," she whispered. Taking his hand, she led him to the bed and motioned for him to make himself comfortable.

Her heart skittered wildly. Would he think her completely shameless and wanton if she took charge, even if only for a few minutes? No, not Tate. It would only make him realize just how much she truly did love him!

She took several steps back from the bed, her eyes not straying an instant from his, and began to pluck the first button, then the second and third with exaggerated slowness. The more labored his breathing became, the bolder her words and gestures.

"Tonight, I am your slave. Your love slave. You are my master. I am here for the sole purpose of pleasing you. I am yours to do with as you wish. Your every wish is my command."

Hips swinging in a slight but provocative sway, she stripped down to her chemise and pantalettes, making sure she took her time, to let his eyes linger a long time on each part revealed before moving on to the next.

Tate reached out for her, but she backed further away.

"This is torture," he moaned. "Let me touch you. Let me feel your warmth and softness."

"Not yet, my darling, not yet."

Her hands were trembling so she could hardly untie the ribbons closing her chemise, but when she laid it open and her breasts spilled out eagerly from their lace confines, their quivering was not from uncertainty but from eagerness to mold themselves to him.

After stepping out of her pantalettes, then kicking them across the room in one grand gesture, she stood posed in all her proud glory and allowed him one long, intense perusual before making her way around the room to each candle and blowing it out with great decorum, save for the one on the bedside table.

As though in a dream, she floated to him, her toes barely skimming the rug.

"Does my master find me pleasing?"

"Need you ask?"

Nostrils flared with heavy breaths, Tate jumped from the bed and roughly pulled her to him, his hands gliding possessively down her back as he took a firm grip on his domain. Fingers dug into her taut buttocks and pressed her into him even closer. Rapid breaths parted her lips with kisses branding her his forever.

Cam felt herself slowly being transported out of this world and into the next on a cloud of passion. In him, she had found her sole reason for existence. Without him, she could not live but could only go through the motions of life.

Without parting his body from hers, he shucked off his clothes, effortlessly tugging them away until nothing separated bare flesh from bare flesh. His hands played a beautiful serenade over her body, his fingers plucking chord after chord in erotic rhythm. Sweet, breathless moans encouraged him to delve even deeper into the territory into which only he had ever traveled.

Desire pounded her limbs with a vigor she had dared to experience only in her wildest of dreams. He had not yet entered her, not yet taken what was his, what would always be his, that which she could have given no more willingly. All-devouring tremors shook her with such force that she could have sworn the earth was trembling beneath her. Were it not for his body steadying hers, she would surely have collapsed onto the floor.

How she made it to the bed she wasn't quite sure. Had he picked her up and carried her there, or had she walked—run, perhaps—of her own accord? It mattered little, for at last she lay across the bed, her head resting on the satin pillow, and on the verge of passing out from the heavenly torment raging inside her. His lips helped themselves to a feast of sensual delights as they gorged themselves on the ripeness of her breasts and devoured the honeyed warmth further below.

At any moment, she would succumb to the delicious exhaustion swallowing her alive, but she dared not give in to the fatigue for fear of missing the next delectable course.

The moment he was astride her, she reached for him, arms and legs unable to resist the urge to tangle themselves around his powerful frame. How she wanted him! How she craved him! Every part of her hungered for him with an appetite that would not easily be sated. Such urgency, such desperation she had never before known, nor had she known it could ever exist.

She opened herself up to him without shame, and amid mumbled pleas, drew him inside her; his thick, hard shaft caressed and was caressed by the welcoming heat inside.

Arching to meet him with a need that was out of her control, she rode with the gentle rhythm he set, but as his thrusts became more fevered, her need became even more frenzied. Never had she known such desperation. She no longer belonged solely to herself. She was his and her purpose was not only to be satisfied but to satisfy his every whim.

Just when she thought she hadn't the energy to go on, new blood raced through her veins, bringing with it the strength of a high-strung horse, and she found herself coiling and recoiling, returning his thrusts still harder and faster and more demanding until her body was no longer hers alone to control.

She could feel the smile affixed to her face when she returned from her love-induced slumber a little while later. Had she been asleep for a few minutes, or a few hours? Time was precious. Not a moment was to be wasted.

Even before she opened her eyes, she could sense Tate watching her, the single light from the candle gentling his rough features. What a lucky girl—no, what a lucky woman she was. Having experienced such blissful ecstasy time and time again under his expert guidance, she could never again think of herself as a girl. She was a woman. She was Tate's woman!

Instinctively, she reached for that which gave her so much pleasure. The limp flesh came instantly alive at her gentle caresses.

Tate licked the perspiration from her breasts. "There is no rush, dearest. We have all night."

His manhood grew still bigger and prouder with each bold stroke.

"All night," she echoed softly. "And not a single moment of it do I intend to waste!"

17

The same satisfied smile of contentment that lingered on her lips throughout the night was still there when morning came. She should have been exhausted, but she felt wonderfully alive. What a night it had been! They had made love four—no, five times. She couldn't remember. The count was hardly important. What mattered above all else was that each time was better than the last, and the first had been indescribable. She had found paradise in Tate's arms, and having been there, no other place would ever compare to it.

Still smiling, Cam reached out to him. The night might well be gone, but there were still a few hours left before she had to get back to Willow Creek.

Her eyes came open quickly when her arms could not find him. The bed was empty and even bigger without him in it.

She called his name softly, then again, but there was still no reply.

Rising from the bed, she looked into the dressing room, but the sarcophagus-style tub was empty. Where could he have gone, and why had he not awakened her, if only to kiss her good morning?

She looked out the window. Beyond the barn, she could see Jackson happily weeding his vegetable patch.

The smell of ham frying wafted up from below.

Her frown faded quickly. Of course. He was preparing breakfast. It was so like him to be the perfect host and lover. And no wonder! After last night, they had both undoubtedly awakened with quite an appetite. No doubt he was planning on surprising her with breakfast in bed followed naturally by other delicious nibbles. The least she could do was to go down and help him. After all, she wouldn't want him to get all worn out before the main course was served!

Belting tight the claret silk dressing gown she had found hanging inside the dressing room door, Cam hurried from the room. Running through her head were all sorts of daring ways to make breakfast even more satisfying and fulfilling!

Her feet froze midway down the landing. There were voices downstairs. Tate's and someone else's, but she couldn't quite make out whose. Perhaps she'd best just wait upstairs, lest his early morning visitor find her there.

She turned around quickly before she reached the top of the stairs and tiptoed back to several steps above where she had stood a moment earlier. Brows pulled together tight, she strained to hear more.

Tate's early morning visitor was Strothers Bennett! What was he doing there?

Perhaps she should go back to the bedroom. After all, if Strothers found out she was there, he would find some way of making sure the Senator learned of it. Besides, what was the point of eavesdropping on their conversation? Undoubtedly Tate would tell her everything that was discussed when he came back upstairs.

Still, she was powerless to turn her body around. Instead, she found her legs had, all by themselves, taken her even farther down the staircase. Curiosity getting the best of her, she decided to listen just a moment, then she would get out of sight.

"Damn you, Strothers, you mean to say you dragged me out of bed to tell me your old lady kicked you out? What did you expect her to do after you flaunted your whores right under her nose? You're lucky she didn't take a shotgun to you."

Cam frowned. She knew that was Tate talking, but he certainly didn't sound like himself. His voice was tough, abrasive. In many ways, the aggressive tone even reminded her of Strothers'.

"You don't understand," Strothers went on hurriedly. "She didn't just kick me out of the house. Hell, the way she tells it, I don't have a pot to piss in. I don't have any claim at all to Sullivan Mill, or to the Sullivan money despite my rights as a husband. Apparently that son of a bitching Senator stuck his nose in where it didn't belong and got her all worked up over some clause or another in her daddy's will. No husbands' rights! Imagine that! You ever heard of anything so crazy?"

"Well, the Senator is a pretty smart man,"

Tate observed. "I'd lay odds he knows what he's talking about."

"So what am I supposed to do? Go back to hustling rich, fat, old wives who are bored with their husbands?"

"If you don't want to do that, then I suggest you get your ass back to town and sweet-talk Abbey into taking you back. Get down on your hands and knees if you have to. A little feet-kissing where women concerned never hurt a bit."

Cam could hardly believe what she was hearing. Why on earth would Tate advise Strothers to do such a thing, knowing Abbey was far better off without him? It just didn't make any sense at all!

"And another thing, I think you'd best send Nellie along the next time you find a reason for Bud to go out of town. You know how folks love to talk in this hick town."

Hick town? Cam's mouth dropped open. Was that what he really thought of Caesar's Head? Why, he had told her time and time again that he'd be perfectly content living out the rest of his days there! Hick town? What was going on?

"Yeah, maybe you're right. I reckon I ought to cool things down with Nellie for a while, and like you said, begging Abbey's forgiveness beats the hell out of working for a living. Say, mind if I pour myself a drink? I could use something stiff and potent."

"Help yourself, but isn't it a mite early to start hitting the bottle?"

She heard Strothers chuckle amid the clinking of glass on glass.

"I had a rough night, Tate, my man. No, rough ain't the word for it. Fact is, it was downright murderous. Nellie and a gal friend of hers worked me over real good, if you know what I mean. Drained me plum dry, they did. Don't know if I'll ever be able to get it up again."

"Really, Strothers, your escapades in bed are no concern of mine. If you want to get yourself killed by a jealous husband or a jealous woman, that's your business. Just leave me out of it."

Cam heard Strothers snickering that disgusting laugh of his.

"Poor fellow. Who's the one's that jealous? I told you that sweet little Cam was nothing but a tease, but no, you wouldn't listen to me. You had to find out for yourself."

"Need I remind you I did not come to Caesar's Head to seduce the Senator's daughter?"

"That's right. You just came to find some way of getting that land of his, not his daughter's cherry, but I tell you this, it wouldn't hurt to get either one. Hell, if you did give her a tumble or two, it might make getting those timber rights a lot easier."

Getting timber rights? Cam wasn't sure she heard right. What was he talking about? Tate knew how they stood about that. He'd not even mentioned it after she set him straight that time. What on earth had gotten into him?

She could feel the anger festering inside her ready to break open at any minute. And Tate—why was he standing there letting Strothers say such awful things? He should have punched him in the mouth.

"Tell you what I'll do, Tate, my friend. Seeing as how you've been so good with all this chaste wooing and courting, I'll get Nellie to arrange a little excitement for you. Hell fire, maybe she can come up with two gals to pleasure you all at once. There's this black-headed gal down at the mill . . ."

Strothers voice lowered; his words were suggestive, and Cam could picture that bulging-eyed leer of his.

". . . Or better yet, I know an old gal down at Sally Rose's place that'll take her turn with me and you both while the other one watches. What do you think about that?" Strothers slapped Tate on the back. "Pretty hot stuff, huh?"

Cam heard Tate take a deep breath and exhale it impatiently. "I am touched at your concern over my lonely nights, but if it's all the same with you, I believe I'll just spend them the way I want to and with whom I choose. Now, unless you have something important to discuss, I think it's time you get moving before somebody sees you here."

"If by somebody you mean Jackson, don't worry. He'll keep his mouth shut. He knows better than not to. A few of my boys will meet him in the woods after dark and give him the beating of his life."

"Strothers, don't talk like that!" Tate did nothing to mask the anger in his words. "I told you that as long as you and I are in business together, I don't want to hear of you arranging any mishaps for anybody. You understand me? Well, answer me. Do you?"

"I told you a long time ago to get rid of that no-account nigger," Strothers said bitterly. "But no, you wouldn't listen to me. You just had to have him around. Well, don't say I didn't warn you!"

"And don't say I didn't warn you." In a less threatening voice, Tate added. "Don't get so riled up over Jackson. He's an old man. He's not going to cause any trouble for you or anybody else."

"No, and he wouldn't either, not if you'd let me take care of him my way."

"Strothers!"

"All right, all right. Damn. I didn't know you were so opposed to tying up a few loose ends to protect yourself."

"Your idea of tying up loose ends would be to have that poor darkie dragged behind a wild horse from one end of the county to the other, and I'll not have it. You lay one hand on him and—"

"Hey, don't get so upset. I gave you my word, didn't I? He ain't going to be harmed. Though I don't know for the life of me why you insist he stay here. Hell, you'd think Hunter's Glen belonged to him the way he carries on."

Tate's words were cool and deliberate. "I have my reasons."

"Well, I have mine, too," said Strothers, still sulking. "Like I told you before, I don't like black niggers or white horses."

"I guess everybody's got their own bugaboo."

"What's yours, Tate?"

"I don't know. Sometimes I think you are."

Cam could almost hear Tate smiling.

"And sometimes, I could swear you don't much like me, Mr. Carruth."

"When me and you went into this little partnership of ours, Strothers, I don't remember signing a contract saying we were bound together by eternal friendship. Do you?"

Cam could hardly recognize Tate's voice. He was sounding more and more like Strothers. It was hard to tell if he was play acting, or if he was for real. Something very strange was going on, something very strange indeed.

"I know why I like you so much," exclaimed Strothers in words that were getting more slurred by the minute. "It's because underneath all your charm and polish, you're just like me. However, the way I see it, we don't have any business venture unless you can swing a way to get those timber rights."

"You just leave that to me. Like I told you when we got started, these things take time."

"Maybe Carruth Lumber has the time, but I don't. I'm used to getting what I want when I want it."

"How, by burning down houses?"

The awkward pause that followed could be felt throughout the house. Cam held her breath, wondering what Strothers would say to that. After a long time, she heard him give a nervous chuckle.

"Reckon I could deny it, but I won't, seeing as how me and you are partners and all. Hell, man, don't look at me like that. I did those folks a favor. Mrs. Winthrop, why, she all but kisses my feet when she sees me. The way she carries on you'd think I was an angel."

"The angel of doom maybe." Tate let out a heavy sigh. "Trust me. My way's the best, and we both get what we want without breaking the law. All right?"

"Well, you're as crazy as my old lady if you think the Senator is going to just turn that land over to you without putting up a fight."

"If you remember, it was you who told me he was on the verge of losing everything and would jump at the chance to sell off those rights. As a matter of fact, I believe those were your very words. Jump at the chance, you said."

"He is, or rather was, on the verge of losing it all. Damn, I don't know what happened. One day he's busted and broke, and the next day he's paying off debts all over town. Can't for the life of me figure out what happened."

"No, neither can I. Needless to say, his sudden run of luck has slowed things down quite a bit for the time being," Tate remarked thoughtfully.

"So what did you find out the other day when I saw you out in the fields with him? He trusts you. You should have been able to find out a lot."

Cam had to sit down on the step before her legs gave way. Surely what she was hearing was all a dream, and a very bad one at that. Tate plotting with Strothers to get part of Willow Creek? My God, that was a nightmare!

"I did not want to ask many questions," Tate replied quietly. "No point arousing suspicion, but I can tell you this much. There's no cause for him to be worried about money, not when he's just put up a healthy crop and has a gold mine in the one that's been two years curing. If he's facing financial ruin the way you led me to believe, you couldn't prove it by what I saw."

"Damn!" Strothers sounded frustrated. "I just can't for the life of me figure out what's happened. I was so sure. So what's this going to do about our partnership? You're not going to try and cut me out, are you?"

There was no mistaking the panic in his tone.

"What would you do if I did? Burn Hunter's Glen to the ground? Maybe have one of your boys work me over?"

Cam couldn't tell if he were joking or serious.

"Don't talk stupid, Strothers. I can't afford to have you as my enemy. I told you you'd own a quarter interest in any Carruth Lumber holdings you help me get. You've just got to be patient."

"Yeah, but right now a quarter interest in nothing ain't enough money to buy me a night at Sally Rose's. Maybe you can afford to be patient, but I sure as hell can't. Don't forget I don't have a mill or a rich wife anymore." He sounded desperate. "We've got to do something, Tate, and fast! No more of this pussyfooting around. You understand?"

"And just what do you propose to do?"

It took Strothers a long time before he answered, "Well, you could sweet-talk Cam into marrying you. After all, that land will be hers when the old man dies."

"That could be years. He's one tough old codger."

"Even tough old codgers have been known to have accidents—fatal accidents."

Cam's heart sank to her stomach. Scheming to steal Willow Creek was bad enough, but talking about killing off her father! Just how low would Tate stoop to get what he wanted?

"I hear your friend Clayton Griffin was a

tough old codger, too. Too bad he got trampled by his horse."

"What do you know about all that? Huh? That nigger's been spreading a lot of manure, hasn't he?"

"Jackson hasn't said one word about you, and quite frankly, Strothers, I don't want to hear one. If you had a score to settle with the old fellow, that's your affair. You have your ways of taking care of business and I have mine."

Cam could hear Strother's sigh of relief all the way up the stairs.

"So what about marrying Cam?" he repeated.

Tate laughed. "I need a wife like I need a hole in the head. Neither one is good for a whole hell of a lot."

"Come on, man. Be reasonable. What choices we got left? You want that land, don't you? And the Senator, he ain't going to live forever anyway, so it don't much matter if we help him along or not. Hell, you've seen the way that gal rides that horse of hers. A man would be crazy not to jump at the chance to have her stradling him like that."

"That's enough, Strothers. Why don't you use your brain to think with?" The disgust was evident in Tate's voice. "A wife is not what I came down here to get. That's one burden I don't want or need."

Cam could feel her blood boil. He was going to regret every word he said. She'd see to that!

"You came after timber land and right now marrying it seems the best way of getting it."

"You thought you were marrying the Sullivan Mill and the Sullivan money and look what happened to you. No, thanks. I'd rather do things myself—my way!"

"But your way costs time and money."

"It will be my way or no way at all," said Tate with determination. "Have I made myself clear?"

"Yeah, yeah, but I don't have to like it, do I?" Strothers' tone became more passive. "Guess I'd best be getting on back to town. Say, you don't want a houseguest for a while, do you? I don't much like living at that hotel."

"Sorry, can't help you out there. I don't think it's too good an idea for us to be seen together too much, not if we're going to pull this off."

"You're right. Wouldn't want anybody putting two and two together, now would we? What about dinner later on? Or better yet, why don't we just mosey on down to Travellers' Rest, seeing as how you don't like to do your catting around in these parts. I know a couple of gals down there that'll make your mouth water."

"Don't you ever think of anything else?"

"Hell, no, man. I ain't got where I am today being a choirboy."

Approaching footsteps made Cam run back up the stairs. Had they not been laughing so hard over Strothers' last remark, they might well have heard her tripping on the top landing.

Cam ran back into the room and closed the door softly behind her. Damn it to hell! Now what was she supposed to do? She would have liked nothing better than to get dressed and out of there as fast as possible. She needed time to herself, time to think and sort out everything she had just heard.

The man she heard downstairs was not Tate, not the Tate she was in love with. Had it all been play-acting on his part, or was there a dark side he kept hidden? After all, there had been so much left unexplained about him, and when questioned, he always evaded her with remarks that implied he had set out to snare Strothers in his own trap.

But what if she were the one he hoped to snare, or rather Willow Creek was? From the beginning Tate hadn't been completely honest about his reasons for being in Caesar's Head, and it was only after Strothers brought up Carruth Lumber's interest in the timber rights to the land across the river did Tate admit the possible acquisition of such rights had been the lure drawing him there. And just the other day, when they rode with the Senator to see the last of the burly being cut, he had asked a lot of peculiar questions, most of them pertaining to the farm's finances.

But how could he be so ruthless, so cruel, so callous? How could she have misjudged him so? He couldn't be cut from the same pattern as Strothers no matter how tough he sounded. If he were, he was a damned good actor to keep his true nature from her for so long.

What to do? Should she comfort him and demand explanation? No. If he really were out for blood, he'd just lie to her and do so ever so convincingly. Should she pretend not to have heard anything and go on as usual, waiting for him to slip and catch himself in his own devious plot, if he indeed had treachery on his mind and malice in his heart? No, she couldn't very well do that either. After hearing the horrible things she had just heard, how could she possibly go on pretending nothing was wrong? How could she revel in his embrace if there were the slightest suspicion she were being used as a pawn in his game of deceit? Still, would it not be better to carry on as before so as to keep track of his every move and not be caught off guard and unprepared? Oh, if only there were simple answers to such complicated questions!

The weight of the world could have been no heavier on her shoulders as she paced the floor. Was she so selfish that she couldn't bear to have ended what she and Tate had so intimately shared? She might pretend his caresses meant nothing, but would she be able to stay in control of the situation, in complete control, and keep her wits about her even when they shared the most intimate of embraces? No, of course not; if she did that, she'd be no better than one of Sally Rose's girls. But what a mockery he had made of what they had shared!

And just what had they shared? If he were indeed playing her for a fool, then their lovemaking had been as meaningless as his empty declarations of love—nothing more than the means by which to achieve an end!

At the sound of footsteps coming up the stairs, she jumped back into bed and dove under the covers. Too late to do anything now! She should have run when she had the chance!

Face down, head buried between the pillows, she waited and waited, wondering how after what she had just heard she could possibly look Tate in the eye and pretend to be the same person who had shared his bed with such lust and passion only a few hours before.

Damn! Why did she feel, deep down, in spite of what she had just overheard, that she, not he, was the one guilty of betrayal for even thinking him capable of such horrible acts?

The door opened, then was kicked shut.

Cam took a deep breath. Somewhere she had to find the strength to go on with this little charade.

"Good morning, sleeping beauty. Sleep well, I hope?"

Cam rolled over feigning a smile and a yawn. "As snug as a bug in a rug."

Perhaps she was over-reacting just a bit, she told herself. Perhaps the only eyes he was pulling the wool over were Strothers'.

All smiles and humming cheerfully, Tate entered carrying a breakfast tray, which he brought over to the bed and set down on the table beside it.

Cam lowered her eyes and pulled the covers up right around her, but they fell back down around her shoulders. Well, it was too late for modesty now, she thought to herself remembering the wild abandon of the night before. Perhaps she should have stayed wrapped in Tate's dressing gown.

Tate dropped a kiss on her bare shoulder. His tongue slid down in slow, teasing motions. "Ah, you shiver. That's good. Means you haven't tired of me yet."

Her pulse quickened. Was that shiver a shiver of excitement at his touch or one of confusion, and why had the blood raced to her head?

If Tate sensed any difference, he did not mention it. "For your dining pleasure, my love, I have prepared ham and gridle cakes with hot maple syrup brought especially from the woods of Maryland."

Dropping his robe onto the floor, he fanned back the covers and slipped into bed beside her, making no effort to cover either of them.

"You're unusually quiet," he said between bites. "Cat got your tongue, or is something troubling you?"

Cam met his gaze head on. She couldn't live a lie, nor could she prostitute herself if it turned out Tate was not the man she thought him to be. She was left with no alternative but confrontation. Tate could not lie to her and get away with it. If he were not telling her the truth, she would know at once, and she couldn't wait another minute to find out the truth.

"Tate, I . . ."

How could she go on? What could she say? And after she had said it, what would be left to say? Would she have the courage to face the consequences?

Tate went on attacking his food with the same vigor, oblivious to the dilemma raging inside her.

"You know, Cam, it's a good thing Strothers didn't see you a minute ago. I shudder to think of the trouble he could get me in with the Senator."

Cam looked at him in disbelief. "What are you talking about? Strothers seeing me when?"

"When you were on the stairs," he replied matter-of-factly. "I must say, that dressing gown of mine does you far more justice than it ever did me."

Her mouth dropped open. "You saw me?"

He nodded.

"You mean, you knew I was there all along?" She still could not believe her ears. "And you still said all those horrible things, knowing I was listening?"

Once more he nodded without looking up from his plate.

"But why? I don't understand."

Tate finished chewing, then put down his knife and fork. When he turned to face her, he met her querying gaze head on, fire-lit jade delving deep into indigo pools.

"Tell me the truth, Cam—did you really believe I meant those cruel things I said about you and Abbey and the Senator? Knowing me as you do, did you really think me capable of such despicable lies?" He gave a troubled sigh. "Good heavens! I believe the thought actually did cross your mind."

She knew she could not lie. She dared not. Tate could see right through her.

"Well, what else was I supposed to think?" she asked in her own defense. "You were so convincing. I was beginning to wonder if I was being played for a fool."

He gave a solemn nod. "I can understand that. Granted, it must have been quite a shock." Then he returned to his breakfast. "I can't say that I blame you. I suppose I was laying it on pretty thick, but that was the only way to make Strothers believe it. Eat up. Your breakfast's getting cold."

Cam did as she was told, feeling a little ashamed of herself for once again jumping to conclusions. When would she ever learn? But after hearing what she heard, what else was she supposed to think?

"I'm surprised you didn't jump out the window and beat a fast path home."

She smiled. He knew her all too well. "The thought did cross my mind, I must admit."

"But instead you got back in bed and pretended to have just awakened." Once again, he laid down his fork. "Suppose I hadn't let on I knew you'd been listening. Just how far would you have carried your little charade?"

"As far as I had to until the truth was out in the open." Her reply was soft but firm. "You know how important Willow Creek is to me and my father. I'd get even with anybody who tried to destroy us or take our land."

Tate's face was all smiles. "Good. I wouldn't love you if you didn't."

"Then you're not angry that I had my doubts?"

"Angry? No. A little hurt, maybe, that you'd think I was like that snake, but considering what you heard, I really can't blame you." He turned her chin to his. "Just look in my eyes now and tell me that you believe me and that you trust me."

Cam had no trouble obeying his request. She did believe him, and she really did trust him.

"Good, now eat up."

"I don't suppose you're ever going to tell me why you let Strothers think you're as despicable as he is," Cam said later, when the empty plates had been set aside and they were holding each other close, her head resting on his chest.

For a long time, Tate offered no reply. Had he

not been knotting her hair around his fingers, she would have thought he had fallen asleep again.

She expelled a heavy sigh. It seemed she had no choice but to resign herself to the fact that he had no intention of ever satisfying her curiosity. Certain questions would go answered, and she just had to recognize that.

"I have reason to believe Strothers was responsible for the death of my father," he announced finally, with remarkable calm.

His declaration took her by surprise. She remembered the night of Abbey's dinner party and the intense pain etched deep into his face when he told the Senator his father was dead.

"Oh, Tate, I am sorry. Truly I am."

"I was wrong not to have told you earlier. I know you've had your doubts about me from the start. Had I been honest with you all along, there would have been no reason for such apprehension." He took a deep breath. "However, I lacked the proof to substantiate my accusations."

"And do you have the proof you need now?"

"I have all the proof I need for myself, but not enough to bring Strothers to justice. Not yet anyway." His jaw set in determination. "But I soon will."

His resolve was almost frightening.

She knew she had reason to fear for his safety. "You must be careful. Strothers will stop at nothing to get what he wants. He has no morals, no conscience. If he finds you out, he'll try to do away with you, too."

"That's why I have to act as if I'm just as wicked as he is." His hold on her tightened. "But don't worry about my safety, my love. I can take care of myself, and by the time I'm finished with that scoundrel, he'll spend the rest of his life rotting in jail for his crimes. I'm just sorry I had to drag you into it."

"Drag me into it? Don't be ridiculous. I walked in on my own two feet."

"No you didn't. Not exactly. Not from the very beginning."

She was confused. "You're talking in riddles. I don't understand."

"Then I'd best explain." His tone became very somber. "I heard the name Strothers Bennett long before I ever met the man, and as you can guess, his reputation preceded him."

"Even up North?"

Tate nodded. "Even up North. When my suspicions were first aroused regarding his involvement in the death of my father," he continued, speaking slowly and carefully and choosing his words, "I decided that I would make his acquaintance on the pretense of wanting him to act as a go-between for me in making land acquisitions in this area. Then I would strike a business deal with him so that I could find out for myself if he were a man capable of murder."

"Timberland in particular?"

Once again he nodded. "That's right, and according to him, he had the perfect property, the choicest pineland in the entire Southeast, which unlike the majority of Dixie woods had escaped Yankee torches. According to him, it was the perfect place for Carruth Lumber to put their new sawmill. With it being on the river, transportation problems would be solved from the start."

It didn't take Cam long for her to understand the rest. "And of course Strothers relayed to you that the land could be bought for a song because the owner was in dire financial straits."

"Well, not exactly. He did tell me about the Senator being in debt, but he warned me that getting him to sell would take some doing. And I said that was fine, that I would come down here myself and help promote the deal. The fact that the Senator had no intention of selling was all the better as far as I was concerned, because that gave me just the time I needed to find out all I could about Strothers." Deep furrows creased his features. "I only regret having involved you and the Senator in my plans. Looking back, I realize just how selfish of me that was, and I am truly sorry."

"There's no need for apologies. You didn't set out to do us any harm." She held tight to his hand. "You should have gone to my father in the first place. He would have known what to do."

"Yes, I realize that now, but when I first came to Caesar's Head, I didn't know who to trust and who not to, and by the time I found out, I was afraid of involving the Senator for fear of subjecting him to Strothers' wrath."

"Yes, I see your point." Deep felt worry shadowed her face. Seeing his concern, she tried to make light of it. "But those two have butted heads with each other ever since Strothers first set foot in Caesar's Head. The Senator had no trouble seeing through him at all."

"Strothers would not dare raise a finger against you or your father," Tate promised solemnly, as if he knew exactly what had been troubling her. "He knows there'd be hell to pay if he did. When it comes right down to it, Strothers talks a big game, but he's a coward, and a greedy one at that. He knows he'd be cutting off his nose to spite his face if he crossed me. Besides, I plan on seeing him tomorrow and telling him I wouldn't have that pineland if I could get it for free. I'll have him look elsewhere, and if he raises any objections, I'll just dangle a higher percentage of interest in front of his nose."

"But surely you don't really intend taking him in as a partner?"

"Tate laughed. "Certainly not. Still, you've got to fight fire with fire and make promises you have no intention of keeping if you deal with that vermin."

"Where do you go from here?" she asked, all cuddled up in his arms. "How do you go about proving he was responsible for your father's death?"

"When I was staying with him, I was able to have a look into his personal file," Tate revealed, smiling. "And certain correspondence and documents I found there gave me the motive I was looking for. They also gave me clues where to look for more answers. Lucky for me, Strothers keeps excellent records of his wrongdoings and isn't smart enough to cover his tracks. It's just a matter of time before we've got him right where we want him, and I give you my word, Cam, I won't stop until he's behind bars."

Knowing that Strothers would soon pay for his deeds was shadowed by the realization that as soon as Tate had accomplished what he set out to do there would be no reason for him to remain in Caesar's Head.

"I suppose you'll be going back to Baltimore as soon as Strothers has been brought to justice," she said quietly. "I mean, seeing as how you do have business interests up North."

"Baltimore, among other places." Tate nodded in agreement. "Carruth Lumber has business involvements elsewhere as well—New York, Philadelphia, Washington, West Virginia—and as a matter of fact an operation here in South Carolina would, I feel, prove quite lucrative, if suitable property could ever be found. Other than Willow Creek, of course," he added hurriedly.

Cam waited, the one question she knew better than to ask on the tip of her tongue. Was business all that concerned him? What about her? Them? Surely their relationship was not merely a way of wiling away the hours during his stay?

Her doubts vanished when he gathered her once more in his arms.

"And last, but certainly not least, there's a small matter regarding one Miss Camille Tranter. She has given me a lesson in Southern womanhood that I'll not be forgetting for a long time."

His kisses made many promises.

"So I guess whether Caesar's Head folks like it or not, Carruth Lumber will most likely expand south of the Mason-Dixon line just as soon as I can find a good location."

She was nearly tempted to ask him if he meant what he had said earlier to Strothers about needing a wife like a hole in the head, but she could not find the courage. Riding steeplechase with all its dangers was a far easier task than asking one's lover just how honorable his intentions were.

Perhaps in time. She sighed wistfully to herself. Yes, time would tell. She just had to be patient. She knew she was the only woman in the world for him, and now all she had to do was convince him of that. Maybe that new dress Ludie Mae was putting the finishing touches on for Tate's big hunt party next week would do the trick. Ludie Mae had promised that after he got a glimpse of her in that gown, he'd never let her out of his sight again. Of course, how was poor Ludie Mae to know he had seen her in far less?

"I'm sure those Baltimore society girls haven't stopped mourning since you left," Cam remarked, trying to make light of what she feared most. A man with Tate's good looks and gentle humor undoubtedly left a lot of sad ladies behind.

"Why, every day the post is full of tear-stained letters just begging me to come back. You wouldn't believe what promises are sealed in those lilac-scented envelopes."

She smiled, but was far from amused. "I can imagine."

He nibbled at her ear. "Why, they promise to do all kinds of wild and wicked things to make sure I come back and never leave Maryland soil again."

"How wild?" She whispered into his throat. "How wicked?"

He pretended not to want to tell her.

Cam rolled over on top of him, her hair

covering her breasts. "Just how wild and wicked?"

"Oh, I fear your ears are much too delicate to hear of such matters."

She trailed teasing kisses down his chest, her tongue flicking his rapidly hardening nipples to attention. "Do they do this?"

"Mmmm."

"And this?" She kissed his stomach, sucking the flesh until little bits of it were blue.

"Mmmm."

"How about this?" Her lips parted his legs.

"Mmmm, that, too."

She bit the inside of his leg none too gently. "Then may I suggest, Mr. Carruth, that you get back to Baltimore as fast as you can before those poor girls drop dead from misery."

Laughing, she swung herself over him and onto the floor.

"Not so fast, my sweet." He grabbed her leg and reeled her back in, pulling her down on top of him. "You're not getting away that easily. You've done some serious damage, and I expect compensation."

Stretching out across him, she slithered down his length, her breasts stroking his flat, hard belly and chest. Velvety swells moved downward to repair the damage she had done. "Just what kind of compensation do you have in mind, sir?"

He sank deeper into the pillow. "That's doing very nicely for starters."

"How about this?" Her fingers began kneading him even harder. "And this?" she asked. Her lips followed suit, driven to be even more daring by his low, soft groans.

"You Southern girls sure could teach our Yankee ones a thing or two."

A blade of jealousy sliced through her heart. Just how many Yankee girls had left him with memories that sizzled hotter than an August afternoon? And was there that one special one who was eagerly awaiting his return? A man like Tate wouldn't be without a woman for long. Of that she felt certain.

But that didn't matter, not now, she decided as her mouth instinctively worked the magic Tate desired. She had him now, and she'd not lose him. She'd do all in her power to keep him, and right at that moment, the power she held over him was as great as that which he held over her.

One hand cupped roughly to a breast, the other tangled in her hair and pulling her face to his, Tate devoured her lips with his, his passion all consuming, setting fire to her mouth and burning uncontrollably all the way down to her toes.

"Let me show you something about us Yanks. Your Rebs are mere boys in comparison."

She was in no position to argue, not when her entire body was a blazing inferno.

She went limp against him, sinking deeper and deeper into his masculine hardness. Their moans or pleasured delight played a single tune. Eyes closed, she drifted aimlessly afloat a sea of white-capped passion.

The next thing she knew he had tossed her over and pinned her so tight beneath him that she was certain her imprint would be pressed into his bed from then on.

Knowing hands commandeered her body,

directing her every quiver, sculpting her lusciousness while molding his strength even closer. He lifted her hips to his, his hands gripping them tighter and tighter as he guided her to meet his demands.

Legs made powerful from years of horseback riding wrapped themselves around his middle, hugging him, embracing him, gripping and grinding and guiding and pulling him closer, still closer. Deeper and deeper, he rammed himself inside her, tormenting her unmercifully with his ravenous urgings until at last their passion rose in unison, then fell, then soared again to heights still higher and winging their way to paradise and beyond.

Heaven could be no sweeter!

18

Cam stepped out onto the porch for a breath of fresh air. Fanning herself with her handkerchief in time with the waltz the band had just struck up, she leaned against one of the big stone pillars and let out an exhausted sigh.

She was worn out! Cross-country riding had never left her as fatigued as Tate's hunt party. She had no idea that being a hostess involved so much work and preparation. Why, so busy had she been making sure all of the sixty guests were having the time of their lives that she hardly had a moment to catch her breath. Men were lined up to dance with her, and so far she hadn't discovered a gracious way to excuse herself. If only there were some way she and Tate could slip away, just for a few minutes, to be alone together.

But from the looks of it, he was just as busy as she, entertaining his company. Her heart swelled with love and pride as she watched through the opened doors as he made his way around the room, stopping to exchange pleasantries with the men and complimenting the ladies. It was plain to see that Caesar's Head society was taken with him, as well they should be. If any one of them had qualms about having a Yankee in their midst, they kept their reservations to themselves.

Smiling to herself, Cam kept her eyes fixed on Tate. What a fine figure he cut in his black smoking jacket with satin lapels! Surely there could be no more dashing a man on the face of the earth. And to think he was all hers! There was no question that she was the luckiest woman in attendance. How envious were the glances the other females cast her way. If only Tate would propose, or at least give her some inkling as to whether or not he intended to ask her to become his wife. Ludie Mae had promised that tonight would be the night for such proposals, and if indeed it happened, she would have to give her old friend all the credit.

Neither did her father for that matter. He very nearly forbade her to leave Willow Creek so attired. But between Cam and Ludie Mae, he had finally been persuaded that the peach silk twill with its skin-tight bodice and low, scooping neckline that did more than just hint at a cleavage was the fashionable rage. She could sense, though, that the cut or the fit had little to do with the Senator's disapproval. That dress had made him realize that she was no longer her daddy's little girl, but a full-grown woman who was ripe for love.

Her smile broadened when Ludie Mae and the Senator whirled passed. No one could be having as good a time as that pair. They hadn't sat out a single dance all evening. If the Senator had a game leg, no one would know it by the way he was high-stepping. If only those two had found each other years before, Cam thought, but at least they had each other now and that would help ease some of the guilt she would feel about leaving Willow Creek if Tate did indeed propose. Heavens, she was beginning to sound like some lovesick schoolgirl who couldn't wait to find a man! What if Tate didn't want to take a wife?

"What's de matter, Miss Cam? You feelin' poorly?"

Jackson stepped out onto the porch looking very elegant in his red tails. "I seen you from inside, and I's worried you be sick. Can I git you somethin'?"

"Oh, no, thanks, Jackson. I'm fine. As a matter of fact, I don't know when I've felt finer. It's just that all those people in there were making me a bit swimmy-headed, and I needed some fresh air."

"I knows what you mean. Ain't it grand, Miss Cam? Why, it's been years since this place has seen the like. Mistah Griffin, he shore knows how to give a party."

Cam nodded. Poor man! He still lived in the past. More than once he called Tate Mistah Griffin, but Tate was so good-natured about it, he just said that if it eased the old darkie's sorrow, it was fine by him to be called by that name.

"Well, if there ain't nothin' I can gits fer you, I reckon I'd best be tendin' to the rest of the guests. Mistah Griffin—lands sakes alive, I means Mistah Carruth—sure got his hands full."

"Yes he does," Cam agreed. "And he is lucky to have you, Jackson. I don't know what he'd do without you."

"Ah, shucks, m'am." Jackson shuffled in place. "He shore is lucky to have you, too, Miss

Cam."

"Oh, Jackson, there is one more thing."

"Yes, m'am?"

Cam hesitated. She wasn't quite sure how to ask the question. She'd been thinking of it all week, and since she had Jackson alone, the time could not be more opportune. Something had been bothering her since the night she dined with Tate. Thinking about it later, she had come to the conclusion that it had been just a bit too convenient for Tate to have given Jackson that particular night off, and for him to have led her out onto the porch where she just happened to see at that particular moment the black-caped mystery man trotting down the drive. Yes, it had all been a tad too convenient. Perhaps Tate had hoped to divert the suspicion from him, but why? Why would he be lurking and in a black cape, and why would he want his real identity kept secret from her, of all people?

"Last Thursday night, Jackson, when Mr. Carruth gave you the night off, were you—I mean did he have you—"

The more she stumbled for words, the wider his big-toothed grin became.

"That Mistah Carruth, he shore is one fine man. He even let me take the buggy over to Olive Grove for the big social that night."

Cam frowned. Olive Grove was the Negro church on the other side of town. Jackson could have hardly been in two places at once.

"Yes, m'am? What about that night?"

"Oh, nothing," she replied quickly. "Nothing at all. I was just concerned you might have been under the weather. I'm glad to know you weren't."

"Why, I ain't never been sick a day in my life, Miss Cam. Not one day. Mistah Griffin used to tell me it was sinful for a body to be so healthy. Now, you shore I can't fetch you a glass of punch?"

"No, thank you, Jackson, but I'll tell you what you can do. How about sending Mrs. Bennett out here if you get a chance?"

"Shore thing, Miss Cam." Heels clicked together, he turned to go. "Lordy me! Ain't this jes the grandest party you ever did see!"

Before she could reply, he was back in the house.

Cam sat down on the steps and waited for Abbey to join her. Poor Abbey had been hesitant to come to the party in the first place. She said it wouldn't look right, seeing as how she was still in mourning. It had taken nearly all week to talk her into it, and now that she had come, she seemed to be having a good time. The black organza with white batiste blouse made her look very matronly, but Cam suspected the mature look was attributable more to the heartaches she had experienced than to her dress.

At least Abbey's Uncle Thurman and Aunt Thelma had arrived from Asheville recently, and they seemed to be doing a good job of cheering her up. How different Thurm was from his brother, Henry! He was big and boisterous and loud and gave the impression that nobody got anything over on him, Strothers included. According to Abbey, Strothers had cornered him earlier in the evening, but her uncle was the one who turned the table and was shaking his fist in Strothers' face and making all kinds of threats. Abbey had kept busy all evening after that acquainting him with all the

Caesar's Head folks. Thurm said he wanted to make everyone's acquaintance because a businessman can never have too many contacts. Cam suspected, however, his real aim was to keep Abbey in circulation and her mind off her worries.

A few minutes later, Abbey came out onto the porch carrying two glasses of champagne punch.

"Thank you for rescuing me," she said, nearly out of breath as she sat down beside Cam with a sigh of fatigue. "That uncle of mine means well, but Lord, he hasn't given me a moment's rest. I feel like a butterfly the way he keeps me flitting about."

Cam took hold of her friend's hand. "But you're having a good time, aren't you?"

"I know better than to say no. If I did, you'd have me out there clogging with old man Kruthers!"

"Not on your life! I'm so tired myself, I'd like nothing better than to curl up on the settee and take a nice long snooze."

Abbey giggled. "Not alone though, right? You and Tate make such a handsome couple. Why, he's hardly taken his eyes off you all evening."

Cam's smile was soft. She knew that was true. Wherever she had gone, she could feel his eyes following her with those invisible caresses.

"You are so lucky to find a man who loves you for you and not for what you can give him."

"Next time, Abbey, that'll be the kind of man you will fall in love with."

Abbey was quick to object. "No, m'am. Not me. I have had my fill of men." Her head dropped. "Besides, what man wants a woman who can't give him a child?"

Cam squeezed her arm. "I don't want to hear such nonsense. If a man truly loves a woman, none of that matters."

"Well, it don't matter much anyway," Abbey announced, trying to sound cheerful. "Starting Monday morning, I won't have much time to be domestic anyway."

"Oh?"

"I've decided to start learning about the mill. Uncle Thurman's got a fellow coming in next week from Hendersonville who's an experienced mill manager, and I aim to learn everything I can from him. Tell me the truth, now. Do you think Caesar's Head is ready for a businesswoman?"

"I'm sure stranger things have been known to happen." Cam was happy for her friend's enthusiasm, but that didn't stop her from worrying. "What about Strothers, Abbey? Has he been giving you any trouble?"

"No, not really," Abbey said, frowning. "He's sent all kinds of messages and messengers, pleading with me to take him back. He said he was a changed man. He even sent Preacher Robinson to intercede on his behalf. The preacher told me it was my duty as a Christian to forgive him, but it will be a cold day in hell before I'd do that."

Cam nearly rolled off the steps laughing. "You didn't tell the preacher that, did you?" she asked, clutching at her side.

Abbey chuckled. "No, I didn't. But I did tell him I didn't care whether Strothers had repented or not, I didn't want anything to do with him. Not ever again. He's no good. Rotten to the core." Her chuckle turned into a laugh. "As soon as he got wind of Uncle Thurm being in town, he arranged a meeting so he could plead his case. He told him I was mentally unstable and he feared I was dangerous to myself, but Uncle Thurm isn't the kind of man who gets the wool pulled over his eyes by some smooth-talking lawyer. No, m'am."

Cam's good humor was quick to vanish. "You just be careful, Abbey. Strothers is a very dangerous man."

"You don't have to tell me that." Abbey looked around, then raised her skirt to reveal a small pistol strapped to her stockinged leg. "Uncle Thurm insisted I learn how to use it, so we've spent the past couple of days target shooting up on the ridge. I don't know how I'd do if the target was alive, but with the paper ones I can put a bullet dead center at fifty paces."

Cam nodded her approval. "My friend, you continue to amaze me!"

Abbey smiled a shy smile. "To tell you the truth, sometimes I even amaze myself!"

"Cam! Abbey! What's wrong? Caesar's Head's two most beautiful women not enjoying my party? I am hurt!" Tate reached around them both and placed a kiss on each cheek.

Laughing, Abbey allowed him to help her to her feet. "I fear I am enjoying it too much. All that dancing has worn me out."

"And you, Miss Tranter?" He pulled her up as well and kept a possessive hold on her arm even after she was upright. "What do you have to say for yourself?"

"Oh, I agree that it is a wonderful party—perhaps even the finest this county has ever known—but like Abbey I am tuckered out."

"What a shame. And just when I've managed

to break away from my guests long enough to take my favorite girl for a stroll in the moonlight."

"Well, if that's the case, I suddenly feel a new surge of energy coming on."

"Care to join us?" he asked Abbey.

"Oh, no. I believe I'll go round up my relatives and head them toward home. Good night." She excused herself with a wink and a pinch on Cam's arm as she breezed past.

As soon as they were away from prying eyes, Tate drew Cam close and kissed her long and hard.

"Do you know what my one and only regret is about tonight?"

She could taste his hunger. "No. What?"

"That I haven't been able to spend every minute with you." He sprinkled kisses down her throat and across the satiny expanse of flesh above plump, out thrust breasts. "You are so beautiful! I haven't been able to take my eyes off you all evening. Every time I saw another man looking at you, I wanted to poke him in the mouth and tell him you were already taken."

"But, darling, you did ask me to be your hostess," she teased him. "Remember? And part of that job is to make sure everyone, men included, is having a good time."

"Right now, the only two people I'm concerned about having a good time are me and you." He grabbed hold of her hand and started running. "Come on before we're missed."

Laughing, Cam ran with him, her new slippers pinching her feet so she could hardly keep up.

The moon was full. The path was lit by its reflections.

"Where are you taking me?"

"You'll see. Shake a leg! I know you can move faster than that!"

They didn't stop running until they were at the boathouse beside the river.

The sound of the Kagle boys' fiddles grew fainter and fainter. The chirping of the crickets all but drowned out the merry-making behind them.

"Tate, just what are you doing?"

Smiling to herself, she watched as Tate brought out a quilt inside the boathouse and spread it on to the river bank. Then, after disappearing inside the tiny rock building a second time, he brought out two glasses and a bottle of champagne.

"What a lovely, lovely surprise." Cam flung her arms around him and gave him a big hug and kiss. "What a romantic you are!"

"Just a lovesick fool, I fear."

"What are we celebrating?" she asked once they had settled down on the ground and toasted each other.

"Us. To our love and happiness forever and a day."

"Oh, Tate, I do love you with all my heart. Truly I do." Excitement rose inside her. Dare she hope he was about to ask that all-important question? "I don't think any man could make me as happy in a hundred years as you have these past few months."

Gentle fingers caressed the strand of pearls around her neck.

She knew what he was about to say even before he said it.

"I see you're not wearing your good-luck charm tonight."

"I wondered if you'd notice. Taking hold of his hand, she kissed each finger, allowing her tongue to lightly skim the rough knuckles; then she rested his palm against her breast.

He couldn't fool her. Not for a minute. Jackson's absence that night had been just a little too well planned, as their stepping out on the porch at just the right time had been. Tate was the mystery man, but he wasn't about to admit it to her or explain his actions. Not yet. Not until he was good and ready.

Cam pressed herself closer. "I decided I don't need any good-luck charm. Not when you're around."

"You mean that; don't you?"

She nodded, hoping she could keep a straight face for what she was about to say. "I must admit at one time I was quite smitten by the man in black, but I was a girl then, a girl whose head was filled with romantic fantasies about being swept off her feet and carried away on a white steed, just like in fairy tales."

Teasing fingers kneaded the muscular cords beneath the white ruffles of his starched shirt. "But I am a woman now, a woman who belongs to you and only you. I'll never belong to any other man." She molded herself still closer and rubbed her flesh suggestively against him. "I belong to you, Tate. You must believe me. For me, there is no other man." She could feel his need growing against her. "You do believe me, don't you, my darling?"

His mouth smothered her words. Hungry lips attacked hers in a frenzy of fevered kisses while starving hands roamed intimately over her breasts. Yearning grew with each muffled moan.

Arms tangled around him, she fell back onto the ground, pulling him down with her, welcoming his weight and pleading silently for its full force.

Legs wrapped tight around him and back arched with silent promises, she pulled him still closer. She did not want him to leave even one part of her untouched.

"This is not at all what I had in mind," Tate remarked, nearly out of breath.

"No?" she giggled. "I find that hard to believe."

"Actually, I was going to save the big seduction scene for later when we were alone to love each other properly without the confines of party attire."

She kissed his ear, her tongue tracing its outline. "Why don't we just rehearse a little for later?"

"You mean a dress rehearsal?"

Before she could reply, anxious hands dove inside her gown, kneading the ivory globes that fell out in hot welcome.

His fiery tongue was maddening! Her senses reeled completely out of control at his knowing touch. Would her flesh never stop flaming, no matter how familiar his caresses became?

"Will I never get my fill of you?" he asked as his lips drank from the sweetness of her breasts.

"Oh, I hope not! I truly hope not! Don't stop, my darling! Don't ever stop!"

Kisses, frantic and swollen with passion and desire, shouted their needs, their hunger. Hands caressed and urged, directed by the unrelenting need pounding inside them, while their bodies pressed closer and closer though the layers of clothing separated them.

It was all she could do to keep her fingers from ripping his clothes into shreds, and it was obvious from the urgency building inside his trousers that he would like nothing better than to jerk off her gown and take once again what was his just for the asking. Their bodies arched and thrust, coiled and recoiled, moving in fast-paced rhythm, trying in vain to quell their tempestuous ardor.

With a loud groan, Tate rolled off. "Damn! This is torture. I want you so badly."

Hovering above him, she made sure her breasts spilled over onto his chest. "Then why don't you take what you want?"

"Don't you dare tempt me, Camille Tranter, or I might just surprise you."

Hot palms caressed the inside of his thighs. "What's stopping you?"

"We'd be mad to make love here, with a house full of people, not to mention your father, only a short distance away."

Ever so slowly, she plucked the first button, then the second and third on his shirt, confident she'd get her way. She could taste the submission in his kisses.

"Tate! Taaate! You down here, you son of a bitch?"

Cam hit the ground, flattening herself as close to the earth as she could get. There was no mistaking Strothers' drunken drawl.

"Tate! You hear me? Where are you, man? I got to talk to you!"

He was getting closer, so close Cam could

hear every slur and all but smell the whiskey on his breath.

"Son of a bitch! Where is that no-account bastard! Never around when I need him! Tate!" He mumbled a few obscenities under his breath. "You're gonna kiss the ground I walk on when you find out what I'm gonna do for you! I'll show you what a good friend I am, you Yankee bastard!"

Cam held her breath, waiting for the footsteps that had come so dangerously close to go away again. When they did, she let out a sigh of relief.

"What do you suppose all that was about?"

Tate rolled over onto his back and stared up into the cloudless sky. "Who knows? But if we're lucky, he'll pass out before he breathes on anybody." After a quick kiss, he leapt to his feet. "Come on, before we have any more close calls."

She knew he was right. They really should be getting back to the party. Still, she couldn't help but feel just a little disappointed. Her look told him what she felt.

He pulled her to her feet, his hands lingering suggestively on her hips. "Later, my darling. We'll make up for it later."

"Promises! Promises!"

She returned to the party ahead of Tate, satisfied that their absense had gone without notice. Abbey, after finally managing to tear her uncle away from the group of local businessmen, had time only to give an exasperated wave before ushering her chatty relatives outside.

Threading her way through the crowd, Cam searched for her father. Instead, she found Ludie Mae sitting in the corner fanning herself with her handkerchief.

"Looks like you dosey-doed one time too many," Cam said with a chuckle as she sat down beside her old friend.

It took Ludie Mae a moment to catch her breath. "That father of yours has worn me plum out," she complained, fanning herself even harder. "I keep telling him he's going to keel over dead if he keeps this up, but no, he won't listen. You know how stubborn he is. He thinks he's still a spring chicken."

"The way you two have been high-stepping it all evening looks to me like you're both in the spring of your years." She scanned the room again. "Where is he, anyway?"

"I had to send him after a glass of punch before I passed out from exhaustion," Ludie Mae said, giggling.

Cam took her hand and gave it an affectionate squeeze. "I am so glad you two finally tied the knot. I don't know when I've ever seen my two favorite people any happier."

Gray lashes swept across flushed cheeks. "It was worth waiting for all those years. Why, I don't think there's a luckier woman in the county, maybe even in the whole state."

"Oh, I might argue with you there." Cam could feel her eyes dancing, and there was little she could do to hide it.

"I saw the two of you sneaking off," Ludie Mae remarked, chuckling. "Guess that dress did the trick, did it?"

"Tate didn't propose, at least not yet, but I have a feeling he just might before too long. And when he does," Cam added as she lowered her head to her friend's. "I'm sure this fancy frock you created will have a lot to do with encouraging him."

"Shhh. Here comes your father now. If I were you, I wouldn't say too much about wanting Tate to pop the question. I'd break it to him slowly. After all, you're still his little girl."

"And she'll be my little girl until she's full of gray hairs," announced the Senator in exceptionally good humor as he limped up to them and gave them a big wink. "You forget I got ears like a horse. Well, gal, has he asked you yet? If he does, you tell him I expect him to get down on his knees and ask my permission."

"You mean to tell me you'd give a Yankee your blessing to marry your only child?" Cam teased him. "I do declare! What is this world coming to?"

"You mark my word, young lady, that fellow has some rebel blood in him somewhere." Thumbs hooked onto the sleeves of his vest, the Senator scanned the room as he rocked from his heels to his toes. "Say, where is Tate, anyway? He promised to show me those fancy hounds he just had sent up from Travellers' Rest. He claims they're real blue-bloods, those dogs. Reckon we'll see just how good they are come Sunday, when the foxes put them to the test. You still going to ride with the hounds, ain't you, Cami?"

"And why shouldn't I? After all, I have ridden every year since I was old enough to sit a horse." She knew what was on his mind. Still, he loved to tease her, and if that made him happy, that was fine by her.

His blue eyes twinkled mischievously. "I just figured now that you've gone and gotten yourself a fellow, you'd be staying home cooking and sewing and being all prim and proper."

"Not on your life! I can still outride any man in this county, and don't you forget that."

She tried to keep her laugh hearty. What she wasn't telling her father was that even though her intentions were to start with the hunt, she wouldn't be pursuing the fox. Why Tate had not admitted before now to being the man in black still baffled her, and she had a feeling that the answers to all those questions she was dying to ask were there at Hunter's Glen. Tate's riding in the hunt was going to give her just the opportunity she needed to do a little snooping.

The Senator gave his daughter a loving slap on the back. "That's my gal! Glad to see love hasn't turned you into a sissy!"

Cam started to give him a poke, but he jumped back out of reach before she had a chance.

"Tate!" he yelled halfway across the room. "Wait up." He gave Ludie Mae a quick peck on the cheek. "Think I'll go have me a look at some of them blue-blooded hounds. See you ladies later."

"Don't be long, Cameron. It's getting late."

"Now, Ludie Mae, don't you start fussing over my health."

"It's my health I'm worried about, sir."

"I'll not be long, darling."

Ludie Mae's smile vanished the instant his back was turned. "You know he's hell-bent on riding with the pack day after tomorrow. I have talked until I am blue in the face, but he won't listen to a word I say. He promised me last year and the year before that he'd ridden in his last hunt. Lordy, he's an old man. He could break his fool neck jumping hedges. Why, that crazy horse of his could spook and throw him and trample his head in and . . ."

Cam quieted her with a pat on the arm. "Now don't you go getting yourself all worked up for nothing, Ludie Mae. You know how he loves to tease you. Why, he hasn't jumped a hedge in twenty years, and as far as his horse spooking—why, old Lucky's got no more get-up-and-go about him than Beggin' does."

"I know. I know. I just worry about him, that's all. I reckon that's what lovin' a man's all about."

Cam nodded in agreement. How well she knew that feeling. "I reckon it is."

"Miss Cam, Miss Cam. You seen Mistah Griff—I mean, Mistah Carruth?" Jackson asked a short while later. "We be running a mite short of sparkley and de way dese folks is guzzlin' it, I best be brangin' more up from the cellar."

"You go right ahead and do that," she told him. "I'll see if I can find Mister Carruth."

Cam surveyed the room with a weary eye. Tate's guests were having such a good time, they might never leave. The Kagle boys had just returned from the buffet table and punch bowl and were about to get at their fiddles again. If anyone was tired, certainly no one was showing it. Without a doubt, it was going to be one, long night! It could well be daylight before she could lose herself in Tate's arms.

"Excuse me, Ludie Mae. I guess I'd best see if I can track Tate down."

"You go right ahead, honey. I've got a feeling I won't be moving from this spot for the rest of the night." Ludie Mae gave a big yawn. "I should have brought a pillow."

Cam made her way through the crowd once again, begging off dancing as graciously as she could. She had half a mind to announce that the party would end at midnight but decided against it. After all, she wasn't mistress of Hunter's Glen yet.

She stepped off the back porch, then hopped back on all in the same quick motion. Strothers was standing at the side of the house talking to two men who, she could tell by their attire, had not been invited to the party. Crouched in the shadows, Cam listened and watched.

Strothers handed the tall, skinny one an envelope. "Don't bother counting it, Pole. Half now, half when the job's done. Nice and neat, understand? I want it to look like an accident."

"Yes, sir," the men replied in unison.

"You can count on us, boss."

Cam recognized the voice but couldn't quite place it. Strothers' words were enough to make her shudder. No matter how slurred they were, there was no mistaking their intent. Strothers might be drunk, but he wasn't too drunk to be up to his old tricks. What was it this time? she wondered. And who would be the unlucky devil who fell victim to his devious schemes?

She had to get to Tate! He'd know what to do. He'd know how to stop Strothers before he did any more damage.

Cam waited until the two had ridden off into the night and Strothers had stumbled his way back inside before moving from her hiding place behind the well house. She had only taken a few steps when she remembered just where she had heard that voice. It was the night of the Winthrop fire when one of the riders who came barreling across the clearing had bragged about having just made the easiest money of his life.

Cam stopped dead in her tracks. And that wasn't the only time, either. Now she knew why the tall, skinny one called Pole looked familiar as well. The night she had ridden up to Mill Hill in search of Strothers, he had been the one who was so quick to smart-mouth her until she sent him sprawling to the ground.

Her heart sank to her feet. That wasn't all she remembered, either. What was it that Strothers had been shooting his mouth off about earlier when he came looking for Tate? Something about making Tate proud of him? Just what was that "something" that he had done?

She turned back and ran the other way. There was no time to waste! There was no doubt who Strothers had just targeted as his next innocent victim. She had to get back to Willow Creek. The future of the Tranters was hanging in the curing barn. One strike of the match, and it could all go up in flames.

"Miss Cam, Miss Cam! You find Mistah Carruth?"

Cam ran past Jackson as if he wasn't there. She had no choice but take to the woods on foot. The trip home would take twice as long by buggy if she had to stick to the road.

Her slippers pounded the earth, the tight satin cutting deep into her heels.

In the distance, she could hear Beggin' barking. The closer she got to their land, the louder his howling became, and there was no wondering the reason for it. No one ever set foot on Willow Creek property without him alerting the entire valley.

Spurred on by his barking, she ran as hard and as fast as she could. She ran until her legs were about to give way beneath her, but somehow, she managed to press on. She had to stop them before it was too late! If only she were wrong! But in her heart, she knew she was right. If Strothers got his way, all that would be left of the farm come morning would be a pile of ashes!

Burning the farm to the ground would take little effort, since low-burning wood fires in the barn were needed to slow-cure the burley hanging in there. It wouldn't take any time at all for the dry leaves and the hogsheads where prime tobacco had been two years mellowing to go up in flames. And the worst part was that Strothers and his cronies might well get away with it. Accidents of that sort were common to tobacco farmers at that time of year, especially if one of the field hands left to stoke the fire got a little careless or couldn't keep his eyes open during the night.

Cam stopped at the spring house to catch her breath. A pair of horses were tethered to a shrub nearby. Praying that they would make no sound to give her away, she tiptoed over to them and untied them. Silently, the two grays ambled off into the woods.

Cam waited, listening to the sounds of the night. She could hear Traveller pawing at his stall.

Even the chickens in the coop sensed something was wrong!

She waited a moment longer. She knew what her next move was going to be, but first the location of the trespassers had to be determined. Undoubtedly, they had arrived just ahead of her and were still nosing around the place. If only she could make it to the porch without being caught! Once there, she could crawl in the window and take down her shotgun from the deer antler rack in the front room.

One quick glance around her while hurriedly discarding her stockings and slippers, and Cam took off running towards the house. There were no 'ifs' about it. She had no choice. She had to get to that shotgun before it was too late. Her life depended on it!

She hit the ground a few feet from the porch and crouched as close as she could to the rose bush hedge. The thorns prickled her flesh, and she could feel blood beading up across her face, but she did not flinch, for if she did, the two men coming down the steps would be sure to spot her.

"Come on, Pole. The sooner we get this job done, the better. I don't like nosing around here."

"If that gal wuz here, I'd have done more poking than nosing. I got me a little score to settle with her." Pole took a swig from the brown jug he had carried out of the house. "You worry too much, Buster. Hell, everybody's over at that party. We got us plenty of time. What's the matter? You chicken?"

His friend jerked the jug away and turned it up to his mouth. "Chicken, hell. I can do you one better any day of the week."

Beggin' came tearing across the yard barking and growling and snarling at the intruders. Cam held her breath.

The skinny one whipped out his pistol, but before he could aim it, his friend grabbed the gun from his hand. "You crazy, man? What you want? To alert this whole damn valley?"

Beggin' stood his ground, not heeding his mistress's silent pleas.

"Shut up, you ole hound!" Pole shouted.

His friend threw the jug at the dog, and the hound scurried out into the woods yelping. "That ought to take care of him for a while."

Cam dared not breathe a sigh of relief. Those two had passed so close to her she could all but count the creases in their boots.

"Hell fire, Buster. Let's get on with it. Then maybe we'll take some of this hard-earned money down to Sally Rose's and buy that cute little squaw gal for the night. I bet she knows a war whoop or two."

"Now you're talking sense."

When sensation finally returned to her numbed body, Cam sprung into the house. After making sure the gun was loaded she rushed back outside and keeping a safe distance behind, followed the two down to the curing barn. Rafe Johnson, one of the field hands, was supposed to be doing his turn stoking the fire. She almost wished one of the less dependable workers was on that shift. Rafe was fiercely loyal to the Senator, and she didn't want to see him hurt on that account!

"Hey, whut you boys doin' 'round heah?" she heard Rafe call out. "This heah's private prop'ty.

you heah me? You better git walkin'."

"Shut up, nigger, or you're liable to wake up dead," Pole shouted.

"Why, Pole Miller! I'd know that voice anywhere," Rafe said, undaunted by the threat as he came sauntering out of the barn. "Now you jus skeedaddle on home, and I'll forgit you wuz heah."

Pole snickered. "Sorry, boy. But you know who I am, and I can't chance you going to the sheriff." He raised his pistol.

"Come on, Pole. We didn't agree to do any killing," said Buster, his voice thick with fear. "Let's get out of here. Bennett can do his own dirty work."

Cam closed in behind them. "Drop it, mister. Both of you, turn around nice and slow." She cocked her gun to let them know she meant business. "I'd just as soon shoot you in the back as not."

"Sure thing, m'am. Anything you say." Buster threw his gun over to the side.

When Rafe rushed to retrieve it, Pole turned his gun on Cam. "Come on, sweet thing. Now you drop it."

Cam fired without aiming, and Pole went sprawling back onto the ground, cursing and crying out in pain.

"You try something like that again, and it won't be your shoulder that gets hit," she told him angrily.

Cam kept her gun pointed at the intruders. "Rafe, you get some cord and tie them up good and tight."

The field hand did as he was told.

"Now lock them in the smoke house and go

fetch the Sheriff. He's most likely still over at the old Griffin place."

"You want to tell me what all this is about?" Buster demanded. "Me and Pole here wuz just minding our business, that's all. If'n we wuz trespassing, I do apologize, but that ain't no cause to go shooting us. Hell, m'am, you put that gun down, and we'll get this little misunderstanding cleared up."

"There has been no misunderstanding, I assure you." Cam's words were as cold as her eyes. "I know why you're here and who hired you. And believe me, if it weren't for keeping you alive so you could take Strothers Bennett down with you, I'd have shot you both dead and left you for the buzzards to pick."

"You're crazy." Pole held onto his shoulder as blood oozed through his hand. "You can't prove nothing."

Her smile was frigid. "We'll see." She motioned to Rafe, who dragged them both to the smoke house. After checking to make sure the outside bolt was locked, she sat down cross-legged on the ground and waited, her shotgun pointed at the door of the small rock building.

Rafe hardly had time to get to Hunter's Glen before Tate came galloping up on Tristram. He hopped off his horse and ran over to her.

"My God, Cam, are you all right?"

She nodded. "I'll be even better when those two are behind bars, and Strothers is dangling from the nearest tree."

"Had anything happened to you, I would have never forgiven myself." Tate hugged her close, all but robbing the breath from her weary body. "I should have never have dragged you and your father into this vendetta of mine. What a fool I was. I could have gotten you killed!"

She laid her head against his shoulder. How secure, how protected she felt in his arms. His strength became her strength, his blood her blood.

"It's over now," she said. "That's all that matters."

"No, it is not over." His whole body went tense. "Not by a long shot!"

She could feel the ice in his declaration. Never had she heard such hate in anyone's voice.

Ever so gently, he disentangled her arms from around him. "But it will be soon; I promise you that."

"Tate! What are you going to do?" Suddenly she was afraid, even more so than a little while earlier when her own life had been threatened.

"What are you going to do?" Her voice was frantic. Tate had the wild-eyed look of a madman. "Answer me. What are you going to do?"

"I've had enough of this play-acting." He took the gun out of her hand and cocked it. "I'm going to do what I came here to do two years ago."

She hung onto his arm. "No—you can't! Let the Sheriff handle this." Her words grew more frenzied with each passing second. "I won't let you, Tate. You don't know Strothers. He'll kill you. He'll kill you and not think twice about it."

"Not if I get him first."

One final kiss and he tenderly pushed her away. "Don't worry about me, darling. I'll be careful."

Tears spilled from her eyes as she followed

him to his horse. His mind was made up. There was nothing she could do to change it.

"You don't understand." She hung onto his leg long after he had mounted. Her eyes pleaded with him to listen to reason, but she knew in her heart her words were futile. "No matter how low-down Strothers is, no matter how much he deserves to die, if you kill him, you'll be the one they'll want to string up. You're still a Yankee, Tate, and no Southern court will take kindly to you killing one of their own. Oh, Tate, I couldn't live if something happened to you. Please, for my sake, don't go!"

He leaned down and brushed her cheek with his lips. "Nothing will happen to me, my darling, Cam, not when I have you here waiting for me. I'll be back. I swear. You have my word as a gentleman!"

19

I give you my word as a gentleman . . . My word as a gentleman . . . my word as a gentleman . . .

Tate's parting words when he took off after Strothers in spite of her pleas echoed inside Cam's head the rest of the night and on into the next day and night as well.

My word as a gentleman . . .

Had there been the slightest doubt before, there was none now. Tate Carruth was the mystery man! He was the man in black who for two years had dominated her every thought. And he had indeed kept that vow he made that first night she laid eyes on him. He had returned to her.

All that was left to do now was to find out just why he had kept up the deception, and why he had even begun it in the first place. Why had he not revealed his secret identity to her, and why had he thought it necessary to continue the charade after he had established himself in Caesar's Head? There were so many questions, they made her head spin!

Cam dressed quickly in the traditional dress

of the hunt, then stepped back to survey her appearance in the hunter's-green riding shirt with short, matching jacket and white-laced blouse with ruffles around the cuffs and high neck.

Satisfied with what she saw in the wardrobe mirror, Cam added the finishing touches—of the tiny green veiled hat that sat perched atop her rolled curls and the long, satin streamers down her back. Usually, she complained bitterly about the kind of attire tradition decreed for the few women who participated in the hunt, but not today. Even though she would start with the pack, she wouldn't be riding with them for long. There would be no jumping creeks and hedges and chasing the hounds across the countryside as in hunts past. No, there would be many more hunts during the season when her skill as a equistrienne would be challenged. Today, she, like all the other riders, would be summoned by the hunt master's horn, but unlike her companions, she would leave the group at first opportunity. The answers she sought were at Hunter's Glen, and this was the day to find them!

Tate was waiting for her on the porch. His fox-hounds sat obediently at Tristram's side.

Her heart skipped several beats, then fluttered and began pounding all over again. How dashing he looked in his spit-polish black knee boots, black jodpurs and scarlet coat! Sometimes when she looked at him, she could hardly believe her good fortune. He was all hers! What a lucky woman she was!

He greeted her with a chaste peck on the cheek as a smiling Ludie Mae looked on with approval.

Cam felt herself blush. What havoc reigned inside her, however innocent his kiss! It had to be love. Why else would she go all giddy when he was near? There could be no other explanation. Thank heavens he had kept the vow he made night before last and returned to her safe and sound, for she could not even begin to imagine life without him.

What a relief it had been to learn that Strothers could not be found anywhere. He had disappeared the night of Tate's party, and if Nellie had any suspicions as to his whereabouts, she was keeping them to herself now that her husband was back in town.

Tate wasn't the only one looking for Strothers. So was the Sheriff. Pole Miller and his pal, Buster Coggins, were more than eager to confess all to save their own necks. Just as Cam had known all along, Strothers had been behind the Winthrop fire, as well as a few more unexplained mishaps at the lower end of the county and had paid his boys handsomely for, as he put it, happening along Willow Creek that night and accidently dropping a match in the vicinity of the tobacco barn.

If Strothers did have the guts to show his face in Caesar's Head again, he would no doubt have some plausible tale concocted in defense of his innocence, but Cam was satisfied that the Sheriff had already drawn his own conclusions as to his guilt. It was just a matter of time before he did come back to town, and when he did, there was no doubt that he would be brought to justice for his crimes.

Cussing under his breath, the Senator came limping around the corner leading Traveller. The horse was already tacked up in his saddle and bridle; even the silver buckles snapping the reins to the bit had been polished until they shone like new. The horse's beautiful chestnut coat glistened in the early morning sunlight. His mane was sectioned into tiny, neat braids, and his tail hung in long plaits.

When Cam noticed her father holding his thigh, she winced, feeling herself the tremendous pain he must be enduring. Knowing how much he hated having a fuss made over him however, she pretended not to take any notice of his discomfort.

"So why are you not dressed and ready to go?" she asked her father as she kissed his cheek. "That fox isn't going to wait for you to show up."

"Damn rheumatiz! That little cold snap we had last night got these old joints into one hell of a mess." He braved a smile. "But you don't worry none about your old pappy, you hear me? You two go on, and I'll catch up with you later." He handed Cam the reins, then gave her jacket a tug. "I said don't worry about me! I'll be along directly just as soon as I've had a few more swigs of my medicine."

Cam nodded. She hated leaving him, but knew he'd have it no other way. At least he had Ludie Mae to look after him.

"I'm expecting one of you to bring home the fox tail," he called out cheerfully after they were mounted.

Cam made a fuss. "Not me. I'm on the fox's side. It's the spirit of the chase that excites me!"

The Senator winked at Tate. "Sounds like she's gone all soft on us, heh, boy?"

Tate chuckled. "Your daughter? That'll be the day! Why, she's hard as nails."

Cam whirled her horse around. "You bet I am! Race you to the bend."

Without waiting for a reply, she urged her horse from a standstill into a slow canter, then on into a gallop as she charged down the willow-shaded lane, her skirt tails fanning the breeze.

"Catch me if you can," she called out over her shoulder.

Tate caught up with her at last, but not before she had reached the corner of Willow Creek property that was marked by a centuries-old oak tree draped in Spanish moss.

Without a word, he rode up alongside her and pulled her over to him. His kisses were rough and demanding as his mouth swallowed hers in a hunger that was insatiable.

Heat rose in her breasts. She threw her arms around his neck and pressed as close to his powerful form as she could get. Two torturously long nights had passed since they had lain together, and the desire for his raw, naked possession so tormented her that it was driving her mad!

"It seems like years since I've held you in my arms," he mumbled between soul-consuming kisses. "One more night without you, and I'll turn into a raving madman!"

"But darling, we were together last evening," she teased him. "Remember?"

His hands kneaded her breasts with a possessive roughness that made her go weak all over.

"What I remember is a very pleasant dinner

with you, your father and Ludie Mae, followed by a very pleasant chat in front of the fire with the Senator while you and Ludie Mae played backgammon, then a very pleasant little stroll in the moonlight with you, your father and Ludie Mae." He gave a labored sigh. "How quickly I forgot. We did spend the evening together after all."

"And a very romantic evening at that, wouldn't you agree?" Her fingers danced along the inside of his thigh. "I told you I'd slip out after they went to bed, but if memory serves me correct, you didn't think much of that idea."

"Oh, quite the contrary, my sweet. I thought much about it. All night in fact. However, I had visions of the Senator sitting on the front porch in his rocking chair with that shotgun of his across his lap."

Cam chuckled. Actually her father had spent most of the night in that very position, but it was Strothers or one of his "boys" he was hoping to fill full of holes, not Tate.

"Yes, m'am. Last night got me to thinking a whole lot about us," he announced as he returned her hand to her own knee. "And I came to the conclusion that if we were going to keep carrying on like we have been, we had better get your father's consent and the preacher's blessing."

Cam could hardly believe her ears. Had he really said what she thought? "You mean you want to . . . to . . .

"That's exactly what I mean. I want to marry you." He chuckled. "Why so surprised? This can't come as any great shock. You know I've loved you since the first time I set eyes on you."

For once, Cam was at a loss for words. He wanted to marry her! He really wanted to marry her! Her dreams were about to be realized. She would become Mrs. Tate Carruth.

"You haven't given me your answer."

She threw her arms around him and held on tight. "Was there ever any doubt what my answer would be?"

"I want to hear you say it."

"Yes, yes, yes, I will marry you." She squeezed him as hard as she could. "I would be honored to marry you, Tate Carruth!"

One more quick kiss and he picked up the reins. "Good. Now that that's settled, let's go see if these hounds of mine were worth the pretty penny they cost me."

Before she could answer, he had shot out ahead of her.

Cam trotted to catch up. That wasn't all that had to be settled. Granted, their future together might no longer be under question, but he still had not admitted to being the man in black. Given time, he might, but she couldn't wait. She had to find out for herself, and she had to find out now!

When they arrived at the big Colonial mansion of the master of the hunter, Roland Winterthur, the riders had already assembled on the front lawn and were sipping hot cider from silver stirrup cups. It came as no great surprise that Tate was given a more welcoming reception than she, for Cam suspected most of the participants, the master of the hunt included, felt her place was inside with the womenfolk playing backgammon or doing needlepoint in front of the fire. No matter! They wouldn't have to contend with her presence for very long. She only hoped the fox went nowhere near Hunter's Glen.

The horn sounded and the command was given for riders to mount their horses. The master of the hunt strutted his big black stallion to his rightful place at the front of the troops. Everyone steered clear of the horses that had red ribbons braided into their tails, for those were the kickers and were best to avoid. Masters issued commands to their hounds, and the packs ran off into the woods.

Tate flashed Cam a big smile, and she blew him a kiss in return just before they were swallowed by the horses and riders as the group lunged forward in pursuit of the dogs. The hunt had begun!

It didn't take long for the hounds to catch scent of the fox, and when they did, the frenzy of the chase took over. Riders spurred their mounts on, jumping creeks and hedges and stone fences and galloping across pastureland as onlookers and well-wishers watched in delighted awe.

Separating herself from Tate proved easier than Cam had expected, for the moment his hounds had taken to the trail of the fox, he had shot on ahead, shouting to her to keep up. Soon he had lost himself in the hunt, and when she saw that the pursuit of the fox had become foremost in his mind, Cam let herself drop further and further behind to the rear of the pack. She was the last to jump the rock wall at the Hamilton place, and rather than press on in the direction of the old grist mill as the others had done, she turned

Traveller to the east and doubled back to Hunter's Glen.

Once there, Cam was confident she would meet with no surprise interuptions, for Jackson was back at the Winterthurs' awaiting Tate's return.

She hopped off Traveller, then on second thought led him around back rather than leaving him grazing out front. If by chance the hunt party did come near Hunter's Glen, she certainly didn't want to arouse any suspicion by having her horse spotted there!

Even though the old stone lodge had become a second home to her since Tate had taken up residence there, she still felt like an unwelcome intruder as she stepped inside, and there was little wonder why. Before she had been a guest, an invited one, and now she was hardly better than a trespasser!

Cold shivers raced down her spine and back up again as she stepped into the library, where Tate had moved the big mahogany desk that had been in the master suite. If Tate caught her snooping around, she'd just die from embarrassment! But that was one risk that had to be taken. She had to find out the truth, regardless of the consequences, and his unwillingness to tell her himself despite ample opportunities to do so had left her with no alternative but to go after the answers herself!

She wasn't sure exactly what it was she was looking for as she shuffled through the papers atop his desk, but she knew for certain that she would recognize it if she did find it. Hidden somewhere in all that clutter was the evidence she needed to confirm her suspicions and offer some kind of explanation for Tate's actions, as well as for his silence. Somewhere! But where?

Cam quickly scanned the contents of one bundle of papers, but they were no surprise to her. Tate had already told her of the letters he had found between the railroad company and Clayton Griffin several years before regarding the acquisition of Hunter's Glen property. What she hadn't expected to find was correspondence between the railway and Strothers, who claimed to be acting as intermediary on Clayton's behalf. Undoubtedly, that was the file Tate had discovered while staying at the Sullivan house, that same file that had somehow found its way into Tate's bags when he left! Obviously, Tate had taken the letters as evidence, but evidence of what? How did Clayton Griffin's death figure into that of his father, Philipp Carruth? What link did he possibly hope to establish between the two?

More confused than ever, Cam flipped through stack after stack of papers, most of which held little interest or relevance, then rummaged through the desk drawers. Nowhere among the bits and pieces could she find any proof to substantiate that which her heart knew was true.

Discouraged by her lack of success, Cam slumped down into the big wing chair behind the desk, her chin resting on her fist. Exactly what was it she was hoping to find anyway? Some signed admission by the man in black that stated he was really Tate Carruth? Perhaps she'd best just ask Tate point-blank for the truth. Considering that they would soon be wed, there really should not be any secrets between them. Surely he would agree with that!

Cam picked up a book with a silhouette of a rearing horse embossed in gold on the crimson leather cover and, as she deliberated her next move, absently thumbed through the pages.

An envelope, yellow and fragile with age, suddenly appeared stuck between two pages. It was addressed to Clayton Griffin in an unmistakably feminine hand.

She hesitated. She really shouldn't read it. The contents were more likely than not very personal, and just because Clayton Griffin was dead did not give her the right to intrude on his privacy.

Ever so timidly, she lifted the letter from its place and examined the faded lettering, half expecting at any moment to hear Clayton's booming voice demanding an explanation for her presence there. For the longest time, she just sat there holding the letter tenderly, for fear it would crumble at the slightest touch.

Instinctively, she knew that what she had in her hand was a love letter. She had never really thought of Clayton in any romantic sense, but then, she had never really known the man. He might well have possessed a side never seen even by those like the Senator whom he considered his friends.

With much care, Cam lifted the envelope to her nose. An ever-so-faint scent of lilac still lingered there. No doubt what she had come to Hunter's Glen hoping to find would not be revealed in a love letter, and as she told herself over and over, she really should just put it back between the pages and close the book. But the urge to satisfy her curiosity was much too compelling to ignore. What harm would be done if she did read the letter? She certainly wasn't about to announce its contents all over Greenville County. Perhaps what it contained would help her to better understand the man to whom it was addressed. Perhaps it would make her see him in a totally new light.

Before any more second thoughts about what was right or not assailed her, Cam carefully slipped the letter out of the envelope, surprised at finding not one letter, but two inside. The first was dated nearly thirty years before.

MY DEAREST CLAYTON,

It began.

IT IS WITH GREAT JOY THAT I WRITE TO YOU OF THE BIRTH OF MY SON . . . OF OUR SON. HIS FEATURES ARE STRONG AND DARK, JUST AS YOURS ARE, AND LIKE HIS FATHER AS WELL, HE POSSESSES BIG, WIDE EYES THE COLOR OF A CAT'S. MY FATHER HAS DECIDED I MUST LEAVE GREENVILLE. THE SHAME I HAVE BROUGHT ON MY FAMILY IS TOO GREAT FOR THEM TO BEAR. SO WE, MY SON AND I, MUST MOVE TO MARYLAND WITH RELATIVES WHO BELIEVE ME TO BE RECENTLY WIDOWED. I LOVE YOU, CLAYTON. I ALWAYS WILL. I LIVE FOR THE DAY WHEN YOU AWAKEN WITH THE YEARNING TO HAVE YOUR SON AND

ME BY YOUR SIDE. I KNOW IN MY HEART YOU WILL, AND WHEN YOU DO, I WILL COME TO YOU.

WITH LOVE ETERNAL,
LENORA.

Cam blinked quickly. She could all but feel the pain the poor girl must have suffered.

She then turned her attention to the second letter. It was dated five years later. From the tone of it, Lenora had grown from a love-sick girl who had been forced by the man she loved to bear alone the burden of her guilt into a sensible woman who no longer entertained such foolish notions about the man who had abandoned her in her hour of greatest need.

In the letter, Lenora told Clayton of having married a kind, wealthy businessman who knew the truth about her and her son, and who wanted to give the boy his name. She cautioned him about ever making any attempt to see her or her son and swore to destroy him if he ever went against her wishes.

Cam slipped the letters back into their resting place and returned the envelope between the pages where she found it. With a heavy-hearted sigh, she closed the book and held it close to her breast. No wonder Clayton had become such an embittered man! Without a doubt, he had realized too late that what would have made him happiest was beyond his reach. The family he might have had was lost to him forever, and he had only himself to blame.

For a long time, Cam remained in the chair, her legs curled beneath her and her chin resting in her hand. Tate had told her the truth after all. He really had come to Caesar's Head to avenge the death of his father—his natural father, Clayton Griffin. In time, the time he deemed right, he would tell her the whole truth. Until then, she would just have to be patient.

She stood up slowly. Her heart grieved for Clayton and for the woman whose desperate love had in the end turned to hate. Thank heavens the love she and Tate shared would withstand all trials and tribulations. She'd see to that. Nothing would ever drive a wedge between them!

She walked towards the door with a heavy sigh. Her gaze came to rest on a bronze statue on the sideboard that, oddly enough, she had never noticed there before. Perhaps Jackson had only recently retrieved it from one of the many crates that had been stored for years in the cellar. Still, the half-lion, half-eagle creature did look familiar.

She took several steps toward it and eyed the statue more closely. It took but a moment to realize why it did look so familiar.

Her fingers reached instinctively for the pendant she no longer wore around her neck. That same design was etched on the gold button cover she had found by the old mine that long-ago night. The answer had been staring her in the face all along. Why had it taken so long to figure it out? Of course! In Greek mythology there was a creature that was half lion and half eagle, and that creature was called a griffin. Since Clayton Griffin could not possibly have been wearing the black cape that sultry July evening, there was only one person who could have been, and that person could be none other than his son!

20

Cam stood at the opened bedroom window and gazed silently into the black stillness cloaking the woods. An slight breeze rustled the fallen leaves that lay scattered across the ground. The night was chilled, the autumn air crisp and alive.

She pulled her cape snug around her bare shoulders and sighed a smile. So much had transpired in the past four months, so much more than she had ever dreamt possible. The vow she had made to her father back in the summer would be realized tomorrow when she wed the only man who had ever been able to outride her. Tomorrow, she would become Mrs. Tate Carruth. It all seemed too wonderful to be really happening, but it was. It truly was. Cam Carruth. Camille Carruth. Mrs. Tate Carruth. Yes, it definitely had a ring to it!

She held her hand close to the single flame for the hundredth inspection of the day of her band of diamonds and rubies that glowed with resplendent beauty even by candlelight. Hardly a moment had gone by since Tate proposed when she didn't pinch herself to make sure she wasn't dreaming. Even with the ring on her finger and the beautiful lace-and-tiny-pearl wedding gown hanging in her wardrobe, she still had trouble believing such good fortune was hers! She really was not dreaming!

Dreams and fantasies! There would be no more of those for her. Her dream had come true. Her phantom lover truly did belong to her and her alone. He had indeed returned to her just as he had promised on that July night two years before. If Tate knew of her suspicion that he was the mystery man in the black cape and hood, he had made no mention of it. Patiently, she had waited for him to admit his secret identity. She had given him every opportunity to do so, but he had remained silent. No matter. Another hour or so and that, too, would be resolved.

Blaming mountain superstition and old wives' tales for her decision, she had refused to see him that evening. But how difficult it had been to keep a straight face! More than once an uncontrolled chuckle had nearly given her away. Tate had acted more than just a little strangely and had all but demanded she meet with him after dark. It was obvious he suspected something was going on, and all the better, too, for it meant he had found the note she had left in the old mine entreating her mystery man to join her for what must be their final rendezvous. If he did think she was about to be unfaithful, so much the better. It would serve him right! Just how long did he expect to keep her in the dark?

True, after the hunt supper at the Winterthurs', he had of his own free will confirmed what she had already deduced by her own sly means—that Clayton Griffin was Tate's natural father—and he had also cleared up several uncertainties that had continued to taunt her even after her discovery.

It had been the man who had raised him as his own son who encouraged him to go south and make the acquaintance of the man whose blood flowed in his veins, if for no other reason than to satisfy a curiosity that otherwise might well plague him the rest of his days. At first, Tate had objected. He wanted no part of the man who had abandoned him and his mother at the time they most needed him, but his father's deathbed insistence that he at least show his natural father the kind of man he had become finally convinced him to travel to Caesar's Head.

He had arrived at Hunter's Glen only to learn that Clayton Griffin had just been laid to rest. He had felt no grief or remorse and had shed no tears at the passing of the man who had chosen to deny him. Yet, after spending many hours with Jackson, he had come to view Clayton Griffin with far more sympathy.

Jackson had been far more than a servant, as Tate soon discovered. He had been Clayton's closest friend—sometimes his only friend. Clayton had told him what he had told no one else. He had taken the old darkie into his confidence about the son he had never seen. From Jackson, Tate learned that Clayton had indeed begged Lenora's forgiveness through countless letters and had pleaded with her to let him see his son, but she had refused time and time again. Jackson had even shown proof of these attempts to the numerous letters that had been returned from Baltimore unopened, letters that the old servant had refused to throw away, so sure was he that Griffin's son would one day take his rightful place as master of Hunter's Glen.

But Clayton's misery at having given up his one true love and their son was not all Jackson had revealed. He had also witnessed a violent struggle between Strothers and his employer, a struggle that ended in Clayton being struck on the head with a poker, then dragged into the stall of his beloved white stallion, Apollo. Fearing his own life would be taken if he made the truth known, Jackson had kept silent for years. Then he had pleaded with Tate to find other means of bringing Strothers to justice, and Tate had set out to do just that, feeling that he owed his natural father that much at least. It had taken two years for him to cultivate a friendship and business relationship with Strothers, while all the while plotting to avenge his father's death.

In the end Strothers' wicked deeds had caught up with him, but it had not been Tate's hand that caused his demise. Several days before he had been found down by the waterfall on Mill Hill with a butcher knife stuck in his chest. He had already been dead a couple of weeks by then. Some said Bud Cooper was the guilty one. Others believed Nellie, after catching her lover in bed with another woman, was responsible. Cam supposed no one would ever know for sure, since both Nellie and her husband had disappeared. She herself had her own idea which of the two was to blame. Bud wouldn't have used a knife. He wouldn't have had to. He would simply have crushed Strother's skull with his bare hands. Anyway, what was done was done. Whatever he got, Strothers had coming.

Her thoughts returned to the missing pieces of that puzzle she'd spent the summer trying to solve. As it turned out, Tristram and Apollo were one and the same horse. As a young stallion, his coat was the color of snow, but as he matured, it had dulled to gray. The sheriff had ordered the horse shot, and Jackson, knowing his master's favorite mount was innocent of trampling him, offered to perform the task. Instead, he had hidden Apollo in the woods and, when Tate arrived, had convinced him to take possession of the horse. Unable to take him back up North, Tate had kept the horse boarded at a farm near Travellers Rest. That horse was one of the few links he had with his father.

All that was left to clear up now was why Tate had begun his masquerade as the man in the black cape and why he had not admitted to his secret identity even after Cam had at last removed the pendant from around her neck.

She pulled her cloak even tighter around her unclothed flesh. Most likely, Tate had first donned the black cape two years ago to be sure his real identity was kept secret for when he later returned to Caesar's Head to snare Strothers in his own trap. And Cam had her own idea why he had continued wearing it, especially at those times when he suspected he would encounter her. True to his word, he had fallen in love with her the first night he laid eyes on her, but he feared it was the romantic notion of the man in the black cape she had come to love, the man of her fantasies, not the real flesh-and-blood man. He could never be quite sure, she supposed, whether superstition or devotion to a love she could never have had kept her from removing the necklace for so long. It wasn't until she had taken it off for good that he proposed.

But why hadn't he admitted to being the man in black after that? Was it because he feared she still entertained some silly schoolgirl dream about her phantom lover? Did he doubt just which one of them she would be thinking of when they made love?

No matter. A little while longer and it would all be over with. She'd show him! She'd teach him a thing or two about deceiving her!

Cam slipped out of her room and tiptoed down the stairs as the mantel clock chimed twelve. Laughing to herself, she ran into the woods. That fiance of hers was about to be taught a lesson he'd be a long time forgetting!

He was waiting for her at the clearing, his long, black cape swaying in the night air.

"Please. Do not turn around. Not yet."

Her words were quiet, her voice aquiver. It was neither the chill nor the eerie figure in front of her that made her tremble. It was the thrill of what was about to come!

"I cannot look you in the eye and say to you what I must, my darling."

She stepped closer very slowly as she continued to speak.

"For two years, I have loved you. I have loved you desperately with all my heart. Every night, alone in my bed, I have dreamed of the time when you would take posession of my body and of my very soul. That time never came, and I have been condemned to an existence of endless nights yearning for your touch."

Cam took a deep breath. "But I can wait no more. No longer can I live for that which can never be. You see, my darling, tomorrow I am to be married. The man I am to wed is a kind and wonderful man who loves me more than anything else in the world, and I love him, too—I suppose—in my own way, for you see, my heart can belong but to one man, and that man, my elusive lover, is you."

Standing only a few feet behind him, she untied her cloak and let it fall open. The chill night air caressed her bare skin, but she scarcely noticed, for raging inside her like a blazing inferno was a desire that demanded instant and total fulfillment.

"Please grant me one last request, my darling. I beg you. Make love to me now, just this once, so I will have the memory of you and of our loving to get me through those long, lonely nights I must spend with my husband."

She slipped her arms around him and pressed close to his back. Daring hands roamed inside the cape across familiar territory.

His breathing grew more labored. His body hardened at her touch.

"Please, I beg of you, do not deny me this one last wish."

Edging around to his side, she took his hand and placed it on her breast. Her heart pounded furiously.

"You won't regret it, I swear. I can make you

so very, very happy. Make love to me, my darling, please. We shall have one glorious night to remember before locking ourselves inside our prisons, never to see each other again."

He turned to her, his hood shielding his face from her eyes.

Ever so slowly, she eased the cape down around her shoulders and let it drop to the ground. Opening her arms wide, she beckoned him closer.

"Come, my darling. Come."

He did as she commanded.

She let out a moan of ecstasy as he pulled her close.

For a moment, Cam let herself go limp against him. Then, feeling his urgency mounting, she slid her hands up around his neck.

"Damn you, Tate Carruth!" she cursed softly as she jerked back the hood. "Just when did you plan on ending this little charade of yours?"

He stared at her in shocked dismay, then threw back his head and roared with laughter. "You knew all along, didn't you, my sly little seductress?"

"I had my suspicions." She stood with her hands defiantly on her hips. "Well, what do you have to say for yourself?"

"For a moment there, I must admit you had me worried." He chuckled to himself. "What was it you said again? Make love to me so I'll have memories of you to get me through those long, lonely nights with my husband? Really, Cam! Am I that much of a bore?"

She reached down for her cape.

Tate grabbed it first and threw it into the bushes. "Not so fast, my dear."

She eyed him suspiciously. "Just what is it you have in mind?"

His caresses were as possessive and demanding as his kisses.

"One way or another I am going to teach you a lesson you won't forget any time soon."

Cam smiled. She herself had set out to do that very same thing. "Oh? And dare I ask what that lesson might be?"

He stepped out of her embrace only long enough to shed his clothes.

"You don't need fantasies, Cam. Not when you have me."